STARGATE
SG·1

HYDRA

"Off-world activation," Hammond answered. "It's Bra'tac's IDC." No sooner had he explained than Bra'tac stepped through the wormhole, heavy boots clanging on the ramp. Teal'c stepped forward, ready to exchange traditional greetings, but Jack put a hand on his shoulder, a subtle command. Bra'tac's posture was stiff, and he barely glanced at either Jack or Teal'c. Beneath Jack's hand, Teal'c tensed.

"Welcome, Master Bra'tac," Hammond said.

No answering smile came from Bra'tac. Instead, he nodded to Hammond and said, "Hammond of Texas. I have come to ask for an explanation for your actions on the mountain world of the Eshet and to tell you the trust of the Jaffa has been broken."

Jack had never heard Bra'tac express mistrust of the Tauri since those very earliest days. The hair rose on the back of his neck. "Bra'tac, what the hell are you talking about?"

"I am speaking of the massacre which occurred on Eshet yesterday—the massacre led by your team in pursuit of technology owned by the people of that world."

D1462580

STARGATE
SG·1™

HYDRA

**HOLLY SCOTT AND
JAIMIE DUNCAN**

FANDEMONIUM BOOKS

An original publication of Fandemonium Ltd, produced under license from MGM Consumer Products.

Fandemonium Books, PO Box 795A, Surbiton, Surrey KT5 8YB, United Kingdom
Visit our website: www.stargatenovels.com

STARGÅTE
SG·1.

MGM TELEVISION ENTERTAINMENT INC. Presents
RICHARD DEAN ANDERSON
in
STARGATE SG-1™
MICHAEL SHANKS   AMANDA TAPPING   CHRISTOPHER JUDGE
DON S. DAVIS
Executive Producers JONATHAN GLASSNER and BRAD WRIGHT
MICHAEL GREENBURG RICHARD DEAN ANDERSON
Developed for Television by BRAD WRIGHT & JONATHAN GLASSNER

STARGATE SG-1 © 1997-2008 MGM Television Entertainment Inc. and MGM Global Holdings Inc. STARGATE: SG-1 is a trademark of Metro-Goldwyn-Mayer Studios Inc. All Rights Reserved.

METRO-GOLDWYN-MAYER TM & © 2008 Metro-Goldwyn-Mayer Studios Inc. All Rights Reserved.

Photography and cover art: Copyright © 2008 Metro-Goldwyn-Mayer Studios Inc. All Rights Reserved.

WWW.MGM.COM

No part of this publication may be reproduced, stored in or introduced into a retrieval system, or transmitted, in any form, or by any means (electronic, mechanical, photocopying, recording or otherwise) without the prior written consent of the publisher. Any person who does any unauthorised act in relation to this publication may be liable to criminal prosecution and civil claims for damages.

If you purchase this book without a cover, you should be aware that this book is stolen property. It was reported as "unsold and destroyed" to the publisher and neither the author nor the publisher has received any payment for this "stripped book".

ISBN: 978-1-905586-10-3 Printed in the USA

For Joyce and Allen
who are greatly missed, and remembered with love

PROLOGUE

doli capax
Eshet (P3X-5S2)
October 29, 2002

Carter hadn't told them to prepare for a dead-of-night arrival. The wavering backlight from the gate sent their shadows writhing over the fitted stones of the platform, twice as big as life, like something from one of those slasher movies — the ones with the shadows that rose up and did the real killing, shocking a scream out of the audience because they were busy looking for the danger someplace else. Carter could have calculated the timing this way if she'd wanted to — and probably had, in some corner of her brain — but O'Neill was happy to chalk it up to good fortune. Nothing like a good approach from the scary darkness to make an impression on the locals. Things were looking up, finally.

"What a difference a day makes," he sang under his breath.

Beside him, Jackson snorted. "Uh huh. That's what I love about you, Jack. Nothing so momentous that you can't sum it up in a cheesy show tune."

"Hey," O'Neill snapped. "That is not a cheesy show tune. That is a classic. Dinah Washington would so kick your girly ass."

With a dismissive shrug, Jackson set off down the steps. "Somehow I doubt it."

"You know, Jackson, hubris is an ugly quality."

Jackson raised his eyebrows and paused to look at O'Neill as the gate shut down. "Jack," he said, all surprised, sunny pride. "Have you been reading again?"

"The dictionary came standard with the software."

Carter's expression was neutral as she followed Jackson off the platform and onto the road, but O'Neill knew she was smirking on the inside. Teal'c had nothing to say, but inclined his head a fraction when O'Neill added, "I'm just sayin': Dinah Washington was no pushover." He turned to his left. "Carter! Time?"

She tilted her head. "Forty-seven hours, 19 minutes... mark."

"Okay, kids. No dallying in the gift shops. Find the magic doodad and make it home in time for breakfast." He heard Jackson say "Eggs" wistfully and had to order himself not to think about hash browns and coffee. "Keep your head in the game, Jackson."

Jackson flipped him a mock salute and kept walking. "Yessir, *mon capitaine.*"

O'Neill sighted along the snub barrel of the P90 so that the laser danced its jittery dance in the middle of Jackson's flak vest and let his finger tighten on the trigger. "One of these days, Dr. Jackson," he muttered. One of these days. But not today. Today they had doodads to collect, natives to awe, et cetera, and so forth.

Despite the rousting from their beds in the middle of the night, the locals were not as awed as O'Neill would have liked, given that he did not have all day to dick around with the subtleties of interrogation. Time was tick, tick, ticking audibly in his head while the mayor or the czar or whatever he was quivered in the mud with his hands behind his neck and promised in a quavering voice that he had no idea what the magic doodad was or where it might be. The old guy looked vaguely like somebody O'Neill would expect to find smiling on a Swiss cheese wrapper, right down to the milk-fed rosy cheeks and the shorts with suspenders—"Lederhosen," Jackson said. O'Neill rolled his eyes, and, for convenience's sake, named the guy Von Trapp. The village was a nice enough place, lots of sharply angled roofs and a communal well and a schoolhouse with a bell and everything. Not exactly post-card material, what with the mud and the way all the build-ings seemed to lean downhill, their doors darkly open so that the barnyard animals could go in and out, but nicely situated in a little notch where the river sluiced ice-blue down from the snowy mountains in the distance.

True to the intel on P3X-5S2, aka Eshet, there were no antennae or power sources more sophisticated than the water-wheel churning away, grinding whatever passed for grain, and none of the men lined up on their knees at O'Neill's feet looked like they could win a fight with Jackson's little sister, if he'd had a little sister. The most dangerous objects they'd seen so far were a pitchfork and an ax, and Teal'c had pretty handily taken care of both the ax and the guy who came at him waving it.

So they were left with a bunch of guys kneeling in the mud, a few women on the edges of the square in the shift-ing torchlight hiding tow-headed kids behind their skirts, and Mayor Von Trapp making some very, very bad choices in terms of handling the situation.

O'Neill crouched down to the guy's groveling level. He put a knuckle under the mayor's chin and raised his head so that they could see eye to weepy eye. "Look," O'Neill said in a low, calming voice. He pressed his knife into the crease between the mayor's two chins. "You don't have to be scared. We don't want to hurt you." He raised his gaze to take in Carter and Jackson and Teal'c standing behind the row of men. Teal'c's scowl alone looked like it could flay skin to the bone. Jackson had those worry lines starting but didn't seem too inclined to step in. Carter was Carter, ready for action and not much expression on her face beyond wary attention. "Well, maybe we do, but only because you make us. You don't have to make us." He added pressure to the knife and felt the may-or's quivering ramp up to eleven. "Just tell us where it is, and we'll be on our way. Make us look for it, and you won't have much left to protect." O'Neill smiled. "See? Easy."

Surprisingly, the mayor stiffened and his eyes got less weepy and more determined. "We will give you nothing."

O'Neill's smile faded and he bowed his head, disappointed. The guy had picked a bad time to develop guts. "You'll give us nothing. Which presumes, of course, that you do have *something*." A tiny twitch of the knife, and blood gleamed on its edge. "Where is it?" The guy's eyes widened and his hand came up to close like a claw around O'Neill's wrist. His voice low, O'Neill repeated, "Where is it?"

."We don't know! We don't know anything! Leave us a—" The woman's protests were cut off by the butt of Carter's P90. She went straight down like she was cut off at the knees, collapsing in a puddle of skirts. Two kids swarmed out of the hovel nearest her and covered her with their skinny bodies; Carter's arm fell slowly. Strafed by Teal'c's scowl, the little crowd retreated farther into the shadows. Jackson stared blankly at the mountains or at whatever it was he looked at inside his head at times like these.

The mayor's grip loosened and he fell away onto his back, leaving O'Neill there with his knife still poised, the blade dark with blood. "Why's it always got to go the hard way?" O'Neill asked the glassy eyes as he rose to his feet. He caught Carter's gaze and nodded. "Find it. Do what you gotta do." As the three of them moved away, he added with a tap on his raised wrist, "Ticktock, folks."

In retrospect, the fire was probably a really bad idea. No doubt the flames from the burning houses licking up against the black sky alerted the Jaffa to their presence. When the lintel over his head exploded with a staff blast, O'Neill vowed to have a little word with Carter about the status of their intel. While he was busy separating tree shadows from Jaffa shadows and then putting as many bullet holes in the latter as possible, he rehearsed his speech. He had time between revisions to get his foot under a fallen Jaffa and roll him over to check out the tattoo. Some kind of dog, maybe, or a deer. As he made his way back to the center of the village—pausing to work his knife through the narrow spaces of a Jaffa's chain mail and into his kidney—he checked out a couple more. The Apophis tattoo he recognized. The one that looked like a scimitar he didn't.

Back at the well, he waited patiently while Teal'c twisted a guy's head round backward and then asked, "You get it?"

Teal'c shook his head. "I did not. I have not seen Daniel Jackson or Captain Carter."

"Speak of the devil," O'Neill said, and turned to watch Carter vault herself across the back of a burly Jaffa before back-handing him. Behind her, Jackson strolled along, stepping carefully over the bodies she left on the ground as she made her way across the little square.

"I don't understand it," Carter said as she got within bitching distance, anticipating O'Neill's pointed question. "There was nothing in the intel about a Jaffa encampment."

"Rebels," Jackson offered, his head tilted so that he could see the tattoo of the nearest Jaffa right side up. "They're all different." Shaking his hair out of his eyes, he aimed a finger at his own forehead. "The tattoos, I mean. Probably rebels. They must be hiding, which explains why they aren't in the intel."

Waving the explanation away with a gloved hand, O'Neill demanded, "Where's the thing? I'm not leaving here without the damn thing."

Jackson held up a black lump about the size of a baseball, smug smile on his face, and waved it at O'Neill.

"That's more like it," O'Neill said. "Time to go." He ducked to avoid another staff blast, but it didn't matter. A grenade spun across the square, fetched up against the well, and blew them all to the ground.

Twisting around in the mud to riddle the forest between the burning houses with bullets, O'Neill shouted the order to retreat and kept firing until he could see the rest of them picking themselves up and making hell-bent for leather up the hill toward the gate. Then he got up and followed them, firing more or less blindly as he went.

"What a difference a day makes," he hummed to himself.

PART ONE

alibi
elsewhere

CHAPTER ONE

Stargate Command
October 30, 2002; one day after invasion of Eshet

Jack O'Neill signed off on the last mission report with a flourish and slapped the cover shut. Months of backlog, finally attended to. He threw it on the pile of reports to his right and sat back in the chair with a sigh of relief. Getting caught up was the only silver lining to a four-day quarantine and lockdown. Maybe SG-10's new historian had used the time to learn all about the SGC's handy protocols for dealing with weird alien artifacts. The one he brought back was harboring a virus that turned skin blue and shrank the vocal cords. They'd all been trapped in the mountain for the better part of a week, waiting to see if they'd start squeaking.

In the meantime, Jack had taken over someone's office—eminent domain, he told Carter—and begun banging out reports. It was either that or climb the walls. Or play chess with Daniel, who had perfected the art of playing with one hand and typing with the other, which distracted Jack to the point of losing.

There were only so many matches he could spar with Teal'c before he lost some teeth, and Carter…well. She was all excited about the blue virus.

Now that it was cured, Jack was itching to get on the departure roster and back to business as usual, but they were bringing in teams that had been stuck off-world, and the delayed missions were bottlenecked. So it was a relief when the alarm klaxon went off and the call followed: "Colonel O'Neill to the gate-room."

He met Daniel jogging down the hall toward the stairs to

the gate-room, his sleeve dangling as he shrugged his jacket on. "Didn't hear them calling you," Jack said.

Daniel just gave him a look. "They called you, which means I'm next," he said, pulling a smile from Jack right about the time they ran into Carter and Teal'c. The four of them peeled around the corner and stopped shy of the ramp where General Hammond was waiting behind a phalanx of SFs.

"Sir?" Jack said.

"Off-world activation," Hammond answered. "It's Bra'tac's IDC." No sooner had he explained than Bra'tac stepped through the wormhole, heavy boots clanging on the ramp. Teal'c stepped forward, ready to exchange traditional greetings, but Jack put a hand on his shoulder, a subtle command. Bra'tac's posture was stiff, and he barely glanced at either Jack or Teal'c. Beneath Jack's hand, Teal'c tensed.

"Welcome, Master Bra'tac," Hammond said.

No answering smile came from Bra'tac. Instead, he nodded to Hammond and said, "Hammond of Texas. I have come to ask for an explanation for your actions on the mountain world of the Eshet and to tell you the trust of the Jaffa has been broken."

Jack had never heard Bra'tac express mistrust of the Tauri since those very earliest days. The hair rose on the back of his neck. "Bra'tac, what the hell are you talking about?"

"I am speaking of the massacre which occurred on Eshet yesterday—the massacre led by your team in pursuit of technology owned by the people of that world."

"What?" Jack's sense of disquiet was growing, tingling low in his belly. So far, not one word of what Bra'tac had said made a bit of sense. More than that, the utter conviction in his voice knocked Jack flat. Since when did Bra'tac believe the worst about them? About Teal'c? "Bra'tac, whatever massacre you're talking about—we've been stuck here at the SGC for almost four days. SG-1 hasn't been off-world since…"

"Eight days, sir," Carter said, from behind him.

"Yeah. Eight days." Jack waited for the skepticism on Bra'tac's face to ease, but it didn't change at all.

Teal'c said, "I give you my word: whatever has occurred, SG-1 is not responsible."

"You swear this?"

"I do."

Bra'tac's deep frown seemed to pull the next question from Daniel. "Bra'tac, what world is this?"

"It is a mountain world, full of people once enslaved by the Goa'uld. They gave freely of themselves when the rebel Jaffa arrived on their world and have since built an enclave there. These people lived in peace. Until yesterday."

His voice pitched low, Daniel said to Carter, "Aren't we scheduled to visit a mountain culture in a few months?"

"Yes," Carter said. "P3X-5S2. It fits the description superficially, but without a more in-depth description I can't be sure."

"Well, if it's on the schedule, there you go," Jack said. "Haven't been there."

"This troubles me," Bra'tac said. "O'Neill, the Jaffa who were present described you and your team in great detail. Some of them have met you previously in battle and believed you to be honorable warriors. Do you think they would implicate you if it were not so?"

"Do you think we would lie to you?" Jack had had about enough of the implications, and he was damn well going to get an answer to that question. He was willing to wait all day in fact without letting Bra'tac off the hook, but Daniel broke the moment.

"There's an easy way to resolve this. Let's just take a trip to P3X-5S2 and see for ourselves. Once they meet us, that'll put this to rest."

"If that's the planet," Carter said. "We don't know that yet."

"I'm sure Bra'tac will be kind enough to point out the gate address, and then we'll know. General?" Jack looked to Hammond. "Permission to go and prove we're not mass murderers?"

"Granted, Colonel." Hammond focused his attention back on Bra'tac. "And once this has been resolved to your satisfaction, I hope we can talk again about what has made you assume the worst of us."

Bra'tac didn't bother to answer the question. He met Teal'c's eyes and said, "I will wait here while you retrieve your battle gear."

Jack held off on saying anything else until they were in the corridor, and then he directed his question to Teal'c. "Do you have any idea what's going on here, or has Bra'tac just lost his mind?"

"I have never known Master Bra'tac to jump to conclusions or make false accusations," Teal'c answered, but Jack could see he was feeling the same stunned doubt that was sitting like a cold lump in Jack's own gut. "There must be some truth to prompt it."

"Sir," Carter said, "I'm confident that no one from the SGC has visited any world matching that basic description in months. It's rare for the Goa'uld to have chosen very cold worlds to settle slaves."

"The cold disturbs the symbiotes," Teal'c said.

Jack had a flashback to being half-frozen while one of those things was squirming around in his head a couple of years back, thanks to Hathor, and a shiver ran down his spine. "Gear up and be ready for departure in half an hour," he said. "We've got name-clearing to do." As Carter passed him, he told her, "If this is one of your time-travel conundrum paradox things, I'm going to get cranky."

Daniel was third out of the gate behind Jack and Bra'tac, Reynolds and the other marines still behind him, so the scream of dismay and warning was shrill in his ears as he cleared the event horizon. Not the first time people had run screaming when they showed up. Usually a little diplomacy meant SG-1 could talk their way into a friendship even with people who'd become accustomed to getting nothing but pain from the visitors stepping through the gate.

He shouldered his way past Jack, ready to perform the dance of meeting, greeting, and getting information, and caught sight of a girl running fast back toward the village, slipping in the mud as she scrambled down the hill. She half-ran, half-slid down slope but left her shoe behind. She was still shrieking. Nothing intelligible Daniel could pick out, just panicked noise.

"Well," Jack said, "that was quite the welcome."

Daniel turned his attention to the village. The houses had steeply tilted roofs, much like Alpine chalets but a bit less sturdy and whole lot sadder than the average tourist resort. Mountains surrounded the village. Glaciers and snowfields dimmed to purple shadow against the blue of the sky, barely gleaming in the weak light of a distant sun. A few trees marked the wide skyline here, and farther down slope the forest proper was a dark swath of unbroken green. The air was thin, but the voice of the girl carried clearly, sharp with fear.

"Yeah," Daniel said, meeting Bra'tac's stern, accusing gaze before stepping down off the gate platform. He turned and gestured to Jack, who thinned his lips and stepped down beside him.

"Carter," Jack said. "Take point." Bra'tac stepped in front of them all and began striding toward the narrow path. "Dammit," Jack said, and Daniel and Sam exchanged a quick smile as they followed.

Then Daniel looked up.

"Uh, I think we could just wait here," he said, pointing. A group of men streamed up the hill from the village, half of them Jaffa in armor. Jack and Sam lifted their weapons and shifted into covering positions, while Teal'c moved sideways to cover their flank. Behind them, Reynolds and his guys fanned out, crouching and looking vulnerable in the absence of good cover. Daniel didn't move. If there was any chance of making sense of the accusations Bra'tac leveled, he'd need to be as conciliatory and open as possible.

"Stay mellow, kids," Jack said, elbow braced to level his weapon.

"Jack," Daniel said. "Let me take the lead."

The group of men was closer now, and they were running. Never a good sign. Daniel counted twelve, maybe fourteen. The girl lagged behind them. She slowed down and stopped in the middle of the road, watching the spectacle up the hill.

"You!" one of the men shouted, and pointed a long ax at Jack. "You will surrender your weapons to us now and step away from the *kreis*!"

To Daniel, it sounded like a German variant. "Circle," he told Jack, who didn't acknowledge him. The men—five Jaffa among them who leveled staff weapons at SG-1, Jack in particular—surrounded them. Daniel wasn't surprised, but he did note that the DHD was cut off as well as the gate. Not a huge problem, and he knew Jack was already thinking them through it, but Daniel couldn't imagine a way that wouldn't involve a lot of bullets. He'd have to find a way to prevent that.

"We mean you no harm," he said to the man who had spoken. "There's been some kind of mistake."

"The mistake was yours for returning to this place. After what you have done." The man's voice cracked with horror, and Daniel processed that, the utter finality in it. The man stared at Jack with haunted eyes. "On this day of all days, when we bury those you took from us. You, with your hands and your knives."

Jack said, "Daniel, you've got about ten seconds to—"

"I can see you believe we've wronged you, but it wasn't us," Daniel said urgently, stepping forward, hands outstretched. "We haven't—"

"You dare," the Jaffa nearest him said. "You, whose crime was worst of all. You stood by and did nothing."

"That's it," Jack said. Voice pitched just for his team, he

said, "Daniel, stop talking and be ready to dial." He raised his voice to normal speaking levels for the benefit of the villagers, and Daniel glanced to his left. They were slowly encroaching on the team, backing them away from the gate. "Listen, folks, you've made the mistake, and we're going to go now. We'd rather do that without a fight, but—"

"Do not let them leave!" The girl's voice, high-pitched and plaintive, wavered like a bird's cry.

"Oh, crap," Jack said.

They all moved at the same time, different directions in order of priorities: Jack, Bra'tac, and Teal'c for cover; Carter and Daniel for the DHD. Jack rolled to the side and crouched behind the gate's stone pedestal. The first staff blast passed so close to Daniel he could feel the heat of it on the side of his face, and he dived for cover, groping for his Beretta.

So much for negotiation skills.

Daniel scrambled into a low ditch, clumps of grass clinging to his face and hair like wet seaweed. He brushed them off and straightened his glasses. A staff blast shattered the ground not ten feet away, raising the smell of boggy peat on a bonfire.

"Defend your positions," Jack's voice said, crackling out of Daniel's radio.

"Some position," Daniel muttered, as he scooped out a miniature trench for his arm to rest in, the better to aim at angry Jaffa. Goopy mud trickled down from the channel. He hunkered down against the shallow wall of the ditch, waiting for a chance to rise up and return fire.

Another staff blast gouged a hole in the dirt right next to Daniel's head, and he threw himself into the brackish standing water in the bottom of the ditch to protect his face from the debris. Gravel and mud pattered down around him, sounding almost like rain. He took a moment to wish he'd worn his helmet instead of the boonie.

He was inching his head up to ground level to get a look at the battlefield when a fresh cascade of gravel clattered down on his back, followed by the thud and splash of a body hitting the bottom of the ditch beside him.

Completely covered in the thick, gray mud, Jack rolled onto his knees, and straightened long enough to send a short burst of P90 fire over the edge of the shelter before hunkering down with his back against the sloping side of the ditch. "Clip," he ordered, trying to wipe mud from his eyes with a gloved hand and instead leaving more mud behind. "I'm out."

Daniel was, for once, grateful that Jack forced him to go into the field with extra ammo. He lifted a magazine from his vest pocket and tossed it to Jack, who slapped it into place.

"What the hell is going on with these people?" Daniel demanded, slouching down and wincing up at the darkening sky. "I don't get it."

O'Neill grunted and pulled out a telescoping mirror so he could get a look over the edge of the ditch. He grunted again and passed the mirror over. "See for yourself."

The field was churned mud. On the other side of it, Sam was strafing the treeline from the shelter of a blast crater—the Jaffa had a cannon. Fabulous. Teal'c was beside her, reloading. A new clip in place, he popped up and neatly dispatched a Jaffa creeping up on their right flank. But there were more Jaffa coming. Many more. And that wasn't even counting the ax-swinging villagers. Daniel had only one more clip himself, and he wasn't feeling too great about using them on civilians.

"This doesn't look good."

"Oh, cheer up, Daniel," Jack answered. "I'd say we're about two steps past terrible. Far cry from hopeless." He got off two quick spurts of fire and then ducked down with a whoop as another staff blast sent up a fan of debris two feet away. Jack's teeth were white in his dirty face when he grinned. The grin had no amusement in it.

Daniel's radio let out a burst of static. "Daniel! What's your position?"

Jack's grin disappeared quickly.

Daniel's mouth fell open and he lifted a hand to point at Jack, like he could pin him to the dirt with the gesture. Then with the other hand he keyed the radio. "Uh, hi. Who is this?"

"What? This is your *commander*, who is currently getting his ass shot to hell south of the Stargate!" Jack's voice was fuzzy with static but recognizable. "Reynolds is in position. We're gonna make a push for the gate, so be ready!"

In the ditch beside Daniel, not-Jack gave Daniel a one-shouldered shrug. His mouth twitched up, and this time the grin was embarrassed. "Oops," he said, and in a second he had clambered over the edge of the ditch and onto the field. By the time Daniel had dodged another blast and the debris had cleared, Jack—or whatever was passing for him—had disappeared into the chaos of battle.

Between them, Jack and Reynolds managed to get both teams rallied and through the gate without having to take out more than a few of the locals. The Jaffa…well, to Jack's mind, they were well armed and capable, and they had started it. Whatever had gone down on Eshet before, there was no telling how much of today's fight was opportunistic on the Jaffa's part. SG-1 had done its fair share to tick them off in the past, and maybe the Jaffa weren't above a little collateral payback. But, no matter how Jack turned it in his head, it looked bad and smelled worse.

In the end, the SGC personnel scrambled through the gate less than elegantly, but, according to the head count Jack did from the top of the ramp, more or less intact. Reynolds was hopping down the stairs between two of his men, holding up what was probably a broken foot. Carter, who was now moving under her own steam, had let go of Teal'c and Daniel and was shaking her head vigorously and twisting her finger in her ear.

"Carter! You okay?"

"What?" she shouted over the bells that were probably still ringing in her head. "Oh. Yes, sir. Fine." Fine for somebody who'd gotten up close and personal with a Goa'uld grenade. Her face was smeared with mud and soot, her eyes bloodshot but both spinning in the same direction.

On the whole, they didn't look fine. They looked like a bunch of sorry cases, all of them covered in gray mud so he could tell them apart mostly by shape and stature. But they were all standing, so he was going to count that part, at least, a win. He'd be happier about that if he had any clue what the heck they were fighting about. Even standing in a nonthreatening way in front of the gate and shouting, "Hey, you guys! We're *on the same side!*" hadn't made much of an impression on the Jaffa, and Jack had the bruises and the mild concussion to prove it. In short, it sucked. He scowled accusingly at the gate before stomping down the ramp, and saved a little bit of the scowl to aim at Bra'tac's turned back.

"Infirmary. Showers. Briefing," Jack ordered, and waved them all away. Bra'tac paused, opened his mouth to say something, but apparently thought better of it. Good call. They'd have an opportunity to get into it soon enough.

Daniel stood at the bottom of the ramp and looked past Jack at the empty circle of the gate, chewing his lip, eyebrows furrowed with worry. He'd lost his glasses somewhere and he looked naked without them. As Jack stepped around him, he put a hand on Jack's arm. "Wait. Jack—"

The alarm sounded and Harriman announced an unscheduled wormhole activation. The iris wheeled shut. Everyone waited.

"SG-1 IDC, sir," Harriman said over the intercom.

Jack did another head count. All present and accounted for. "Anyone missing a GDO?"

His team members shook their heads.

Up in the control room, Hammond was frowning. Teal'c and Carter raised weapons, and Reynolds's men followed suit as the gate-room squad moved quietly into position. It had to be a trick.

Soon there'd be a thump on the back of the iris.

"Open it," Daniel said urgently, just loud enough to be heard over the ripple of the event horizon. He met Jack's eyes. "Open it now, Jack."

Another second for consideration, while Jack pondered whether Daniel had lost his mind completely. It violated a million different protocols. "Daniel," Jack said tightly, but Daniel shook his head hard, stepped closer to Jack. His eyes were an intense, unearthly blue in the gate light.

"I'll explain later. There's no time. You *have* to open it."

Despite his unease, Jack nodded up at the control room and Hammond nodded back. The iris swirled open. A second later, Daniel—another one—stumbled through the event horizon and, with his first Earthly breath, shouted in that wounded, exasperated, wallpaper-peeling tone only Daniel could achieve, "Whatever happened to not leaving people behind?"

Jack got that feeling. That one that told him he should've stayed retired.

"We did not leave anyone behind," Teal'c said as he swung his P90 around to aim at the Daniel beside him.

Carter's aim wavered between the two Daniels and then returned to the mud-spattered Daniel on the ramp. She shot Jack a quick look that clearly communicated her regret at not taking up that job at NASA.

Barely missing a beat, which said a lot about what a guy could get used to in this job, the new Daniel yanked off his boonie and used it to point at his double. "Okay," he said, "*that* is not me."

"Maybe *you're* not you," Jack said.

"I am. You can tell."

"How?" Jack put his hands in his pockets, cocked his head and added his best narrow-eyed quizzical expression for good measure.

"I have glasses. He doesn't."

"Ah, yes," the other Daniel said. "My clever disguise." He pulled off his bandanna and fluffed his hair so it fell over his eyes.

Jack put his fists to his temples and groaned.

Daniel had assumed the old "I'm fine, really, so stop looking at me" pose—namely, the one where he folded his arms around his chest and stared stonily at some spot halfway between himself and whatever it was that should be freaking him out. It was the pose that made Jack think of the academy, the Wall of Hell he'd hoisted himself over a hundred times, wearing out the toes of his boots scrambling against the worn wood of the planks. Fort Daniel. *Guy might as well have a moat,* Jack thought. *With moat sharks.*

It did not help one bit that the other Daniel was sitting on the edge of the bed in Quarantine 1 with precisely the same look on his face—a younger face with that scruffy Daniel hair and no glasses. Even with those slight but significant differences, there was a weirdly familiar fatalism there in the slump of his shoulders that made Jack feel tired. He'd seen that slump a thousand times in his long career, when things went FUBAR and the adrenaline had peaked and left a guy still two days behind enemy lines running on nothing but duty. Jack looked at his Daniel—the Real Daniel—reflected in the glass of the observation window and couldn't blame him for taking a time-out behind the battlements. But Jack was not at all happy with the way Daniel's shoulders were slumping.

He nudged him with an elbow.

"Yeah," Daniel said.

"'Yeah' what?"

In the reflection, Daniel eyes were focused now on the scene in the quarantine bay. "Yeah, it's freaky. And no, I'm not excited to have someone around who might be able to beat me at chess." He unfolded his arms and stuffed his hands in his pockets instead. "Maybe he doesn't even play chess."

Below them in the quarantine room, Fraiser was shuffling back and forth in her vacuum bag suit, stepping around the marine stationed at the end of the bed in his super-sized vacuum bag suit. The other Daniel watched her as she assembled her instruments on her tray.

"I'm not going to hurt you," he said, tilting his head toward the marine. "Really." His mouth twitched up in an ironic grin. "I come in peace. And I have an explanation for everything."

"I'm sure you do," Fraiser said with that same professionally soothing tone she used on all her patients, even the really bad ones, and motioned for him to take off his shirt.

"Oh, yes," Jack replied into the microphone. "I'm sure you have a wonderful explanation for everything. Especially the dead bodies."

Beside him, Daniel shifted his weight uncomfortably. "Maybe he does."

Jack's grunt was noncommittal.

Before Daniel could go on, Teal'c came in and stood behind them. His reflected frown looked like the scary, suspicious Jaffa equivalent of "Hmmm." Then, before the door had even latched, Carter stuck her head in and shouted, "So, what's the verdict?" Clearly it would be a little while longer before her hearing recovered. Otherwise, she looked scrubbed and none the worse for the wear. Coming up beside Daniel, she put a comforting hand on his arm for a second, then dropped stiffly onto the stool in front of the window.

"We're taking bets," Jack said. "Daniel's thinking parallel universe. Teal'c is abstaining." He twisted a little to give Teal'c a withering look. "Abstainer."

Carter was nodding thoughtfully. "Could be. If so, we'll have to consider cascade failure, which won't be very comfortable for you, or him." She waved a hand to indicate the second Daniel, who was now looking up at them. He lifted a hand to wave back, and she quickly dropped her own and caught it between her knees. Then, because Carter was Carter, she gave the guy a little wave after all and finished with the flash of a guilty smile for Daniel's reflection.

Daniel shrugged it off. He wasn't worried about loyalties, evidently. "You'd think by now I'd be more used to this kind of thing," he said. He was back in the Fort Daniel pose, but Jack could tell his curiosity was going to be too much for him. Jack could almost hear the high-speed whirring of his disc spinning up. Sooner or later, there was going to be fast-paced lecturing, with or without the laser pointer and the incomprehensible slide show. Jack shifted his weight, bracing for it. Daniel opened his mouth, but all he said was, "But, you know, the whole doppelganger thing, it never stops being unsettling."

"How do you think I feel?" Jack asked. "Like one Daniel wasn't enough to give a guy gray hairs."

Daniel focused on Jack's reflection in the glass. "I saw another you there, too, remember. So maybe we all get to have gray hairs."

Wrinkling his nose in distaste, Jack shifted his shoulders uncomfortably, raised his chin at the reflections of Carter and Teal'c, and said in his best singsong Dorothy voice, "And you were there, and you were there."

"Maybe it's not so bad. Maybe you'll even like this one better." Daniel lifted his fingers off his elbow and waggled them toward the double. "Maybe he loves things that explode."

"Maybe he likes poking sticks at Jaffa. I wouldn't call that better." The monitor over his head showed the same scene as the window did, but somehow Jack found it easier to look at. "Similar, but not better."

Speaking of poking, Fraiser was about to stick the other Daniel with one of the many needles he had to look forward to, but he put his hand on her arm.

"Look," he said, his voice sounding a little tinny through the speaker. "I can save you a lot of time."

"If you're gonna place your bets, do it now," Jack said, leaning forward and feeling the others do the same.

The other Daniel was looking directly at them now. "We

need to talk," he said distinctly, like enunciating would somehow make the words carry the weight of an order. Then he
pressed his thumb to a spot in the middle of his sternum.

"Great," Jack muttered as he looked at the blinking lights
exposed when the other Daniel's chest opened outward like a
book. There was stuff there that reminded Jack of the inside
of his stereo.

Surprised, Fraiser stepped back. Then she leaned in a bit
and aimed her pen light into the workings. She was reaching
out a tentative, curious finger when the robot advised mildly,
"I wouldn't." She snatched her hand away.

Leaning back awkwardly so that she could see into the observation booth from inside her hood, Fraiser said, "Colonel, I
think we can say that my services aren't going to be relevant
here."

"But," Carter said, "the duplicates of us were destroyed
last year, on Juna. That Daniel is—" She looked at Daniel.
"Isn't it—he?"

Daniel just raised his eyebrows at her and then looked at
the robot. He opened his mouth and closed it again. "Well,
maybe—I mean obviously—there are...more." His eyebrows came down again in a frown, and his fingers did a little dance that Jack assumed was meant to indicate somebody
making knockoffs of *real people* in his basement. Of course,
Daniel would put it more diplomatically.

"Harlan," Teal'c said.

"Harlan." Jack's hands made a choking motion around an
imaginary neck in the air in front of him. "I do believe that
I'm going to kick his jolly ass." He went to the phone and
ordered a nice, sturdy cell for their guest and, remembering
the strength of the robot duplicates they'd watched expire on
Juna, added a double detail of extra-burly marines for good
measure.

As he stalked out of the observation gallery, he heard the
robot say, "Lock me up if you have to, but I need to talk to
General Hammond. It's important."

The team followed along as Jack headed down the corridor. "I knew we should've destroyed that equipment when we had the chance," he muttered.

They were in the elevator before Daniel opened his mouth to make the standard speech about respecting boundaries and sovereignty and not being the ones in charge of the whole universe and everything in it, but Jack raised his hand to silence him. Daniel faced the door with the weary sigh of the man who never gets to finish his speeches about boundaries and sovereignty yadda yadda. Jack stared at the numbers on the panel and tried not to grind his teeth.

"All I'm saying," Daniel blurted, because he had no sense of self-preservation whatsoever, "is that we need to hear his story."

"Remember the bodies, Daniel," Jack said. "Remember the angry, angry Jaffa."

"Indeed," Teal'c said. "We cannot allow such violence to be done in our name."

"Obviously." Daniel wisely kept the "but" to himself.

As they filed off the elevator on level 28, Jack stopped Daniel with a hand on his arm. "Just keep that in mind when you're talking to it."

"Him." Daniel's jaw had that stubborn set to it that made Jack want to try out retirement again.

"That," Jack said, "is not helping."

CHAPTER TWO

NID Primary "Hydra" Project Site, Perseus (P66-421)
May, 2002; six months prior to invasion of Eshet

Carlos Mendez missed his cell phone. He missed his email, and his recliner, and Sundays spent in front of the TV with a beer, watching his two favorite football teams consistently lose. He even missed his father, who hadn't tried to understand why Carlos was going to be gone for months and had resorted to family guilt to try to keep him from leaving. Family honor was a big thing with Joe Mendez, perhaps the only thing that had ever mattered to him. Carlos had looked his dad in the eye and told him this was the most important project he'd ever been assigned. After all these months, he was actually starting to believe he'd told his father the truth.

The base was fully functional now, all the bells and whistles in place, and more personnel were arriving every day. Most were arriving via transport from Earth or from the roundabout network of gates set up to bypass any potential conflict or interaction with the SGC's scheduled off-world visits. The team handler was on his way and would soon be directing off-world missions, one more invisible cog in the vast network being built around Operation Hydra. He smiled at the thought of the name. Clearly someone higher up in the NID had a sense of humor. Possibly they thought this operation was the stuff of legend.

If Carlos had his way, he intended to make it memorable as well as successful.

He pulled a small bag out from under the desk—more of a table, really, with sturdy, ugly metal legs—and sifted through it. None of his personnel were permitted to bring personal items off-world—less chance of being identified, should their operations ever be uncovered. There was a standard party line, and all the loyal were expected to follow it. But Carlos had his own ideas about the party line.

He pulled out a small statue of an angel, kneeling, her wings outspread and her hands clasped, and placed it on the shelf behind him, next to a stack of start-up manuals and readiness reports.

"Guardian angel?"

Carlos turned his head. A young man in a black T-shirt and regulation BDUs stood in the doorway. He wore an overshirt that seemed two times too large for him, and his hair was a little too shaggy. His hands were in his pockets, mostly, Carlos figured, because they were habitually fidgety.

"Something like that," Carlos answered. "Can I help you?"

"Was told to report to you." The kid—probably in his twenties, but he was still a kid to Carlos—took a couple tentative steps into the room, then moved a little faster when Carlos didn't stop him. He pulled up short in front of the desk, almost at attention, but not quite. Just enough off the mark to suit Carlos. "I'm Mike Talbot."

"Ah. You're the operations expert." He cocked his head and gave Talbot the once-over. For someone recruited straight out of the ranks, he seemed a little off-kilter, the kind of guy who'd wear a uniform but chafe under it.

Talbot smiled, as if he could tell what Carlos was thinking. "Army was a way out of where I started off," he said. "But this is a better opportunity, where I can do what I do best."

"Which is?"

"Manage people," Talbot said. "Procuring things. That's what I'm good at."

"Not good at taking orders?"

Talbot's smile flashed into a grin, then retreated. "Not really."

"Better get good at it," Carlos said, as mildly as he knew

how, and was gratified to see the smile dim a little. Not that he wanted to eat the kid for breakfast or anything, but he was not a fan of undisciplined soldiers. In his experience, they only slowed things down. Fortunately, the NID had been careful about their screening. Only the cream of the rebellious crop was coming in now.

Talbot had a good reputation. The file said he'd served with distinction in the Army in two intelligence assignments, but he'd been languishing at Area 51 as a lackey to the scientists there. The NID had seized its chance. No one was more ready to be useful than the bored and underutilized, or so said the recruitment doctrine.

"You're being given an enormous responsibility," Carlos said. "You'll be the handler for up to ten operational teams. Their every communication will be through you. You'll be their lifeline, their point of contact. They'll come to trust you."

"But they're robots, right?" There was an interesting light in Talbot's eyes, a spark of deep curiosity. "That's what I was told."

"Not exactly. They're duplicates." Carlos handed Talbot a thick file. "Study up. These are your best friends from now on."

Talbot opened the file and turned pale. "These are…I met Major Carter, once. She's…I…" He shifted the file, as if it had suddenly become heavier. "You made a robot of her?"

"Duplicate," Carlos said, in a tone he hoped would convey that he didn't want to have to correct Talbot again. Talbot swallowed and nodded. Carlos pushed in his chair and came around the desk. "Your handle will be Piper. That's the only identifying name you need. Understand?"

"Yeah." Talbot closed the file but tucked it under his arm.

"Mr. Mendez?" He turned toward the urgent call. One of the technicians, Peterson, stood in the doorway, clipboard clutched tightly to his chest. "We're about to activate the alpha team, sir. I think you should be in the observation room when it happens."

Carlos gave Talbot—Piper—a quick glance. "Study up quickly on your new project. You'll be meeting them in just a few minutes."

Piper swallowed hard, but fished the file back out and began flipping through it. The look of intense, earnest concentration on his face made Carlos think back to his own early days with the military, when he still thought doing a good job was what counted.

"Let's go," he said, pointing at the door.

Carlos followed Peterson down the narrow corridor of the building, Piper behind him. He wasn't sure what this place had been before they took over the abandoned structure, but clearly their architecture wasn't about space and light. Everything was damp and dark and reminded him of concrete bunkers. It served its purpose, however. They wouldn't be there forever.

"By the way, stop calling me 'sir,'" Carlos said, offering Peterson what he hoped was a less scary smile than the one his superior often gave him.

"I'll try," Peterson said, eyeing him.

"The technology is operating properly?" Carlos asked, as Peterson shoved open the steel door separating the duplication lab from the rest of the facility.

"With some minor bugs." Peterson waited for Carlos to pass him, then slowly pushed the door shut. "We still don't understand all the proprietary code, but it hasn't been an issue. We do understand the programming, and that's been a simple matter to change."

Carlos nodded. The danger of any stolen technology was hard to see until they began using it. This technology had been one of the NID's best steals, even if its operatives took several years to get around to it. No question, Jack O'Neill's intervention two years before had set back off-world operations a decade or more—so many personnel lost, and others gone underground until the smoke cleared. It gave Carlos some satisfaction to think how O'Neill would react to the knowledge his duplicates would be doing the work he'd tried so hard to undo. Eventually they'd figure out how to make new duplicates, instead of using the stored patterns from SG-1 again and again, but it was all a useful experiment; they were nearing the day they'd be able to completely control the programming.

"Then let's get this show on the road."

When Jack opened his eyes, he blinked at the bland white ceiling tiles overhead, their long expanse broken by suspended fluorescent lights, and knew he wasn't anyplace where he should reasonably be flat on his back unconscious. Where the hell had they just been? Were they off-world? Why couldn't he remember what they'd been doing? He twisted his head experimentally. Nothing seemed to be out of alignment. No reason not to sit up and look for his team.

Except for the skinny guy looming over him, squinting at him the way someone might clinically examine a bug. "Take it easy, Colonel," Squinty said.

Jack took one quick glance around the room: glass windows on two sides looked only into other rooms pretty much the same, consoles doing that blinky thing consoles did. Security forces were scattered around at strategic locations, their weapons lowered, but they were watching Jack carefully. Their posture was entirely military, their uniforms devoid of identifying patches or ribbons. All of them were too far away to make grabbing for a weapon very practical.

Jack pushed up, forcing Squinty to quickly back up a few paces, like he didn't want to be within reach. Smart man. He was wearing basic fatigues, no name tag. His hair was a little long around the ears, and he seemed both nervous and eager. No clues as to who he was, though he was speaking unaccented English. No epiphanies about where they came fast enough for Jack, so he stood up. Better to have his feet under him, whatever was going on. His naked, oh so very naked feet, at the end of his naked legs, which were below his naked—

"Damn," Jack said, trying to approximate clothes by artfully arranging his hands. Which were too small. There was a joke in that. For some other time. Meanwhile, his assets were hanging out.

"Uh, we have these for you," Squinty said. He held out a blue plastic bag at arm's length, an expression of embarrassed sympathy on his face. Jack snatched it from him, dumped the contents on the floor, and picked through them: one black T-shirt, skivvies, a pair of olive BDUs, a belt, some socks, and some slipper-looking things. The skin on his back was prickling, and he did his best to keep everyone in sight, backing up against the bed while he yanked the clothes on as fast as humanly possible and stood up again, twitchy at having started out vulnerable and not even noticing for a half-minute. Squinty wasn't actually staring; he seemed to be trying hard to look everywhere but at Jack. Even so, the level of Squinty's interest gave Jack the heebie-jeebies.

Jack stepped out from the bed a little way. Although they made no overt movements, he could *feel* the soldiers tensing, practically hear their heartbeats kick up a notch. "Who the hell are you?"

Squinty shifted his weight from foot to foot and offered a small smile.

"I'm Piper."

At the left edge of Jack's peripheral vision, Carter sat up, rubbing at her eyes. Jack diplomatically lifted his gaze to her face, the better to not see her. She wrinkled her nose, eyes darting from Squinty to Jack, just as Daniel crashed up and out of his own bed on her right. He was blinking like an owl. They caught sight of each other and turned away, saying in identical tones, "Oh, boy—sorry," before noticing their own nakedness.

"All right, there, Carter? Daniel?"

"Fine, sir," Carter answered, hands flying up to her own

assets, though she sounded confused. Waking up naked in a room full of strangers would do that to a person. A couple of guards tossed bags to Daniel and Carter, who disappeared out of Jack's line of sight for a minute to throw on their own clothes.

Jack contemplated asking another question, but with his team in various states of undress, maybe waiting would be best. Instead he measured the distance from where he was standing to the only door he could see—20 feet—and estimated the odds of taking out enough of the guards to make it that far. Not good.

Daniel moved closer to Carter, hair flopping in his face. He raised a hand to adjust his glasses and, since he had none, ended up staring at the hand for a second like it belonged to someone else. "Jack? Where are we?"

"Don't know." Jack pivoted back to Piper. Behind him, some guy in a white lab coat was furiously making notes on his clipboard, pen going a mile a minute. To both of them, Jack said, "How about it? A little explanation?"

Lab-coat guy flinched, as if startled to have been addressed by Jack, and raised his eyebrows at Piper, who said, "You bet. As soon as…" He looked significantly past Jack's right shoulder, to where Teal'c was now sitting up, only to be met by a guard roughly his size, holding a bag.

"O'Neill," Teal'c said. "I am without a symbiote."

The full implications of that rattled around in Jack's head and sorted themselves out into the simple conclusion that someone didn't care much if Teal'c lived or died. That upped the stakes of whatever game this was considerably.

"Please follow me," Piper said, making it sound like a pleasant picnic invitation.

Jack fixed Piper with a narrow gaze. "Lead the way."

Piper gestured to one of the guards, who swiped a card across the access panel. "Through there," he said, stepping aside as the door slid slowly open. Jack collected his team with a glance.

The corridors were military gray. Jack felt like he'd been in a hundred bases just like this one. It was a pretty good approximation of standard issue military quarters: lots of closed doors marked with numbers, few windows that opened only into other rooms. The others were quiet. Jack could practically feel Teal'c getting ready to pounce, given the right opportunity.

Through a pair of wide blue non-secure doors, Jack found himself in a straightforward briefing room with one large circular conference table and about a dozen chairs. At the far end of the table, a man in a navy blue suit was standing, smoothing his silver tie. Jack disliked him on sight.

"Come in," the suit said, gesturing expansively at the table. His black hair was slicked back neatly. He looked spit-polished but not in a military way. Manicured. Civilian. "Have a seat."

Jack walked around the table and pulled out a chair facing the door. The others filed around behind him and sat to his left. Piper sat down next to Jack. To his credit, he didn't scoot his chair away, though his body language made Jack think that was just an act of willpower.

Suit smiled a smile that under other circumstances might seem genuine. Hard to tell. "My name is Carlos Mendez," he said. "I'm going to get right to the point. I'm sorry for the way you had to be…awakened…but we weren't actually certain everything would go as planned."

"Cryptic," Jack said. "Not exactly getting to the point."

"You're duplicates," Mendez said bluntly. "Let's just get that out of the way. You are not the real SG-1."

Beside Jack, Carter gasped softly. Jack stared at Mendez for a long moment, trying to put some context to the words. "What are you talking about?" he said.

"We created you from off-world technology." Mendez had the nerve to look apologetic.

Jack immediately patted his chest, then jerked up the edge of his T-shirt and stuffed a hand under it, palm pressed flat to where his beating heart should be. His skin was warm, but there was no heartbeat.

"Duplicates." Teal'c raised his eyebrow.

"Androids," Mendez answered. "Sophisticated ones." This time the smile that twitched the corners of his mouth looked real and proud.

Jack turned sideways in the chair to Carter, who was pressing at her pulse points. "You're not you," Jack accused her, and not until he heard the words did he realize how ridiculous it sounded, or how a thin, sharp line of anxiety had tightened around his throat. It wasn't possible. But something in his brain told him that it was. If he concentrated on it, he could almost bring it into focus, a running patter in the background. He thought of the blinking consoles in the lab down the hall, programs running silently, click click click. For the tiniest fraction of a second, something flashed in his eyes — numbers, maybe — but he denied it. The patter receded. He fisted his hands on the table in front of him. Not the time for an existential crisis.

"I feel like me," Carter said, meeting his eyes with her own wide blue stare. As if trying to prove it, her hands traveled over her fake skin, looking for…what? Seams? "But I don't… I'm not…"

"No. You're not." Mendez pulled out his chair and sat down, leaning forward to clasp his hands and rest them on the smooth wooden table. "We created you to serve a need."

"Created us how?" Daniel, of course, interrupting as per his usual pattern. Or the usual pattern of the original. Jack tilted his head to one side and shook it. Too bizarre. In the back of his mind, or whatever it was, he was preoccupied with his own series of questions: where they were, what the real deal was here, and how he could immediately terminate his existence if he didn't like the answers to questions one and two.

He grabbed the pen clipped to the edge of Mendez's folder, clicked it open, and plunged it into his leg. It hurt, a brief flare of pain, and then it just…didn't. He pulled the pen out, ignoring Carter and Daniel's shocked looks and Mendez's thinned lips. The pen dripped a viscous gray goo.

"Ugh," he said, flinging the pen back on the table.

"You can be damaged," Mendez said. "Make no mistake: you can die."

"You mean be terminated," Carter said coldly.

"Whatever terminology suits you, Captain." Mendez assessed her for a moment, then directed his attention back to Jack. "We represent Earth's interests. The SGC has been closed down for some time now. Bureaucrats and paper-pushers have seen to it that the value of Earth's Stargate goes unrecognized. SG-1 is presumed dead." He paused to let that sink in. "No one is going out there, looking for technology to save our world. We couldn't stand by and see this happen, so we took matters into our own hands."

"And created a bunch of robots?" Jack pressed his fingers experimentally into the hole he'd made in his robot leg. He needed a Band-Aid. Or a glue gun.

"Yes — can we get back to my question? Created us how?" Daniel again, persistent.

"We used duplicating technology SG-1 originally found off-world."

"Our team…originally…" Carter frowned. "What year is this?"

"2002."

Carter said, "Sir, it should be 1998."

"That's when SG-1 stumbled across this technology, yes. The team was duplicated, and when that matter was resolved, they left the technology behind. Fortunately for us."

"Yes, isn't that nice," Jack said. "What was that about the SGC?"

"Closed," Mendez said. "Shut down. No one looking out for Earth."

"I sense a 'but,'" Daniel said.

"Oh, yes," Mendez answered. He smiled. "Looking out for

Earth is your job now."

Jack folded his arms across his apparently empty chest. "And we should believe you why, again?"

"Because it's the truth." Mendez looked from one to the other of them, ever so earnest. Jack couldn't get a clear read on him. That bugged him. "We will give you access to SG-1's essential mission files. Everything you've missed. New languages, Dr. Jackson. New technologies, Captain Carter. Many new things, new projects."

"And then?" Jack said.

"Then you'll begin going off-world. You'll need to earn your keep."

"This is not a life," Jack said. "This is…"

"This is your duty," Mendez said. He stood up, which was apparently some kind of signal. The guards pushed the doors open and stood waiting. "You've been designated SG-Alpha. You've already met your handler."

Piper pushed back from the table and stood up. He cleared his throat and moved down the table, shaking their hands in turn like some kind of perverse receiving line. The expression on his face told Jack this was a brave new world for him too. He seemed a little stunned by the whole thing, and when he caught Jack watching him, his eyes shifted away.

"Handler?" Carter said, as if the whole thing was too surreal for words.

"For your missions. You'll be going off-world regularly."

Jack glanced at Piper. Piper looked away again. Suspicion took up a nice permanent spot in the back of Jack's brain.

"And what world would this be, exactly?" Jack was working pretty hard to maintain a dispassionate attitude about the fact that he wasn't Jack O'Neill, wasn't on Earth, and had no idea who the hell these people were, but it was getting more difficult by the second.

"All in good time."

"Now seems like a good time," Daniel said.

"We'll need to get you outfitted. Tell you a bit about your

enhancements. Then we'll answer more of your questions."
Mendez nodded to Piper, who smiled nervously at them.

"Come on," Piper said. "I have some stuff to show you."
He popped open the door with one hand and held it, waiting.
Jack had the impression that he was an overeager kid about to
play with his new toys on Christmas. He finally looked right
at Jack, this time not so much meeting his eyes as trying to
look inside his head. "Have you accessed it yet? The heads
up?" He swirled a finger in front of his own eye. "Pretty useful in the field. Pretty cool too."

Ignoring the question, Jack backed away from the table
and as he passed Daniel, said, "Maybe there will be an army
of robot women." Carter's scowl was the best, most normal
thing Jack had seen all day. He thought that was probably
going to be the high point; it was bound to be all downhill
from there.

Ignis (P9T-166)
May, 2002

The moment they stepped out of the Stargate, spikes of
crimson fire exploded along Jack's fake skin, like flaying
acid. He looked down at his arms, expecting to see blackened skin shriveling back along gears and circuits, but they
looked perfectly normal. The pain would have taken his breath
away, if he still needed to breathe. All Mendez's speeches, all
the pretty pictures of red gases swirling in the breeze on this
strange little planet where the magical alien doodads were
hidden, and he hadn't mentioned how it would *feel*.

"Oh, my God," Daniel said next to him, shaking his arms
as the wind cut across them again. Jack grimaced in empathy.

"It's the pain response," Carter said faintly, shoulders
hunched in as if she hoped to curl in on herself, defend her
body against the assault. "It's there to tell us there's danger

to the mechanism."

"Just like being alive," Jack said, wallowing in the lovely irony of it. Meanwhile, his fake eyeballs were burning like sulfur was being streamed into them. "Let's get on with it so we can get the hell out of here."

"Sir," Carter said, pointing to her right at something Jack vaguely interpreted as *primary target .238 kilometers buried 10.6 centimeters beneath the surface.* He blinked, annoyed at his own supposed brain going into stealth analytical computer mode without him asking it to. He had no idea, anyway, how he knew all that. He just did.

Teal'c stepped away and set off at a rapid jog across the wasted burnt-red landscape, Daniel right behind him, and Jack loped along with them. The contrasting joy of having no pain in his knees, his back, or his neck was overwhelmed by the beating agony of the ferocious radiation, the heated wind battering at him. He couldn't even properly appreciate not having to feel old for a change.

It wasn't a high price to pay for doing something his real live counterpart could never do, even in a protective suit. But pain without a real purpose made him sad because it didn't make much difference if he melted on the spot. There were other kinds of pain, and there was a debate for people like Daniel in that, but Jack didn't have time for it.

The ruins around them were scrubbed a sickly gray-green. The squat buildings, their tops blown away, had singed edges crumbling into the gusting wind. Someone had lived here once, in this place that reminded Jack of hell; the idea of it seemed impossible. Jack had tuned out all the scientific stuff about the what and who of it, but he couldn't imagine how anything breathed here.

Of course, he was proof that what lived didn't have to breathe. The irony slapped him upside the head, hard.

Ahead, Daniel stopped and scrubbed furiously at his arms and chest like he was brushing away flies. The same sensation assaulted Jack, sharpened-glass pinpricks all across his body, overloading him with the desire to scratch. He stopped, focused on forcing the sensation away, and it receded. "Come on," he said to Daniel, with gritted teeth. "Think your way through it."

"Sir," Carter said, pulling up short beside him. Ahead, Teal'c continued on. "Sir, it isn't that easy, it's—" She gestured to her neck, where it looked as if seams had opened up along the once-graceful lines of her throat, and her head looked in danger of toppling off.

Daniel held out his arm. The skin over his wrists and below his shirt cuffs had a strange grayish char to it, the kind of thing that had stopped turning the real Jack's stomach years before, but it looked pretty horrible. "So much for indestructible," Jack said, noting the stoic way Daniel's jaw was set, no complaints finding voice. "Let's move it, people."

Teal'c knelt beside a free-standing wall where the invisible crosshairs in Jack's brain said *X marks the spot* and began moving dirt with his bare hands. Daniel crouched beside him, not digging, his hands tucked down between his legs. Carter turned to take up a defensive position, though there wasn't much to defend against, other than the atmosphere.

Carter closed her eyes and said, as though reading from the inside of her eyelids, "Atmospheric pressure and temperature are increasing, sir. We have two minutes before system integrity is compromised."

"Nice," Jack said, thinking that "compromised integrity" was such a pleasant way of referring to imminent death. He noticed his clothes were starting to disintegrate now, bits of thread flying breezily off into the ether.

"O'Neill," Teal'c called, and then a blaring shout inside Jack's head: *O'NEILL.*

"Ahhh," Jack hissed, heel of his hand coming up to knock against his temple.

"Internal comms," Sam said urgently. She held one hand to her throat, covering the damaged area. She closed her eyes and her voice blared inside Jack's head, as Teal'c's had a second before: *CAN YOU HEAR ME?*

"Dial it down," Jack said, through gritted teeth.

I have the object, Teal'c said, and through him Jack understood it was small enough to fit in the palm of Teal'c's huge hand, a round ruby with hash marks scored across its face. There was nothing about it that seemed to make it worth this little trip into the furnace, beyond giving Mendez a chance to see how well his new toy soldiers were going to jump through his hoops. For all Jack knew, the little jewel was a championship belt buckle for alien rodeo-riding. It'd look good on the shelf in Mendez's office. He felt a sudden pang of empathy for every MALP he'd ever watched tip over an event horizon. Careful not to touch its surface, Teal'c slipped the jewel into a pouch Daniel held out, and Jack pivoted on his heel, what was left of his boot flapping around his foot.

The DHD was off-center of the gate, some of its symbols excoriated by the elements, but intact. Jack punched the symbols fast, so fast his blackening hand was a blur. The wormhole popped to life, an odd purplish color, wrong and weird like everything else in this place. Carter passed him, her uniform hanging off her shoulders in a patchwork of sooty green and gray. Jack hit the bottom step and turned to see Teal'c doubled over, whatever cranks that turned the machinery having apparently given up. Daniel bent beside him.

Jack had barely moved two steps toward them when Daniel slipped an arm under Teal'c and dead-lifted him from the ground to throw him over his shoulder. Jack took a moment to properly appreciate how wrong that was. A moment was all he had; one of his eyes gave out, a misfire of green sparks and then darkness. "Go!" he told Daniel, unnecessarily, and Daniel threw him an impatient look as he took the steps two at a time and barreled through the wormhole.

Jack followed, and on the other side he met the steaming, charred heap of his friends: Teal'c flat on his back and half-clothed, Daniel looking as pissed as Jack had ever seen him, and Carter staunchly ignoring the fact that her skin had opened up in maybe a dozen places, all her innards sparkling silver out at them in ways that made Jack turn away. The stoic part of him that had gone along in the name of duty, of being useful, morphed into an ineloquent rage. He had to resist the urge to put his hand on Carter's shoulder, to pat Daniel on the back.

Mendez stood at the low edge of the ramp watching, the antithesis of Hammond in every way. His smile seemed lopsided, the first evidence of actual humanity Jack had seen out of him, as he made sharp gestures sending technicians to their side. "Welcome back," he said. "Congratulations on completing a very difficult first mission."

First. Many more to come. Jack submitted to having his blackened pieces peeled off, his arms wrapped, a blanket thrown around him for the sake of appearances and practicality, no real comfort or need, and pictured an unending life filled with moments just like this.

He thought next time he might just take the chance to get in the way of an incoming wormhole.

But then Daniel made a noise, something that might have been a cry of pain, and he remembered: his team, his duty, his responsibility. For as long as the last of them were in existence. And maybe one second longer.

In Carter's eyes, he saw the certainty that the time was going to come sooner rather than later.

CHAPTER THREE

SGC
October 30, 2002; one day after invasion of Eshet

Daniel had no love for the interrogation rooms. Aside from the fact they were cold and claustrophobic, he'd spent enough time on the wrong side of the table over the years. He shared at least some of those unpleasant memories with the Daniel Jackson facsimile waiting to be debriefed inside Room A. Daniel watched him through the small rectangular window and tried to keep in mind that this other Daniel might have a knowledge gap of four years. A great deal had happened in that time.

"You really think this is going to be productive?" Jack leaned closer and looked through the window, then pulled back like he was afraid he'd be caught staring. Daniel glanced in again and saw a small smile on the facsimile's face. It was unnerving to recognize it, and the sentiment behind it: Jack was never subtle, and that never ceased to amuse Daniel. Either Daniel, apparently.

"Well, if he's willing to give up information, I don't see why it wouldn't be." Daniel held up the tablet he'd been curling in front of him like a shield. "I have a long list of questions, some from General Hammond, some from Sam. You want to add anything?"

"No," Jack said. "Unless maybe he can tell me how to get you to stop arguing with me when you're clearly wrong."

"Very funny." Daniel gave him a look and nodded to the airman at the door, who swiped his security card and pushed the door open for Daniel.

Airmen bustled around, setting up cameras and microphones, but Daniel's attention was focused on his duplicate, who glanced up at him once and then looked back down at his hands. Daniel couldn't help staring at the robot, at the fine lines on his skin approximating the same lines Daniel saw on his own face every morning when he shaved. The hair on the back of his neck rose.

"Um," Daniel said. He set his notebook and pen down on the table and nodded to the airman. "You can go."

"We'll be outside, sir. Colonel O'Neill's orders."

"Right," Daniel said. All the arguments against it wouldn't get him anywhere, and to make matters worse, he wasn't entirely sure the guards weren't necessary. He pulled out his chair and sat down in front of his imperfect mirror image. This Daniel was a retro model with longer hair. The uniform was current, though, and the anomaly jarred Daniel. He pointed to it. "You have the most recent SGC patch. You shouldn't."

His counterpart smiled, a little lopsided. "I wear what they give me. And this is what they gave me."

Daniel nodded slowly. "Guess you're going to tell me who the 'they' is."

"The NID, we think."

"Ah." There were more questions in Daniel's head than he could sort through or articulate, so he abandoned the list and settled on the easiest first. "I'm not quite sure what to call you."

"I can see how that'd be strange." The robot's eyes narrowed, something Daniel recognized as a tic of his own, an outward sign of working on a problem. "To me, I'm you. To me, you're not really me anymore. But to you, I'm not me."

"Well, that's…confusing."

"Try being me for a while. Then let's talk about confusing."

"I see your point." Daniel shifted in the chair and glanced at the camera, which wasn't on. Yet. "How about if I just call you Dan?"

"That's fine." Dan smiled. "Odd, but fine. No one's ever called me that."

"That's why I chose it," Daniel answered, saw the understanding register on Dan's face. A name that wasn't his, for someone who wasn't him.

"Of course it is." Dan didn't smile, exactly, but close enough for Daniel to know there was no resentment there. Daniel wasn't sure why; if he were the duplicate, he wasn't entirely sure he'd be so gracious. Only one of them could be Daniel Jackson in the world Daniel knew and embraced. "I guess I don't really feel much like a Dan."

Daniel cleared his throat. Jack would have a field day with the idea of giving Dan a name at all. *It's a thing, Daniel,* Jack would tell him, at his earliest opportunity. *It's not human.* Daniel batted the little Jack voice in his head away with a frown.

"You still hear Jack, don't you? Disagreeing. Editorializing." Dan was watching Daniel with the kind of intensity Daniel usually reserved for things he had to decipher and translate, and he twitched a little to think anyone could understand the inside of his head so well.

"Sometimes."

"Be glad you can turn it off." Daniel tapped his ear. "I hear Jack in real time. When he's nearby."

"Internal radios, right."

"Thinks out loud, sometimes," Dan said.

"Huh." Daniel picked up his pen and said, "So you were created…where?"

"I'm not sure, actually. The handler calls the planet Perseus, but that's not all that illuminating. I woke up in a lab, surrounded by officers wearing military uniforms. We were all there. They gave us uniforms and we got dressed."

Daniel's eyebrows gave him away. "You woke up naked?"

"No one there seemed surprised by it, so we tried not to be."

"We? So, there's...the team..."

"We were all duplicated."

"So, the Jack I saw on the battlefield on Eshet?"

Another nod. "My team. They called us SG-Alpha."

"I see."

"You should stop that," Dan said. "Those little asides to indicate you're listening. I know you're listening."

Daniel opened his mouth, closed it. He tapped the pen on the paper. This really wasn't going the way he'd hoped it would. But what had he hoped, really? That they'd strike up a friendly conversation, exchange war stories about where they'd been all this time, what they'd done? He hoped like hell Jack wasn't outside watching. The whole thing left him unsettled in ways he'd rather Jack not know, because it would just be fodder for a hundred of those arguments Jack found so tedious.

"If you're wondering when I was created—5 months, 24 days, 11 minutes, and 5.4 seconds ago."

"By the time you say it, the time is inaccurate," Daniel said. "That must be annoying."

"I try not to think about it that way," Dan answered. "It's just one more tool, like your pen or your paper. One more way to catalog the world around me. Whatever world it may be." He pointed at the wall clock. "The one in my head is more accurate than any of yours. For instance, it tells me I have 23 hours, 6 minutes, 37 seconds and change of power left."

"And then what?"

"Then I die."

"But you can be taken back and recharged...right?"

"Doesn't work that way." Dan took what appeared to be a deep breath. For some reason, that made Daniel's hair stand up again. He half-expected Dan to be a wax statue, and statues don't breathe. "It's...I'm an alkaline battery, not a rechargeable. Once the juice is gone, it's gone."

"But you can leave your power source for short periods

and return to recharge, can't you?"

"Something like that." Dan's impatience smoothed into a tolerant look, like a parent gives a confused child. "As long as we aren't drained completely. It's complicated."

"Should I get Sam?"

"She wouldn't understand either. Which, actually, might be a problem." Dan tapped his chest. "Power sources are the real issue, we think. That's why I came here. To warn you. And because I'm pressed for time, I'll have to hit the highlights. You can connect the dots."

Daniel drew his pen across the paper and wrote in Asgard: *sounds more like Jack*.

"You try having only Jack as your primary source of company and see what happens to you," Dan said, which gave Daniel the creeps because he was reading upside down and in a language Daniel had learned after the first set of duplicates was left behind on Altair, and getting the gist anyway.

"How do you know this language?" Daniel asked, pointing to the Asgard scrawls.

"They gave us access to some of your mission data," Dan said. With an apologetic twitch of his eyebrows, he tapped his head. "I, uh, learn fast."

Daniel sighed. 'Fast' probably meant milliseconds. It was enough to make him wish for an upgrade. "So you woke up naked in a lab, and…"

"Ah. Right. Naked in the lab, with my team, and they gave me a uniform. They told us we'd been created as a last resort, that the real SG-1 was dead and we were needed to find alien technology for the defense of Earth at all costs. It all sounded convincing, at first."

Daniel thought about waking up in a lab and knowing he wasn't himself, the real Daniel, and still having to carry on, create a life independent of what Daniel Jackson is. Was. "You thought you were all that was left of me."

"Well, it's difficult to think of myself as anyone but Daniel Jackson, as you might imagine. Especially when I thought you were dead and I was the only Daniel Jackson of any kind around." Dan tilted his head back and looked at the ceiling. "Turned out that was wrong too."

A low, sickening suspicion was churning in Daniel's stomach. "How many other teams are there?" he asked.

"Not sure. I know of eight. Well, there were eight manufactured. Not all of them woke up. Four of them lasted. That's…not relevant to what we need to discuss. They aren't a threat to you, and I don't have time to play it all out for you right now." There was a whole history there he waved away with his hand as he leaned forward to level his gaze at Daniel. Daniel found himself searching the blue eyes for some sign of artificiality. He wasn't sure if he was more or less disturbed to find none.

"Why would they need so many teams? I don't understand."

"We can go where human teams couldn't — or so they told us. We traveled to gates underwater, worlds on fire, any place human lungs would burn with the toxins in the air or collapse from the pressure. We understood we were disposable." Dan went back to looking at his hands, but the bitterness crept into his voice. "Jack reminded me every time we went through the gate that it was no different than what it was before. Every mission's a risk."

"He's always been about the mission," Daniel said, thinking of the horror any version of Jack would feel at being a carbon copy, and a disposable one at that. "About protecting Earth. We all are."

"Even if you aren't privileged to be a part of the thing you protect anymore," Dan said. "Ever again."

Daniel's stomach turned over, eating itself with acid. "Why not just make your own power sources and take off during a mission? You must have known a thousand gate addresses."

"Couldn't. There were key bits of knowledge erased from our programming. Earth's gate address, for one. The practical understanding of our power sources, for another."

"You're saying the NID tinkered with Harlan's original programming?" Daniel stopped taking notes and stared. It should have occurred to him from the moment the robot mentioned the NID. They never had pure motives for anything. "To keep you from discovering the truth?"

"We were the first team off the table. The ones that came after us were...different." Dan winced. "Harder. More callous. They were working to take all the humanity out of the teams, make us pure soldiers. It didn't take with all the teams. But the last team, the theta team...something is wrong with them on a fundamental level. The moral center of their programs is gone. They *are* a threat."

"So you were the prototype, but the NID wanted something a duplicate of any of us wouldn't give it." Daniel rubbed a finger over the bridge of his nose, warding off the incipient headache. "And they had to strip away everything we are to get there."

"Worse than that." Dan rested his arms on the table, hands folded in front of him in their restraints. To Dan, with strength far beyond that of a normal human, they had to be just a formality, a symbol of his position here. "The theta team has gone rogue, off the radar. We were sent to find them. That's why we were on Eshet. We tracked them there but arrived too late, got cut off from the gate by your friends, the angry Jaffa. Finding you was just good luck." His thin smile didn't reach his eyes. "And confirmation once and for all that everything we'd been told was a lie."

"They're killers," Daniel said, thinking of the village, the screaming girl in the middle of the trail, the terror on her face. "It was them, in the village."

"Yes."

"Those people must have been half-insane," Daniel murmured. "Three versions of the same people. My God."

"One SG-1 is enough," Dan said wryly.

Daniel nodded. "But what was the rogue team looking

for?"

"Autonomy." At Daniel's questioning look, Dan added, "They want technology to enable their Sam to build an independent power source." More softly, he said, "They know they've been lied to, just like we do. They have nothing left to lose."

"And once they get the power source..."

"Try to imagine a version of Teal'c or Jack—or you—with no conscience," Dan said. "There's the answer."

Daniel didn't have to do much imagining; he'd seen bits and pieces of that nightmare in various forms. "Tell me how we can stop them."

"I can't help you," Dan said. "I can never go back. The gate on Perseus has an iris, and my GDO codes will have been locked out. None of the off-site bases will be accessible to me either."

"But you know where they are?"

"Yes. We figure the thetas will try to hole up in one of them. I'll give you all the intel I have, and maybe you can make something of it." Dan reached for Daniel's pen, then seemed to think better of it. "A laptop would be better. I can type much faster than I can write it all longhand."

Daniel pushed back the chair and went to tap on the door. When the airman stationed outside opened it, he said, "Please arrange to have a laptop and several external hard drives brought down. And get Colonel O'Neill."

"Okay, Dr. Jackson." The airman clicked the door shut and set off down the hallway at a loping jog.

Daniel turned back to the robot, who was watching him with sadness in his eyes. It wasn't difficult for Daniel to think of him as human, as his own being, and Dan would be dead in a day. He looked at his watch. Twenty-three hours. Less than a day. He gestured at Dan to raise his hands. When he did, Daniel pulled out his penknife and sliced through the restraints. "You knew you wouldn't make it back," Daniel said. "You came anyway."

"Someone had to warn you. We saw our opportunity the minute you came through the gate." Dan's thin smile was back. "We still love Earth, even if we don't belong here. Even if we were never meant to be."

"That's Jack talking," Daniel said.

"That's all of us." Dan stood up and went to the back wall, pressed his fingers against it. "We're prisoners of our own desire to be alive as much as we were prisoners of the NID. None of us wants the lives we have. We're not grateful for them. They aren't any kind of lives at all. We don't...we aren't...like you. Like SG-1 is. Should be."

"What do you mean?" Daniel waited, but Dan said nothing more. The weight of Dan's way of life, the isolation and lack of anything they'd ever wanted or known, settled on Daniel's shoulders. It struck him then that Dan didn't know about Sha're, hadn't asked about her.

It might have been kinder to leave the truth unsaid, but Daniel couldn't imagine a version of himself who wouldn't want to know. "You haven't asked about Sha're," he said quietly.

"She's not mine to ask about," Dan answered.

"The feelings are the same," Daniel said. "The need to know."

A long silence, and then, not looking at Daniel: "Yes."

"She died," Daniel said, stopping there because even now, after so many years, to speak of it brought the raw anger and grief rushing up as if it had never been dealt with or set aside. "Teal'c killed her to save me when Amaunet attacked me. He had no choice."

"So he took her from you twice."

Daniel bristled, a bit. "No. The Goa'uld did that. Teal'c saved my life."

Dan sat down on the cot in the corner and stared at a fixed point on the floor. "I never allowed myself to think of her," he said. "She could only be one man's wife. I'm not even a man."

For a moment, Daniel had a flash of having the same conversation with every one of the Daniel duplicates, and bile rose in his throat. "I'm sorry," he said, though it felt empty, and there were no better words to ease the moment.

"So am I," Dan said. "For you, I mean." He looked up at Daniel. "We thought we were doing something to help Earth, you know. Something important, to give our existence meaning."

Daniel bit back the urge to apologize again for the misery this version of himself had gone through. One purpose in his life, and now he knew even that was a lie, that there was no greater good being served by his actions.

"Anything else about your life you'd like to share?" There was bitterness in the question, and just a bit of envy. Daniel supposed Dan was allowed.

"I'm going to take what you've told me to Jack. There might be something we can do."

"Hope so," Dan said. He jerked his chin toward the clock. "Time's running out. And my team isn't expecting me back."

To hear such a casual acceptance of death threw Daniel. "What's going to happen to the rest of your team?" he asked.

Dan looked away, and in the silence that followed, seconds slipped away, irretrievable. "They'll continue with the mission. Keep looking for the thetas. After that..." He spread his hands and let them fall to hang limply between his knees. "They have as much reserve power as I have. And as many options."

"I'm sorry," Daniel said softly, but he bit back the rest of the platitudes and thanks he wanted to give. They couldn't comfort Dan, just as they wouldn't comfort Daniel if the shoe was on the other foot. "I'll be back shortly," he said instead, and Dan nodded.

In the corridor, Daniel watched the airmen parade by with their arms full of cords and computers and drives, and concentrated on the breath filling his lungs, the too-rapid heartbeat pulsing beneath his warm, live skin. Amazing how grateful and guilty it made him feel, in equal measure.

NID Secondary Outpost "Hawaii" (P7A-025)
October 30, 2002, one day after invasion of Eshet

"You know," Jackson said, with just enough of that bored condescension in his voice to make O'Neill's hackles rise, "dead people aren't exactly the best source of information."

The body at his feet was a heap of broken angles held together by a lab coat. On the far side of the room, the technician's glasses lay on the floor against the wall, and one of her hands was stretched out along the floor, as if reaching for them. Jackson stepped over the body and went to retrieve the glasses, then held them up to the light to squint through the lenses. He cleaned them briefly on his shirt before brushing the technician's hair out of the blood on her forehead and settling the glasses back on her startled face. In O'Neill's mind something stuttered, an image of another Jackson shoving his glasses up his nose and looking owlishly at him, his mouth opening to protest, or to argue, or maybe to laugh. That was the meat-memory, not his own. In his short life, O'Neill had never seen Jackson laugh.

"We could've interrogated her," Jackson continued.

"She wasn't gonna talk." O'Neill knew the look. The technician was a worker bee and a true believer; no way she was going to spill without authorization from five levels of superiors.

"I could've gotten through to her."

"We don't have time for that," O'Neill said, turning his back on him and leaning over the monitor to watch Carter's fingers blurring with motion over the keyboard. "Besides, we don't need a meat-brain. We've got Carter. Right, Carter?"

She flicked him a glance and went back to "getting through" to the outpost's mainframe. "It would've been quicker to have the access codes," she observed dryly with a little nod toward the dead technician.

Enunciating clearly, O'Neill reminded her, "She wasn't going to talk."

"Nor were the others."

They all turned to watch Teal'c come into the lab, and O'Neill grinned to see him weighed down with goodies.

"Brought presents, did ya, Santa?" O'Neill took the zat Teal'c handed him, checked the charge, and passed it along to Jackson. He slung a second P90 over his shoulder and stuffed the extra magazines into his vest, leaving a few for Carter on the top of the monitor. He lifted his chin toward Teal'c's prize. "They equipping marines with staff weapons these days?"

Teal'c swung the weapon up. "There is a storeroom at the end of this corridor beyond the mess hall. There is not much of use, but they had this."

The nose of the weapon crackled as he activated it a few inches from O'Neill's chest. With his index finger, O'Neill pushed on it until Teal'c gave in and let it swing away. "Might want to watch where you're pointing that," O'Neill advised mildly.

"Who says he wasn't?" Jackson's smile was thin and did nothing at all to convince O'Neill he was joking.

"Ah, the banter," O'Neill sighed wistfully. "The bonding. The camaraderie." He aimed a piercing glare at Jackson and went back to looming over Carter. "Captain, the clock is ticking." *And*, he added to himself, *some of us are in danger of dying sooner than others*.

"I know the time. Sir." Over the last few weeks, O'Neill had measured to the millisecond the various increments of that delay between the reply and the 'sir.' Someday he'd have to make a chart, calculate the maximum interval so that he'd know when the time finally came to duck.

In the meantime, he propped his chin on his fist and looked around. As he knew from their first stroll around the joint, there wasn't much to the installation. Besides this room, with its banks of computers blinking away as they slowly churned raw data into useful intel, there was the mess, still smelling of bacon, a deck of cards scattered around the bodies of another tech and a marine. A bunk room held five empty beds and one still occupied by a dead guy — whether a soldier or a tech, it was hard to tell. Finally, there was the gate-room, with two marines full of holes lying where they fell at the foot of the ramp, and on the ramp itself, the body of the NID operative the thetas had used to give them a foot in the door. Having taken the brunt of O'Neill's frustration, the body of the operative was in pretty bad shape, but O'Neill figured it was the operative's own fault for poking his nose where it didn't belong. The guy had trashed the thetas' back-up power plant — Carter's pride-and-joy — and as far as O'Neill was concerned, anything that the thetas did after that could be laid at the operative's feet. When he'd blown up the power plant, he'd taken their only chance at a peaceful exit scenario. Now, they were going to have to find some other way to stay out from under the NID, and taking over this miserable outpost was a start.

The gate itself was zipped up tight behind its iris, so at least the thetas wouldn't have to worry about the cavalry showing up here for a show-down. That was a plus. But, for all its strategic value, and even without the addition of the dead bodies, the place was depressing: gray concrete blending into gray bedrock. Secondary Outpost "Hawaii" — so named, apparently, by someone with a healthy sense of irony — was just a way-station for shuffling NID personnel and equipment through the gate system, with all the comfort of a glorified galactic bus station, and no backup power units to warm the circuits of the weary traveling robot. A klick above them, as the monitor behind Teal'c showed, ground level was silent and still in the vacuum. The stars were more than half obscured by the oppressive, rust-colored bulk of a gas giant. Beside the monitor was a poster inviting them all to visit beautiful Hawaii, the real one, with the palm trees and the clear, blue water. Comparing the two views, O'Neill was willing to bet that this planet hadn't seen liquid water in a billion years. Even Perseus, with its milky, listless sunlight that never penetrated into the endless warren of corridors and labs, was a gem compared to Outpost Hawaii.

Aiming with his finger at the poster, O'Neill blew an imaginary hole in the paper beach. Not like he was ever going to see it.

"Bingo," Carter said suddenly, lifting her hands off the keyboard and sitting back in her chair. "We're in."

"It's about time," O'Neill muttered and, ignoring her irritated look, came around the desk and yanked a chair over to sit beside her. "So, what's interesting?"

As it turned out, O'Neill's idea of interesting and Carter's and Jackson's were all different. In the end, he had to concede the field, shoving himself away from the desk and letting Jackson take his place. There was a lot of stuff to sift through, most of it packed away in little encrypted boxes. For about the millionth time since he'd known her, Carter repeated her low-key rant about not having some kind of direct interface with computer technology, because fingers — even her fingers — were slow, and the computer's buffer was even slower. Of course, there was no way the NID was going to give them that kind of easy access. They were lucky the bastards left them enough brains to make sentences, let alone the wherewithal to get cozy with their computers. He told Carter to quit bitching and left them to it.

By the time she called him back to the lab, he'd gone over the installation again, with Teal'c in tow to tell him, "I already looked there, O'Neill," every time he opened a door or a drawer. He counted their ammo ten or fifty times and finally lay down in the bunk room to stare at the ceiling and watch the time ticking by inside his head. In the next bunk, the dead guy stared at the ceiling too. Finally, Jackson pinged him on internal radio, inviting him back to the control room.

"Okay," Jackson said as O'Neill came around the desk

again and looked at the monitor over their shoulders. "We've been able to access the mission logs and to dig into some of the status reports. This one—" He clicked open a window and sat back to crane his neck at O'Neill. "—is the background intel on that device we were sent to Eshet to retrieve." On the screen was an image of the bagel-sized device Jackson had held up smugly in the burning village, the one a whole bunch of people had died to protect. It was black and round and covered with a fine network of curlicues O'Neill figured were numbers or letters. He could feel his brain already working on the translation, but he looked at Jackson for the explanation instead. Jackson had the context to make sense of the data. "And you can see that I was right about it," Jackson was saying, "and why our friends at the NID didn't want us to know what it really was."

O'Neill looked at the squiggles and lines on the device. "Wow, that is fascinating. It's all so clear."

Jackson opened his mouth, but Carter cut him off. "It's a power source. Or, at least, it's part of one. The idea is that there's at least two pieces that work together. According to the records, the guys on Perseus speculated that this one is like a key, it grants access, primes the pump so to speak. Somewhere, there's a control device that regulates the energy, converts it into something useable. In time I could figure it out—"

"If we had time, Captain, we wouldn't need to figure it out." O'Neill stood up and scowled at the Hawaii poster. "It's moot, anyway. We don't have the other piece. Or this pump thing that needs priming."

"True," Jackson said, "but those people were trading partners in a group of three other planets. According to the log, the NID suspected that the pieces might have been hidden on one or more of them."

He brought up a series of gate addresses, and O'Neill slotted them into place in his memory. Three planets. "Crap." The ticking clock in his head sounded like thunder.

Shrugging, Carter said, "Well, it narrows the field, anyway. Three is a heck of a lot better odds than a few million. In the meantime, here's something you might like." She shifted her chair over to displace Daniel and opened another window.

In it were another gate address and a series of images of what looked like the gloomiest hospital in the galaxy. Leaning forward and squinting (although more from habit than necessity), O'Neill could make out a number of beds sticking out like spokes from a central hub. In the background were pipes and ductwork and a lot of dingy concrete.

"Okay, again, fascinating."

"It's the first," Jackson said, pointing at the screen as though O'Neill wasn't already staring at it.

"The first what?" O'Neill shrugged off his irritation at the obliqueness, because he also knew that this sort of thing happened when Jackson was excited, when his brain was leaping ahead to implications and forgetting to make his mouth explain for the class.

"The place of our origin."

O'Neill could feel Teal'c moving in behind him to look at the screen, too. "That is untrue," Teal'c said. "We originated from the NID lab on Perseus."

"Not *us* us." Jackson made a little circle with his finger to include the four of them. "I mean *us* us." The circle got wider. "Our kind. This is where it started. Altair."

O'Neill rocked back on his heels and frowned skeptically. "*That's* the Garden of Eden? Sorry, but that does not look to me like the home of state-of-the-art android manufacturing." Even as he objected, though, there was another stutter in his head, a fragment of a not-memory, something from the meat-memory that felt like déjà-vu. He chewed his lip for a moment and stared at the image on the monitor, the vast sprawl of machinery fading into the shadowy distance. "They were there," he said. "The original SG-1."

Nodding, Carter clicked through a few more shots of the installation, stopping at the picture of a round-faced guy with a big, somewhat uncertain smile. "Meet Harlan, our maker," she said.

O'Neill braced himself on the back of her chair and leaned closer to the screen to tap Harlan's forehead with a finger. "I always thought God would be, I dunno, more imposing."

"I did not," Teal'c answered. "In my experience, gods are less impressive when personally encountered."

Carter backed up to a long shot of the cavernous interior of Harlan's installation and zoomed in on a sparkly metal disco ball-type thing floating near the ceiling. "Maybe he can make it up to us."

"By teaching us the Hustle?"

"By giving us this power source."

O'Neill smiled. The day was starting to look up.

SGC
October 30, 2002, one day after invasion of Eshet

Jack found Carter in her lab, perched on her tall stool at the counter leaning close to her laptop screen and chewing on a pencil, which wasn't exactly a decent substitute for the lunch she'd skipped.

"More nutrition in a power bar," he said from the doorway.

Jumping at the sound of his voice, she dropped her pencil. He picked it up off the floor on his way in and handed it back to her.

"Thanks, sir." She took the pencil, almost put it back in her mouth, but thought better of it and dropped it into the cup beside the laptop.

He circled around behind her so he could get a look at the screen. It was filled with what looked like one giant paragraph. "Light reading?"

She shook her head like she wished that were true. "No, actually." She paged down. The paragraph continued without a break. "This is some of the material the Daniel duplicate provided. I'm just trying to sort through it." After highlighting a section, she cut it and moved it to another window. "The duplicate organizes information just like Daniel does."

"Illogically?"

Carter flashed him a grin and went back to shuffling information between windows. "Daniel's not illogical, sir. He just has his own way of putting things together. He thinks in terms of narratives. In his mind, things only make sense when they're laid out like a story. Apparently the duplicate thinks the same way."

"But the robot is a robot." It didn't seem right. Jack expected to see charts and graphs. Something more...mechanical.

"I know!" Now Carter was all aglow with that geeky excitement that meant that in fifty words or less she was going to rocket out of the range of normal-guy understanding. He braced himself internally and got ready to deploy his cut-to-the-chase expression. "It's fascinating," she went on with a nod toward the screen. "You would think that the programming — and that's not even counting the differences in somatic response to stimuli, and the way that information is delivered and processed — would result in some kind of radical restructuring of the duplicate's worldview."

"*You* would think that," Jack said, but Carter was on a tear and continued like she hadn't heard him.

"There must be an incredibly sophisticated system for converting that kind of input and processing into the simulation of Daniel's consciousness." Struck by an idea, she stopped abruptly and lifted her head, gazing into the middle space. "I wonder if he's aware of it. If he can experience the technology *as* technology, I mean, or if it's all seamlessly translated into simulated human responses." Another pause as she worked it out. "No, he must have some awareness, or how would he be able to consciously access his enhanced abilities?" She turned to Jack like he might have an answer. "Unless it's not conscious. I mean, you don't have to consciously think about every little thing in order to, say, access your hand-to-hand training, right?"

"Hmm," Jack said, simulating deep thought.

Carter recognized the gambit for what it was and grinned again, this time a bit self-consciously. "It's really interesting," she finished, somehow managing to look as though after all these years there was still some unquenchable hope in her geeky heart that he might actually agree.

"*Fascinating.*"

She clearly didn't buy it, but her mouth quirked up in an acknowledgment of this minimum level of effort. The smile faded, though, as she contemplated the screen.

"What?"

"It's weird."

"What is? Besides the obvious, I mean."

She slumped for a second, thinking about it, then sat up straighter. "We never really got a chance to study the original duplicates that died in the conflict with Cronus, and while we were with them, well, there was other stuff on our minds."

"Like saving the galaxy. Again."

She nodded and scrolled text up the screen and back down again. "The robots went off to Area 51 in crates and...I don't know. It was different. This—" She pointed at the screen. "It's like reading Daniel's own reports, his journal."

"It's a machine, Carter."

"I know that, sir. I do. But the way he talks about the conditions he's lived under. The restrictions."

"We all live under restrictions." Jack stuffed his hands in his pockets and went around the other side of the counter. He couldn't see the screen from over there.

"I know that, too. But they don't have anything but missions and waiting for missions."

"Neither do you."

At that, she gave him a look that was calculatedly blank and therefore not the least bit insubordinate. "The difference is I can leave anytime I want."

"You wouldn't."

"I could resign my commission." She slid off the stool like she was going to prove it to him and waved an arm at the door. "I could do a...a tour of Europe on my Harley if I want to. I have a say."

Jack came back around the counter and stepped between her and the door. "But the Harley has no say. *That's* the point."

They stood toe-to-toe for a long moment.

"So," Carter said finally, tilting her head a little and looking at him like she was trying to see inside his head. "Do you dislike them because they're not enough like us, or because they're too much like us?" When he didn't answer, she let out a long sigh and turned to climb back up onto her stool. She kept her eyes on the screen. It wasn't until he was almost to the door that she added, not quite to herself, "The Harley's not *conscious*. That's the point."

Daniel was doing his level best to give Jack a headache. At least, that's how Jack thought of Daniel's approach to explaining just exactly what the hell had happened on P-whatsis, Eshet. Despite the fact that Daniel was hoarse from talking with the robot for the last four hours, he didn't seem to have a lot of answers to the important questions. Like, for instance, how to go about turning off the fake Jacks running around in the universe.

What bothered him most was the idea that the NID was behind this thing. It had been two years since he'd pretended to be a traitor in order to infiltrate their ranks. They'd taken down over twenty of the core personnel, including at least one mole inside Stargate Command itself. It had been a significant victory, or so they'd thought at the time. Considering that they'd recently exposed Senator Kinsey's connections to the remnants of the NID's black ops, he was starting to think the network was much more decentralized and dangerous than they'd suspected. Which was saying a lot, because

Jack knew exactly how calculated each covert ops decision was and how determined the NID would be to reach its mission goals.

It made his skin crawl to think of any version of himself out there dancing to the NID's tune, little robot puppets at the whim of people who wanted the wrong things for the right reasons.

Jack put his hands flat on the conference table, waited for Daniel to pause in his briefing, and launched in. "So to recap: nothing we've done has made a dent in the NID's operations, and there are a bunch of robots that look like us going around killing people. Does that sum it up?"

Daniel blinked. "Well, it's somewhat of an oversimplification, but…yes."

"Okay. Then as I see it, the first priority is to, I don't know, stop them from killing people?"

"That's going to be easier said than done, Colonel," Carter said. She glanced at Daniel. "Especially now that they're working from their own agenda. We have no idea where to find them, and we can't gate to Perseus without a working IDC. If the duplicates have occupied one of the NID's off-site bases, they're protected by an iris there too."

"We could take a ship," Jack said. "The Tok'ra must have a couple spare *ha'taks* laying around."

"Unlikely," Teal'c said. "It would take several weeks to reach this world by ship."

"If that's all we've got, then that's what we do," Jack answered, but Daniel was shaking his head in that infuriating, invalidating way he had.

"The situation is too urgent. We have to take action now—we have no idea what they'll do if they become autonomous or how many others they'll kill to get there."

"Why do we not simply wait for them to exhaust their power?" Teal'c asked. "If in fact they have only a limited supply to work from."

"Because Dan thinks theta Sam might have rigged up some

kind of temporary portable supply, or maybe they've already found some technology to solve the problem, at least partially," Daniel answered.

Jack stared at him. "Dan? You're giving it nicknames now?"

Daniel stared back. "I have to call him something."

"It's not a him, Daniel. It's an it."

"It's not an it, Jack. He's exactly like me. How am I supposed to treat him any differently than I'd want to be treated? Do you think I don't know what he's going through? How I'd feel is how he feels." Daniel's voice was steadily rising with the full force of his passion behind every syllable.

"I get it," Jack said. "I just don't want to get it. It's a mistake to start thinking about them as being the same as us. They're not, Daniel."

"Enough," Hammond said. "Let's get this back on track, please." He waited a beat. Jack didn't break gaze with Daniel, who seemed bound and determined to stick to this until he had Jack convinced. Which, as everyone except Daniel seemed to realize, wasn't ever going to happen. Hammond broke the deadlock by asking, "Dr. Jackson, what do we know about the technology used to create the robots?"

"Not much," Daniel said. "We have no idea how the duplicates are made or what they're made of. Some components are trinium. Beyond that—" He raised his shoulders in a shrug and looked to Sam who simply nodded in agreement. "We know they aren't indestructible, obviously, and they're much stronger, and are impervious to pain to some degree, though they clearly feel it. But we don't know how they're powered. If they're seeking a permanent power source, it might be helpful to know what they need."

"The place to find such information would be with its original source," Teal'c said. "Perhaps a visit to Harlan's world."

"Excellent idea, Teal'c." Hammond flipped open the folder Daniel had placed in front of him. "Dr. Solja's report on Harlan's original robots, and the Daniel Jackson currently in custody, shows some small but significant changes to the operational model. Major Carter, you have additional information on this?"

"Yes, sir." She opened her own folder and revealed copious notes scribbled there. To Jack it looked like a bunch of hash marks and doodles, which is more or less how he thought of the inside of Carter's brain — very bright, brilliant doodles that he had little to no chance of ever comprehending. "There have been adaptations to the core mechanisms. I haven't had time to go over it in detail, but based on comparisons to the scans of the duplicates we housed on base several years ago, I can tell their programming has been changed."

"Changed how?" Jack said.

"Based on my conversation with Dan, I'd say they're being changed to be more compliant with orders, more ruthless in pursuit of goals," Daniel said. "I'd guess that the changes are being perfected with each team created."

"The perfect obedient soldier," Jack said. "One more way they aren't like us."

"Truer words were never spoken," Hammond said with a small smile. "Very well. We need more information, and it would appear we don't have much time. Gear up and pay a visit to Harlan's world. Perhaps you can obtain information on power sources for these duplicates. That's one place to start."

"Yes, sir." Jack nodded. The prospect of seeing Harlan again gave him the creeps. "Assuming the place is still there." He remembered the anguish on Harlan's face, the imminent demise of his world without anyone to help him save it.

"There's only one way to find out," Hammond said.

Before he could give the order, though, Harriman trotted up the stairs and handed him a slip of paper. "This call just came in, sir. He was particular about the wording."

Hammond pulled at his lip while he read it, then handed it to Jack. "I think this message is for you." While Jack looked it over, Hammond asked Harriman, "Did you get a trace?"

"Tried, sir, but he bounced the call through half a dozen links. No joy."

Jack lifted the paper and read aloud. "Starsky: Ever feel like one of you is just not enough? Buy a guy a hot dog and maybe you'll learn something. Hutch."

Jack closed his eyes and let his head fall against his seat back. After a cleansing breath, he opened his eyes and looked up through the mountain at the sky, where there seemed to be an evil god looking down at him, pointing and laughing. "Just when you think the day can't get any more fun." He sat up and slid the paper back to Hammond. "Permission to go meet Maybourne and punch him in the face, sir?"

"Granted. Take Teal'c with you."

"Thank you, sir."

"Major, you and Dr. Jackson take some backup and make that trip to Altair."

"Sir." Daniel didn't get up when the rest of them stood with the general. "Maybe we could bring Dan with us. If there is a power source still on Altair, it could—"

Hammond started shaking his head before Daniel had even gotten to his second sentence. "I'm sorry, Dr. Jackson," he said, not unkindly. "Until we know more, the duplicate will have to stay here. If the situation warrants it, we'll revisit your suggestion."

Daniel opened his mouth to protest, but Jack's glare shut it again. Instead, he nodded and gathered his notes.

Hammond headed for his office. "Maybe Harlan will be forthcoming. We don't have a lot of time, people. Make it count."

Carter was getting the short end of the stick. Thank God. Anything to avoid dealing with Harlan, even if that meant having to look Maybourne in his beady eyes. "Have fun, kids," Jack said.

Daniel was giving Teal'c a wary glance. Fun was all in the definition.

PART TWO

et sequentia
and those that follow

CHAPTER FOUR

NID Primary "Hydra" Project Site, Perseus (P66-421)
July, 2002; three months prior to invasion of Eshet

The sudden blaring of the alarm made Piper drop his break-fast tray on the desk. Not that he was on edge or any-thing. Cursing, he looked around for a napkin and ended up snatching a few blank requisition forms out of the middle drawer to dab at the spilled oatmeal. What he couldn't blot up with form QY-041-D, he wiped up with the sleeve of his BDUs. He pressed his headset to his ear and listened in, but nobody was calling for him. Lab accident, probably. Maybe those guys would learn not to turn weird alien gizmos on until they had some clue whether or not they'd tune you in to Intergalactic Easy Listening or burn your face off. He went back to his oatmeal-sticky specs, but the sound of running feet and gunfire got him to his feet.

Out in the hallway, he had to jump backward to avoid a pile driver in the form of an ex-marine with a skull and cross-bones shaved into his hair, and then two more running jar-heads spun him in the other direction. Opting to exercise self-preservation, he backed up against the wall. "What's going—?" he asked the lab coat that blew by him, and then, "Where's the—?" as another dashed after the first. At that point he realized he was looking an awful lot like Bugs Bunny, and lowered his hand and its pointing finger. "Never mind," he muttered, and set off at a jog. "Go back to your specs," he told himself, but his feet kept going in the direc-tion of the crisis, whatever it was.

He rounded the corner into the lab section and stopped short—barely—of plowing into Mendez from behind. For a moment, all he could see was the boss's impeccably pressed navy blue suit jacket. Gunfire from further down the hall made Mendez jump sideways toward the wall, so Piper had a real nice view of the troops herding the beta team down the corridor. Piper had his mouth open to ask the obvious question, but his teeth snapped down into his tongue when Mendez grabbed him by the back of his shirt and yanked him into the shelter of Siebert's muscled back.

Siebert shot Piper a grin full of teeth and went back to sighting along her P90 down the corridor. "Stand back, little man," she ordered and squeezed off a short burst of fire.

"Damn it," Mendez said gruffly.

"What happened?" Piper asked. And why didn't anybody *tell* him? If there was a loop he should be in, this was it.

From his spot around the corner, Peterson said, "It looks like the introduction of the Goa'uld code has produced some unintended results."

"No kidding." Piper edged forward a bit so that he could get a view of the action. "Aw, crap."

The betas had a hostage. Karen. Karen something. Mechanical engineer. Piper tried to remember more about her, but the wild look of terror on her face—Jeez, he could actually see the whites of her eyes from way down here—blotted out anything he'd ever known about her. Her boots kicked frantically back against the beta Teal'c's shins as he lifted her up by her waist and retreated with the rest of the betas through the blast doors into the development lab. Karen's scream was abruptly cut off when the doors slammed shut, but it kept ringing in Piper's head.

He followed Mendez out of their shelter and into the hall. Two marines were lying on the concrete, one in a slowly spreading pool of red, the other on his back, his neck obviously broken. Piper mouthed a silent *ouch*. "Some unintended results," he said.

Mendez snorted in disgusted agreement. "Get the medics," he ordered softly as he knelt to feel for a pulse on the fallen marines. The one who was shot was still hanging on. For the one with the broken neck, the gesture was a formality. "They've disabled the security cameras. Get me eyes in that room."

Siebert nodded curtly and headed back toward main control, barking orders into her headset mike as she went.

Half an hour later, the medics were rolling the bandaged marine onto a gurney. The dead one was covered by Mendez's jacket. Piper followed Mendez around the corner to watch Siebert working a fiber-optic cable through the ventilation system. Peterson was perched on a chair he'd dragged from one of the offices. A clipboard on his lap, he was scribbling furiously and muttering to himself. Piper knelt on the floor to help Siebert hook up the feed from the camera. As Piper tapped keys on Siebert's laptop to bring the images up on the screen, Mendez put his hand to his headset.

"What!? Oh, sorry, sir. No, not good. Three dead so far. Yes, *so far*." He started off toward main control but turned on his heel to jab a finger in Siebert's direction. "I want a solution by the time I get back."

"Sir," Siebert said. She took the laptop from Piper and worked the trackball to pan the camera across the room. "Piece of cake," she said grimly. "Not."

The fiber-optic with its camera had snaked along the vent shaft and was now poking down through the grating near the ceiling. Below the grating, so that they could only see a shadow, beta Teal'c was pacing. Further into the room, Carter and Daniel stood over Karen and three other techs who were on their knees with their hands laced behind their heads. O'Neill was over by the door. There was no other exit. The betas didn't say a word out loud, but that didn't mean they weren't talking.

As Siebert adjusted the focus, beta Carter reached down, grabbed the hand of the closest tech, and twisted hard. The tech—a young guy named Jameson—let out a howl and fell over, cradling his broken wrist. When Karen leaned down to him, beta Daniel clipped her a good one on the chin with the heel of his boot. She sprawled on her back with her hands over her face. No one made a move to help her. Piper looked away with a hiss of sympathy. Peterson glanced up at the sound and then went back to scribbling.

"This is not going to end well," Siebert said.

If the knot in Piper's chest was any indication, he agreed with her, no matter what his more optimistic side might be hoping. "We have to get those people out of there."

Piper looked sidelong at the feed. Karen was still laid out. Unconscious or maybe just playing dead. As if he could feel Piper looking, beta O'Neill stepped around the hostages and glared up at the camera. After a moment of consideration, he moved out of the frame. When he came back, he must've been standing on something because his face filled the entire screen. The expression he wore, the utter coldness of his eyes, made Piper shudder. Then O'Neill's fingers loomed close and adjusted the angle of the camera so that the hostages were right in the middle of the frame. Piper wasn't able to close his eyes fast enough, and the lurid afterimage of beta Carter shooting Jameson floated and doubled behind his lids. When he opened his eyes again, the feed was dead.

"Son of a bitch," he breathed.

"We open those doors," Siebert said with flat conviction, "we are all going to die."

"That's why we're going to burn it." Mendez's voice came from right behind them.

Although Siebert's hesitation was barely noticeable, it spoke volumes. But she shifted the laptop over to Piper, rose smoothly to her feet and snapped a salute. "Yes, sir."

Piper was less graceful, and the laptop clattered to the floor as he clambered upright and steadied himself with a hand on the wall. "Wait a minute! Wait just—there must be something—there's got to be—" He let go of the wall and pointed through it at the lab. "There's *people* in there. We could negotiate."

"We tried negotiation," Mendez answered. "They killed

two techs in the clean room."

"But there must be something we can bargain with."

Grabbing him by the front of his shirt, Mendez put his face about an inch from Piper's and growled, "They don't *want* anything. They want to kill, starting with everyone in this facility."

"How—how do you know?"

"Because they *told me*." Mendez's voice was hoarse, but behind the anger in his eyes was something else, something close to horror. "They're wrong inside. They're *broken*."

"Gee, I wonder why."

For a second, Piper thought Mendez was going to put a fist through his face, but instead he let him go and stepped back. Then he was classic Mendez again, slick as ice. "I have my orders," he said stonily, and shifted his gaze to Siebert. "And you have yours."

Mendez stepped out of the way so that Siebert could bring in the charges. Behind her, Kutrell was setting the timer.

"Move it, Piper," she said when he stood his ground under the vent opening. Her voice hardened when she repeated the order. She added, "I can have you in the brig in ten seconds flat." She handed the charges to Kutrell.

Piper tried to stare her down for about half a second, but he wasn't much of a match for her steely blues, which seemed likely to bore a couple of holes through his forehead. "This is so messed up," he said.

"Clearly, we'll need to introduce the Goa'uld code in stages," Peterson said to no one in particular. "Yes, that's it. Next iteration, if we introduce it in stages we can..." He trailed off, and for a long moment there was just the sound of his pen scratching on his clipboard and of Kutrell taping the charges to a remote-controlled robot small enough to track through the vent.

Piper gasped out an disbelieving laugh. "Next iteration?"

"Move it, Piper."

Siebert took a step toward him, and he held up his hands

in surrender. "Fine." He edged sideways along the wall until he came to the corner and followed it around into the main corridor. In front of the closed lab doors, the concrete was stained with an almost perfect circle of dark blood. Red boot prints led away toward the infirmary alongside the double tracks made by the gurney wheels. The dead marine was still there, under Mendez's coat. Two more marines were at the door, welding it shut. Piper slid down and rested his elbows on his raised knees, pressed the heels of his hands into his eyes. "*Next iteration.* You gotta be kiddin' me." The sparks from the welding danced around in Piper's brain.

Piper dropped his hands and stared at Mendez's shoes when they stopped in front of him in the hallway. Nice shoes. Italian, probably. The pair of sneakers that followed them were Peterson's. Piper rested his chin on his folded arms and listened.

"Don't try to lose me in the technobabble, Peterson. Just get it done." Mendez's voice was tight. Piper could picture the tendons standing out in his neck above his starched collar.

"It's not so easy as you seem to think, sir," Peterson answered. He sounded a little bit breathless. Piper let his gaze climb up past the wrinkled lab coat to the round face, the perma-creases in the brow above the washed-out eyes.

"I want an off switch, a way to shut them down. How can that be hard?"

"Because." Peterson pulled a tissue out of his pocket and dabbed at his forehead. "It's because of the primary technology. The duplicating system is predicated on two basic principles: survival and autonomy. Those principles inform the process at every step."

"So bypass them."

Peterson poked his fingers and thumb up behind his glasses and pinched the bridge of his nose. "We could do that." Maybe it was exhaustion, or maybe he just had some kind of death wish, because his tone was just a hair shy of patronizing. "But then you've eliminated the very qualities that make the units useful. It's the point of the project."

"I know the *point* of the project," Mendez said acidly.

Peterson blinked like Mendez had just slapped him across his face. It took him a few long seconds to collect himself. "I think that the problem here…" He peeled a hand away from the clipboard and waved vaguely in the direction of the lab. Piper noticed that his hand left a wet print behind. "What I mean is, I'm certain that the break—not a psychotic break, exactly, but something comparable—has entirely to do with the way we introduced the Goa'uld code. If we can make modifications in a more controlled way, progressively, we can avoid this kind of response."

"Response," Mendez repeated. When he lifted his hand to rub it across his face, Piper was surprised to see that it was shaking.

Down the hall, the marines had packed up their welding gear and were pulling back to the intersecting corridor. Inside the lab, the betas must've figured out what was up, because they were pounding on the door. More than human power in each blow of a fist made the blast doors ring.

"Listen to me, Peterson," Mendez said. "You are going to figure out how to make me a switch."

"Fire in the hole," Siebert shouted.

Mendez's voice was barely a whisper. "I do *not* want to do this again."

Piper put his hands over his ears, but it didn't matter; he could feel the blast through the concrete, in his bones. He couldn't hear anybody screaming. Not really.

CHAPTER FIVE

Colorado Springs
October 30, 2002, one day after invasion of Eshet

"We are being followed," Teal'c said, his eyes hidden behind his shades.

"Yeah, I see 'em."

Jack kept his own eyes on the hot dog stand at the foot of the winding path, but part of his attention was on the two shapes ghosting along beside them, darting from bench to tree for cover. The park was busy for a weekday afternoon. Probably the unseasonable heat. He squinted through the mostly bare branches of the trees at the bright sun sliding fat and orange toward the roofs of the apartment buildings on the other side of the park. Even this late in the day it was warm enough to go in shirtsleeves, but he kept his jacket on to hide the holster on his shoulder and the 9mm snug in his armpit. There were kids in the park, which lay adjacent to an elementary school. After school day-care was still in full swing beyond the chain link fence. Thin screams of laughter scored the high, bright air. No way he wanted to get into a firefight here.

Which was why Harry picked the spot, of course.

The ghosts split up, one heading around the back side of a thick-trunked cedar, the other dashing across the path behind Jack and Teal'c to crouch behind a garbage can.

Willing them away with his mind, Jack counted benches, found the third one down the path, two up from the hot dog stand, and sat down, just like he'd been instructed to do in the note he'd found on the windshield of his truck back at the mountain. There was no sign of Harry, but the two ghosts had joined up again and were now hunkered down together behind the garbage can, whispering.

"This is inconvenient." Instead of sitting, Teal'c strode to the near side of the garbage can and looked over it. Caught before the jig was up, the two ghosts made the best of it by leaping up in their bedsheet shrouds and, with widespread hands waving, shrieked, "BOO!"

"Boo," Teal'c said mildly, and the kids froze for one long second before screaming identical screams of terror and taking off at a run, their costumes whipping around their sneakers.

When Jack turned back, Harry was next to him on the bench, smiling that infuriating smile.

"Trick or treat," he said, around a mouthful of what had to be half a hot dog.

Jack cocked his head and contemplated him for a moment. He looked pretty good for a guy on the lam, smug and well dressed. "How 'bout I just beat you to death instead?"

Harry laughed, giving Jack a view of the hot dog that would make him lose his appetite for a year. "You could try, but then you wouldn't hear what I have to tell you." He craned his neck a little to look up at Teal'c, who had stepped back to the bench to block out the sun like an incoming space cruiser. Harry didn't try a smile, but he said to Jack, "I had no idea you thought I was worthy of the serious muscle."

"You're not. I bring him along to protect me from the fourth graders." Jack shifted around so he could rest his elbow on the back of the bench. "C'mon, Harry. Spill it. I'm kind of in a hurry, in case you didn't know."

"Hmm, I hear you're having a little trouble." He dabbed at a spot of mustard on his jacket. "Of the doppelganger kind."

"For a guy out of the loop, you sure seem in the loop."

"I hear things. Like to keep up, you know. Helps me know who's likely to kill me this month." He paused to watch the schoolyard on the other side of the fence, where there were children in costumes lining up by twos for early Halloween hijinks. Frankenstein was holding the hand of the princess, while Batman hooked up with SpongeBob. "You stop to wonder how those duplicate teams know where to go, Jack? How they're avoiding crossing paths with your SGC teams?"

"Actually, no," Jack answered. "Been a little preoccupied with other things."

"Maybe you should start. The answer is closer than you think."

"A mole."

Harry aimed a finger gun at him. "Head of the class."

Jack scratched the back of his neck. "We shut down their off-world programs," he said. "You admitted as much when they tried to get Hammond reassigned."

"Jack," Harry said, reproachful. "Do you really think these people can be shut down? We're talking about the best liars in the known universe. Half of everything they say is disinformation."

"By 'they' you of course mean 'you.'"

"There's someone you could talk to," Harry said. "Someone with more current information than mine."

"You mean Makepeace," Jack said.

"Very good, Jack. The more channels the NID has to off-world operations and technology, the better off they are. And I hear they're flying in comfort these days."

"A ship," Teal'c said. The rumble in his voice left no doubt about his opinion on that matter. Possibly the worst news Harry could have given them.

"Amazing what you can get ahold of when you've got SG-1 working for you."

The kids were making their way toward them across the park now, two straggly lines of sparkles and spandex like party favors blown along by the late October wind. Jack looked away from them, turning his scowl on Maybourne. "Anything else you want to tell me to brighten my day?"

"Just that the thought of unlimited duplicates of you out there frightens me." He stood up and brushed crumbs off his pants. By the time he was done, the ranks of kids had broken down into a generally cohesive gaggle. Before Jack could even think about putting a hand to the gun in its holster, Harry was in their midst, shouting "Trick or treat!" and tossing candy at outstretched hands. The teacher was wading back toward Harry, but the momentum carried the group on down the path. Just before they turned the corner at the base of a knoll, Harry waved over his shoulder and grinned.

Jack leaned his mouth close to his lapel mike to let his own ghosts know where to pick Harry up, but after a couple of minutes a voice came back informing him that the kids had left the park and there was no sign of Maybourne at all.

"Of course not," Jack muttered, and headed for his truck.

While Jack was speed-dialing the mountain, Teal'c said, "It is two hours' drive to Clearwater."

"Yeah, I know." They didn't have two hours to waste getting to Makepeace. He spoke into the phone. "General. Maybe he gave us something. Won't know 'til we go check it out. Think you can find us a chopper?"

Jack pulled his sunglasses down over his eyes, the better to pretend he wasn't spending this sunny day headed toward a maximum-security holding facility to interrogate a traitor. He tossed the keys to Teal'c. "You drive," he said, climbing into the passenger seat. Even though it was just a couple of miles to the rendezvous with the chopper, he never could resist a chance to watch Teal'c drive. Teal'c approached driving with the ease and determination of someone who'd flown spaceships through hostile space. Cars and freeways were just more of the same.

In several ways, it was a relief to be doing this particular task with Teal'c, because Jack thought they were on the same page with it. Carter would have some issues with Jack's planned approach, and Daniel...well, if Daniel had been assigned to this, he'd be wearing the reproachful look already, and there would be talking and reasoning and *feel-*

ings and *rights* all the way to the prison, and that would only throw Jack off his game. Not because Daniel was right, but because he had an insidious way of making Jack ask the wrong kinds of questions. He couldn't afford to question what he was about to do.

Teal'c drove in silence for a while, and then defied Jack's predictions by pitching an opening to a conversation Jack wasn't sure he wanted to have. "You consider Colonel Makepeace a *shol'va*?"

That brought Jack up a little straighter in the seat. He squinted out the window at the passing landscape. Some nice little irony, sending one civilization's traitor to extract information from another's. "It's not the same," he said finally.

"Is it not?" Teal'c changed lanes, giving the words time to sink in like barbed hooks, and said, "He disobeyed orders in the hope that he could keep this world free."

"It's different," Jack said. He peeled off his shades. "You disobeyed orders to save your people. Because there wasn't any other way."

"Do you not consider the NID's mission to have been one with Earth's protection as their foremost goal?"

"No," Jack said automatically, though he could already see where Teal'c was going with this. More than once, Teal'c had told Hammond the SGC wasn't doing enough to secure Goa'uld technology, and he felt their methods were ineffective. Granted, he'd eased off on that after the first year, but sometimes Jack could still see it in his eyes.

Jack knew how he felt. He'd been conflicted while he was undercover, and he was still a little conflicted now. It hadn't been hard to steal technology from the Tollan people. He'd enjoyed it. He hadn't had to act much.

But unlike Makepeace, he knew a bad order was still an order and shadow ops never ended well, regardless of how well executed they were or what they managed to accomplish. Someone always paid; the cost was usually too high.

He was thinking of platitudes about honorable methods,

but honor wasn't a word Teal'c took lightly, and he knew it was bullshit anyway. He was talking to a man who'd chosen betrayal himself, who'd chosen right over honor, and had redefined honor, given it new context.

"You do not fault the motive," Teal'c said, same question, different angle.

"No," Jack answered. "Not the motive."

No more was said on the matter as they secured themselves in the chopper for the short hop to Clearwater. Jack occupied himself by picking out landmarks below. By the time the chopper settled outside the gates of the facility, he'd put everything else aside and had his game face on.

Teal'c scanned the fence as they walked through, eyed the guard towers. Jack had the distinct impression Teal'c found the security less than adequate. He kept the impression to himself, just as Teal'c kept his opinions quiet. Jack often wanted all the nonessential details Teal'c noticed, all the things he didn't deem important enough to say, but he had to be content with those few things Teal'c felt were critical enough to pass the filter of his long decades as First Prime.

Makepeace was housed in a cellblock with few windows. Interrogation rooms encircled the common visiting area, their windows darkened. Jack pushed open one of the unlocked doors; the light flickered on dimly overhead as if called into service by his presence alone. Two chairs on either side of a small table. Jack looked up at the ceiling, at the mirrored wall. "Couple beers, a jukebox, could be a popular vacation spot."

"How would you like to proceed?" Teal'c was watching him in that way he had of making Jack feel like a junior Jaffa.

Jack sighed. "Let's see what I can talk him into giving up."

"And if he will not comply?"

Jack looked him in the eye. "Then I guess we'll take it as it comes."

Teal'c inclined his head. Once, a long time ago, Jack had come close to asking Teal'c if he'd been an interrogator among the Jaffa, if he knew how to torture. He was pretty sure he knew the answer, and he hadn't wanted to make Teal'c go back into those memories, but the curiosity nagged at him sometimes. He had the feeling if he and Teal'c ever compared notes, the black pages in their books would look pretty similar. He'd seen it in Teal'c's posture, in the tilt of his head when he looked at some of those he'd left behind. He'd seen the way they backed away from him, old memories surfacing in their fear.

Technically, they weren't allowed to employ those methods to obtain information. Jack was pretty sure, however, that nobody would be watching. And if they were, they wouldn't care. The only thing standing between Jack and that information would be…Well, 'ethics' was such a clear-cut word, and Jack hated to be boxed in.

The door on the far end of the cell buzzed, calling to the guard behind, who pushed it open. Makepeace swaggered through with as much of an arrogant strut and turn of the hips as the belly chains would permit, looking just as military and self-possessed as Jack remembered. His hair was a little grayer, his frame thinner, but there were no other visible effects of almost two years of confinement. He dismissed Teal'c with a glance—Jack was sure he thought he'd figured out all there was to know about Teal'c in the time he'd supervised him, because Makepeace really was just that arrogant. He saved the full force of his attention for Jack.

"I figured I'd be seeing you soon," he said. "You run out of other sources to burn there, Jack?"

Jack ignored the jab and gestured to the guard to remove the chains and cuffs. Makepeace made a show of rubbing his wrists and dropped his hands to his sides, though Jack knew he'd been through far worse.

"So," Jack said. He pointed to the chair on the opposite side of the table and pulled out his own. Teal'c put his hands behind his back and stood very still. "Keeping busy?"

"Very funny." Makepeace kicked the chair out from under the table and sat down, his posture braced, his body slightly turned toward Teal'c, who deliberately moved to place himself behind Makepeace. A strategic decision, one that would allow him to see Jack, read his intentions. Makepeace twisted in his chair, his level of discomfort increasing with every moment Teal'c stood behind him.

From Jack's perspective, Makepeace was right to be uncomfortable.

"What do you want, Jack?" Makepeace glanced back at Teal'c, who had not moved. Jack could hear the determination in Makepeace's voice, but there was a thread of something thinner, more fragile.

"Rumor has it there are several versions of me running around the cosmos," Jack said. He leaned back in the chair and crossed his arms over his chest. "Thought you could shed some light on things, seeing as how it's your cronies from the NID who're behind it."

"And why exactly would you think I could do that?" Makepeace leaned back, mirroring Jack's position exactly. His lips twisted in a half-smile. "I've been out of commission for the better part of two years. You know that better than anyone."

"You put yourself here." Jack kept his tone smooth, even.

"Semantics." Makepeace jabbed a finger at Jack and said, "If you think anything you've done since you locked me up has kept Earth safe, you're delusional. You know damn well that procurement operation was both necessary and important. Shutting it down did nothing but leave Earth defenseless."

Jack's lips thinned to a straight line. Never mind his own sympathy for the argument. He hated to hear it thrown back at him by Makepeace. "Whether I agree or not isn't the point. We didn't have a choice. You alienated our allies. Only someone as arrogant as Maybourne would think it's possible to trick and steal from the most powerful races in the universe and get away with it. We needed their goodwill."

"Sure we did. Because they've given us so much, right?" Makepeace snorted. "Wake up, Jack."

"Come on, you can't think everything the NID did was worthwhile." Jack frowned. "Procurement, sure. But replication of human beings?"

Makepeace looked away.

Jack leaned across the table. "How long has this thing been in development?"

"You'd love it if I gave everything up, wouldn't you?" Makepeace turned his head to look Jack square in the eye. "But what are you going to give me in return?"

"Nothing for nothing, Makepeace. You don't get many chances to do the right thing anymore, do you? I don't think you even recognize them when they come your way."

"I tried, once." Makepeace looked away again.

Jack stood up slowly, and as he did, Teal'c pressed in behind Makepeace, so close he was touching the back of the chair. Makepeace tried to shift away, but Teal'c's hand landed on his shoulder, an iron anchor.

"So this is how it is, now?" Makepeace shrugged, but the hand remained in place. "You gonna tear little pieces off me, make me beg?"

"I will be considerably more efficient than what you describe," Teal'c said, and even Jack could feel the chill behind the words. Teal'c's fingers tightened, his grip bearing down on the muscle, then the bone. Makepeace gasped, face scrunched into a rictus, collarbone in danger of snapping under Teal'c's relentless pressure.

"I could offer you the same deal I gave Maybourne," Jack said, as though Teal'c wasn't presently engaged in his own kind of persuasion. "Life instead of death."

Makepeace said nothing. Jack shrugged, sat back down. Teal'c didn't move. Only his hand shifted, and Jack couldn't hear tendons snapping, but Makepeace turned white.

It went on for almost a minute, the pain producing ever wilder grimaces from Makepeace, and then Jack nodded to Teal'c, who released his grip. Tears leaked from the corners of Makepeace's eyes, but he only looked at Jack with something like admiration. "Guess Maybourne was right about you after all," he said.

Jack was only a little surprised to find he had to suppress a wince. He'd thought he was long past that.

Makepeace was slumped sideways in the chair. Teal'c hauled him upright, and Makepeace made an impatient sound. "Everything I knew is useless now."

Jack braced his hands on the table and said, "Let me be the judge of that."

"The mission to steal the technology on Altair was on our agenda months before you came on board. I guess they continued on with the plan, even after you busted up our shop." Makepeace eyed Teal'c, who was watching him carefully, his hand poised just above Makepeace's vulnerable elbow. Jack had no idea what he planned, but he was certain now it wouldn't leave lasting marks. It didn't matter. Jack didn't think for one second Makepeace was talking because of the pain. "All I know is that they wanted invulnerable soldiers, and they wanted the code. Guess they figured once they got it, they wouldn't have to recruit on-world anymore."

"Where were the additional teams based?" Teal'c asked. He moved his hand, subtly.

Makepeace hissed through his teeth. With a glare improperly directed at Jack, Makepeace said, "They never told us. Every off-world cell operated independently. Our job was simple: steal, report back, reverse engineer, ship the goods. But I did have additional contacts in the chain of command, in case Maybourne was ever eliminated."

"Names," Jack said.

"Washburn and Farmi." Makepeace smiled. "You know there's always another one. And another one in his place. You catch me, somebody else steps up, funnels the information through. Right this minute, there's a mole scuttling around the SGC, picking up stray bits of information and sending it on." He paused, tilted his head. His eyes gleamed. "How's it feel, Jack? Knowing there's a version of you doing the job you should've done in the first place? You like it?"

"One of me's enough." Jack stood up. Teal'c let go of Makepeace. "Who's the mole?"

"Don't know." Makepeace met his stare. "Couldn't say."

Jack sighed. They had enough. It wasn't especially useful, but it confirmed Harry's tip at least. "I'll talk to Hammond, see if I can get your sentence commuted."

"Doesn't matter." Makepeace lifted a hand to his shoulder and rubbed. "Dead or good as dead, it's all the same to me now."

CHAPTER SIX

**NID Primary "Hydra" Project Site, Perseus (P66-421)
August, 2002; two months prior to invasion of Eshet**

Piper sat up straight in the chair, blinked hard, and cracked a huge yawn. Somewhere on Earth, it was around one a.m., but not on Perseus, Land of Eternal Morning, where the days were 18 Earth-standard hours long. Not that he ever got to see the sun, of course. The gate-room was just outside, close enough to shout information back and forth to the security guys and the techs, but he might as well be on the moon for all the human interaction he actually had. He'd been stuck in the cubbyhole that passed for a communications center and bunk room for going on two days, ever since the incident with the epsilon team. Six teams in rotation and already two down. Beta and epsilon. Not exactly a stellar success rate, there. He scanned the roster pinned up next to his desk. Gamma and delta were fine. Zeta was fine. Alpha was fine. *Fine, fine, fine* stumbled around inside his head, going nowhere helpful. He needed caffeine.

He groped around on the top of the console, fingers reaching through assorted debris and empty coffee cups, and came up with half a power bar. Enough to keep him going a little while longer. The yellow legal pad in front of him was covered with scratched-through scrawls, the outline of a situation refusing to lend itself neatly to an organized explanation.

The facts seemed clear on the surface: epsilon Teal'c had suffered a catastrophic power failure while on the team's last mission. Some of the technicians had an idea that the power failure was a result of the weird way the Teal'c units integrated their programming, but Piper had a sinking feeling it wasn't that at all. He'd been watching the teams for four months now, listening to their chatter, and there had never been a single sign that the Teal'cs were having power issues. They gutted out harsh conditions stoically, just like the file indicated the real version would, and came up swinging on the other side after minor repairs.

There were signs, though, that they weren't taking well to being under such strict controls. Piper didn't have a good word for it, but the term "enslaved" screamed around in the back of his head a lot. That's what it was, really. He was pretty sure how Teal'c would take to that. Maybe Teal'c had just gotten tired of it. The technical phrase was "cascade failure in the emotional circuits of the duplicate," but Piper couldn't bring himself to write it down. It seemed so... impersonal. So inaccurate.

Piper sighed and rolled his pen around on the tablet. The epsilons had relayed the information back about Teal'c and then gone quiet, not a word from them in over twelve hours. Mendez had finally sent the gammas to have a look around and report back, and now it was just a waiting game, listening for a report and hoping nothing else had gone wrong.

"Hi."

Piper twisted around to see Daniel Jackson—the alpha version—standing in the doorway, watching him. "Uh, hi," he said, flipping his tablet over. Daniel's lips curved up in a small smile. "I'm actually not supposed to talk with you except in the course of duty."

"I know." Daniel nodded, as if he'd taken the hint. Then he grabbed a chair and rolled it up next to the console. "Mendez is in his quarters, though. What's the harm?"

"Mendez turns up sometimes when you least expect him," Piper said, pulling all his junk to one side as Daniel settled into the chair.

"He make you nervous?"

"No," Piper said. Daniel's eyebrows lifted just a hair, and

as if Daniel had called him a liar, Piper suddenly felt guilty. "Okay, yes. But I'll deny it."

"It's okay. I think he makes several people here nervous." Daniel was taking a casual look around the room, like he came visiting every day, which was weird.

"But not you?"

"I'm not a people, technically speaking." Daniel didn't look back at him to see whether Piper agreed. "Besides, the original Daniel has dealt with all sorts of aggravating authority types over the years. I have all that experience to fall back on."

"Right," Piper said. He tried to keep the wince off his face.

"So. You sleep here too?" Daniel asked, nodding to the cot in the corner.

"Just sometimes. When I have teams out."

"Like now." When Piper nodded, Daniel asked, "So what do you think really happened to the epsilons?"

Piper fidgeted in the chair, looked down at the bland gray cardboard back of his tablet, on which nothing of any use was written. He really needed a sounding board, and the temptation to talk to Daniel about it was pretty strong. "I don't know," he said. "Why don't you tell me?"

"Come again?"

Piper looked up at him, at the open, friendly expression on his face. Kind of funny, considering, so Piper answered, "I know you guys are talking on comms channels I can't monitor or record. You're keeping secrets."

"Wouldn't you, if you were in our position?"

Piper shrugged. It hadn't escaped him that Daniel was really good at answering questions without actually giving any information. "Don't know." He thought briefly of all his pledges of secrecy to the US of A, and the long nights of self-struggle, trying to figure out what the greater good would be if he broke those pledges. "Maybe I'm not the best person to ask."

"Maybe you're exactly the right person to ask."

Two techs went by the door, but neither of them so much as glanced into the room. Piper scooted away from Daniel a little anyway. Daniel didn't budge. "I can't really trust you," Piper said.

"Look at it this way," Daniel said. "What do you think you'd be telling me that I don't already know?"

"Kind of not the point." Piper put an arm over his closed laptop. A whole chorus of warning bells was ringing in his head. Obviously Daniel was looking for some kind of information. But what could he do with it, really? It wasn't like anything was a huge secret around here. Well, except for the one thing he really couldn't give away. But he had enough sense not to say one word about Earth. Or the SGC. In any iteration, Daniel Jackson was smart, and all he needed was a tiny clue to make the connections.

Daniel leaned forward in the chair. "Did you know they tried to activate the eta team yesterday?"

"What?" Piper frowned. "No. Usually I get an introduction to the team right after."

"Would have been hard to do, this time." Daniel's expression remained entirely composed. "They didn't wake up."

"That's...really?" Implications fluttered through Piper's mind. Bad programming, maybe the cascade failure he'd been thinking about, or the power issues. Could be something about all those code manipulations they'd been doing too. Really, Daniel's team was the only one that still seemed true to the originals, which was interesting, come to think of it.

"Interesting, isn't it?" Daniel said. Piper twitched. He was pretty sure the robots couldn't read minds, but Daniel seemed too perceptive.

"Yeah," Piper admitted. "Yeah, I guess." A twinge of sadness poked at him. Each of the teams, no matter how different from the one before, had become his responsibility. It was weird to think one of them was, in essence, DOA.

"So, the epsilons."

Piper grinned. "You're a persistent SOB."

"So I've been told." Daniel smiled back, not a big smile, but one that suggested he didn't smile all that often.

Lowering his voice just in case, Piper said, "I've been thinking something's wrong with the Teal'c circuits. If they don't get it corrected, it's just…we'll keep losing them, and I…" He cleared his throat. "I hate to see that happen, you know?"

Daniel's expression softened then. "I know. We all appreciate how hard you've been working to keep us safe."

"Yeah, well." Piper shrugged. "Anyway, I don't know what else I can—" The gate alarm klaxon cut him off, and he swiveled back to the panel, threw on his headset. "It's an incoming wormhole."

Into the earpiece came the tinny voice of the gamma Jack. "Piper, SG-one-niner-Golf."

"I read you, Colonel."

"Found the epsilons," Jack said. "In pieces."

Piper's stomach dropped. He swallowed hard. "Say again?"

"No sign of any resistance or obstruction here at the gate," Jack came back. "Seems they sat down on the platform and… waited."

Waited until their power ran out maybe, or…Piper closed his eyes. "Can you check their power levels?"

"Already did. They had plenty of juice." Jack didn't say it, but he didn't have to.

Intentional self-termination. An image popped into Piper's head—the team sitting down to die, just waiting for an incoming wormhole to take them out. "But why," Piper whispered.

"Heading back now," Jack said. "Bringing in the remains."

"Understood." Piper pulled off his headset, hands shaking. The taste of bile lingered bitter in the back of his throat. He should go to the gate-room, be there when the gammas brought in whatever was left of the epsilons, but he couldn't seem to make his legs work. Maybe he had failed them somehow; maybe there was something he should have seen, predicted.

Daniel put a hand on his shoulder, gentle comfort.

Carlos was having a hell of a bad run.

He'd lost the beta team to psychosis, the epsilons to something he refused to call suicide, and the etas had failed to activate. According to Piper's report, the deltas and gammas were in various stages of what amounted to a robot nervous breakdown, questioning their orders and acting oddly, which only complicated things — particularly since he couldn't pull any in from the field right now. The push was on to secure additional technology. The word from on high had been clear that he needed to produce results *now*.

Calling in to explain how he'd lost valuable assets — and not even due to mission-related danger — had not been the high point of his career. They were expendable, sure. But the project's resources weren't infinite.

Peterson was sitting at the briefing table, going on and on about why the eta duplicates didn't switch on as planned, and all Carlos could think about was the mangled remains of the epsilon Carter. For some reason, the image of gamma Teal'c carrying her down into the gate-room was stuck on an infinite loop in his head.

"Sir?" He looked up to see Peterson, frustration written all over his face, obviously waiting for him to answer a question.

"Sorry," Carlos said. He drew himself up, smoothed his tie. "What was that?"

"I asked if you're ready for us to attempt activation of the theta team." Peterson flicked the corner of his project file with a thumbnail. "We want to see if we've solved the coding problems."

"You have the alpha team standing by to debrief?"

"Yes, sir," Peterson said.

"You're still calling me 'sir,'" Carlos said.

"Sorry," Peterson said, though he looked as if it was killing him not to add the 'sir.'

Carlos left his briefing materials on the table and followed Peterson out into the corridor, as he had seven times before, for teams alpha through eta. He glanced into the debriefing room as they passed by. Alpha team was milling around with the bored, restless expressions he'd come to understand so well. He would have had them out there searching a hundred worlds a week if they could get the intel to guarantee the missions were safe, but intel was coming slow these days. He had to be patient. The alpha team was his ace in the hole for breaking in each successive team. He wouldn't have to lie over and over about the mission and worry about how much of the lie might show on his face; the alpha team had already swallowed the story, and now he relied on them to carry the torch. Nothing like looking into the face of your duplicate self to convince you that every word was true. Or so Carlos assumed. He hoped to God he'd never have a reason to know for himself.

The theta team—the most recent incarnation of these duplicates—seemed to be sleeping in the racks designed for them, their expressions peaceful and at rest. Carlos never ceased to be amazed at how lifelike they were and how easy it would be to forget they were as disposable as the toy robots he bought for his nephew. Except they were a hell of a lot more expensive. Hence his problem.

"Wake them," he said to Peterson, who nodded and set down his clipboard.

"It'll just be a minute or so while I power them up." Peterson bent over the panel the engineers had rigged up. He was one of the brighter talents recruited from Area 51. His genius was tweaking technology, making alien gizmos do things they were never designed to do.

The O'Neill duplicate's eyes blinked open, and it turned its head toward Carlos. Even though Carlos knew the cause was artificial, the spark of intelligence in its eyes unnerved him. O'Neill stared at him, then sat up and looked around until it saw the other duplicates nearby. Already the Carter duplicate was stirring to life. "Where the hell are we?" O'Neill said.

"You're in a secure off-world base," Carlos answered.

"Well, that clears everything up," O'Neill said, his stare never wavering. Sarcasm was the one thing all the O'Neill duplicates had in common. The robot swung its legs over and stood up, lightning quick. "Now let's move on to who the hell you are."

"I'm Carlos Mendez. As soon as the rest of your team is awake, I'll explain everything."

"You're damn right you will."

"Jack?" The Jackson duplicate sat up quickly and practically launched itself off the platform.

"See about Carter," O'Neill told it, still watching Carlos, who was sure that if O'Neill had a weapon, Carlos would already be dead. There was something about the expression on this one's face that was different from the ones that had been created before him. This version seemed…colder.

"She's fine," Jackson said, helping Carter up.

"Teal'c?" O'Neill turned its head to the side and waited for the response.

"I am uninjured," Teal'c answered, standing up.

"Guess you'd better get started on those answers," O'Neill said to Carlos.

"Sir," the Carter duplicate said, stepping up beside him. "Something's happened. Our uniforms are different."

O'Neill glanced down at its chest, saw the THETA designation on its pocket. "Start with this," he told Carlos, tapping it.

"I will. If you'll follow me?" He gestured to Peterson, who went ahead of him to open the blast doors. He turned and led the way out of the lab, all four of the duplicates following behind him at a distance. He could hear them talking softly to one another, and then O'Neill swore suddenly, and the team fell silent. It always happened that way when the new group of duplicates realized they could hear each other thinking. It never took long for them to realize what had happened after that.

He rounded the corner to the debriefing room and stepped inside, let the reveal take care of itself. The alpha team stood up to welcome the newcomers, who filed slowly into the room, watching their counterparts with wary, angry expressions.

"I know," alpha O'Neill said. "Believe me, I understand exactly what you're thinking."

"You should have a seat," the alpha Jackson said. "This will take some explaining."

"Get to the bottom line," theta O'Neill answered, throwing out a hand to stop the theta Jackson from sitting down. "What's been done to us? What are we?"

"You're duplicates of the original team," alpha Carter said. "Just like we are."

"You were created, like we were, because the SGC has been shut down on Earth," alpha Jackson said. "We were created in order to continue the mission: find technology to protect and defend Earth, since the SGC can't or won't do it."

"You believe that?" Theta O'Neill turned to Carlos. "This guy been feeding you that line?"

"We don't have any way to disprove it," alpha Carter said.

They all turned to look at Carlos, his customary moment in the spotlight, but this time he was thrown. The alpha Carter duplicate hadn't given her unqualified endorsement. She'd only said they couldn't disprove what they'd been told. This was new.

"Political pressure on Earth forced the closure of the Stargate program," Carlos said. "The original SG-1 was... well, let's say they were no longer able to do the work they started. So we did the next best thing: carbon copies, made from technology on Altair."

"That's the planet we just gated to?" theta Daniel said.

Alpha O'Neill snorted. "If by 'just,' you mean four years ago. The original versions of us gated there and were copied when they arrived. We come from patterns of the original team."

"I see," theta Jackson said. It knocked theta O'Neill's hand aside and sat down. "So we're...not human. We..."

"Your lives are over as you knew and understood them," Carlos said. All the alpha team members were staring at him, but he ignored them. Sugarcoating things only drew it out, and these weren't humans anyway. They would adjust.

"What's to prevent us from leaving here and taking back our lives?" The theta O'Neill stepped closer to Carlos, a move so smooth he didn't see it coming until O'Neill was inches away. "Just snapping your neck and getting the hell out of here?"

"You'd never make it," Carlos said, looking directly into those dead, angry eyes. "Can you think of a single gate address?"

The theta's eyes narrowed. "Daniel?"

"I can't," the theta Jackson answered.

"I don't remember any of them either," theta Carter said.

"You'll learn them as we give them to you," Carlos told them. "Oh, and there's the matter of your power supply. It's here. Leave here, and you run out of energy. No options."

"Son of a bitch," theta O'Neill said. Carlos stepped back. He knew that look, and he didn't want to be a quadriplegic for the rest of his days.

"Save it," the alpha O'Neill said. "There's work to be done. A chance to be useful."

"A chance to help Earth," alpha Jackson said.

The eight duplicates looked at each other, one of the many signs Carlos had learned to recognize. They were communicating internally. He never had any idea what they said to each other, and it always unnerved him. But whatever the alpha team was saying, it seemed to be working. Theta O'Neill turned away in disgust and sat down at the table.

Phase one—introductions—was over. Now they would

begin to acclimate. Within a week, he'd be able to test them in the field.

It took a little doing to throw a blanket over the seething chatter leaking into the comms from the theta team. Daniel was used to it by now, that first wash of disorganized exclamation as the new teams got a grip on who—what—they were. That panicked static would eventually resolve into questions, some of them philosophical but most of them mundane. In fact, it was surprising to him how quickly the teams could progress from existential angst to the issues of food (unnecessary), privacy (none except in comms), and operational structures (detailed and unbending). Maybe it was the military training kicking in, knocking them back to pragmatism. That pragmatism certainly made it possible for the Sams and Jacks to settle in, in spite of the individualism of their source culture. The Air Force had directed all their energy toward a commitment to duty. Ultimately, the structures in place, they would follow orders; their programming had started long before they'd become machines. Predictably, the Daniels always had a harder time adjusting, and the unanswerable questions about what it all *meant* tended to lie underneath the details like standing water.

Most surprising, though, were the Teal'cs. At first, Daniel had thought that the original Teal'c's roots in Jaffa culture would have made him ideal for the program, since he was used to being the tool of another's will. On the contrary, though, he realized that, having sacrificed everything for independence, the Teal'cs did not let that go easily.

Theta O'Neill's "voice" cut through the chatter like a blade through canvas. *All right. Everybody shut it. Except you, Daniel, or whoever you're supposed to be. I assume you're still doing the presentations with the pictures and the long-winded explanations.*

Daniel didn't know how to interpret the disgusted look on the theta's face as O'Neill dropped into a chair. The rest of his team followed and the eight of them sat in outward silence until Mendez and his pet scientist left. Of course, they weren't alone. Daniel could feel the unwavering gaze of the installation's ubiquitous security cameras sweeping the room.

Theta O'Neill leaned forward against the table and spoke out loud. "You tell us everything." He lifted a stiff finger and aimed it at Daniel's forehead. "Don't make me go rummaging around in there."

There was an immediate red flare from the alpha team, and theta O'Neill sat back, but the cold light in his eyes didn't change. Daniel shot a look over his shoulder at his own Jack and found him watching, narrow-eyed.

Hinky, alpha Jack said into the narrow alpha team band of comms. *This one's* — There was no word for it, but Daniel got the general impression of napalm.

Terrific, Carter said.

So, after a hurried debate with his team, Daniel didn't tell the thetas *everything*.

He told them about their missions, the worlds they'd visited: worlds with radioactive atmosphere to sear the false skin from their bodies; seas of blue flame that licked at the base of the Stargate; skies livid with the streaking trails of falling debris as the planet's gravity devoured its own blasted moon; a watergate they'd returned to only to find it entwined in the tentacles of a vast, eyeless monster; the low-walled cities on landscapes pressed flat by crushing pressure; storms of unbreathable wind driving glass sand into towers whose upper spires reached beyond the atmosphere.

He told them about the artifacts — toys, Jack called them, sometimes grinning and sometimes grim — they'd been sent to retrieve. Sam let treasures go reluctantly because she never got to poke at their insides or take them apart. They disappeared to some other installation, some shady equivalent of Area 51, they suspected, where scientists backward-engineered them — or blew themselves up.

Of course, this was just speculation on the alphas' part, because they never got news from the other installations, never heard a word about anyone beyond themselves and the other teams with whom they shared comms in those brief moments when the gate was open and the signals could get through. But a few seconds was a lifetime in terms of a data burst. Daniel was starting to get a perverse sort of pleasure from watching Mendez's or Peterson's face when the teams suddenly froze, inaudibly ranting and sharing information or just saying hello because it was good to know someone other than yourself was listening when you spoke.

Until the epsilon team's suicide, alpha Daniel had been engaged in a game of chess with epsilon Daniel, one move per burst in order to keep the game going as long as possible. There was a rumor that delta Carter and gamma Teal'c were engaged in some kind of stilted dork-stoic flirtation, but if they were, they'd encrypted it so well nobody could hear anything more than the occasional flutter of contact between them. The O'Neills tended to remain silent in shared comms, especially the later iterations, unless there were operational details to discuss. There was a lingering sense of distaste in their communiqués, concentrated in their tendency to lapse into referring to the other duplicates, especially one of the other O'Neills, as "it."

But alpha Daniel didn't tell the theta team that. Nor did he tell them about the last burst they'd received from epsilon Teal'c in which he'd declared that he was dying free, or the silence that followed it.

He never said explicitly that, in some small way, the entire alpha team envied him.

CHAPTER SEVEN

Altair (P3X-989)
October 30, 2002, one day after invasion of Eshet

The first thing to go when he became king, O'Neill decided, would be the damn siren. The noise ricocheted around the vast, gloomy chamber like a bunch of hysterical birds shrieking at each other. The second thing to go would be the dust. And the rust. And the mildew—one of those galactic constants, like rats—and the gloom. The place was even gloomier in real life than it had looked on the computer monitor back at Outpost Hawaii. It was also clammy and it smelled bad. Like feet. Like thousand-year-old army boots. As he was opening his mouth to shout over the wailing, the siren cut off so his voice was loud in the sudden silence.

"Some Garden of Eden. Definitely does not live up to the brochures."

The echoes agreed with him until they wandered off to die, probably from depression. A couple of levels down, something gave up or gave in with an anguished groaning sound, and a cloud of greasy steam billowed up through the grating, turning the team to ghostly shadows.

"Yuck," Carter said from somewhere off to the right.

"You okay?" Jackson asked.

"Yeah, just put my hand in...actually, I don't want to know."

As the steam cleared, a different sort of siren started, far off, a heavy-hearted moaning that stuttered, cut out, started again, and then seemed to give up with a resigned sigh.

"Even the sirens sound miserable," Jackson observed. "This does not look good."

For once, O'Neill had to agree. The place was clearly two bolts and a rubber band away from complete collapse. The odds that there was anything here to help them seemed pretty slim.

"Carter?"

"Yeah. Sir." She was standing in the open space in front of the gate, her head tipped back and the light mounted on her P90 aimed up at the ceiling.

"You've got 30 minutes to find something useful, and then we go try our luck with the one of the Von Trapps' trading partners."

"Okay." She waited a beat and added, "Found it."

Teal'c raised an eyebrow at O'Neill and then fell into step with him to join Carter and Jackson. As one they all looked up into the shadows where Carter's light was playing across the dully gleaming surface of the holy disco ball. It was 1.4 meters in diameter, divided into quarters, its pockmarked silver skin split along the seams to let out a pulsing orange light. It wasn't exactly beautiful but somehow just standing there looking at it made O'Neill feel even better than when he jacked in for a recharge on Perseus. He could feel some of the peripheral sensors that had powered down to conserve energy pricking up their ears. He could feel acutely again, all across his skin instead of just in the key use areas of hands, head, feet. The low-grade numbness he'd been getting used to was giving way to a sort of sizzling sense of *presence*, like he'd been suffering from a head cold and was now suddenly cured.

Beside him, Jackson had stopped looking at the disco ball and was inspecting his hands, closing them into tight fists and opening them again, turning them over and wiggling his fingers. "Wow," he said. "It's like battle readiness only—"

"Better," Teal'c said.

"Yeah. Better." A grin pulled up the corner of his mouth, and O'Neill thought that on this red-letter day, he might actually see Jackson laugh. No such luck, but he did look like he'd just taken a hit of the good stuff. The really good stuff. "Wow," he repeated. "This is really, really..."

"Good," Teal'c said.

Carter was still looking up along the shaft of light. "It's the power source. This is what we're supposed to feel like, I bet."

"Sweet," O'Neill said. Then, "How the heck do we get it down from there?"

Carter's shrug made the light waver. "I have no idea," she answered vaguely, although he could practically see the gears spinning away in her head. He didn't mention gears, though, because that tended to set her off on rant number 2038 about how referring to what they had in their heads as "gears" was just insulting and maybe they should realize what a work of art they were, since the violation of the uncertainty principle alone yadda yadda and so on. O'Neill had never managed to listen to that one long enough to find out what the cat had to do with anything, although he knew that it would take no effort at all to recall exactly what she'd said. He could find out all he wanted to know about Schrödinger's cat if he wanted to. He chose not to.

"Perhaps Harlan will know," Teal'c suggested.

"Perhaps, perhaps," O'Neill said. "Anyone see a burning bush around here?"

Jackson rolled his eyes.

Waving them off down the corridors branching between the shuddering hulks of mysterious machinery, O'Neill said, "Fan out. Keep in touch. Don't break him."

He stood for a moment until a new siren hiccupped and settled into an adenoidal wheezing that mostly drowned out Jackson's ongoing patter about the level of technology and unfamiliar architecture. He headed in the direction of the siren, on the assumption that someone would eventually show up to fix whatever it was squawking about or, failing that, he could shoot at it until he achieved blissful silence.

The installation didn't get any more attractive as he

moved beyond the gate area, and even with the happy glow
he was getting off the disco ball, he reconsidered the whole
being king option. The massive machinery that lined the corridors seemed mostly inert. The occasional hunk of corroded
metal showed signs of life, mostly by venting steam or leaking goo. Some of the ductwork that snaked along the ceiling and writhed between the machines looked like it had
been repaired multiple times, layer after layer of scrap metal
bolted and strapped and welded into place. Whatever this
world was like outside the installation, it must've been *really*
bad to motivate anybody to want to keep this derelict going.
"Reminds me of my first apartment," he murmured to himself.
When Carter pinged an inquiry about that over the internal
comms, he told her to mind her own business. Jackson, however, took the opportunity to remind O'Neill that his first
apartment was, in fact, an incubation unit on Perseus.

O'Neill took the opportunity to remind Jackson that he
was breakable.

If this guy, Harlan, is such a technological genius, O'Neill
asked, *why's this place such a dump?*

Carter's virtual shrug came across as a looping inquiry
ping. *The file wasn't complete. Pertinent data like, for
instance, schematics for the power source and the duplicating technology, are pretty carefully firewalled back at the
NID mainframe on Perseus. I guess we'll just have to ask
Harlan.*

If we can find him, Teal'c said in that neutral tone that
meant he was getting ticked.

O'Neill climbed a ladder to the top of what looked like
some kind of water storage tank and tried to get a bird's-
eye view. At twelve o'clock, Jackson was heading deeper
into the installation, trailing a hand along the flanks of the
machinery and still muttering away to himself about how
the whole place was simultaneously fascinating and disappointing. To his right and one level up, Carter was crouched
in front of an open panel, poking at its innards. A shower of

sparks made her jump away, but a second later she was back to sticking her fingers in the light socket. *Rats learn faster than that, Captain,* O'Neill observed, and it wasn't at all possible that she flipped him the bird. To his left, Teal'c was making his way across a catwalk, his shadow enormous and imposing on the wall behind him. The siren was still wheezing away, so O'Neill dropped from the tank onto the rattling grating and followed the sound.

Getting more than a little ticked himself, he called, "Harlan! Come on, we just want to talk." The sound of rapid footsteps one aisle over made him stop and back up to peer through a gap between machines. "We're not going to hurt you!" Then, when no Harlan obediently appeared, he added, softly, "Much." He sent out a ping to the team and ducked through the gap just in time to catch sight of a leg and a bit of quilted coat at the turn at the end of the aisle. "Look, don't make me chase you," he advised. "I'm not in the mood."

Truth be told, though, he was in the mood. All kinds of zippy energy surged around inside him, and what he really wanted just then was a 30-klick footrace with a cheetah. A quick wrassle with a bear. A tall building good for leaping. As he scrambled up the ladder of another tank and dropped silently down on the far side, he stopped himself shy of anything stupid like breaking into song. He did whistle a little, and called out in a friendly voice, "Come out, come out wherever you are!" The footsteps grew fainter, and he loped along behind, just fast enough to keep a bead on the prey and to make sure the prey could keep a bead on him. *A little further. Keep running, pal.* Now he was close enough to hear a repeated litany of "oh, dear" in time with the patter of scurrying feet. If he hadn't been in such a good mood right then, that might've hurt his feelings. He put on a last little burst of speed, adding some good foot-stomping, and pulled up as Teal'c dropped from the catwalk practically on top of the roly-poly, bald-headed guy and knocked Harlan flat on his back in a puddle of something slick and smelly.

Looking down at his squinched-shut eyes and his pudgy fists held tight up under his chin, O'Neill might've felt sorry for him, if he'd been capable. "Harlan," he said in his smoothest and least intimidating voice. The eyes didn't open, but Harlan's head did start to retreat like a turtle's into the high, stiff collar of his coat. O'Neill nudged him with his foot. "Harlan," he repeated, this time without the friendliness.

At a nod from O'Neill, Teal'c bent down and heaved Harlan up by the front of his coat. No sooner were Harlan's feet planted than he was darting for the stairs. Unluckily for him, he ran headlong into Jackson, spun away in the opposite direction, and fetched up against Carter.

"Oh, dear," he wailed softly. "No, no, no, there's no *time!*" He made another attempt to get by Carter but she wouldn't budge, so he gave O'Neill an appealing look over his shoulder while pointing in the direction of the siren. "You must help! The pump on the secondary coolant tank is not working! The gears in the heat exchanger will fuse!"

"So?" Jackson asked.

Harlan looked at him like he was the dumbest kid to fall off the apple truck this month. "So? So if the gears fuse, the heat cannot be expelled, and then—" He made an expressive "poof" with his hands. "—it will explode!" When nobody seemed to take this terribly hard, he added, "And it will be very bad. Very hard to repair. Very, very hard."

"Okay," O'Neill said, coming close to pin Harlan between himself and Carter. "You give us what we need, and we'll let you go fix your whatsis. Although why you'd *want* to is honestly beyond me."

Harlan's mouth fell open and then closed in a tight, sad frown. "Want to? It is my home. I'm the last!" His hand fluttered up to pat O'Neill's chest and away again like he'd touched something hot. "Except for you. Of course." His gaze slid in Carter's direction. "You have a servo loose in your left shoulder." He leaned a little on her outstretched arm. "I can hear it. Not serious. Easily repaired." Turning back to O'Neill, he continued, "But I am the last, the only one left to remember Hubbald, the last of my people." As he spoke, he looked nervously in the direction of the faulty coolant pump and bounced a little with anxiety. "Please. If you have not come to help me, why are you here? Not, of course, that I'm sad to see you. I am so happy!" Putting his palms together, he said, "Comtraya!" and pulled them apart in a circular gesture of celebration. "I was told you were dead. Dead, gone. So sad—"

O'Neill slapped his hand across Harlan's mouth. "Maybe somebody's dead, but it's not us." He gave Harlan's head a shake. "We're not them. We're us. And we don't have a lot of time."

Harlan's eyes widened.

"The power source. We want it. Now."

Against O'Neill's palm, he said, "Oh, no. Oh, no, no, no."

"Yes, yes, yes, Harlan." O'Neill nodded Harlan's head up and down in time with the words. "And you're going to tell us how to make it work so we can get the heck off this piece-of-junk planet."

O'Neill pulled his hand away as Harlan set off on another agitated filibuster. "I can't do that! It's impossible. Quite, quite impossible. And even if it wasn't, if you take it I will die and all of this will be lost." He swept an arm in a wide arc to take in the installation in all its rusting, stinking, oozing glory, and his expression brightened from panic to hopeful cheerfulness. "But you could stay! You could stay and help. I need help. This place, it's so big for one person to handle." As if in agreement, another siren started whining in counterpoint to the first, making Harlan shake visibly with distress.

"By this time," Teal'c observed, "the NID have discovered that they have lost contact with their outpost. They will know we have accessed their computers. It is likely that they will come here to retrieve us."

"Good point. Sorry, Harlan, we can't stick around. We want the power source." O'Neill was looming so close that Harlan started to shrink into himself like he was expecting to be crushed, which was probably true. "Talk, Harlan, or I'm going to have to resort to plan B."

"Plan B?" Harlan repeated timorously.

"Yeah, that's the one where Carter takes your head off and we figure it all out someplace else."

Behind him, Jackson snorted his disgust, but Carter obediently wrapped her hand around Harlan's throat.

"But it can't be done!" Harlan squeaked as the pressure increased. "The power source is integrated. Fully integrated into the station's systems!"

O'Neill leaned even closer. "Then unintegrate it."

"I don't know how."

"Who knows?"

"Hubbald! He's the creator of all of this. He knew everything. Everything. But he's gone! Gone for so long now and I am all alone here."

Narrowing his eyes, O'Neill studied Harlan's face for a moment, then reached down and untwisted Harlan's hands from each other. He raised the left one by the thumb. "Answer me this, then." He began to apply pressure, feeling the resistance as the joint strained against the motion. "How come this Hubbald left us with the capacity to feel pain?"

"Jack—"

O'Neill stabbed a finger in Jackson's direction to shut him up. Jackson lifted his hands in resignation and went to sit on the stairs. O'Neill turned back to his task. "It's a design flaw, Harlan."

"It—it makes us more—" His mouth opened wider but nothing came out.

"More what?"

"More alive."

Placing one gentle hand on the side of Harlan's face,

O'Neill used the other to snap Harlan's thumb backward. When Harlan stopped screaming, O'Neill said, "It makes you weak."

The gate light didn't do much for the decor, although Sam figured it at least gave the place a nice Gothic atmosphere, just in case anybody was feeling relaxed or anything. She took a moment to wonder whether she and Daniel had actually pulled the short straw, winning the maddening job of chasing Harlan around while he twittered and fretted and evaded questions in that cheerily desperate way he had. As she nodded to the marines to take flanking positions at the foot of the ramp, she decided that, no, even coming back to this depressing place had to be less awful than Colonel O'Neill's task. She wouldn't be surprised to gate home to discover Maybourne stuffed and mounted over the colonel's mantelpiece.

She felt the marine to her left—Rickert, more bear than man—raise his P90. A second later, the one to the right—Hassan, terrier-fast and ferocious—did the same. A siren was groaning and, in that direction, a red light was flashing in a panicked, erratic rhythm.

"Huh," Daniel said from behind them. "I don't remember it being so..."

Sam could picture him opening and closing his mouth a couple of times, trying to find a nice way to say it.

"Horrible?" Hassan offered helpfully, her lip curling. Sam sympathized. The place had acquired a distinctly decrepit smell since they were last here.

Daniel's shadow rippled as he shrugged, and then it disappeared when the gate disengaged. "Not Netu horrible. More... old abandoned installation inhabited by B-movie zombies horrible."

"Are there any other kind of zombies?" Hassan asked. She was at the bottom of the steps now, aiming the P90 down through the grating where, on the next level down, it sounded like an industrial washing machine was eating a Volkswagen. Steam billowed up and she stepped back, coughing. "Nice."

"Okay, let's just find Harlan." Sam waved them toward the flashing light on the assumption that, if he wasn't at the gate beaming and waving his arms around and singing "Comtraya," Harlan was probably gluing bits of the installation back together. "And remember, there may be duplicates running around, so stay alert and don't shoot the good guys." She lifted her arm to indicate the orange band tied around her bicep. In case there was any confusion on this score, Daniel did the same. His band had written on it in the colonel's hand, "Annoying but not evil." Sam hid a smile.

Hassan and Rickert nodded and fell in, Hassan behind Sam and Rickert behind Daniel.

"Do you really think they're coming here?" Daniel asked, although from his tone, he already knew the answer.

"If I was hunting for information, I'd look into my origins, go back to the source."

Daniel made a noncommittal sound that was almost lost in the moaning of the siren. "If they know about this place."

"Some source," Rickert said as he sidestepped a slick oozing from the bottom of a shuddering machine, only to step into another slick oozing from an identical machine on the other side of the corridor. "What's that stink?"

"My guess is the scrubbers are malfunctioning," Sam answered. "We probably don't want to be here too long."

"Or at all."

"Easier to keep your ears open when your mouth is shut, Ricky," Hassan said.

"Ma'am."

Not bad advice on Hassan's part, except there was practically no chance they'd hear something coming. The siren was still grating away and the washing machine was still gnawing at its dinner. Something flickered in Sam's peripheral vision. She raised her fist, and the team came to a stop and lined up against the hot flank of yet another machine. Cursing the siren, which blotted out more important sounds, she edged up to the next gap and peered into it. Another flicker of motion, but the pipe near her head was hissing steam and she couldn't make out what it was. The strobing red light that went with the siren made the steam alternately an opaque wall and a shadow box filled with menacing shapes. Just as she was bending to get a better view, a shot from the next corridor over ruptured the pipe. The belching steam drove her back into Hassan, who caught her before she fell and pulled her away as the end of the alley filled up and another siren yelped in alarm.

As she waved the team back the way they came, another shot gouged the concrete at Sam's feet. A third caught Rickert in the shoulder and spun him around so that he landed on his knees, but he was up again in a second. It was unclear whether he was letting Daniel help him or was shielding Daniel with his body. Either way, they were heading back along the alley, sticking close to the minimal cover of the machines.

They didn't get far before the floor in front of them was strafed in a precise line of staff weapon fire. Rickert let Daniel push him into the space between the machines and then shuffled around to get Daniel behind him. Hassan and Sam ducked into the corresponding space on the other side of the alley.

"There!" Hassan pointed up at the catwalk spanning the alley above them.

Blinking condensation from her eyes and ignoring the sting of the burn on the side of her face, Sam followed Hassan's gaze just in time to see a familiar shape disappearing up the stairs to the next level. "Teal'c," she said, and saw Daniel nodding across from her, confirming. "Rickert?"

The marine's scowl was eloquent, but he unclenched his teeth long enough to say, "Arm's no good, but I got another one."

"Sheep," Hassan said.

Sam grunted her agreement while Daniel raised his eyebrows and mouthed "Sheep?"

"They're herding us," Sam answered. "Can't go forward. Can't go back."

"Ah," Daniel said. "Sheep. Right."

Sam edged to the corner and risked a peek back along the alley. Steam was still hissing from the ruptured pipe, but it was starting to clear a little. She got her head tucked in again in time to avoid a shot from that direction. "Harlan's control center is back that way." Leaning her head against the metal side of the machine, she peered up through the slice of catwalk she could see from this angle. It seemed empty. Somewhere off to the right were footsteps, but she couldn't tell if they were coming from the gate or from the control center. The first siren stopped abruptly, and a low rumble shook the floor under her. The second siren yawped one last time and cut out, and with it the warning light. In the sudden silence, she heard Hassan swear under her breath when the floor under them shuddered, followed a moment later by a percussion Sam could feel in her bones. Her ears popped.

Sam turned to Hassan and said, "Take Rickert and get back to the gate." She pointed with her P90 past Daniel and through the gap between the machines at the next alley. "Dial out and apprise Hammond of the situation. Tell him we've engaged the thetas. We think." She looked the question at Daniel and he nodded again.

"Seems a reasonable assumption," Daniel answered. "Dan said that the other teams weren't a threat, and these guys are definitely threatening."

"Okay." Deciding safe was better than sorry, Sam looked from Hassan to Rickert. "If you see any of them, take your shot."

"Yes, ma'am," Hassan responded while Sam checked to make sure that Rickert had the catwalk covered.

On Sam's signal, Hassan dashed out across the alley, shoving Rickert back and taking his place. Then Sam followed. A bullet tore a hole in the concrete at her heels, and Hassan fired a sweeping burst into the thinning steam at the end of the alley. After taking a second to look Rickert over—he was sweating and pasty but alert—Sam climbed over him and then Daniel to check out the next alley. It was clear in both directions, and the catwalk above ended in an empty staircase. No overhead vantage there. There was still a chance that someone could pick them off from atop one of the machines, but the floor was shuddering continuously now and staying put wasn't doing them any good.

She covered Hassan and Rickert as they darted across the alley and into another gap. No fire. Turning to Daniel, she said, "You good to go?"

He nodded. "Go where, exactly?"

"We do a quick check of the control center, try to find Harlan." She paused, unable to be heard over the whining, groaning sound of stressed metal giving way. The floor shuddered again, but there were no sirens. That was a bad sign. "If he's not there—" She couldn't hear Daniel's reply, but his frown said it all. No help for it. Given what they knew about the duplicates, Harlan's chances weren't good in any case.

Covering each other, they leapfrogged their way across three more alleys and then crept back toward the control room, keeping as much as possible under the crazy web of pipes and cables that made a virtually solid canopy in this part of the installation. They were almost back at the point parallel to the ambush and ready to cut across to the control center when the colonel's voice rose gate-ward in a loud whoop, followed by a burst of P90 fire. Sam keyed her radio and Rickert answered.

"Got two at the gate," he panted.

"Who?"

"O'Neill and Teal'c. Jeez, Major, they look just like—" A succession of staff blasts drowned him out.

"Do you control the gate?" Sam asked.

"No joy. But we will."

Hassan's voice cut in. "Damn, these guys are *fast!*" More gunfire.

"Okay, hang tight. We're close to the control center. We're gonna check it out and head back." Holding onto Daniel to keep her footing, she waited until the floor stopped rolling underneath them and pushed him toward the control room. "Two at the gate. So where're the other ones?"

"You mean us."

"I mean them."

Just then Daniel tripped and fell headlong with a muffled "Oomph," then rolled over to get a look at what had gotten under his feet.

"Oh, God," Sam said.

"That's—"

Sam bent down and picked it up. "Harlan's arm."

"—disturbing," Daniel finished.

As she lifted it, still in its quilted sleeve, the arm uncurled and the fingers opened beseechingly. "Hopefully the rest of him is still in one piece," Sam said.

He was, more or less. Somehow, even with only one arm, Harlan managed to convey hand-wringing. As they came around either side of his console, he looked up at them with a start and lifted his hand up to shield his face. "I have no more! It doesn't matter what you do! I cannot do what you ask!"

He hunched defensively away as Daniel leaned in and said in his soothing voice, "Harlan, it's okay. It's us." He shot Sam a quick glance. "The flesh-and-blood us, not the—" A wave of his hand in the direction of the gate. "—you know, 'them' us."

Sam left Daniel to coax Harlan out of the emotional fetal position while she did a quick survey of the console. It took only a second to see that the thing was useless, every interface and monitor fried. No wonder there were no sirens. Harlan's rising wail, half relief, half dismay, did the same job.

"Harlan, what's going on here?" Sam demanded as gently as she could, given that whatever had exploded was belching smoke into the main complex and gunfire was still popping like fireworks from the direction of the gate. The decrepit stench was worse now, and she was pretty certain that whatever counted as an atmosphere planetside was leaking in.

"Them!" Harlan cried, pointing with a wavering finger toward the gate. "They wouldn't let me—the coolant leak—overheating—and then they destroyed—" His gesture began with the console and ended up taking in the whole place in a wide arc. He raised tearful eyes to Daniel. "How could they? They are Hubbald's children, too!"

Another explosion, this one closer, almost knocked him out of his chair. Daniel and Sam clutched the console for balance.

"He made this place! He made this body, the technology—"

"They're not Hubbald's children, Harlan," Daniel said. "He never made something like them, okay?"

Harlan squeezed his eyes shut and bobbed his head in agreement. "No. Hubbald would never." When he opened them again, his gaze was clear and as accusing as Harlan was capable of. "*Your* people! You Earth people! Months ago they promised to help me, and instead they took my duplicating equipment, your templates, and left me here alone with no help! They made these ones!" Even with the anger in his words, Harlan looked more hurt and confused than furious.

Daniel glanced at Sam, his brow furrowed deeply. "Not us. Not our people. Not exactly."

Sam shook her head. They didn't have time for this. "We've got to go."

Between the two of them, they got Harlan on his feet and moving in the direction of the gate where the occasional burst of gunfire could be heard over the groans and squeals of collapsing infrastructure and the rumble of secondary explosions.

"And then they came—the duplicates—bad, very bad malfunctions, I think—and wanted to take the source, the power source—that's mine, all I have to keep me alive—and they wouldn't believe me when I said that it was integrated. The planet—it draws its power from the planet—and they were so angry. So angry." Harlan's litany broke as he bent to collect his arm from where Sam had left it in the alley, and then it started up again. "The others, the first ones I made those years ago, those first duplicates, they were angry sometimes but they were never, never *cruel*."

Sam was just opening her mouth to tell Harlan to save it for the debriefing when his sudden silence made her spin around. He was clutching his severed arm to his chest, the lifeless hand open on his shoulder like a bizarre gesture of comfort, and looking back the way they'd come. In the flickering light, Sam just caught sight of Daniel, backpedaling awkwardly as he was dragged away by...himself.

The duplicate flashed her a grin and shouted, "Hi, Sam!" He disappeared around the curve of a water tank before Sam could contemplate a safe shot.

She and Harlan caught up to them in the next alley. Sam sighted along her P90, pacing evenly to close the distance between herself and the duplicate who was still walking backward, the muzzle of his 9mm pressed against Daniel's temple. She didn't shift her aim when Carter dropped from the top of a water tank and mirrored her stance, her P90 aimed steadily at Sam's head. The patch on the duplicate Carter's shoulder read: THETA.

"Let him go," Sam said.

"Or what?" theta Carter said.

"Oh dear, oh dear, oh dear," Harlan muttered.

"We can work this out," Sam said over his fretting. "It doesn't have to go this way."

Theta Jackson tipped his head to say to his hostage, "Diplomacy. Isn't that supposed to be your routine?" When Daniel pressed his lips together in a stubborn line, the duplicate sighed, and kept dragging him backward. They were close to the gate now. "Cut your hair, I see," he said to Daniel. "You think that will make them respect you? Think they'll

STARGATE SG-I: HYDRA　　　　119

let you in their little club?" In response to Daniel's silence, he added, "Sell out," and gave Daniel a gratuitous jerk that made him grunt in pain.

They kept moving, Sam and theta Carter mirror images in the alleyway as theta Jackson continued to drag Daniel backward. Sam kept a bead on theta Carter while she listened to the sporadic gunfire, close now as they neared the gate. Behind her, Harlan followed them, his voice thin with fear as he repeated, "Bad malfunctions. Very bad."

Sam opened her mouth to tell him to run, but theta Carter flicked a look in his direction and said, "I don't think that would be a good idea. We're going to need you to get that power source disconnected."

Harlan's fretful muttering stretched even thinner to become a querulous wail. "I told you! I told you and told you. The power source is integrated. It won't *work* outside of this place. Why won't you believe me?"

Neither of the thetas had time to answer. One more turn and they emerged into the open space before the gate. Sam hesitated before stepping out of the alley. A quick glance around the corner showed her Rickert to the left, hunkered down behind a control panel that was already smoking and gouged by repeated staff weapon fire, and Hassan to the right, stretched out on a downward flight of stairs with her eyes at floor level. Good positions, defensively speaking, but they weren't going to be able to access the DHD from there. When the thetas and their hostage got as far as the DHD, theta O'Neill and theta Teal'c broke cover. Sam felt a sick sort of satisfaction to see that theta Teal'c was wounded, his left arm dangling and coated with the sticky gray-white fluid that served as their blood.

Coming down the steps from behind the gate, theta O'Neill barked, "Carter, dial us up." When he met the two Daniels he added, "I'll take that," yanked Daniel from the duplicate's grasp and, wrapping his arm across Daniel's neck, put a 9mm to his head. "Hello there, Carter," he said to Sam, like they'd just run into each other in a grocery store. When she took another step toward them, he tightened his choke hold so that Daniel's hands came up and pulled fruitlessly at his arm. "Ah ah ah. Not too close." He waggled the gun a little and left the rest of the threat unsaid.

Behind him, the event horizon billowed out and settled again. Sam tried to make out the glyphs on the DHD, but theta Carter's body was blocking half of the panel.

Way off at the other end of the installation, something substantial gave way with a roar. Twisting girders wailed. A greasy breath of wind pushed Sam's hair away from her forehead.

"Go," theta O'Neill ordered, and the theta team headed up the stairs. Sam kept pace at a wary distance as theta O'Neill backed up to follow them, Daniel's reluctant feet catching on the steps. The gate gulped as it swallowed theta Carter and theta Teal'c. Right next to the event horizon, theta Jackson stood waiting, like he was interested to see how it would all turn out.

"I will shoot him," O'Neill warned Sam.

Gasping in a breath against the hold on this throat, Daniel said, "No, you won't."

O'Neill raised his eyebrows. "Oh, really?"

"You could've killed us any time," Sam said.

"But you didn't." Daniel sagged a little in O'Neill's grip, still clinging to his arm.

"The day is young." O'Neill squeezed harder, and Daniel's eyes closed tight.

In her peripheral vision, Sam could see Rickert sliding his 9mm up over the edge of the control panel. The angle wasn't great, but if he was steady, there might be a chance. On the right, Hassan was in a better position. Sam didn't look directly at her but was able to see her point two fingers at her own eyes and then toward theta O'Neill. Theta Jackson still had his pistol out but was too absorbed by the spectacle on the stairs to pay much attention to the marines. Although,

Sam admitted, it was hard to know how the duplicate was processing sensory data.

"You won't," Daniel was saying. They were almost at the event horizon now.

"And why, pray tell?"

"Because no matter what's been done to you, somewhere in there, you're still Jack."

O'Neill's blandly interested expression turned suddenly venomous. "I'm not him," he said, each syllable clipped and precise.

"Then who are you?"

That seemed to stop him in his tracks and for a second, as he contemplated the answer, O'Neill's face fell into lines of sadness. Just for a second, though, and then he sneered, his mouth close to Daniel's ear, "I'm what's left when there's no more Mr. Nice Guy."

O'Neill lifted his elbow and shoved the gun harder against the side of Daniel's head, ready to pull the trigger. Turning to Rickert, Sam shouted "Now!" Just as she'd hoped, O'Neill shifted his aim in Rickert's direction as Hassan bolted upright and took her shot.

The bullet caught O'Neill in the side, under his raised arm, and his own shot went wild. At that moment, a massive explosion in the lower levels of the installation made the floor heave. As O'Neill lost his balance, Daniel squirmed out of his grip and rolled down the stairs to fetch up under the DHD. Sam's own shot missed theta Jackson as her feet went out from under her and she crashed down on her elbow with a yelp of pain. Through the grating, she could see a fireball blooming upward, searing heat waves rippling ahead of it. She was back on her feet in a few seconds to find the gate empty and the duplicates gone. Daniel was staring at the DHD.

"I got the address," he shouted above the receding rumble of the explosion. Under her feet, the gate platform lurched and she almost fell again. More screeching as the girders underneath it began to buckle.

Sam shook her head. "Dial us home!" She signaled to Hassan to help her with Rickert, who was slumped barely conscious behind the control panel. As they got him to his feet, she hollered at Harlan, "Come on! Harlan! Let's go!"

Another explosion rocked the gate platform. Standing at the edge with his severed arm still clutched to his chest, Harlan looked out into the billowing smoke. Ignoring Daniel's shout, he headed down the stairs and was immediately lost in the roiling darkness. Daniel had only time to take one step in his direction before another explosion tore up through the grating and threw him backward onto the stairs.

Sam shoved Hassan and Rickert through the event horizon, then came back and dragged Daniel to his feet just as the remainder of the platform tilted with a deafening shriek toward the flames. They scrambled up the increasing incline, the watery surface of the gate looming impossibly over them, and leaped into safety.

PART THREE

corrigenda
things to be corrected

CHAPTER EIGHT

NID Secondary Outpost "Hawaii" (P7A-025)
October 31, 2002, two days after the invasion of Eshet

"Ouch!" O'Neill yelped and jerked away from Carter's hands. "Go easy, will ya?"

"Sorry," she mumbled. When she went back to poking at his innards through the gaping hole left by the sneaky marine's sneaky bullet, her touch wasn't any gentler than before. "It's not too bad. I think you're going to lose some functionality in this arm. Not much, but some. And the internal radio took some damage. If I can just—" She wiggled something and the adjustment registered in O'Neill's brain as an alert message carried on an arc of lightning. He hissed, but managed to stay still while Carter cut away more of his shirt and then his skin to get a better look at the damage. She wiggled the thing again, and this time his raised arm jumped upward and came down again so that his elbow connected hard with the back of her head.

"Ouch!" she shouted and pulled back to glare up at him.

"Sorry. Robot thing," he said with a thin smile. "Maybe you shouldn't wiggle that any more."

Carter sat up and stared at him a moment, then shook her head and turned away to rummage loudly in the toolbox on the table next to O'Neill. "It doesn't matter anyway," she grumbled. "I don't have what I need here." She raised her eyes to him again, but this time the ire was pretty much gone. "If we're going to get you patched up for real, we'll have to take you back to the lab at Perseus."

"Where we will be welcomed with open arms, I'm sure," O'Neill said. "Just fill the hole and make sure nothing's going to corrode or explode." He gritted his teeth as she ducked down again and started going at his delicate insides with a pair of needle-nosed pliers. "And while you're in there," he added, "be a pal and deactivate the pain response, okay?"

Carter shook her head. "Can't, unless you want me to open up your head." She waited for the order for a second, then went back to her work with a distinctly disappointed shrug. "Even if I could, though, I wouldn't recommend it. You need it."

"Why? So I can feel more 'alive'?" He made quotation marks in the air with his fingers for the last word, and raised his voice an octave to mimic Harlan's panicky squeak. The quotation marks turned into clenched fists when Carter wiggled the whatever-it-was *again*.

"So you know when you're pushing your systems past their limits," she answered. One last wiggle sent twelve different alerts zinging across O'Neill's vision, and she sat up, only to duck again out of the range of his killer elbow. "Although the alive thing isn't exactly inconsequential, either."

O'Neill grimaced and lifted his arm a last time to let Carter patch him up with duct tape. Then he leaned back so that she could toss the roll to Teal'c, who caught it one-handed and started tearing off strips with his teeth to wrap around the hole in his bicep. At the same time, Teal'c was monitoring the NID's radio chatter on his headset. O'Neill watched him for a moment, calculating the effect of the damage on their operational readiness, and said, more to himself than the rest of them, "I could use a little less of that kind of alive right now, thanks."

Jackson didn't look up from the monitor as he said, "Wait 14 hours, 3 minutes, and you'll get your wish." Then his gaze flicked up toward O'Neill and away again. "Unless you want to try that out sooner."

"Almost did, thanks to you. Way to go with the whole watching my back thing there, by the way."

Jackson swung his chair around to face him more directly

and narrowed his eyes, thinking, but not, apparently, about letting this go. "Actually, I was just a bit distracted by the spectacle of you putting a gun to my head."

"It was not your head," Teal'c corrected.

"No, I suppose it wasn't." Jackson turned back to the monitor.

Teal'c continued, "And it was you who did so first."

"True. But I didn't have quite so much fun with it."

"Shut up, Jackson," O'Neill said.

"Very snappy, Jack."

"Daniel," Carter warned, and he waved a hand over his shoulder, maybe surrendering, maybe just wiping them out of his conscious space. Even with the damage to the comms, O'Neill couldn't miss the brief fugue of vague, unpleasant images that leaked into comms from Jackson's end.

With a growl, O'Neill yanked his cap off and scrubbed at his hair. He couldn't feel it, not the way he remembered feeling it. Away from Harlan's magic disco ball, his peripheral systems were powering down again, leaving behind the numbness that now seemed even worse by comparison. Sensors indicated proximity, pressure, direction of movement, in a stream of data that his brain could interpret, but that *thereness* he'd felt in Harlan's installation was fading already, like he was an island and his real estate was shrinking with each lapping wave. Still, the pain response was doing just fine. And it was this in-between-ness that was making him nuts: not enough like a man, not enough like a machine. He watched Teal'c fixing a hole in his flesh like he was repairing damaged drywall and felt the very familiar heat of anger and frustration sizzling along veins he didn't even have. If he needed to, he could ramp up to battle readiness, occupy himself fully again, but only if he wanted to trade duration. The shootout in the Garden of Eden had already eaten up most of the extra reserves they accrued from their exposure to the disco ball. And all he had to show for it was a pain response any really decent evil overlord should've edited out of him, a fist-sized hole under his arm, and 14 measly hours.

"Fourteen hours," he muttered and slid off of the table with a wince. He walked around Teal'c and stepped over the body of the tech to stand in front of the poster by the big wall monitor. Palm trees leaned out over the waves, and happy pink and yellow letters invited him to Hawaii. He stared at it for a few long seconds and then slammed his fist through it. Buried to his wrist in the concrete, his hand flared briefly with pain and another series of alerts cascaded across his vision. A little avalanche of dust and debris clattered out of the hole when he pulled his fist out of the shattered beach.

"Feel better?" Carter asked. She'd been closing up her toolbox but opened it again.

O'Neill waved her away, and she closed the case. "Much. Thanks for asking." He turned away from them and yanked his T-shirt off over his head. The fluid that had leaked out of him had hardened to a crusty plastic-like consistency, turning blue as it dried and making the shirt stiff and brittle. Weirdly, the smell of it reminded him of something, something that belonged to another life, like pudding or candy—cloying, sweet, and a bit unnatural. Not at all like blood, in any case. According to Carter, the fluid had something to do with data transfer. She thought it was the height of interesting. He thought it was creepy. Frowning with distaste, he balled the material up and tossed it into the corner before pulling on a spare shirt he'd found in the bunk room. It was a little big, but he wasn't planning on going on a date anytime soon, and it didn't matter so long as the duct tape was covered and he could pretend that he wasn't patched up like one of the derelict machines in Harlan's installation.

While Teal'c finished his own repairs, Carter put her toolbox away and pulled out the black stone pump primer they'd scored from the Von Trapps on Eshet. Since the trip to Altair had earned them a spectacular load of nothing, the gizmo was their next best bet. The thought of Harlan's disco ball and all its feel-good energy going up in flames and down in rubble was enough to make a grown robot cry. A lump of black stone seemed a miserable substitute, especially since it gave off no feel-good vibes at all. With a grunt of resignation, O'Neill hooked a chair with his foot, dragged it over to the monitor, and straddled it.

"Okay, kids, what's the news?"

Jackson had about forty windows open on the monitor and was clicking through them at a rate of about one every two seconds, opening more as he went. It looked like he was assimilating anything that had even the vaguest connection to the gizmo Carter was turning under the light at her table and poking with her pliers.

Teal'c tossed the tape into her toolbox and came to stand with his hands behind his back on the other side of Jackson's monitor. "There is a high density of radio traffic. It seems that the handler is in the process of recalling the remaining teams and support personnel. Piper's code repeats at regular intervals. We are ordered to return."

"Right." O'Neill tried the smile again. "We'll just pop back home then, shall we? Catch up with the gang. Get back to work." He folded his arms, but stopped himself from picking at the edges of the duct tape through his shirt.

"I vote no," Jackson said, and added hastily with mock deference, "not that we're a democracy or anything." The rapid flutter of changing screens reflected in his eyes and made him look, well, like a robot.

O'Neill focused on Teal'c instead, who was waiting patiently for his turn. O'Neill's fingers weren't itching to tug at the tape, but there was enough remembered sensory data from the original template to make him think they were. He unfolded his arms and locked his fingers across the back of his neck. "Okay, so how's that going? The recall, I mean."

Teal'c answered, "The gamma versions of O'Neill and Teal'c are unaccounted for, but gammas Carter and Jackson have returned. There has been no sign of the alphas. The zetas remain inoperative on Perseus."

O'Neill's smile was thin with mean satisfaction. "Things aren't going so well for Mendez, it seems. All those tin soldiers defunct, AWOL or half brain-dead." He cocked his jaw. "The alphas are a problem."

Looking up from her work, Carter nodded. "Somebody must've tipped off the SGC. Why else would they have been at Harlan's installation?"

Daniel agreed. "The alphas are the likely candidates. They're the closest to—" He lifted one hand off the keyboard to wave it in the general direction of Earth. "—you know, them. And I doubt Mendez would do it, although that doesn't rule out someone else on Perseus, I suppose."

Jack's gaze slipped sideways to the flashing data on Jackson's screen. Without even trying, he was reading each page before it was replaced by the next. He closed his eyes, but he could feel the data swarming around in some virtual space that wasn't really a brain. "No," he growled, "it's the alphas." He opened his eyes and dropped his fists to his thighs with enough force to leave bruises. If he could still bruise. "And that is not a good thing. They'll be on our asses."

Carter dropped a tool into her box and felt around for another, never taking her eyes off the pump primer. It didn't seem to care one bit what she did to it, though. It just kept sitting there, a lump of stone, doing nothing. "It's a sure bet that if the alphas are working with the SGC, they've spilled the beans about the whole power supply issue. Maybe they even know about this." She picked the primer up and held it closer to the light. It was so black it seemed to suck the color out of the room. She glowered at it and went back to poking at it with all the pointy things she could find.

Jackson's hands lifted from the keyboard and hovered there.

"What?" O'Neill asked.

"You know, we could turn ourselves in."

"To the people who most likely want to grind us into itty-bitty pieces? I thought you voted no to that plan."

Jackson wagged his finger at him. "No. No, not to them. To the SGC."

O'Neill narrowed his eyes at him. "Now *that's* a stupid idea."

"Think about it. If they know about the power source, well, the alphas are *them*, and they'll want to help them. I mean the alphas are the good guys, aren't they? At least, they're pretty much identical to them. And so are we." His lips twitched in a qualifying smile. "Sort of. They could save us. It's what they do. The SGC won't countenance the systematic destruction of a whole race of sentient beings."

"Really." O'Neill leaned forward and clasped his hands between his knees. "Ever heard of the Goa'uld? What do you think they want to do to them? Invite them over to play bridge?"

Jackson blinked. "That's different. The Goa'uld are evil snaky things. We're *them*."

"All the more reason to have us destroyed," Teal'c said.

O'Neill wondered if everything he said would sound equally dire. "Say 'Mary had a little lamb,'" he ordered.

"Mary had a little lamb," Teal'c responded. It sounded dire. He continued as though there had been no interruption. "They are real. We are not."

"I'm real," Carter said from her workbench.

"Right," O'Neill said. "But I bet you a—" He couldn't think of anything worth betting that didn't belong to someone else's life. "—whatever, that the flesh-and-blood Carter wouldn't be on your side."

"Maybe she would. It's not like I want to *be* her."

"Don't you?" Again, the ghost of memory made an agitation of static in O'Neill's head, like faint chatter in comms, a whole context he could sense but that didn't belong to him.

Jackson put his fingers back on the keyboard and sighed in resignation. The sound made anger sizzle again inside O'Neill. There wasn't any need for breath, except to make a better lie, a finer illusion of humanity they had no right to claim.

"Nobody's turning themselves in," O'Neill said with finality. "Unless you actually *want* some geek to make a career
out of poking at your bits to see what makes you twitch."

Jackson frowned. "Vivisection," he said. "Now that sounds
like fun."

"Well, then," Carter announced as she slid off her stool
and stuffed the doodad into her vest, "we'd better get a move
on, because this thing is useless without the other half, and
we have a little over thirteen hours to find it and figure it out
before the debate about our future becomes moot."

"Dr. Jackson? Ideas?" O'Neill leaned in to watch the data
zipping across the screen.

"I can tell you what the other half looks like." He paused
at an image of another doodad made of the same material.
Photographed in bad light, it looked like an oversized cock-
roach and was nestled in folds of rough blue and gold fabric.
It was hard to see in the grainy picture, but, like the one in
Carter's vest, it definitely had markings on it.

"You recognize these?" O'Neill asked, his fingers drifting
across the screen.

Jackson shook his head slowly. "No. But I saw markings
similar to this in the database somewhere." He started rummaging around in the directories. "Somebody was speculat-
ing that they were related to markings found on another artifact."

While he was looking, Teal'c lifted the headset off his ears
and said, "It appears that Mendez has been ordered to evac-
uate Perseus. They've dispatched the ship to transport the
equipment to the beta site."

"Do you think they terminated the ones who followed
orders and reported in?" Carter asked.

O'Neill considered and shook his head. "Mendez hasn't
got a lot of assets left. But the gammas are a wild card. Maybe
they'll play nice, maybe not."

"If the alphas are with the SGC," Daniel began,

"they'll—"

"Die slow instead of fast," O'Neill said. He got up and stabbed a finger at Jackson's screen. "Screw 'em. We knew we were on our own. So let's get to it."

Jackson's mouth gaped for a second, then snapped shut. His hand drifted up to his face like he was about to adjust his glasses and then fell again. "Okay, here. We know the device was split up and hidden on two of these three planets." He indicated three addresses and highlighted one. "The gamma team already searched this one. So that leaves these two." He sat back. "Your guess is as good as mine."

O'Neill tapped the second one. "We start there." Then he pointed to the image Jackson had isolated on the screen. "What's that?"

"It's the other artifact that had the same markings. It's in storage on Earth somewhere."

"Huh," O'Neill said. "What's a quantum mirror?"

SGC
October 31, 2002, two days after
the invasion of Eshet

Interior briefing rooms always gave Jack the hives. At least Hammond's general-purpose conference room, outside his office, gave the illusion of space and comfort. Having a direct view of the gate didn't hurt that feeling, the reason for it all just a stone's throw away. But secrecy forced them into a level 22 conference room barely big enough to contain Daniel's laptop and Jack's pen—and strictly speaking, only the laptop was necessary since the pen was for chewing and doodling.

Carter finished up her synopsis of her recon on Harlan's world. It was one of the most blindingly unsuccessful missions Jack could remember sending her on. "To recap," he said, letting a little of his frustration out, "you came back injured, without Harlan, without any of the rogue team, and no information."

"That's about it," Carter said. She lifted her chin and gave him a one-eye-narrowed look that bordered on downright testy. Of course, it could be that she was just wincing from the pain of the steam burn that covered that side of her face. "If it weren't for the fact that they beat us to the punch, we could have surprised them when they arrived."

"Spilled milk," Jack said, glancing at Daniel.

Daniel's fingers rubbed at the small, round bruise on his temple, left behind by the muzzle of the theta's 9mm. "But at least we saw them for ourselves." He caught Jack watching him and dropped his hand to his keyboard. "We know Dan was telling the truth."

"At least part of it," Jack said. Where the NID was concerned, truth was a tricky, tricky thing.

Even Daniel had to admit that, and he did, with a tilt of his head and a suppressed sigh. He looked tired, his eyes a little too bright, his hands a little too jittery as they tapped the keys of the laptop. Self-medicating with caffeine again. What he needed was a good eight hours sack time. They all did. Except Teal'c, of course, who didn't have the courtesy to show a little wilting around the edges, even when listening to technobabble at one in the morning.

Speaking of technobabble, Carter launched into a diatribe about power sources and schematics, what technology the NID could have captured, and what they might have done with it. Jack leaned back in the chair, trying to find a position that didn't make his tailbone ache since they seemed likely to be at this a while. And they still hadn't gotten around to discussing the critical piece of information he and Teal'c had obtained from Makepeace—the names of his contacts hadn't panned out, and they'd probably been removed or replaced months ago, but that didn't mean they couldn't make the situation work to their advantage.

"So, a mole," Daniel was saying, and Jack had the distinct feeling he'd missed about a paragraph of nonessential information before the word "mole" caught his attention. Eyebrows raised, Daniel was watching him with an expression both expectant and slightly miffed, and Jack sighed, long-suffering. Next to Daniel, Major Davis—the president's favorite Pentagon emissary—was sitting at attention in his regular uniform, hands clasped in his lap, waiting for... something...from Jack.

"Yes," Jack said, sitting up straighter. "A mole. Which only makes sense, if you sort of take for granted that we didn't actually break up the NID operation. We just disrupted the part we could see. Like...killing bugs on the kitchen floor. For every one you see, there's a hundred more."

Davis blinked and looked over at Hammond. He said, "That's not a bad analogy, actually. We believe there might be as many as forty cells, scattered on and off-world, and each has a separate chain of command."

"Our priority has to be uncovering the mole passing on information through this particular chain," Hammond said. "Suggestions, people?"

"There's one tried and true method," Carter said. "Plant information and watch where it travels."

"Yes." Davis swiveled in his chair, facing Jack. "But for that plan to be effective, we would have to know who to target, and I don't think the suspects have been narrowed sufficiently—have they, Colonel?"

"There were eleven people who had knowledge of the upcoming mission schedule and unconfirmed gate addresses..." Daniel trailed off, having apparently realized his title wasn't "Colonel," and shrugged apologetically, depriving Jack of an opportunity for picking on him. Jack waved a hand, and Daniel continued on. "SG-1 and General Hammond account for five of those. The other six are all long-term employees: two civilians, four career military."

"Much like Colonel Makepeace and Colonel Maybourne were before they were recruited." Davis took the folder

Daniel offered but didn't flip through it. Jack admired his attention span. "None of them show any particular resentment toward the military?"

"No," Daniel answered.

"One of them, however, did serve with Colonel Makepeace in a previous assignment," Jack pointed out. Three pairs of eyes turned toward him expectantly. "Aaronsen, the gate tech."

"That's a place to start," Hammond said. "Work on it, Major Davis, and put the plan in motion once you've chosen the information to pass on."

"Yes, sir." Davis nodded to Hammond.

"Anything else?" Hammond asked.

"The president's highest priority is the capture of the remaining active duplicate teams and the remains of the other five, if possible," Davis answered.

"Capture, or destruction?" Jack asked, ignoring Daniel's pointed stare.

Davis cleared his throat. "Whatever is necessary to remove the threat."

"Understood," Hammond said. He stood. "Let's get this done. Dismissed."

The five of them stood as Hammond left the room. Carter and Teal'c stepped out into the corridor for a sidebar; Carter always did have an excellent sense of the strategic withdrawal, Jack thought.

Davis looked from Jack to Daniel and said, "If you'll excuse me." Quick as a rabbit, he was gone, and Daniel couldn't wait two seconds to open fire.

"Dead or alive, Jack? Is that really how you want to do this?"

"You heard the major." Jack shoved all Daniel's report-filled folders back across the table. "Not my call."

"Yes. I think it is." Daniel ignored the mounting pile of dead paper.

"Listen, Daniel, just because you've been talking with your mirror image, don't start feeling sorry for it. Them.

Whatever."

"That has nothing to do with it."

"Of course it does." Jack shoved his hands in his pockets. "You can't help feeling sympathetic. I get that. I really do. I watched mine…kick off on Juna, remember? But they aren't human, and they have to be eliminated."

"You said it yourself, Jack. I've been talking with my duplicate. And he's me. Don't you get that?"

"No. He's a corrupted copy. He's not you." Jack waited a moment, let that sink in. Then he said, "We can never be sure of them. Any of them. All of them could be changed. This one could be lying, too. We'll never know their true agendas. They are a threat, Daniel. A *threat*. We answer threats with force."

"We could help them," Daniel said.

"With what? What are we gonna do, plug 'em into the wall? You were there, Daniel. We can't get a lock on Altair. No gate connection, no access to Harlan's power source or his fancy robot factory — if it even survived."

"Maybe it did. And if it didn't, we could find a way. The NID obviously have a way."

"Right. And what then? We wind up their toy soldiers and let them rattle around the galaxy wearing our faces, with who knows what kind of crap in their heads?"

"It doesn't have to be like that."

So damn stubborn. It made Jack want to vault the table and shake sense into him, but he just shook his head instead and looked at his boots while Daniel barreled on.

"We could reverse the changes to their programming. They deserve a chance, Jack. A chance to live out some kind of life."

"Some kind of life? You mean our lives? Sorry, but it's mine, and I'm not giving it up."

"No, that's not what I mean. Not…I know they can't live our lives. But they can have a life, Jack. They can do meaningful things."

"Like what? Crocheting? Basketweaving?"

Daniel's jaw set. "Research. Daniel is still Daniel. Sam is still Sam."

"And what about Jack?" The idea of it made Jack want to puke—the thought of sitting around, not able to work, not able to live his life. See his friends. Drive an open road and know where he'll be at the end of it. Have a *purpose*. "I guarantee you, Daniel, no robot version of me wants to go on living without some reason for being."

"You don't know that."

"Oh, yes. I do. And if that Jack wants to live that way, he's not *me*. He's something else. Do you *get* that?"

"But he's still sentient. He's alive. We don't have the right to end that. We can help to give them meaning."

"Oh, for—" Jack bit it off, because there was no point. All these arguments with Daniel had the same rhythm, the same annoying patterns. All the talk of real and alive was just the same old crap.

But Daniel never caught the hint. "They have a contact. They call him the Piper."

"As in 'Pied'?"

"Yes. And he has contact with all the other teams. If we can somehow get to him, maybe he can help us find the others. Then we can figure out what to do."

"How can you be this naive after all these years?" The words were out before he could stop them, and Daniel's accusatory glare made him a little sorry, but not as much as he should have been. "If we find them, Daniel, we are shutting them down. End of story. End of argument. Not one more word."

He was saved from having to hear his order contradicted when the alarm klaxon sounded, and Harriman's voice echoed through the corridors: "Off-world activation. Colonel O'Neill, General Hammond to the gate-room." He went, confident Daniel would follow—because it suited him. He had no illusions about that. Jack wasn't the naive one anymore.

"Colonel O'Neill," Harriman said, the comm system making his voice thin. "We have a transmission coming through from SG-13."

"What now?" Jack muttered. He jogged the few steps up to the control room, the rest of his team right behind him.

Harriman turned and said, "They're doing recon on P3N-113. The locals call it Dunamis. When you're ready, sir."

"Lynch?"

"Colonel O'Neill." Static threaded through Lynch's voice, breaking it into insubstantial splinters, and he sounded little like the man O'Neill knew. In the background, he could hear others talking. "Sir, I've…we've seen…that is, we just spotted a team here that we thought was SG-1. They've got SGC patches, but they're not identical." A sharp staccato sound raised the hair on Jack's neck, and he locked eyes with Teal'c just as Lynch shouted, "We're under fire, sir! We could use some backup!"

"Hold them there, Lynch," Jack said, gesturing to the others, who were already moving, headed out to gear up. He glanced at Hammond, sure already of his permission. "Keep them there at all costs. Do not, I repeat, do not let them access the gate. We're on our way."

"Understood."

On his way to the locker room, it occurred to Jack that he might have to kill this version of himself. Not like he hadn't contemplated cutting parts of himself out before. The irony wasn't lost on him.

Dunamis (P3N-113),
same day

Daniel emerged from the event horizon into blinding sun. He threw up one hand to shield his eyes and moved to the side to clear the gate, but he tripped over something and sprawled onto crimson-spattered sandy ground. Lynch was dead beneath Daniel's tangled feet, staring up at him, unseeing. Daniel scrambled to his feet and squeezed his own eyes shut, phantom pain shooting through his skull in sympathy. He willed himself not to vomit.

The air was filled with a low keening sound—women wailing. Daniel looked up, half-startled by it, and realized a woman was crouched a few feet away, waving a bundle of what looked like blue and yellow cloth at him or at Lynch, he couldn't be sure which. Her eyes were wide and filled with disbelief, her dirty face streaked with tears.

"No one will hurt you," he said automatically, but she shook her head and covered her face with the cloth, flinching. The veil effectively hid him from her sight, instead of providing protection from his gaze.

"Fan out and provide cover," Jack ordered the marines, cutting a hand at the two teams backing them up. He eyed the woman and pointed left, where other women were milling about, a clear signal to Daniel to get busy.

Daniel turned to his left. Carlson was curled into the brush. Daniel couldn't tell without turning him over, but it looked like one of his arms had been severed. "Jack," Daniel said, but Jack was already kneeling beside the body, forcing the two women there to back away or be shoved aside. The look on his face raised the hair on the back of Daniel's neck. "I don't think this is the work of these people," Daniel said quickly. "Look at them, Jack. They're grieving. They're...I think they're praying for our dead."

Sam was peering down into a ditch. She jumped down into it and disappeared for a moment, then called, "Farlow is over here." Teal'c eased down the embankment and disappeared as well. Daniel turned back to the woman nearest him, but she was running away, her gray robes flying up in the dust where her feet met the road. A few others turned to follow her, and the cries of those who remained died down until an eerie silence fell in the clearing.

Frowning, Daniel took a longer look at the people gathered on the plain near the gate. It was hard to know for sure because most were cloaked head to toe, but he thought the majority were women, and scattered thoughts about matrilineal societies and other things he hadn't had time to check ran through his head. This had been a mission he wasn't acquainted with, one of the many briefings he'd trusted staff to prepare and had only glanced at peripherally, and now he was up against a near-complete information vacuum. The women had grown still, most of them watching either him or Jack with wary eyes. They were slowly retreating toward a small group at the back of the clearing, a cluster of dark blue and gray robes now formed into a thick circle, obscuring something from view.

Sam reappeared at the edge of the ditch and Teal'c clambered up behind her. To Jack, Sam said, "Farlow's neck was snapped clean."

"Sir!" Sergeant Cooper was gesturing wildly to them from some stones to Jack's right, but Daniel left whatever grisly discovery that might be to Jack and took some cautious steps toward the cluster of women. His steps sent them into a flurry of reorganization, like birds crowding closer on a wire when startled instead of taking flight.

"Please," he said, holding one hand out. "I promise you, we are peaceful. I don't know what happened here, but no one here is going to harm you. You have my word."

They rustled, and Daniel had the distinct impression words were exchanged, or maybe just signs, because he didn't see them speaking to each other. There was one, a woman in white robes with a fringe of ebony beads obscuring her face, who focused her attention on Daniel even as the others shifted around him. From behind her, a soft sound in a familiar voice—his name, drawn out hoarsely: "Daniel."

The owner of that voice was currently twenty feet behind him, talking to Cooper, so he couldn't be—

"Daniel?"

"Oh, my God," Daniel said. He shouldered into the crowd,

noting only distantly how they parted, then closed behind him. "Oh, my God."

Jack O'Neill—or a version of him that Daniel remembered from his first days on SG-1, brown hair, but with a patch on his chest reading ALPHA—was in pieces on the ground. Like something from a horror movie, a remembered atrocity. His torso had nearly been severed, his neck bent awkwardly at an angle no human Jack O'Neill could survive, and a puddle of gray fluid spread wide beneath him. "You're not Daniel," the duplicate said to him, rasping, his brown eyes settling on Daniel's face, assessing him.

"Yes, I am," Daniel said, before he grasped its meaning. "I mean, I'm Daniel—the real—not yours," he finished, breath short in his chest.

"Did he make it?" The alpha Jack's fingers twitched in the grass, provoking a sharp intake of breath from Daniel.

"He's alive," Daniel said. "He told us everything."

"Good." The robot made a horrible gurgling sound. Daniel stared at its mangled legs, burned by what might have been a staff blast. "Got something else you might want," the not-Jack said. His body jerked. "Need to..." He fell silent then, lips moving but no sound emerging.

"Need to what?" Daniel dropped to his knees beside the duplicate, warring with dual impulses, to touch or to shrink away. *That's not Jack*, he told himself, but it looked like Jack, and he was suffering, and Daniel couldn't bear to kneel there and do nothing. The robot's lips were still moving, and its expression was agonized. "Can you...what can I do?"

The robot grabbed his wrist and squeezed hard enough to make Daniel gasp. When it met his eyes, Daniel tried to read something there, anything to understand what it wanted to tell him.

"Daniel, what?...Oh, my God." Sam crouched beside him, one hand on his shoulder. The robot's glance flicked to her, then back to Daniel, but he didn't release Daniel's wrist. "Is it the original...the alphas?"

"I think so, yes. Something must have...Jack was trying to tell me, but he's lost the ability to speak. It might be his power source, or...I don't know." Daniel turned his face to Sam and saw the mirror of his own stricken feelings on her face. "Can you do something?"

"I don't know. I don't think so." She bent to the task, hesitating only a moment before she put her hands deep into the mechanism of his chest. The robot's grip tightened on Daniel's wrist, and he shook it hard. Daniel met its eyes and tried not to think about its pain, tried to get the job done and understand what it wanted him to know.

He looked at his wrist, where his pulse thumped hard against his skin and the robot's fingertips, and suddenly he knew. "Dan," he said, the solution so obvious he could kick himself for taking so long to realize. "Alpha Daniel?" The robot gave a tiny nod and released him. Daniel stood and turned in the same movement, headed for the gate at a dead run, and didn't stop until he'd finished dialing home.

"Daniel," Jack said, the real Jack this time, at Daniel's elbow as though drawn there by something Daniel didn't say. "Whatcha doin'?"

"I have to get Dan — the Daniel duplicate — here now," Daniel said, well aware he was saying it as though he were talking to a five-year-old, and he felt a pang of regret. "*Now*, Jack. Your duplicate is dying, and he can't talk."

"Uh huh," Jack said, nodding like he was told every day his doppelganger was kicking off mere yards away. "SG-one-niner calling Stargate Command."

"This is Hammond. Report, Colonel."

"Sir, all of SG-13 are dead, but the area is secure. I'm not really sure what the hell is going on, but Daniel thinks it's urgent that you send the Daniel robot through to the planet." *Now*, Daniel mouthed at him, and Jack's lips thinned, but he said, "Right away, sir."

"Stand by," Hammond said, and a moment later, the gate shut down.

"There had better be—" Jack began.

"Yes, Jack, there is."

The gate roared to life, wormhole pushing out into the air, and a few seconds later Dan stepped out, flanked by two marines. He stopped, and then ran toward the DHD, the escort jogging to keep up. "Where," he said, and Daniel pointed the way, running behind him as Dan sprinted toward the Jack duplicate.

"Okay, that's not weird or anything," Jack said, as he kept pace.

This time the women parted for them as if asked to step aside, and Dan dropped to the ground beside his teammate. Just as he had with Daniel, alpha Jack grasped Dan's wrist and held on, but Dan put his hand over alpha Jack's. Neither of them spoke, but Daniel knew now that they were talking.

"What is this—?" Jack stopped, and his face wrinkled up in recognition. "They're talking on some kind of communication system, aren't they."

"Yes. At least, I think so," Daniel said, watching Dan's face intently. Sam moved to stand silently at Daniel's shoulder, Teal'c at Jack's, and all four of them stood by while the duplicates communicated in silence. The story flashed through Dan's eyes—sorrow, anger, worry, in all too human flickers of anguish.

Dan reached into the alpha Jack's jacket and fished around, then produced a piece of torn blue and yellow cloth. Daniel recognized it as the same type of cloth the woman had held across her face when he arrived. This cloth was wrapped around something, and Dan shoved it at Daniel, who took the heavy, small object carefully. "It's what the theta team was after," Dan said. "My team was tracking them. They came here to take that, and my team stopped them. SG-13 blew into the middle of this mess and the thetas...they..." Dan stopped and lowered his head. "They tore your people apart on their way out of here. Apparently they wanted to be gone before you arrived. I guess the fact that Lynch called for backup scared them off."

"But why?" Daniel knelt down next to the duplicates. "What is this all about?"

"I don't know their ultimate goal, but whatever it is, they thought that was important to it."

Daniel unwrapped the piece of cloth and stared down at the heavy black object and its inscribed words. "This looks familiar," he said, handing it up to Sam.

"Very," she said, passing it across to Teal'c.

"Share with the class," Jack said, reaching out a hand.

"It's similar to the quantum mirror device," Dan said, causing a visible flinch from Jack.

"If you don't mind, I'd like to hear it from the one who's not a carbon copy," Jack said.

Daniel glared up at him. "Quantum mirror," he reiterated, forcing an irritated squint from Jack.

"Whatever they are looking for, if it's tied to that mirror, it's technology we don't have a true grasp of," Sam said, passing the item to Jack. "Which…"

"…could be a problem," Daniel finished for her.

"Clearly." Jack handed the thing back to Daniel.

"Is there anything else you can tell us?" Daniel asked his duplicate. Dan jerked his head up, as if he'd forgotten Daniel was there, and then returned his attention to the Jack duplicate, completely distracted. Dan put his hand on the duplicate's chest, left it there for long moments until the duplicate had stopped moving, eyes open, eerily still, the spark of whatever life it had gone completely.

Jack turned and walked away. Sam shifted, cleared her throat. Daniel stood up and looked at her, at the tears in her eyes, then back at Dan, at his hand still resting on the duplicate's chest. He looked away and followed Jack back into the clearing.

"I could have gone a long time without seeing that again," Jack said, when Daniel stepped alongside him.

"It's…" Daniel reached for a word, thinking of the utter

sorrow on Dan's face.

"Yeah." Jack cleared his throat and nodded at the black stone. "You know what that is?"

"I have no idea." Daniel wrapped the cloth around it. "But the people here must know."

"They will want the return of their property," Teal'c said, as he joined the circle.

"Too bad," Jack said. "This thing is ours until further notice."

"Jack, I think —"

"Don't think, Daniel, please. It will only get us into trouble."

"Sir." Sam called their attention. She was still standing over Dan, but the group of women had dispersed, and only one remained beside the "body."

Jack tapped Daniel on the chest. "Stow that thing," he said, and Daniel stuffed it into his vest for lack of a better option.

The woman moved toward them, white robes shifting around her feet as she walked. Because he couldn't see her eyes, Daniel couldn't get a read on her intentions, but she seemed calm. In charge. She held her hand out, palm up. "You have the *kei*," she said. "It is not yours to take. Please give it to me."

There wasn't any question in Daniel's mind what she was referring to, but Jack's hand landed on his chest just then, a warning to keep back. "Can't do that," Jack said. "Sorry. Normally we would, but the, uh, the *kei* is dangerous."

"It has been ours always, and it is not dangerous to us." The woman lowered her hand slowly to her side and tilted her head, her veil of beads shifting and sparkling in the light. "It is not yours to take."

"Technically true," Jack said, the depth of his discomfort apparent in his posture.

"We don't intend to keep it forever," Daniel said. "This is an unusual situation. The people who came to your world, who killed these people — you must recognize that even though they looked like us, they weren't us. Not exactly."

Bead-woman was still as a statue, and Daniel suppressed a shiver. It was like she was staring straight through her veil and his skin directly into his soul. Which was ridiculous, but he had the urge to reach out and yank those beads aside to see what he was dealing with. "You live," she said softly. "They were merely alive."

Daniel nodded and added a wince. "A good way to put it. Sort of."

"I do not understand why you must keep from us this thing we need."

"Because we need it also, or many more people might die." Daniel stopped, his heart in his throat because it had only just occurred to him that he had no idea if the rogue team had harmed any of her people. It wasn't like him to forget to ask, but the feel of Lynch's dead weight, the sight of his blood, and the drama of seeing the likeness of his friend torn in half—he wasn't focused. "Did those who came here before us hurt your people?"

"They hurt us, but they saved us. And now they steal from us."

Daniel saw himself through her eyes in an instant—copy upon copy upon copy, each exhibiting behavior so different from the previous ones. And yet not so different at all. A flare of shame curled in his belly.

"We aren't…we don't…" Sam stopped trying to explain almost as soon as she began, and Daniel wished she hadn't tried. The moral conundrum twisted in on itself endlessly, right and wrong supplanted by "must." Must find the answers. Must save their people. Must not care about the cost.

"I'm Daniel," he said softly. "What's your name?"

"I am called Asha." She turned away from him. "I do not speak for my people. There is one who must know you before you leave this world."

"We're not going to give you back your *kei*," Jack said. Daniel had a brief impulse to slap his hand over Jack's mouth to stop whatever might come out next so they would actually be allowed to leave, but Jack was right. There was no point in beating around the bush. "And we don't have time for this."

"If they are possessed of knowledge about the device, we would be wise to meet with them," Teal'c said. "Even if only briefly."

"Teal'c's right, Jack." Daniel nodded to Asha. "We have no idea what this thing does."

To his right, Sam slipped away from the group. She dropped down beside Dan and the Jack robot and spoke to Dan quietly. Dan staggered to his feet, braced by Sam's hand on his elbow, and turned toward Daniel, who flinched at the sight of him, gray fluid wetting his face, his eyes.

Artificial tears, shades of gray.

"That thing is part of a power device," Dan said, in a voice cracking hoarse with very real sadness. "Jack didn't know what it is, or what it does. Only that they wanted it, and would have done anything to get it."

"Did he say anything else we can use?" Jack stood beside him, hard as nails on the outside, but Daniel had felt him flinch too.

"There's nothing human left in them." Dan's face crumpled, the picture of angry grief, and tears pricked the corners of Daniel's eyes in response. "What they did to your people... to my team...they are only machines. Dangerous machines." He looked up and stared at Jack. "You have to destroy them. No matter what it takes."

"I know," Jack said in an entirely different tone, one Daniel had heard him use mostly with children and dogs.

Dan nodded, just one jerk of his head. Then he pulled away from Sam and headed straight for the DHD, in response to an order Jack hadn't given.

"Carter, send the IDC and get him out of here. Tell Hammond to find out everything the robot told him. And keep the marines on the search. There's still two alphas unaccounted for." Jack pointed at the robot torso in the grass. "Have the marines take that back with them. See if there's something they can get out of it at Area 51."

"No," Dan said, turning toward them with his hand already on the first glyph. He stalked back over to them, wiping at his face. "He gave his life for Earth. He deserves better. Don't you let them tear him apart, you son of a bitch."

Jack's eyes narrowed. "We can't leave him here."

"I didn't suggest you should." Dan stared him down. "Let me take him back, but just…I know they have to examine him, but…please, just bury him when it's over. It's what you'd want done for you."

All of them had wills, letters, orders hidden away. All of them hoped their friends would never need those documents, but there was comfort in knowing their last wishes would be followed. Daniel blinked and looked at Sam, at the lines and shadows on her face, and then back at Jack, who was avoiding his gaze. Two Daniels was at least one too many.

"All right," Jack said finally. "Carter, handle it."

"Yes, sir."

Dan's jaw was set, but he said, "Thank you," like it cost him. This time when he turned his back, he went to the Jack robot, bent down, and picked it up in his arms.

Daniel couldn't watch.

He turned to Asha and said, "We'll come with you." But she was already moving away, as if assured of his compliance. He glanced back at Jack. At Jack's tiny nod of permission, he followed, Jack and Teal'c behind him and Sam at the rear, a line of dark green on the harsh plain.

CHAPTER NINE

NID Primary Project Site, Perseus (P66-421)
September, 2002; one month before the invasion of Eshet

"Is this all of it?" Carlos sorted through the color-coded files, losing bits of stray paper as he shuffled the folders. He'd asked for a comprehensive briefing. It was getting more difficult to wrap his head around the scope of what they were creating, and he was going to have to fully account for the technology acquired (or lack thereof) soon. It was impossible to predict when he might be visited by someone higher up in the chain of command. It was also impossible to predict who that person might be. Carlos loved the job but not the uncertainty. Better to be prepared. He held out the thin sheaf of papers marked ALPHA to Peterson and said, "After five months of accumulating data, shouldn't there be more on the first team?"

"These are briefs and summaries," Peterson told him. He looked like a guy who'd been staying up a little too late and not eating enough to compensate. There was a pinched look around Peterson's eyes, and his complexion was grayish. "I didn't think you'd want entire project files on every team."

"I'm most interested in your analysis of the theta team," Carlos said. "Whether or not the programming changes are effective."

"I have some mission video for you," Peterson said. He flipped through a stack of DVDs, selected four, and handed them to the lab technician standing beside him. "Load those, please." Peterson sat back in the chair and adjusted his glasses. Behind the lens glare, his blue eyes looked gray. "The alpha team was engineered to be as close as possible to the originals, with some slight memory alterations—no recall of specific gate addresses, no recall of power specifications, short-term perfect recall only."

Carlos pushed one of the folders around in a circle on the table with his index finger. "Has this prevented the teams from engaging in escape-oriented behaviors?"

"Thus far." Peterson produced a flowchart and placed it in front of Carlos with a gesture suspiciously like a proud flourish. "As you can see, each successive team has had their abilities changed as well according to schedule. The results are mixed. The enhanced communication abilities permit teams to speak to one another directly, instead of just within one group, but this has been problematic for the handler. They often leave the handler out of the loop until the last minute."

"A solvable problem, I assume," Carlos said.

"Eventually." Peterson set the team roster on the table and turned it so Carlos could see. "Once all the teams are back in from the field, we'll begin a period of further adjustment."

"The kill switch?"

Peterson angled his head in a reluctant shrug. "We've integrated it in the zetas and the thetas." He slid a folder in Carlos's direction. "The field test on the zetas was less than optimal."

Carlos scanned the file. "You fried them."

"There was no way to reacquire core memory or conscious function once the switch was activated. The units are still intact, and we hope to be able to reload the personalities, but it's going to take some time. It'll be a clean slate with them. We lost a lot of data." Peterson's glasses were slipping down his nose, and he shoved them back up with a knuckle before dabbing at his forehead with a tissue. "As a result, though, we've modified the switch in the thetas. We hope these modifications will allow us to shut them down without sacrificing the memory core."

Hope, speculation, stabbing around in the dark. In Carlos's neck and at the base of his skull, the headache he never seemed to get rid of squeezed him harder. He wondered if it was possible for his own tense muscles to snap his bones.

"Theta team just arrived back from its second mission," Carlos said. He'd chosen the mission himself, a planet with non-hostiles so the chance of active resistance would be lessened. "How have the personality changes manifested?"

"Since the inception of those changes with delta team, each successive team's reaction to the changes has been an order of magnitude greater. Theta team is closest to the desired outcome." Peterson clicked on the wall screen monitor and keyed up the video. He selected one of the images on the screen. "This is delta team's first mission."

Carlos watched as the scene played out before him. He remembered this mission profile: two pieces of technology to acquire, both Asgard devices enabling short-distance teleportation. Onscreen, the delta O'Neill was beating the town elder down into the ground. The delta Carter and Jackson stood by and did not intervene, but both looked as if they were the robot equivalent of nauseated.

"This is footage from Teal'c's internal recorders. As you can see, only the O'Neill duplicate was capable of immediate aggression. The remaining duplicates did not participate."

"But they didn't attempt to stop it," Carlos said.

"No."

Carlos nodded. This was a key benchmark in the operational development. "You've introduced the Goa'uld code into the program now?"

"Most of it. We've extracted what we can from the symbiote code captured during the first duplication attempt of the real Teal'c. Portions of it were given to the theta team during the duplication process."

"Has it been fully integrated?"

"See for yourself." The screen briefly darkened, then lit again, to reveal theta team advancing on a row of villagers kneeling in the snow. The villagers' faces were almost hidden inside fur-lined hoods, but their postures clearly indicated their fear. In the background, long, low boats nosed up onto a rocky shore. Skin tents leaned into the wind, and in the open flap of the one just at the edge of the picture's frame, there was a small, round face, all wide, dark eyes and an open mouth. Crying. The sky above the water was a piercing blue Carlos knew would make his eyes tear up if he were there. These folks didn't have much to offer, beyond themselves and a passive resistance that made a useful test of the thetas' limits. Carlos watched as theta O'Neill and Teal'c argued briefly, then turned their anger on the villagers.

After a few moments of the vivid carnage, Carlos nodded to Peterson, who switched it off. He had a strong stomach, but such calculated death wasn't what he'd signed on to do. He was only a facilitator. "They're certainly more aggressive, but will they continue to take orders?"

Peterson hesitated, and then set down the remote. "Their handler has documented a marked increase in oppositional behavior. They're like teenagers. They feel free to do as they please without long-term consequences."

"What did you expect?" Carlos sat forward, stared Peterson in the eye. "When you engineer out morality and conscience, why wouldn't they do what they want to do, and the hell with orders?"

"We tried to achieve a balance," Peterson said. "Complete obedience and no ethical compunctions."

"Are they all similarly impacted?"

"The Daniel Jackson of this team has shown marked reluctance to comply with certain kinds of orders. He is usually in direct conflict with the O'Neill duplicate."

"Conscience?"

"Expediency. He seems to feel violence is not the fastest answer to the problem. He prefers..." Peterson hesitated, looked away from Carlos. "He seems to prefer psychological torture."

"So you've bred me a unit of psychopaths and one sociopath for good measure," Carlos said. He tilted his head back in the chair and laughed. "Perfect."

"They get the job done," Peterson said, his tone turned frosty.

Carlos sighed. As usual, he joked and the lab rats thought he missed the point. "Kidding," he said, and waited for Peterson's face to relax as much as it was capable of. The guy was a walking heart attack waiting to happen. "All right. Recall the remaining teams one at a time and begin adjusting their programming."

"I recommend you leave the alpha team as is, for baseline comparison," Peterson said. "In case we have to revert to the original state, for safety reasons."

"Agreed."

Peterson gathered up his materials and left Carlos sitting there among the piles of atrocities done in the name of protecting Earth. Strange that he no longer saw any of it as optional.

NID Primary Project Site, Perseus (P66-421) September, 2002; one month prior to invasion of Eshet

Daniel still wasn't able to think of himself as "alpha Daniel," no matter how many times the lab rats called him by that name or how many different nicknames Jack ascribed to him (Jack had already abandoned "action Jackson" and "alpha-falfa," and his current favorite was "robogeek"). Daniel thought of himself as Daniel Jackson, which complicated things immeasurably by a certain emotional standard, even though there wasn't much Daniel couldn't measure in the blink of an eye these days.

No doubt he wasn't supposed to think of himself as human since he wasn't, but he couldn't help that either. The technicians they dealt with daily were polite, but Daniel always had the feeling that he was like a very expensive vegetable peeler to them; useful and time-saving but ultimately replaceable with a hundred identical models. To them, the plethora of Daniels and Jacks and Sams and Teal'cs were tools to be manipulated to their best advantage. It fascinated and repelled him in equal measure. Every day he looked at his hands, with their realistic skin and fingernails, and thought about what makes a human *human* — the life's blood, or their memories, or their spirit. The sum total of everything Daniel recognized as Daniel Jackson was in him, but it was as if time had stopped somewhere and Daniel had been unfrozen out of it, a relic from his own past. He knew the year was 2002, and he knew the real Daniel's life had carried on in ways he couldn't imagine, in whatever time he'd had before he'd died. He wondered about all the things Daniel might have found, in the time before the SGC was shut down. He worried about Skaara and Sha're in his weaker moments.

Holding on to the slender thread of Sha're's memory, to the idea that the human Daniel might have found her, made the prospect of never seeing her again bearable.

He wasn't supposed to feel things as deeply, to want and to grieve, to feel helpless, but all those things were as strong in him as they always had been. The thought crossed his mind — *you've only been alive five months* — and he reminded himself again, as he had a hundred thousand times before: his feelings were only a copy of what existed in the human Daniel.

Sometimes he wondered about the thought processes, the odd way information flowed through his brain. It felt the same, or he guessed it was the same, though most things came to him now with a peculiar crystalline clarity, a sharpness of knowing that left nothing to chance or guesswork, no fuzziness of recall. It took much of the fun out of research; the moment he learned a fraction of the information, much of the rest extrapolated within his logic circuits and took root.

Those were the kind of thoughts that were painful for Jack, so Daniel never discussed them with him. If it was hard for Daniel, it was impossible for Jack, who wanted nothing more than to do these things that were asked of them and earn a blissful release from service.

Daniel had no idea what would happen to his consciousness when that day came. He tried to imagine himself as a bundle of circuits, the image that would have made Jack wince, and dispassionate logic failed him. Not for the first time.

Daniel. Sam, calling him on the internal comms. *Delta team is finally returning.*

The deltas had been on their mission for 4,805.21 seconds. Daniel had no idea why he distilled it down that way. Perhaps because he could.

He made his way toward the gate-room to welcome them back, as the alpha team always did, but stopped midway when chaos erupted, the deltas all talking over each other at once. He automatically separated them out into discrete threads, cataloging the hundreds of emotional cues in their communications. Fear, despair, anguish, grief, betrayal—those were strongest. *They lied to us, they lied,* delta Jack was saying, *those sons of bitches.* Delta Sam's stream of information—planet designation, indigenous peoples, lack of technology—was sprinkled with disbelief: *We saw them with our own eyes,* she said, *all of them.* Jack added to the puzzle, confusion, rage: *They were talking to the SGC. It had to be.*

It was the delta-team Daniel who sorted it out, finally, his voice easing over the others, soothing them down to a dull roar: *We've been played for fools. SG-1 is still pursuing off-world missions, just as they always have. Everything we were told is a lie.*

Daniel stopped dead in the middle of the hallway, caught up by his team's Jack, and the instructions Jack sent out with the force of a shouted order: *Don't give anything away.*

Any of you. Don't report this. They can't know we know.

All the remaining teams were on-site. All of them heard it, Daniel knew. Chatter ceased.

Daniel, Carter, Teal'c. Down here to the bunk room. Daniel turned and followed the order immediately. The human Daniel might not have an appreciation for being ordered around by his Jack, but Daniel had figured out quickly that in this environment, he was out of his depth. This was no equal-opportunity team. He was a warrior here.

They didn't need a bunk room, because none of them slept, but it was a resting spot for downtime and repairs. They didn't even need to see each other to communicate, but old habits died hard, and Daniel supposed it soothed all of them to see each other, to work things out face-to-face. They really were all they had. It was true of their team and to some extent of the gamma, and delta teams, but the teams after that were...different. Less interested in team-work. Daniel was grateful his team had been the first duplicated. It would have been too hard to bear if they had lost even this simple camaraderie.

Teal'c was waiting beside Jack in the bunk room. Sam arrived a few seconds after Daniel. It was remarkable how much could be said with only a look, and the one on Jack's face was eloquent.

What do we do now? Sam asked him, still on private comms, sitting down at the small table where lab gadgets and gear were scattered.

We bide our time, Jack said.

Until we can warn them, Daniel said, following the thread.

Yes. Jack met his eyes, and then Teal'c's, and Sam's.

We don't even know... Daniel began, thinking of the things that had been kept from them, everything they needed to find their way home...to Earth. There was no home. Only a world they had to protect as if it were still their own.

But he stopped, because they would find a way. An

opportunity would come. It always did. And if it didn't, they would make one of their own.

A little over three weeks later, the theta team dropped off the grid.

It was the kind of thing Piper told them in somber tones, as if the alpha team couldn't figure it out on their own, but in fact all the teams were way ahead of the handler. Jack thought they were NID, though they'd never come out and said so. It added up; all the pieces were starting to fit. SG-1 off-world meant there was an SGC functioning, and whatever the duplicates were doing now, it wasn't directly serving the interests of Earth. One of the gammas — their Jack — had suggested that they were just doing what had to be done, and maybe now that they didn't have a code of conduct to adhere to, they should relax and revel in the freedom to procure technology. But alpha Jack had said what Daniel knew he would, an encapsulated speech about honor and duty being the only code they had.

Daniel was pretty sure none of the other teams believed it, and the delta team was totally silent on the issue.

They were summoned to a briefing a few hours after the thetas went off the radar. Daniel sat with his team around an ugly metal briefing table, watching Carlos Mendez in his navy suit and his impeccable tie as he watched them back, and he could understand why the deltas were so quiet.

"Your objective for this mission is simple and non-negotiable," he said. On the screen, a picture of the theta uniform patch appeared. Mendez said nothing else, but the watchful look in his eyes changed, became something Daniel found harder to quantify. Not regret. Resignation, maybe.

"You feel like telling us why? Or are we just your little killing machines?" Jack sat back in the chair, skirting dangerously close to an invisible line that would alert Mendez they were on to him. Sam warned Jack on the comms, in a pointed way the human Sam would probably have envied.

Daniel thought the real Sam probably had bitten her tongue raw over the years trying not to tell Jack what she really thinking.

Mendez pointed his pen at the screen. "This team has gone rogue. We don't know why—"

That's a lie, Sam said, and told the team that via her pattern recognition software she'd identified fourteen separate facial muscle contractions indicating deception.

"—and it doesn't matter. You should all be more aware than any of the personnel on this base that there's no one more dangerous than one of you gone rogue."

"Aren't you worried we're next?" Jack lounged back in the chair, and his internal comms squawked, *Now we're personnel. Nice.*

Mendez smiled the tiniest smile it was possible for a person to smile and waited a beat before answering. "There are other teams."

Daniel couldn't help his sarcasm. *Nice loaded threat. And with layers of meaning, too. Didn't think he had it in him.* Sam hid her smile.

"So there are." Jack nodded, the very picture of defeated obedience. If Mendez had had a clue about Jack O'Neill, he would have been more worried about the version in front of him than the one out there floating rogue. Daniel was grateful for small favors. "When do we leave?"

"As soon as we have intelligence as to their whereabouts. We expect that soon. Delta and gamma teams are checking last known and future departure coordinates." Mendez glanced at each of them. "Just to be clear: your mission is to terminate them. Leave no functioning trace."

None of them asked the obvious questions. None of them voiced the bizarre pain of being told to commit murder on versions of themselves, their teammates. Daniel thought maybe they were so far down the rabbit hole it no longer mattered. Mendez certainly seemed to be waiting for the challenge, and when it didn't come, he stood up from the table. "Get your comms checked," he told them. "We can't seem to hear anything on comms from your team."

"Will do," Jack told him, and Daniel nodded to Sam. Suppressing the comms from outside monitoring was the best idea she'd ever had.

What do you think the thetas are after? Jack said via comms, as they watched Mendez leave the room.

Power source, Sam answered. Daniel turned to her, and she caught his look and added, *It makes sense. It's the only thing we can't do without, the only thing keeping us in check. We've been working on an independent source. You all know that. She must have figured out a way to rig something up. Something temporary, to keep them going until…*

Until they get whatever they're after, Jack said.

Daniel frowned. *Which means she kept it from the rest of the teams for a reason.*

Such deception can only mean they have treachery in mind, Teal'c said.

They fell silent, processing a billion pieces of the puzzle, listening to intermittent chatter from the rest of the teams, with whom Sam hadn't shared her method of suppressing comms. It seemed there was a lot of information being kept close to the vest, which was…unnerving.

We're going to need a plan, and a good one, Jack said. *One of us will have to—*

I'll do it, Daniel said.

You could have let me finish.

Like I didn't know what you were going to say? Daniel fixed Jack with a look. Jack shrugged.

When the opportunity comes up, you be ready, Jack told him. *All of us need to be ready, in case…*

In case Daniel Jackson cannot complete the task, Teal'c said.

Our priority is contacting Earth then? Sam asked. *Are we going to carry out the mission we were given? Kill the thetas? Do you really believe they've gone rogue?*

Jack looked at her steadily. *Guess we'll cross that bridge when we come to it.*

CHAPTER TEN

Dunamis (P3N-113)
October 31, 2002; two days after the theta invasion of
Eshet

For someone who spoke for her people, Yagwen didn't do much talking. Or any, in fact. She sat cross-legged at a low table in her tent and watched them file in after Asha. Like her acolyte, she wore a veil of beads over her eyes. Her hands moved restlessly over the table, collecting and throwing bones, sorting them into groups according to some system Daniel couldn't fathom. Outside the tent, the robed women were gathered around what seemed to be an altar, their heads bowed as they rocked slowly, their hands folded under their chins. As Yagwen sorted her runes, their voices rose and fell in wordless lamentation.

Asha took up a position at Yagwen's shoulder. "Yagwen. These are the off-worlders." She knew their names — Daniel had introduced them all on the way — but she seemed disinclined to introduce them as individuals.

Daniel opened his mouth to speak, but Yagwen held up her hand, then gestured for him to sit. While he settled down, she brushed most of the bones into a pile that Asha scooped into an embroidered bag. The bag disappeared inside her robe. Only three bones, one an impossibly fine needle point, still lay on the table when Yagwen smoothed the cloth around them with her broad, gnarled hand. Daniel had to squint in the dim light that filtered through the heavy canvas of the tent to see the runes against the cloth's intricate pattern of leaves and birds. Behind him, Jack shifted uncomfortably from one foot to the other, his sigh mostly suppressed but still warm against the back of Daniel's neck. The other two bones, one the barbed circle of a vertebra, the other an odd, tiny hook, disappeared under Yagwen's palm as she shook her head, her mouth turning stubborn and thin. Unable to see her eyes, Daniel could still imagine the glint of anger there.

Standing at her side, Asha was unreadable behind her own veil of beads as she said flatly, "You will not return the *kei*."

Daniel bowed his head and stared at the bones on the cloth, the skeleton of some alien animal honed and worn into meaning.

"No," Jack said. "Sorry."

Yagwen swept the bones up and threw them again.

With a pointed glare over his shoulder at Jack, Daniel added, "Not yet. We —" He looked at the bones, tilting his head as though that might make a difference. "You know that others will come to take it from you. We only wish to protect it and to learn from it."

Asha replied in that same flat tone. "Its protection was entrusted to us by He-They."

"Yeah, and a great job you're doing there, by the way."

Daniel didn't bother glaring at Jack again. Instead he sighed. "We understand that. But there's something bigger going on here — well, out there, actually." He waved a hand toward the Stargate. "The *kei* is important to that."

"You are not safe while it is in your possession," Teal'c added from his place by the door.

There was a faint chiming of beads as Asha turned to him and raised a hand to silence him.

Sam stepped into the light and picked up the argument. "Yagwen, you saw what these —"

She looked at Daniel for help, and he interjected "People," earning a glare of his own from Jack.

Sam chose to avoid the issue, saying, "You saw what they can do. Teal'c's right. As long as you have the *kei* in your possession, you're in danger. We can help. All we want is information about the device."

Another throwing of the bones. Asha leaned low over Yagwen's shoulder and peered at them. As she did, her beads swung open a little and Daniel caught a glimpse of her perfectly white, blind eyes. "We see little difference," she said, turning her head as if she was looking at each member of SG-1 in turn. "You. Them." She cut her hand through the air, dismissive.

"For one thing," Jack answered, "the bad guy has brown hair and I have, well, not brown hair. Oh, and also there's the fact that he's a *robot*."

"I don't think that's what she meant, Jack."

"I know what she meant, Daniel. The point is we don't have *time* for this."

As Jack was heading for the door, Daniel pulled the device out of his vest and peered at it. It was oval-shaped, palm-sized, cool to the touch even after being carried next to his body, and a deep black that seemed to suck the color out of the tent. Sweeping his thumb over its surface, he could feel the raised markings there. In the light from the door, where Jack was holding up the flap to usher Sam and Teal'c out of the tent, the markings resolved into something familiar. "This language is similar to that on the control device for the quantum mirror," he said.

The tent flap fell again, and Sam's shadow wavered across the table and its scattering of bones. She took the device from his hands and turned to Jack. "Sir."

"Fine," Jack said, but raised his wrist and tapped his watch. "Ticktock."

To Yagwen, Daniel said, "Who was He-They?"

Yagwen gathered the bones and closed them in her hand.

"Please." He looked to Asha for some help and got nothing. "Lives could be in danger. Please tell us what you know."

The bones fell again.

"He-They was a wanderer who came to us many generations ago. He-They entrusted the *kei* to us and warned us never to let it leave this place. He-They said that it was a thing of terrible power, that it could fold the universe. Or tear it asunder." Asha held her hands palms up and then folded them together with the precision of a ritual gesture. It was the same gesture the women outside made as they mourned the dead. "Then He-They broke into pieces. All who looked on the fragments were struck blind. It is we, the descendents of the blinded, who tend the place of He-They. We are those who see."

And she did seem to see, Daniel thought, as she stared at him through the screen of beads and the opacity of her eyes.

"May we see the place of He-They?"

Yagwen's hands closed into fists on the cloth, but she nodded.

"I will take you there," Asha said. "And then you will go. You will take the *kei* because you have the might. We who have no might will hope that it will someday be returned."

Jack grunted as he ducked through the tent door and then straightened, squinting into the late afternoon sun. He didn't turn around as Daniel stepped out behind him. "Don't even say it," he said as he examined the lenses of his sunglasses and then, deciding against them, let them fall against his chest again. He watched as the small crowd that had gathered outside the tent shuffled backward away from them, leaving them in a wide, empty circle. All of the faces wore variations on the same expression, a mixture of anger and fear. "It wasn't *us*," Jack said testily.

"No," Daniel said, as he watched the people shrink from them. "But it's us now."

Teal'c came to stand beside him. "Our intentions seem to make no difference."

Daniel shook his head. "Not to them."

With a grunt that Daniel couldn't quite interpret, Jack walked up to the crowd and between the people as they scrambled to get out of the way.

When Asha followed him, all the assembled people bowed their heads and covered their eyes with their hands until she had passed. She moved easily in her bare feet across the rutted mud of the camp, stepping surely around obstacles and guiding the team away from the tents and the cooking fires toward the woods. She slipped ahead of them into the shadows and became a ghost in her white robes, a mist drifting between the trees.

"Asha."

The acolyte stopped and turned to Sam.

Sam's hand came up to gesture at Asha's eyes. "The blindness. You got it from looking at He-They? Is there any danger to us?"

For a moment it seemed like Asha was considering a lie, and Daniel figured she was entitled to spin a yarn to scare them away, but she shook her head with a sigh. "You will be safe there. No one has been affected since the breaking day many generations ago. We are born with the eyes of He-They."

They waited. After a moment, it seemed Jack decided to believe her. "Lead on, McDuff."

Asha tilted her head.

"I mean, after you."

Without a word she turned and continued on.

They hadn't gone very far along the narrow floor of a ravine when the ground twisted under Daniel's boots. He dropped to a crouch for balance. Fingers curled into the loam and needles of the forest floor, he watched as the shadows and the bands of sunlight cast across the ground in front of him slanted more and more, like the sun was moving across the sky, time sliding sideways, too fast. "Um," he said.

"That's weird," he heard Sam say from somewhere beside him, just as Jack's hand closed around the shoulder of his vest and pulled him to his feet.

Daniel swayed for a second, keeping a tight grip on Jack's arm until the world stopped seesawing under him. When he opened his eyes, there were two Jacks looking back at him, a double exposure, two left arms united at the hand still curled into the fabric of Daniel's vest. He blinked and then there was only one.

"Weird? Always with the technobabble, Carter," Jack said as he gave Daniel a pat and let him go. His words were out of synch, and his voice continued after his lips had stopped moving. He blinked hard. "That's so not right," he added and split into two again. "There's two of you." He swatted a hand beside Daniel's face, trying to grasp a ghost.

"He-They," Daniel said.

Nodding, Asha pointed at a slash of shadow in the side of the ravine. Her rising arm was ghosted by a fugue of arms, each mirage moving just a fraction slower than the one before and, as she went still, collapsing together like the folding wing of a bird. "Yes," she said, and led the way.

Jack—both of him—followed, leaving Daniel to steady himself with a hand on the smooth bark of the tree next to him. With a snap that he felt in his eyes instead of hearing it in his ears, the world aligned again and there was only one of everyone. He waggled his fingers in front of his eyes and counted only the regular five. He looked through them to find Sam watching him. "How many fingers?" he asked and turned his palm toward her.

"Four and a thumb," she answered. "This might just be perceptual, maybe some kind of energy that's affecting the brain."

Jack stopped and looked back. "Dangerous?"

Sam shrugged. "Hard to say. But Asha doesn't seem too badly affected and she's been here all her life."

Jack pursed his lips, assessing. "Brain rays," he said finally as he continued trudging up the path. "Terrific. Remind me to requisition some tinfoil hats."

"Or," Sam continued as she turned away from Daniel and headed off after Jack and Teal'c, "the universe really is coming unglued somehow." She went on to explain something about the space-time continuum, but Daniel's mind replaced the words with something that sounded a lot like "doom doom

doom" which throbbed in time with the low-grade headache that was gripping the back of his skull. As he fell into step with his team, he wondered if, had he known at the outset that he'd get to a place where brain-damage was the sunnier alternative to choose from, he might have been so quick to sign up for the program.

Probably.

He made a mental note to find a therapist with clearance.

By this time the little procession had climbed over a low ridge, and the gash in the side of the ravine had revealed itself to be the entrance to a cave. Around it, the gray-skinned trees that lined the ravine like the pickets of a fence were contorted, bent away from the gaping mouth as though they had been blown back by a giant exhalation of breath and had frozen there, their whiplike branches and tiny silver leaves splayed on the ground like tangled hair. Without their cover, the clearing was open to the full glare of the late sun that crazed the red earth with shadows and livid slashes of light. When Daniel closed his eyes for a moment, the scene burned behind his eyelids, inverted. Daniel figured it was just his headache that made the sun seem to throb, but, given the whole ungluing universe scenario, he wasn't willing to bet on it.

A few paces ahead of him, Jack stopped, first cupping a hand over his ear, and then shaking his head a few times before looking up into the sky. Just behind him, Teal'c also paused and looked around, scowling. Daniel stepped forward and felt his ears pop. The sudden silence made him stop too. He stepped backward and his head was filled with the low rushing sound of the breeze in the leaves of the picket trees, the chittering of some reptile or insect in the hollowed-out trunk at the side of the path, and, distantly, the continuing keening wail of ritual lament in the encampment beyond the woods. He stepped forward and there was nothing. He cleared his throat to make sure he hadn't gone deaf.

"Some kind of perimeter," Sam said, waving her hand in

the air behind Daniel. "Not a force field. Or not one we've seen before." She stepped around Jack and Teal'c to address Asha. "Is it always like this?"

Asha nodded, setting her beads swinging. "For Yagwen, many years ago, there were voices, but it has been a silent place as long as I have known it. Some claim to have heard singing, but I myself have not. The silence spreads every season."

There was no singing now, but as they drew closer to the dark gap of the entrance, they could hear the now familiar sound of weeping. Barely high enough to accommodate a man of Daniel's height, the crumbling sides and roof of the cave mouth had been shored up by beams which, after who knew how many generations, had been wreathed by the roots of the picket trees atop the ridge as though the forest itself were trying to pull the mouth open against the slump of time and fatigue. Daniel expected the cloying scent of rot and decay, but instead the dry breath seeping from inside the cave seemed sterile, faintly antiseptic like the air in a freezer at a morgue. That made the hairs stand up on his arms under his jacket, and he distracted himself from zombie thoughts by sliding his flashlight out of his vest and playing it along the dirt floor.

Not that he needed it. Light leaked into the low passageway from someplace not too deep inside the cave, a slithery bluish glow that brought Daniel's brain back to zombies again. He made another mental note to cancel his cable. Or to stop letting Teal'c pick the videos for movie night. Involuntarily, he cast a little glare in Teal'c's direction. Teal'c raised an eyebrow but looked otherwise innocent.

"Next mission, I'm putting in a request for a beach," Jack muttered and set off at a lope to catch up with Asha.

Daniel agreed and followed Sam, leaving Teal'c, walking backward, to watch their six.

A few yards in, the passage opened out into a cavern about half the size of the gate-room, and the ceiling in there was high enough that Daniel didn't feel like he had to hunch. Just at the point where the passage ended, three women, also in white with beads screening their eyes, were kneeling around a fourth who lay on her back on the sandy floor. Her own veil had fallen away from her face, and her white eyes looked fixedly up at the dangling and knotted rootwork that seemed to be holding up the roof. Pausing, Daniel noted that she was young, barely a teenager. Her neck was clearly broken.

Raising their heads all in one motion, the three women gazed blindly up at him, unshrinking, although they leaned a little closer together to block his view of their companion.

"I'm sorry," he said to them. They made no answer. He could feel Asha behind him, her silent resentment a cold hand on the back of his neck.

"Whoa."

Jack's voice pulled Daniel around to face the center of the cavern where there was...nothing. Inside Daniel's head, his brain slid sideways, and he bent at the waist to brace his hands on his knees and stare at his boots for a few seconds while the brain righted itself again. Slowly, he lifted his eyes, but couldn't keep his gaze from sliding away from the center of the room and toward the safe solidity of the walls. The blue light seemed to come from nowhere and in spite of it, Daniel couldn't shake the feeling that he was staring wide-eyed into darkness. If he concentrated on his peripheral vision, he could almost grasp the shape of it—whatever it was—a sort of column of blankness. He felt like he was standing at the edge of an open elevator shaft; he couldn't see the empty space, the long, deadly drop, but he could *feel* it. It was paralyzing and, at the same time, it pulled at him. He couldn't help but reach toward it, to touch it, if only to confirm that there really was nothing there.

A hand closed around his wrist.

"You just have to put your fingers in it, don't you?" Jack was mostly turned away from the hovering nothing, one of his eyes squinted almost shut against it. He let Daniel go.

Daniel put both hands in his pockets and tried to keep from tipping down the elevator shaft.

Unlike Jack and Daniel, Teal'c was looking directly into the... whatever it was...and he didn't look happy about it. Finally, as if he'd proved some kind of point, he bowed his head and closed his eyes. "This is most unsettling."

"No kidding." Jack turned to Sam, who was on her knees digging equipment out of her pack. "Carter?" He waved a gloved hand at the elevator shaft.

Sam chewed the inside of her lip as she took her readings, and she didn't answer right away. After a few seconds, she sat back on her heels and let the monitor fall to her lap. "Well, the readings are similar to what we get from the quantum mirror when it's active, but these—" Sam raised her monitor again, wrinkled her nose at the screen and tapped a couple of keys. "—these are way more chaotic. I can tell you one thing, though—there's a lot of energy here."

"Good energy or turn-your-brain-to-goo energy?"

"I don't know, sir." She craned her neck to ask Asha. "Has anyone suffered any ill effects from being in here? Tremors, loss of consciousness, anything like that?"

"Ill affects? You mean other than *blindness*?" Jack asked pointedly.

Asha shook her head. She, too, was staring into the blankness, her hands folded under her chin as if in prayer. She aimed her blank eyes at Jack. "But we are not blind. We see the unseen."

"Like what?" Daniel stole a glance in the direction of the emptiness. "Like this? What does it look like to you?"

"Like—" She opened her hands helplessly. "Like everything."

Daniel was about to pursue the question, but Teal'c spoke up instead.

"Perhaps, then, the theta team intended to use this to escape, as one might with the quantum mirror," he suggested. "The mirror can be said to reflect everything."

Sam shook her head. "I don't think so, Teal'c. The energy from the quantum mirror is far more coherent. This isn't stable enough to function that way." Pushing herself to her feet, she angled her head away and held the monitor out at arm's length, looking at it askance. Again she turned to Asha. "You said that He-They split apart. What do you mean by that?"

Again, Asha made that careful gesture, unfolding and then refolding her hands together. "He became two and three and four, and then he shattered into a thousand fragments, like broken ice. And when they melted, this is what remained. All who looked on became the blind who see as we, their descendents, do." As if to prove it, she turned to study each of them for a moment from behind her veil. Daniel's skin prickled when she touched him with her gaze. "The forest howled, and since then the world has been broken here. He-They warned us of this. He-They knew it was to come."

"How?" Daniel asked.

"This is what happened to the world of He-They. It was supposed to be wonderful, He-They said, a light to burn forever. But there was wildfire and the world broke to pieces."

Daniel met Jack's eyes. "Well, that doesn't sound good."

"This is his world," she finished, gesturing with folded hands at the nothing. "It is to remind us not to reach too far."

"So maybe this is just a side effect, residual…" Sam said, mostly to herself.

Jack's patience was wearing thin. "C'mon, Carter. Give me something here. These guys killed four of our people to get that doodad." He stabbed a finger at Daniel's vest where the artifact was tucked away, a cold lump against his ribs. "If they didn't need it to open this door to Neverland, then what did they want it for?"

Daniel jumped a little as the idea struck him. "The leash."

"What?"

"The theta team doesn't want to escape. That won't solve their problem."

"Which is what?"

"The leash."

"So you said."

Daniel adjusted his glasses. "Dan said that the NID had them on a leash. The duplicates couldn't rebel against them because the NID had the one thing they need to survive. It's what they were looking for when they went to Altair."

"Power," Teal'c said.

"Yes." Daniel pointed at him. "The Goa'uld do the same with the Jaffa. The Jaffa can't survive without the symbiotes, and the Goa'uld control the symbiotes."

"The leash," Jack said. "Okay. So how does your doodad fit in?"

Sam joined them and waited while Daniel pulled it out and unwrapped it. In the blue light, the raised symbols gleamed gently. "The artifact we found with the original quantum mirror is a control device," she said. "But it only works with an interface, the mirror itself. If this works on the same principle, then there must be an interface somewhere, something like the quantum mirror that can focus the energy harnessed from—" She shrugged, and Daniel could actually see her editing out the million details, equations, and theorems that Jack wouldn't need to hear. "I don't know, maybe another universe that's burning hotter and faster than this one."

Tipping his head toward the blankness in the center of the room, Jack reminded them, "But she said there was wildfire and howling."

Beside them, Asha folded her hands again carefully. "He-They warned us that the *kei* must not leave this place."

"Right. The universe. Asunder. We got that." Jack turned on his heel and did a quick survey of the cavern. "You got an interface around here, by any chance?"

Asha looked at him blankly, and it had nothing to do with her blind eyes.

"Okay, so that leaves us pretty much nowhere."

"Perhaps not, O'Neill."

Near the entrance to the cavern, the three women were

preparing to carry the fallen girl away and were bending low over her to wrap her in a winding-sheet. The nearest woman had long, red hair that fell over her shoulder as she bowed down, exposing her neck.

Teal'c tilted his head to peer more closely at her. "Daniel Jackson," he said, and pointed.

Daniel put a hand on the woman's shoulder and asked, "May I?" He waited for Asha's curt nod. Asha held the woman's hair aside so that Daniel could get a better look. There, where her neck met her shoulders, was a design tattooed in blue ink. Daniel smiled.

"Asha, what is the meaning of the tattoo? Do you have one? Is it different?"

She nodded. "In the early days, the first Yagwen came to this place and waited and fasted and prayed, and He-They spoke to her. It is from her that we have the story of He-They. She was the last to hear his voice before he broke to pieces. He-They gave her the symbols. We each wear one to remind us of our duty."

Daniel's smile widened. "And let me guess: there's seven of them, right?"

Carter dropped onto the seat next to Jack at the conference table and handed him the file. He put it on the table without opening it. "So?"

"If the tattoos Yagwen's acolytes are wearing do, in fact, add up to a gate address, it's not on the Abydos cartouche. And it's not among the addresses you entered when the Ancient database downloaded into your brain."

Teal'c raised an eyebrow, and Daniel nodded, sitting forward to flip open the folder and look at the glyphs in the file. "There be dragons," he said vaguely and raised his eyes to meet Jack's questioning look across the table. "Off the map."

"Ah." Jack turned to Carter again. "You think this is where they're headed?"

She shrugged. "I don't know for sure, but it's as good a

place as any to start."

"Except for the universe ripping thing," Jack pointed out.

"And, you know, the blindness thing," Daniel added, waggling his fingers at his own eyes. "Or not-blindness. Or whatever that is Asha and her friends have going there."

"Yes, that too." Jack scowled at the circles and lines of the schematic on the general's office window and at the dots indicating the planets on the current contact roster. "Be nice to catch them *before* they go to a place you can't even look at straight on, don't you think?"

"Agreed," Teal'c said. "We must draw them out."

After sliding the file out from under Daniel's hands, Jack flipped a page and rapped his knuckles on the photograph of the device they'd appropriated from Asha and the acolytes on Dunamis. "And we've got the bait. The thetas want it bad enough to kill for. I think it's time we dangled a worm."

Carter's thoughtful frown faded as she started to nod. "Okay, but how do we let them know we're willing to talk?"

Standing, Jack closed the folder and used it to point at Daniel. "That's where your tin friend in lockup comes in."

CHAPTER ELEVEN

NID Primary Project Site, Perseus (P66-421)
October 2002; one week before the
theta invasion of Eshet

Alpha Daniel hadn't been by to see Piper in over a week, even though the alphas had been on Perseus most of that time. Piper hadn't run into him, either. It seemed pretty odd, because his read on the guy was that he wasn't one of those people who only befriended for information and then turned his back.

But then again, he wasn't the human Daniel, and the things Piper had seen these teams do in the last few weeks…He wasn't sure what the hell to think anymore.

He pulled his duffel out from under his bunk and rifled through it. Very little clean clothing left, but one T-shirt didn't smell too badly. Maybe he'd be able to coerce someone into washing a load for him. More than one person owed him a favor for procuring, fixing, or otherwise hooking them up with something they needed. He was handy that way.

The barracks were empty; Piper was sleeping at odd hours now, all based around the missions. The gammas, deltas and zetas were off-world, which meant he had a lot to juggle, and that wasn't even counting the whole issue with AWOL thetas, but, for the next few hours, at least, he had a break. Someone else was babysitting communications until the first check-in from the deltas was due. Piper should have been out cold. Should have. Couldn't sleep, though.

Daniel had brought him a dog-eared book from the tiny base library of castoffs the week before: essays about superheroes. Thinly veiled message, maybe. Didn't matter. Piper was a comics nut from practically the time he crawled out of his mother's womb. He pulled the book out from under his mattress and propped it on his belly, but after reading the same page ten times and not really getting into it, he gave up.

Ten minutes later, he had the semi-clean shirt on and was nudging Bragg out of the way to reclaim his chair. "I'll take it," he told her, holding out his hand for her headset.

"Okay," she said, valiantly not wrinkling her nose at his stubble. "I cleaned up for you," she added, like she'd done him a favor. Probably she had. The place was a litter dump, or had been before she had hitched a shift for him. The tiny cardboard box under his cot was filled to the brim with all of that now. She'd stuffed it mostly out of sight. She might even have wiped things down. The suspicious brown coffee drips were missing from one of the screens.

"Thanks," he said, snatching the equipment from her hand.

"Whatever," she answered. He noticed she was careful not to touch him when she scooted by him. He lifted his shirt and sniffed: soapy, with a hint of sweaty. So it wasn't the smell, just the sight.

He settled into his chair with a sigh and started scanning through reports and materials. For the past few weeks, he'd been neglecting his routine reports, mundane crap about the search for leftover Goa'uld weapons and whatnot. Some of the teams were showing a marked resistance to orders — still complying, but with attitude. Mendez didn't seem too concerned, but Piper was, especially after that scene with the betas. He just wasn't sure how much of it should go in the official reports. He was getting impatient queries from other teams about their next missions, the schedules, everything under the sun. None of the O'Neills liked sitting on their hands, that was for sure.

When the gate activation klaxon sounded, he breathed a sigh of relief. One more team coming in.

The scream caught him off guard, sent a shiver tearing down his spine. He stabbed at the comms link. "SG-one-niner-delta! Report!"

His only answer was that same sobbing wail, and a grunt, and then...nothing. Static. An emptiness. He shoved back from the console and ran out into the gate-room, where the security forces and two techs were still as statues at the bottom of the gate ramp, staring at...something. Piper pushed through to see.

What was left on the ramp was probably Jack. Hard to tell; it was a melted mess, something out of a horror movie, and it looked like a doll in an oven, misshapen, no longer recognizable.

It twitched.

"Jesus," breathed one of the techs. "We need to...to...shut it down...somebody get me my tools, somebody..."

Behind Piper, one of the security guys was busy puking on the floor.

"Piper," Mendez said from behind him. Piper tore his gaze away, trying to ignore his roiling stomach, and turned to his boss. Mendez was a shade of green that didn't occur in nature, but his features were calm, totally expressionless. "When that wormhole's killed, recall zeta and gamma teams. Tell them nothing about this. Understand?"

Piper nodded. He didn't trust himself to open his mouth.

It took a couple of hours for the techs to scrape up the mess on the ramp. Piper sat against the wall, watching and thinking about Jack, his sarcasm, the brilliantly Freudian doodles he produced by the bucketful in briefings, and the way he'd picked on Daniel mercilessly. And Daniel annoyed him right back.

They might not be alive, but they were living. Had been, anyway. And Piper was watching them die, over and over, one after the other in ways he could never have imagined before he came to this place.

When it was finished, he went back to work. He had orders.

Things he was supposed to do. He gave the dial-up order, activated the comms channel for the zetas, recalled them by rote, didn't even flinch when he told them it was imperative they return immediately. He pretended the voice in the back of his head wasn't screaming, that it didn't matter they were probably going to be put in cold storage, or dissected, or whatever else it was that Mendez did to the duplicates when the teams malfunctioned, and the zetas hadn't exactly been on their game since they got wiped by the kill switch trial and rebooted, anyway. Their future didn't look cheery.

He thought of the thing that had been delta Jack and shivered. No way to know what they'd run into. Or if they'd done it to themselves.

No wonder Daniel hadn't come by to see him. Piper was part of a death machine.

When he activated the gamma channel, he had tears on his face. "SG-Gamma, do you read?"

"We read," Jack came back. Behind his signal, something like a loon hooted, twisting Piper's heart.

"Go to secure channel," Piper said, reaching for the toggle. "I have some things to tell you, and I don't have much time."

NID Primary Project Site, Perseus (P66-421)
October 29, 2002; the day of the invasion of Eshet

Sunshine filtered weakly through the high, thin cloud cover. Daniel shifted around in the grass until he found a comfortable position, then closed his eyes, warmed by the weakened rays of Perseus's sun. He had his shirt off. The grass tickled his back, and he steadfastly made himself believe, just for these few minutes, that this was real skin, that the itch between his shoulder blades and the skin of his body were real, and he could interact with nature the way he remembered he once had. Sort of.

To his left, Jack was sprawled facedown in the grass,

apparently asleep, though Daniel knew that was just a pretense, since Jack did sometimes like to be left completely alone. He sighed and stared up at the sun. No risk of retinal damage. No skin cancer. No allergies, despite all the waving grass beckoning to his nose. It took some of the fun out of it, he had to admit.

To his right, Sam and Teal'c were talking quietly. If he really wanted to, Daniel would be able to hear every word in pristine detail, but he chose not to go there. Sometimes he suspected they were…well, getting closer than their human counterparts ever had.

"Stop thinking so loud. You're keeping me awake." Jack flung out an arm and smacked Daniel on the elbow, then resumed his deceptively naplike pose.

"Like you sleep," Daniel said, one side of his mouth twisting up in a small smile.

"They'll be looking for us soon. I want to enjoy every tiny second of this."

"I don't know why we didn't break out sooner." Daniel glanced back toward the direction of the base. The alpha team had found its way out with surprisingly little difficulty. They'd been gone a full fifteen minutes before someone went looking for them. Hunkered down in the grass, they might be able to escape detection by the goons for another half hour, maybe forty-five minutes.

"Fifteen minutes, tops," Jack said. *Optimist*, he added, without giving voice to it. Daniel rolled his eyes at the way Jack said it, as though it was a dirty word.

"Get out of my head," Daniel answered, though he didn't bother to turn off his comms or say it via the channel. He supposed all the mind-picking Jack did to him now was payback for the annoyances of a previous life. So to speak.

Jack sat up and brushed grass off his T-shirt, then eyed Daniel. "Aiming for a tan, there, Daniel?"

"Skip all the out of uniform jokes, would you? Come up with something new." Daniel glanced toward the rise of the hill. "Besides, someone's coming."

"Mendez," Jack informed him. He lowered his sunglasses and lay back down, hands on his belly, fingers laced casually across the black T-shirt, though Daniel knew he was battle-ready.

They hadn't been able to figure much out about Mendez. He was relatively young, maybe thirty-five on the outside, and sharp as a whittled tack, as Jack liked to say. They had an idea he wasn't the mastermind of the operation, but it was difficult to tell. He definitely had taken charge of things and didn't have much compassion for them. He treated them like soldiers, which was irksome for Daniel, since the guy wore man-in-black suits and didn't even have the decency to skulk about in them. He walked like he owned the place, which Daniel supposed he did, from a certain perspective.

Mendez certainly had an agenda, but beyond procurement, Daniel really had no idea what it might be.

He had enough time to slide on his shirt before Mendez showed, though he left it trailing out of his pants, messy and completely unmilitary, just to piss Jack off if he should happen to notice. Mendez crested the hill, sweaty and fully suited but alone, and stopped dead when he saw them. "Well," he said, scratching behind his left ear with two fingers. It was a peculiarly familiar gesture, like he was puzzled and amused all at once.

"Didn't think we'd stop once we got going?" Daniel asked.

Mendez smiled. "Knew you'd have to. There's nowhere to go." He squinted up at the sun, his charcoal-colored tie flapping sideways in the breeze, gold threads catching the light. "How'd you get out?"

"Dug a hole with a spoon," Jack said. He swatted lazily at the air beside his face, though there wasn't much chance any insect would take a bite of what Jack had to offer.

Mendez loosened his tie but didn't rise to the bait. "What I'm curious about is why you left the complex at all, since

I'm sure you had to know there was no way out."

Daniel sighed, more from reflex than any particular need to do it at all, and noted that Teal'c and Sam were up and edging closer. "Sunshine," he said, jabbing a finger skyward. "Blue sky. Haven't seen these ones in, um…"

"Ever," Jack said, still without moving a proverbial muscle.

"Fair enough." Mendez hesitated, like conflicting impulses controlled him, and then sat down in the grass at Jack's feet. Daniel raised his eyebrows. Mendez didn't speak, just sat there in the breeze and looked out at the horizon. By now, Teal'c was close enough to snap his neck with one lunge. Just like Daniel and Jack had been all along. But it wouldn't serve any purpose.

"You wanted something?" Daniel said. The surreal quality of the conversation wasn't lost on him. The whole thing seemed like some demented fever dream he might have had in college, drunk and under the influence of something offhand and random he'd been passed, while his brain ran uphill a mile a minute.

"I know you're up to something," Mendez said. He didn't look at Daniel. Instead he wrapped his arms around his knees and clasped his hands, a conspicuously out-of-place visitor at their picnic. "I want you to tell me what it is."

Daniel picked at a blade of grass, rubbed at it for a while, and watched it disintegrate between his fingers. Everything impermanent, except the thing encasing whatever passed for his consciousness. That apparently would go on forever, until something ended it violently. Beside him, Jack was so still he might as well be dead. Which was probably how Jack looked at it.

They all sat in silence for a while, until it became apparent Mendez wasn't going to get an answer to his question. Daniel listened to Mendez's soft breathing, the thump of his heartbeat. If he listened carefully enough, he could probably hear the grass growing underneath them. It was a blessing and a curse. Mostly a curse.

Mendez said, "When I started out in this business, everything seemed pretty clear-cut. Good, evil —"

"Could you spare us the lesson on morality?" Jack pulled his cap down over his face, then added, muffled behind the fabric, "It ruins the mood."

Daniel studied Mendez's clenched jaw, the tight set of his shoulders. His pulse was slow, steady. No indicators of deception. "You know, don't you, that at the end of the day, I'll have to choose Earth over any of you."

"Should have been doing that all along. You pretty much suck at your job." Jack pulled the cap down further, like he couldn't stand to be bothered by the conversation any longer. Daniel put his face down into his sleeve to hide his smile.

When he raised his head, Mendez hadn't moved. "No one likes being lied to," Daniel said softly.

Shut up, Daniel, Jack said on comms, his annoyance carrying through. *Don't give away the farm.* So Daniel only met Mendez's steady stare and offered no further commentary.

"We have reliable intelligence on the whereabouts of the rogue team." Mendez shifted uncomfortably on the ground, then shrugged and lay back in the grass, shiny dress shoes sparkling in the sun. "One of our operatives discovered their back-up power station and destroyed it. We've not heard from him since. We're pretty sure they're going to hit a world called Eshet, try to acquire some technology there. It was on their roster already, so they've got the gate address."

Sam moved up. She cast a shadow over Mendez's face. "Which doesn't explain what they're doing, or why we have to go after them," she said. "Some information might be helpful."

"The team is unstable. Their behavior is erratic. It can't be controlled."

"Which is somehow your fault, I'm sure." Jack didn't even bother to remove the cap from his face. "Why should we clean up your mess?"

"Because, left unchecked, we're not certain what their objective will be. But I can certainly tell you it has nothing to do with protecting Earth." Mendez smiled a smile that reminded Daniel in a really horrible way of Jack at his meanest. "And that's the one thing we all have in common, isn't it?"

"I do not think we share any common goals." Teal'c loomed over them now as well, casting Mendez totally into shadow.

"Well, we do now." Mendez opened one eye and looked up at Teal'c. "You're blocking my sun."

Sam rolled her eyes and sat down, and Daniel took a moment to appreciate how bizarre this was. Somewhere in the places where circuitry overruled emotion, his electronic brain was preparing a little flowchart for him, all the possibilities for why the team went rogue, what they were after. If they were really bad. If whatever had happened to them would happen to his team too.

Sam beat him to the punch. "You tampered with them, didn't you? Did you tamper with us too? Are we next?"

"Yes, and yes. But no. You're not. We tampered with all of you. You didn't really think we needed perfect SG-1 clones, did you?" Mendez sat up and fixed Daniel with a stare, as if Sam wasn't sitting right there. "What do you think this is? Some kind of cakewalk? Prance around to the music, come back with trinkets? We programmed you to be what we needed."

"Which was what, exactly?" Jack shoved the cap back with the heel of his hand and sat up, brushing grass off his shirt. "Robots gone wild? Film at eleven?"

"Soldiers in service to one cause only: defending Earth. I won't apologize for that." Mendez rose smoothly to his feet and sidestepped Teal'c neatly, without really giving him an inch. "You are what we made you. This is the life you've got. I would think you'd want to use it as well as you could, since really, we're only asking you to do a variation of what your real selves did."

Do, Daniel wanted to say, but his team were practically hissing at him to shut up, and he did know the value of strategic silence, so he exercised some restraint. "So now you want us to go hunting for ourselves," he said instead. "Because you say they're dangerous."

"Don't take my word for it," Mendez said. "There's some footage waiting for you back at the complex. Have a look. Make up your own mind." He pulled his tie back into its perfectly straight lines. "And then do exactly what I've told you to do."

"We still have free will," Daniel said. He squinted into the sun as he looked up at Mendez.

"No," Mendez said. "You really don't."

He turned and walked back down the hill, breezy as if he'd just been called in to dinner. Daniel watched him go, all sorts of cute phrases about choice and self-determination just itching to be shouted after him, but there wasn't any point.

Jack lay back down. "Wake me when it's time to go kill our doppelgangers," he said.

Mendez was just a dot on the landscape now, moving away at a steady pace, his shadow growing longer across the grass.

Eshet
October 29, 2002

The minute they stepped through the gate, Jack knew everything was FUBAR. Just the look on the faces of the folks scattered around the gate platform told them everything they needed to know—the only time he'd seen that look was in the wake of violence he'd done with his own hands. Down-slope from the gate, smoke twisted up into the thin blue of the early morning sky, obscuring the choppy teeth of the mountains in that direction. The village, which, he guessed, had once been a collection of Swiss postcard chalets, smoldered against the dark forest. The alphas were too late. The thetas had already done their damage. *Cover, people*, he said through comms, and scattered into the woods with the rest of his team. Daniel disappeared into the underbrush, Carter close on his heels, and Teal'c dived for cover with Jack.

Well, this is cozy, Jack sent. He had dirt up to his eyeballs, and he'd pulled half a bush over him. Good thing he had no need to breathe.

What the hell? Amazing how well Daniel's tone transmitted without actual spoken words. *They looked at us like they wanted to murder us.*

Think the intelligence Mendez gave us was a little behind the curve, Carter transmitted.

Jack peered out from the base of the bush. In the distance he could hear something like a cross between a dog and a bear. At least he could be grateful that he didn't have human scents to track. Though maybe the dogs would pick up on forty-weight oil and chassis lube, who could say. *Think we're stuck here, kids. Get comfy.*

Comfy, of course, did not equate to hours of being sniffed and licked by various woodland creatures and the occasional dog while villagers trampled the ground all around them. On one memorable occasion, Carter whined about being peed on by a groundhog-looking thing, which Jack might have found funny if he had had even one iota of his sense of humor left. Teal'c had apparently burrowed down into the ground and was waiting for some indication he needed to come back up again.

Jack was so, so bored, and he would never admit it to Daniel or Carter, not even if the sun went supernova and he was incinerated for refusal to tell, but he started doing mathematical equations in his head to pass the time. Not that it was difficult. He hadn't had a difficult "thought" since the day he woke up.

The gate opened once, and a lone Jaffa—an older guy with a silver skullcap—strode down the hill to the village where he was met by the whole congregation. Jack could pick up the general thrum of agitated voices at this distance, but not the words. No matter. He knew what they were talking about. A little while later the gate coughed open again, and the Jaffa left. Jack pitied whoever it was he was going to see. After that there was a steady litany of lamentation from the village, voices weeping and singing, the sound seeping across the cold earth like spilled ink. He considered adjusting his hearing to block it out, but knew it wouldn't help. In front of the gate, Jaffa paced. No exit.

An hour later, Carter's ping got his attention. *You're not going to believe this, sir.*

Between the stubby spines of the creepy bush, Jack watched his mirror image stepping down the platform stairs. He took an inventory — heartbeat, respiration, brain wave function, human body temperature fluctuations — and as he alerted the others, they were shouting at him on comms as well, one joyful cacophony of *It's them* and *Holy Hannah, our luck is incredible* and *I believe our opportunity has come.* Jack crawled out from the dirt, his hands braced in the earth, and looked for Daniel, aware it was the last time he'd see Daniel alive, if everything went according to plan.

A young girl was shrieking and running away, leaving a very human Daniel standing with his mouth gaping and his hands held out in a familiar, conciliating gesture. And then came the angry Jaffa and the angry men with axes, and SG-1 and the marines took cover, and the whole carnival was up and spinning, fireworks and all.

Daniel smiled at him, and then they were all running, heaving themselves toward the only worthwhile cause they had left to embrace. The only one that mattered.

PART FOUR

inter spem et metem
between hope and fear

CHAPTER TWELVE

SGC
October 31, 2002

"There's no guarantee he'll talk to me." The robot watched the gate spin and the last chevron engage. He tried to shake the hair out of his eyes but had to raise his bound hands to brush it aside with the back of his wrists before he looked up at Jack. "Since I'm technically—" He stopped and his brow furrowed. "I was going to say 'persona non grata,' but I guess that's what I was before, in a way." The blooming event horizon filled the control room with the familiar blue light, and it reflected exactly the same way in the duplicate's eyes that it did in Daniel's, behind the glasses.

Jack winced and shifted his attention to Carter at her console. "Anything?"

"No radio traffic." She tapped keys. "Nothing on subspace." Her eyes on her screen, she asked, "Is Piper at this location?"

Jack watched the robot's reflection in the window. The hair fell back over the robot's eye as he shook his head. "No. This is just a relay. I can access the subspace transmitter remotely. I'm sending the code now."

"Where is Piper?" Teal'c asked.

"I have no idea. He was on Perseus, but who knows if they've abandoned that facility yet. If they have, he could be at one of the off-site stations, or at the beta site." The robot started to raise his hands to point at the sky beyond the weight of the mountain but let them fall again. "Could be anywhere. Could be here on Earth, for all I know." He kept looking up as though he could see through concrete and stone. "Is it night

time? I remember—I mean, I have a schematic of constel-
lations. Orion should be visible now, right? " A brief smile
revealed teeth as he shifted to flash a glance in Daniel's direction. "I wonder sometimes what they let me keep and what
they—hang on. He's responding." He fell silent.

After a few seconds, Jack took a step forward and poked
him in the arm. "Hey. Out loud, if you don't mind."

Without a pause, the robot opened his mouth and started
talking, only not in his own voice. "—hairy back at the barn,
Daniel. I don't know how long I'm going to have access to
this channel. What's your status?" The voice was a little
reedy, a bit breathless, words running into each other like the
speaker was trying to cram as much as possible into a small
space.

Carter caught Jack's eye and mouthed, "Piper?"

Jack gave her a little shivery shrug. It was weird enough
listening to Daniel's voice coming out of the robot; hearing
him playing both sides of a conversation was two steps at
least beyond that.

The robot switched back to Daniel's voice. "I'm okay.
Running low on power, obviously. Oh, and I'm in the custody of the SGC." This time when he stopped talking, Jack
got the feeling there wasn't any kind of silent communication
going on. After a pause Dan said, "Piper? Do you read me?"
He quirked his eyebrows at Jack and followed that up with a
little shrug of his own. "Hello-oo."

Jack took the opportunity to poke the robot again. "How
do we know this isn't just you playing ventriloquist?"

The weary look the robot gave him was all Daniel. "Either
you trust me or you don't. But I'm dying to help you, literally,
so maybe that counts for something."

Jack avoided Daniel's gaze and instead traded scowls with
Teal'c. "Okay, we'll play," he conceded. "If, that is, your
friend ever decides to—"

"Okay, sorry," Piper responded. "Uh, I just...it seems someone 'accidentally' tripped the evac siren." He sounded pretty

proud of himself. "My staunch brothers-in-arms are currently
engaged in running and leaving my ass to fry." The chuckle
was nothing like Daniel. "Losers. They'll be back once the
all clear goes, so I gotta talk fast. I assume we got an audience, right?"

Dan looked up at Jack. "Piper can hear you, if you want
to say anything."

Jack shook his head.

"Yeah, the gang's all here," the robot answered Piper.

A long pause, and then: "I want you guys to understand
something, okay?" Piper—or the robot—took a deep breath.
"I'm not doing this for the SGC, right? As far as I'm concerned, you guys have screwed some stuff up royally. But
I've seen things—" He broke off and Jack's brain supplied
all kinds of images from his own life to fill the gap. "Things
I—well, I didn't sign up for that. Not that. I'm here because
I want to protect people. But these...this organization, it's got
a really narrow idea of who gets to be protected and who gets
to be people. And I'm not just talking about robots. You follow me?"

Piper's voice was husky with intensity, but the robot's face
showed none of that. Based on the robot's aping of Piper's
laugh, Jack got the feeling he could suit his expression to the
voice if he wanted to. It seemed, though, that he was choosing
instead to play the role of relay or translator. The disjunction
was a little unnerving.

Still, even through the weirdness of the relay, the tension
was unmistakable. Piper, whoever he was, was taking a leap
here, a big one he might not survive. Jack imagined Piper
in some bunker somewhere, the evac siren wailing and his
internal scaffolding collapsing, trying to make something out
of the rubble. He didn't envy him one bit. "We follow you,"
he said.

"Okay." Somehow, even though the robot didn't move at
all, Piper seemed to dismiss Jack and turn his attention to
Dan. "What's the status of the rest of your team?"

The robot's controlled expression crumpled and he ducked his head so Jack couldn't see his face. It didn't matter; on the other side of Dan's chair, Daniel was making the same expression of pain. "They're dead," Dan said flatly. "All of them."

A long pause. "Damn, Daniel. I'm sorry."

If the robot replied to this, he did it internally. Jack let that go.

"The thetas?" Piper asked finally.

"Yes."

"Son of a bitch."

"Yeah."

"I got a list of asses to be kicked, you know?"

The faint smile came back. "Yeah. Me too."

"Maybe your new friends there can do something useful for once and help us out with that."

"Maybe. Which is why I'm calling, actually. We need you to pass along a message. I'm sending the first part now, coded, so don't waste your time trying to work it out, okay? The less you know, the safer you'll be."

"Got it. Theta channel, I presume?"

"Yeah."

"They weren't born yesterday." Piper seemed to catch himself. "I mean, not *quite* yesterday."

Dan flicked his gaze to Jack and grinned. "Give me a few minutes and I'll send you some footage that should at least pique their curiosity."

"I hope you know what you're doing, Daniel." Again, the robot lifted his eyes to meet Jack's as Piper said, "You guys better bring the big guns. The thetas aren't going to go down easy." Another pause. "O'Neill — I guess you know you have a leaky boat, intel-wise, huh? If I were you, I'd be looking for the guy who's scared to go home, maybe bought a last-minute ticket to Outer Mongolia. My bosses are going to be doing some housecleaning — I'm talking real wet work — and dimes to dollars the mole knows he's getting mopped, and soon. Like, today." There was another brief silence, and Jack could picture him looking over his shoulder. When Piper came back, his words were even more rushed. "Oh, and here's a little bonus for you. Ask him about the switch. Good-bye, Daniel, and don't let them eat your soul. Piper out."

Dan cocked his head and looked like he was reading the inside of his eyeballs.

"What's the 'switch'?" Jack asked, making air quotes with his fingers.

Frowning, the robot shook his head. "I have no idea. But he sent me a secure subspace frequency. Maybe you should ask the boss."

Carlos stood in the small square of empty space in the cargo hold and glared at the two remaining gammas. Her mouth tight and her chin raised, Carter gazed into the middle space just like a good soldier. The gamma Daniel watched him with slightly narrowed eyes, like he was doing the math—and probably was, although who knew what kind?—and for once was silent. They were compliant enough in the restraint nets, but Carlos kept his distance anyway. Not so much because he was afraid of them, he admitted to himself, as because he might not be able to keep himself from kicking their shins in sheer frustration. He had at least a couple remnants of dignity left though, and he didn't mean to lose them by giving in to his inner five-year-old, who was currently pitching a temper tantrum between his ears.

Six months and eight teams and this is what he had left: two missing gammas, two cranky gammas, a set of more than mildly brain-damaged zetas in cold storage, a Goa'uld cargo ship and all the equipment they could cram into the hold, four military bulldogs, and Peterson, who looked like he was exactly two beats away from a heart attack. Carlos didn't kick anything, but he did growl a little.

"I'm sorry?" The gamma Daniel raised his eyebrows in mock interest. "I didn't quite get that."

In the corner of his eye, Carlos could see gamma Carter smirking, all dimples and lowered lashes, but when he turned his head she was back to parade-ground neutral.

With a glance in the direction of Peterson, who was slumped on a crate with his head in his hands, Carlos made a mental note to get the tech to edit out the smugness code on the next iteration. He took a hand out of his pocket, unclenched it, and used it to smooth his tie. He liked this tie. A gift. His mother had a thing for stripes. Suddenly it occurred to him that maybe stripes were all wrong for outer space, and he wished he were at home in his folks' kitchen, drinking home-made beer out of juice glasses with his dad. The wry smile that image brought with it grew a little dangerous as he put the clenched fist back in his pocket. "It's a long trip, Jackson. Maybe you should go to sleep or something. Reserve your energy. Who knows when we'll get the power units hooked up again?"

The gamma took the hint well enough. Smart robot.

Carlos scanned the crates in the hold, wondering which one held his stash of aspirin.

He was just about to start opening them at random when Kutrell stuck his bullet-shaped head in through the cargo hold doorway. "Sir?" He had a voice like a storm caught in a well, which made sense, since the guy was roughly the size of a mountain.

Carlos turned his back on the gammas, who weren't looking at each other but were clearly communicating about something. He resisted the urge to shout a few choice words at them about bad manners and instead redirected his energy to bark at the mountain, "What?"

Kutrell actually flinched a little, which made Carlos feel better and worse. "Unauthorized, unencrypted communiqué on the secure frequency, sir. You'd better come."

Instead of slouching into a sigh, Carlos straightened his spine and arranged his tie, then wove his way along the narrow path of clear floor between the stacked crates. Peterson stayed where he was, wheezing a little. In the cockpit, Kutrell and the other three mountains were crammed in with the overflow from the cargo hold like grown-ups in a dollhouse. The two who didn't have seats shuffled around to get out of his way. Siebert got up and gave him her place at the console.

In response to his mouthed "Who?" she shook her head. "No ID code, sir."

Carlos fell heavily into the chair and keyed the comms. "This is a secure channel. How the hell—?"

"Let's just say that the SGC isn't the only boat with a leak."

Carlos closed his eyes for a second and watched the distorted starscape of hyperspace streak across the darkness behind his lids. "O'Neill."

"In the flesh." Even across several thousand light years, there was no mistaking the ire underlining the airy tone O'Neill used to deliver that cliché.

Carlos used the pause to feel around in the inside pocket of his jacket, where he found one slightly crumbled and linty ibuprofen tablet. He flipped it into his mouth and swallowed it dry.

"So what should I call you?" O'Neill was asking. "Shady NID Guy is a bit of a mouthful."

"What do you want, O'Neill?"

"Okay, 'Mendez' it is. And what I want is to clean up this mess you and your shady NID friends have made, starting with something called theta team. You've heard of them? Look something like us, only they don't mind kicking puppies and killing people."

"That situation is under control."

Carlos figured the silence marked a certain incredulity on O'Neill's part. Which, Carlos had to concede, wasn't entirely misplaced.

"I think our definitions of 'under control' differ a little bit," O'Neill said. "Listen, unlike you guys, we actually *have* a plan and it would be in everybody's best interest if you would tell me—*please* tell me so I don't have to actually believe you're as dumb as you seem—that you've got some kind of edge on these things. Like, oh, I dunno, maybe a *switch*?"

Subspace hissed gently while Carlos swore in three languages under his breath. After he'd worked through his repertoire, he leaned forward. "Why would I tell you anything?"

"Because I presume you actually want to survive this, and you know that if the thetas get what they want, the very next thing on their to-do list is to come after you. You want to know how I know that?"

Carlos could see O'Neill's humorless smile—he'd been looking at multiple versions of it for months. He was very glad that there was a galaxy of space between himself and that smile right now. Rubbing a hand across his mouth—he needed a decent shave—he ignored the needling attention of the soldiers and worked his options, which weren't great in any direction. Then he twisted around in his chair and shouted toward the cargo hold, "Peterson! Quit dying for five minutes and get your ass in here!"

Kutrell and Siebert exchanged glances, but said nothing.

"Okay, O'Neill. I'll throw you one bone. One. There is a kill switch, a series of commands for each of the thetas. Not field tested on those units yet. The code shuts them down by stages—sensors, motor control, and so on—to preserve core memory. But you don't want to preserve them, O'Neill. If you have any brains at all, you'll blow them into as many little bits as you can manage." He got up and made room for Peterson. "Give them what they need," he ordered, and stalked back to the cargo hold to find the aspirin.

Dan floated in darkness.

In his power-down mode, he didn't dream—that was too simple an explanation for what he experienced—but he did remember. He knew he was processing information, packets of data, but details pushed through his consciousness like sharp splinters, ugly and painfully deep: Jack, torn apart, and the look in his eyes when he died; Sam dead; Teal'c missing. He tried not to look because he wanted to remember them alive, but it was difficult to partition off the data that way. If he tried, he felt less than human, not in touch with what made him essential, and he'd had enough of that to last a hundred lifetimes.

Besides, his lifetime had almost reached its natural end, if the word "natural" could be correctly applied.

Sometimes he had the sense he could feel Sam calling to him, her tattered voice circling around him like a soft wind, touches he could feel in some part of himself where he hadn't completely lost what he was, who he had been.

He supposed when he ended, he would just go dark, be over. He'd never thought much about the afterlife. Ironic, considering how much time he'd spent studying other cultures' interpretations of it. The real Daniel probably had come to some conclusions by now, but then again he might have a soul to worry about. Cosmic questions, and Dan had little time left to ponder any of them, but they were all he had to occupy himself. So he followed the threads, logic overlapping emotion until the two were fused.

Any minute now, the real Jack would be along to give him a lecture and ask him one last time if he was sure he could handle his part of the plan. Infinitely predictable, Jack was, in any incarnation, although this one tended to equate all his Daniels with the one he'd known for six years, and failed to take the variations into account. Dan supposed he was guilty of the same generalizations.

It was hard to look at Jack now and not remember the light going out of his Jack's eyes. Hard to stand next to him and not mourn for everything he'd never had—as well as for the few precious things he'd had and lost. Jack couldn't understand. He'd never think of any of the duplicates as living beings, and it made him as guilty as Mendez and the others. Dan wanted to forgive him that, but with his Jack in cold storage waiting to be picked over by technicians like buz-

zards stripping flesh from a corpse, it was pretty damn hard
to do.

Footsteps approached in the corridor leading to the locker
room. Because the length of stride and the meter of the heartbeat indicated his visitor was Jack O'Neill, Dan didn't bother
to sit up. Every bit of energy he had left would be required to
get through the simple plan Jack and Sam had cooked up. He
opened his eyes when the door opened and turned his head.

"You ready?" Jack said, as the door swung closed behind
him.

"Yes." Now Dan sat up. The new gear felt odd, unfamiliar
against his body. New vest, new weapons. Very strange. He
shrugged his shoulders, and the vest fell into place.

Jack shoved his hands into his pockets. "You're sure
you're up for this?" he asked.

Dan leveled his best scornful look at Jack, the one that
never failed to get a reaction, and was rewarded with pursed
lips and a frown. "Jack, I'm really not the Daniel you're used
to. I assure you, I can take them. Any of them." He had a
momentary flashback to the first time Jack had taken Daniel
to the range and sussed out his capability with weapons. He'd
always had a sure aim. The hand-to-hand stuff had come
more slowly, but then again, Daniel hadn't been especially
motivated to learn it.

That was before he'd become a robot, and his expert
teacher had insisted strength alone wouldn't cut it. One lesson was all that was required.

"All right," Jack said. He fell quiet and looked around the
locker room, as if unsure how he'd found himself alone with
Dan in the first place. Jack had apparently been abandoned by
Carter; she was somewhere else, setting up the sting probably.
Jack cleared his throat. "Listen, I'm...I was...your team..."
He pulled himself up and bit the bullet. There was less emo-
tion in the voice then, but Daniel knew how Jack dealt with
things and how to read that turn. "I'm sorry."

"I know," Dan said. He would have liked to give some

reassurance since he was quite sure the image of him bending over Jack's double was fresh in Jack's mind. But the bitter taste of his treatment by the SGC wouldn't allow it. "Thank you."

"Give it a few minutes," Jack said. "The control room will be cleared out by 2130."

"Understood."

"And look." Again, another hesitation and regrouping. "You're in your rights to want to clock me good, but go easy. I've still got work to do today." A crooked smile almost made him look friendly. "Glass jaw, y'know?"

Dan offered him a little smile. "I promise not to screw it up, Jack."

Jack squared his shoulders, standing straighter against the suggestion of familiarity, and pointed at Dan's head. "It's the hair," he said. "Throws me every time."

"I wasn't so different, when you first knew me," Dan said, but he grimaced. The whole pronoun thing was just creepy. For them both probably, although Jack would only give him that grudgingly. Dan threw a khaki bandana over his hair and tied it tight.

"You don't have much longer left, do you?" Jack asked.

Dan picked up his standard-issue Beretta, holstered it, and sat down on the bench, hands resting on his knees. "We should hurry."

NID Secondary Outpost "Hawaii" (P7A-025)
October 31, 2002

"Home sweet — er, not-sweet hopefully temporary not-home," Jackson said as he kicked at the dead technician, whose glasses were askew over her blindly staring eyes, to move her out of the way so that O'Neill and Teal'c could get into the base control room more easily.

On the monitor behind him, the gas giant had rolled across

the sky and rotated to show the ugly puke-coloured vortex of a violent storm churning in its upper atmosphere. O'Neill avoided looking at it and focused on helping Teal'c manage their burden. Outpost Hawaii was just as bleak and boring as it had been when they'd left it. But, if Carter's little plan worked, the thetas wouldn't have to be there long. She pushed past them and went to start clearing her work table.

"You know—" O'Neill stopped talking so that he could concentrate on helping Teal'c get the prisoner onto the table. It wasn't like it was hard labor or anything—he had the strength of ten men, yadda yadda—but there was something about the whole scenario that made Teal'c's alpha counterpart seem heavier and harder to handle than he should be. There was a jitter in comm space as Jackson made some observation about the weight of conscience. Fortunately, O'Neill's semi-fried comms unit didn't pick up on the nuances of that. Still, O'Neill shot back a blast of static, and Jackson's comms went silent for half a blissful second. While Teal'c heaved the prisoner's stiff legs up and onto the table, O'Neill ducked out from under the prisoner's arm and eased him down. Carter clucked and fluttered, getting her gear out of the way.

"—I'd've thought he'd have a little more loyalty to his own kind," O'Neill continued as he pulled out some zip ties and secured the thick wrists to the table legs. Just in case. Carter was pretty sure she'd managed to trash his motor control, but you never knew. Not that the ties would do anything more than slow the prisoner down if he woke up, but even a second would be enough warning. He hoped. O'Neill shot a glance at theta Teal'c. "That would be us, by the way. His own kind." Side benefits notwithstanding, O'Neill's own trashed comms meant he couldn't get a good read on whether the captured alpha was still active. He leaned over to look closely at the glassy eyes. No sign that the alpha Teal'c could see out at all. But then again, they all had glassy eyes, didn't they?

Lifting his gaze again to his own Teal'c, O'Neill compared

the two. The one standing was watching him back, expressionless, but there was something there behind the synthetic eyeballs. O'Neill wasn't going to name it, though, and he sent another burst of static Jackson's way when he offered up, *Someone. That would be a person in there, Jack*, in answer to O'Neill's mostly unintentional query ping into the ether. If O'Neill was going to wax philosophical, the last voice he wanted to hear from on high was Daniel Jackson's.

Comms practically shivered with Jackson's amusement, and his chuckle followed in real time as he sat down in a chair and shoved himself away from the table and over to the computer. Teal'c blinked slowly at O'Neill and kept on standing not quite at attention at the alpha Teal'c's head, ready to act if it turned out the alpha was playing possum. Whatever Teal'c was thinking didn't make the slightest ruffle in comms, but he was thinking. No doubt about it. O'Neill could see it there in the eyes. Something. Something different from the emptiness strapped to the table. The captured Teal'c was definitely dim inside, if not 100 percent defunct. Out of gas. Nothing left but engine knock.

He was listening for that metallic ping, a scrap of sense memory, and wondering if the other O'Neill ever got the timing checked on his truck, when Carter bent down into his peripheral vision on the other side of the table and said, "Sir?"

"What?"

"We don't have much time. He's almost gone. If we're going to do this, it's got to be now." She had her toolbox open in a puddle of grey goo that had leaked out of the alpha to drip viscously over edge of the table beside the alpha's hip. The alien doodad—their pump-primer—was perched like a fist-sized cockroach on the top tray, trailing wires with stripped ends, ready for the patch-in.

O'Neill nodded, and she placed the doodad carefully on the alpha's chest so she could rummage in the box. Theta Teal'c watched with a minutely raised eyebrow that meant he was on the edge of his seat. Over at the computer, where windows were flashing open every few seconds as the buffer caught up with Jackson's commands, Jackson pushed the headphones off one ear and swiveled to join the audience.

"I'm still not clear why we need to use him," Jackson said, waving a hand toward the alpha. "Why not just interface the device with one of us? Better control that way."

Instead of answering, Carter held up a screwdriver. Then she leaned down and worked it into the corner of the alpha's eye. With a twist of her wrist, she popped the eyeball out of its socket. Trailing a tassel of filaments and a slippery goober of blue data-transfer fluid, it arced through the air and landed on O'Neill's shirt.

"Gah!" he said and batted it off with the side of his hand.

After one squelching rebound off the back of the computer console, it rolled up against Teal'c's boot and sat there, squat and oozing, staring up at him. Teal'c returned the look for a second and then raised his head, unperturbed.

"Oh," Jackson said faintly. "Okay. Never mind."

"Yuck," O'Neill muttered and tried to flick the blue goo off his hand, settling for scraping it against the side of the table. He thought of gears and wires, gears and wires, and carefully avoided the eyeball's accusing gaze.

For her part, Carter was already three knuckles deep in the alpha's brain, her own gaze blank as she felt around for the right connections. O'Neill wasn't sure how she was going to know when she hit it, but got the answer when, even with his compromised circuits, he felt comms go live and wild with a rapid fugue of images and data. Half a dozen alerts flared through yellow to strident red as the alpha's system log tried to dump a report to anyone listening. Involuntarily, O'Neill clasped his hands to his own side to cover the imaginary staff blast hole as the black box replayed the alpha Teal'c's last couple of moments before he went dark. It was a phantom pain, the alpha's pain. O'Neill's fingers slid across the brittle surface of plasticized data fluid that had soaked his shirt when he'd slung the alpha up to drag him to the gate and back here to Outpost Hawaii. He forced his hands away to hang at his sides but couldn't help rubbing his fingers and thumb together, crumbling the drying fluid to dust. A quick glance at Jackson showed him in a similar pained posture, with hunched shoulders and one hand pressed against a wound that didn't exist. Teal'c showed nothing except a deepened scowl. Carter was too absorbed in the joy of discovery to pay much attention to the rest of them.

Bending forward in his chair, Jackson said, "Ow." He looked up at Carter. "Any way to dial that down a bit?"

Carter shook her head sharply. "Sorry. This isn't an exact science." She frowned. "Well, it is, but not here. If you want to do this the nice way, we have to go back to Perseus and get the schematics. Unless you have a supercomputer in your pocket." She grinned and waited. "I didn't think so." Again with the blank look as her fingers did the walking.

Gears and wires, gears and wires, O'Neill chanted silently under the broken drone of the black box report. *Failure, failure, failure*, the alerts flashed as the dimming brain itemized the alpha's corrupted systems. Meanwhile, Carter narrated intermittently as she worked. "Lucky for us, our brains — well his, in this case — are sophisticated enough — that is, if there's enough of him left to —" She winced and cocked her head like she was listening for that telltale engine knock. "I'm trying to get him to query the device, get it talking so that he can process the data."

There was a bright flare across O'Neill's visual field as the march of stats cut out. A moment of static and then, as Carter swore softly to herself — a buzz of irritation in comms — another cascade of sensory data. A groundhog's-eye view of the gate backed by those dear old Von Trapp mountains, another SG-1 hesitating against the blue event horizon, and a weird jittering O'Neill recognized as excitement translated into zeros and ones, Teal'c's emotion robot-style. Jackson's *Witness, the Real SG-1, in the flesh* rose up like a narration on *Mutual of Omaha's Wild Kingdom*, a remnant of comms traffic in the alpha's memory. There was a moment of disorientation when the alpha Jackson's "voice" was overlaid by a murmur from the theta Jackson about *embodied experience* and *consciousness* and the implications of equating the *real* and the *flesh*, and then a bitter swath of pity for the poor alpha Jackson still dreaming of being a real boy. That gem was followed by some yak-yak from Carter about the *uncertainty principle* and *mapping matrices*.

While the deteriorating brain of the alpha Teal'c carried them in a series of disjointed vignettes through the ensuing pitched battle on Eshet with the Von Trapps and some familiar, pissed-off Jaffa, O'Neill tracked the scattered time signatures and put the time line together: this had happened after the thetas' own visit to the planet (hence the pissed-off Jaffa), which meant that the alphas had been pretty close on their tails. Meanwhile, back at Outpost Hawaii in real time Jackson was pulling out the old *ineffable stuff of being* argument, and Carter was countering with a smear of equations dedicated to reducing—*or elevating*, she interjected testily—god to a prime number. O'Neill blocked out the peanut gallery and focused on sorting out the scattered images he was getting, alternately cursing his damaged comms and wishing it were even more damaged as the debate between Philosophy and Science escalated at the periphery of his attention.

Through the alpha Teal'c's eyes, he watched the battle go from bad to FUBAR through a fragmented and looping series of data bursts one after another. "Hel-lo," he said and whistled a low whistle that got the attention of the debating team. The SGC personnel were retreating up the steps and through to safety, taking with them in the crowd one Daniel Jackson who gave off no heat signature at all. This one paused on the steps, and O'Neill caught a burst of...something...in comms. *Good-bye and good luck*, he figured, and was glad that the wave of hollowness that washed through him wasn't his own. Then the alpha Jackson was gone, gulped up by the gate and already being reassembled on the other side.

"Nice gambit," O'Neill said. "The alphas got a man inside. Substituted for the real Jackson. Walked him right through the front door."

"I object to the use of the word *real*," Jackson said, his train of thought, as usual, running at an angle to the main line.

Whatever, O'Neill said, following that up by raising his fingers in a "W" sign.

Deciding not to push it, Jackson tapped his headset to indicate the NID chatter he was monitoring with the part of his brain not engaged in existential crisis. "A bit of news if you're interested," he said. "The SGC managed to get Our Ladies of Blindness on Dunamis to give up the other half of our beetle."

"Crap," O'Neill said. "Carter?"

"Almost there, sir. Even with it, they can't get very far. We have the pump primer. They can't access the power source without our piece."

"And we cannot access it without theirs," Teal'c reminded them.

"Access, yes. Control, not so much," she answered distantly. "If we want to convert the energy into anything we can use, we need their piece. Unless — hang on."

Carter was still fiddling inside the alpha's eyeball, but she stopped suddenly and stood up straight, eyes wide, as the alpha shot out another burst of data. Even attenuated by his comms filters, the intensity of the burst made O'Neill's jaw snap shut with a crack. He groped for the edge of the table to anchor himself as it roared through him. Grief. Enough to take a guy out at the knees — if the knees in question weren't state-of-the-art trinium alloy. A rapid-fire series of images, askew and lanced through with alerts: alpha Carter turning, her hair across her eyes, her mouth open, a shout doubled by a red shriek of warning over the comms — theta Teal'c leveling his staff at his alpha double — alerts, alerts, more alerts as the second blast tore through the alpha Teal'c's side—theta Teal'c spinning, the staff moving in an arc that left a livid smear across the visual field—the blast that lifted the alpha Carter off her feet and threw her into the trees, the saplings snapping and falling, and the alpha Teal'c's grief a howl in comm space whiting out everything, even O'Neill's own face looming into the alpha's field of vision, O'Neill's narrowed, assessing gaze, his grin of triumph—

Nothing.

A low thrumming of something unidentifiable across comms. Carter snatched her fingers out of the alpha's brain, and the thrumming resolved into *Holy Hannah*.

O'Neill caught her arm as she was backpedaling away from the alpha. He waited until her wide eyes focused on him before giving her a shake and pulling her back, guiding her hand to the gaping hole in the alpha's head, the wires snaking from his brain to the device still sitting inert and silent on his chest. "Time waits for no robot," he said.

A jerky nod and she stepped up again. But before she worked her fingers back into the eye socket, she shot Teal'c a look that was a painful combination of venom and wonder.

"It was not I," Teal'c answered. "She was not you."

Another jerky nod. "I know. I know that." Bending low again, Carter worked at the connections, this time getting a hesitant trickle of data as the alpha's brain finally started to make small talk with the device. "Of course I know that," she said to herself, and her stream of comms went pointedly blank.

Jackson, who had remained uncharacteristically silent, pushed forward again as the device opened up and started blabbing. His eyes flicked back and forth just like they did when he was reading incised letters with his fingers drifting across ancient stone, translating touch into knowledge. "Huh," he said.

"Huh?" O'Neill repeated when Jackson didn't elaborate.

Jackson held up his finger, and O'Neill pressed his lips

together. The data—mostly curlicues and slippery gleams like plants growing in fast-motion—meant nothing to O'Neill, but Jackson's lips were curling up on the edges, and his knee was starting to bounce, which were both good signs. "Hmm," he said.

O'Neill pressed his lips tighter.

"There," Carter said and the data ungrew and started again, tendrils winding outward.

"Yep," Jackson agreed.

"There *what*? Yep *what*?" O'Neill hissed through clenched teeth.

The two of them looked up together and said in unison, "Gate address."

O'Neill raised his eyebrows at them in polite invitation to explain what the hell they were grinning about.

"That," Jackson said, pointing into the air in front of him and meaning, O'Neill supposed, the squiggles currently making pretty in comms, "is a marker embedded in the system info for the device. Basically, it's the device's return address."

"Which means we can go there," Carter added. "And I can access all the power we need."

"Access. Control, not so much," O'Neill reminded her.

She shrugged. "I'm pretty sure that if we can get there, I can figure it out. How hard can it be with a brain the size of a planet?"

Always happy to spoil a nice moment with pragmatism, Teal'c said, "We must retrieve the control device in the possession of the SGC." He completely ignored Carter's affronted expression and her finger pointing emphatically at her giant brain.

"Right." O'Neill scrubbed at his hair. "Good plan, Teal'c. Thanks." He swung back around to Jackson, who was still grinning. "*What*?"

Again Jackson held up a finger and with the other hand cupped the earpiece of the headphones. "I think I have an idea." He dropped his hand and said, "Guess who just contacted our boy Piper?"

"Santa Claus?"

"Try alpha Jackson. And guess what he's got to trade?"

"Rookie cards?"

"Try a certain beetle-shaped control device." Jackson folded his arms and grinned some more. "And you said the alphas lacked loyalty to their own kind."

The swirls and curlicues of alien data faded in comms to be replaced by what, according to the ID code, seemed to be a direct visual feed from alpha Jackson. There was a monitor with the familiar schematic of the dialing computer on it, and through the SGC's wide observation window, a gate with chevrons lighting up one after another. On the console itself was what looked like an unconscious tech — O'Neill's favorite kind. The gate erupted and settled and the alpha was on the move. In the gate-room, though, he was met with resistance — marines he toppled easily and, on the ramp, none other than Classic Jack O'Neill. The alpha punched him in the face, and the warm glow of satisfaction suffused comm space. The feed cut out as the gate disassembled the alpha. He sizzled back to coherence again to show them one lovely sight: the control device held up in the alpha's hand. With that, the visual cut out and the alpha said: *Hello thetas. You know, it took awhile, but I finally see what you've seen all along: we mean even less to the SGC than we did to the NID. I'm tired of being expendable, and I'm tired of living for them, any of them. I think we can make a deal.* There was a thrum of dark amusement. *Robot to robot. This important little lump of technology for a share in whatever power supply you can get with it. I'm waiting here, but not for long.* A gate address followed and the feed ended.

O'Neill cocked his jaw. "Right," he said. "Anybody who thinks this is an act of loyalty to robot kind raise your hand." Nobody did. Now he grinned, just a little.

After a thoughtful pause, Jackson said, "Can we afford not to go?"

They all knew the answer to that.

Clipping his P90 to its strap, O'Neill said, "Okay, kids. Time for a plan."

CHAPTER THIRTEEN

Hendek (P2V-861), rendezvous site
October 31, 2002

The second the thetas crossed the event horizon, they were ramped up to battle readiness, all sensors wide awake and singing. For O'Neill, it was disorienting, for a nanosecond or two, as the data flooded in after so many hours of damped awareness. It was like trying to drink from a fire hose. Energy sparked through him and he found himself grinning even though each second of heightened presence took him closer to the dry bottom of the well. They had to make this fast, or they'd have nothing left to carry them through to the last phase of their plan.

The gate was in a clearing. No cover. If there was a sun, it was hidden behind the roiling cloud banks, and most of the light came from the nearly constant discharges of lightning that crackled and forked in all quarters of the sky. The mostly bare trees that hemmed in the clearing on all sides stood out, first black against the white flare of sheet lightning and then as white as jumbled bones scattered on the deep blue-green of the storm. The grass in the clearing hissed and the trees bent away from the force of the wind that ran ahead of the rain. O'Neill could feel it coming, the slipperiness of negative ions and the smell of ozone. Good choice on the SGC's part, O'Neill admitted to himself. If he'd been human, he'd have been momentarily blinded by the light when he stepped through the event horizon, while any soldiers hidden in the trees would have a clear view, clear line of fire.

But O'Neill wasn't human. *Move*, he said to his team, and they did. Carter and Teal'c went left, Jackson straight ahead into the trees, streaks of motion against the dark forest and the convulsing sky.

Only one and a half seconds had elapsed since the event horizon had formed, and already the gate platform was empty.

As he darted sideways, easily avoiding the gunfire that pocked the dry earth behind him, O'Neill did a quick sweep on infrared. In the constant flicker and flare of the light, it wasn't as effective as he'd like, but he was still able to pick out ten hostiles. Teal'c confirmed. Alpha Jackson was ahead of O'Neill, a dull blue shadow next to a crouching figure glowing in yellow and red with a bright white core. Between O'Neill and his target were at least four hostiles, big ones. Grinning again, he swung his P90 up and took out the marine behind the nearest tree. His vision washing out with each flash of lightning, O'Neill parsed the noise around him carefully instead, separating out the immediately threatening from the distant. Behind him, the forest was echoing with gunfire. Teal'c, Jackson, and Carter were doing their best to keep the soldiers busy and out of his hair. Almost lost in the low rumble of thunder, a scrape of a boot on stone to his left — two shots sent the marine ducking back into the cover of a decaying stump, but not before a delicate spray of red in the air confirmed a hit and the marine's heartbeat went from a steady, rapid thudding to a tripping staccato. O'Neill turned and headed around the stump, coming up behind the fallen soldier and finishing him off with ruthless efficiency. He crouched for long enough to help himself to the marine's ammo and tracked the advance of the other two hostiles toward him: one from the front, the other one flanking, their breathing resolving out of the whisper of shifting leaves and pinning them in the landscape as clearly as their body heat did. About twenty meters away, the alpha was now almost hidden by a tree, and the glowing signature of his companion was still in the same position, hunched over something O'Neill couldn't make out. There were two more glowing blobs a few meters away in covering positions.

Status, he said as he faded back around the stump ahead of the flanking marine and slid his knife out to test its balance in his hand. The marine was breathing shallowly, his heart beating in a solid, unhurried thud-thud-thud.

Two down here, Carter said. *No sign of the alpha.*

Teal'c's response was scored by impatience. *I am pinned down and cannot advance. No visual on SG-1 or the alpha.*

Where are they? Jackson asked, managing to sound peeved and exhilarated all at once.

O'Neill snatched the marine by his arm, pulled him in close to his chest and broke his neck. *They're here, south of the gate, forty meters. Jackson, get to Teal'c. Carter, with me. Go quietly. We only need one of them, but two would be better.* O'Neill switched to the common internal comms frequency and said, *Jackson—that's alpha Jackson—I assume you don't actually have the control device with you then.*

How dumb do you think I am?

You really want to know? O'Neill scanned the dancing shadows. There was static in the air, lifting the hairs on his arms and his neck. *So what about all that stuff you said about wanting to live? You can still do that, you know. You have a chance here to live a real life. All you have to do is lean down and snap the neck of whoever that is beside you.*

Not really my style, the alpha answered.

On the theta frequency, Carter pinged for O'Neill's attention, and he switched over. She was circling around and had eyes on him now. O'Neill acknowledged that and switched back to the broader frequency. *You disappoint me, Jackson. But then again, you Jacksons always do.*

I don't really care much what you think of me. The only Jack whose opinion mattered is dead. You killed him.

Nothing personal. Pocketing the marine's ammo, O'Neill stepped over the body and scanned for the alpha. He was completely hidden. O'Neill pinged for Carter, and she reported that she was working her way through some underbrush and had lost visual. The other two blobs were still there in the same positions as before, and the third remained hunched on the ground. He switched back to the common channel. *I killed him because he got in the way. That's it.*

Well, that's not really all that comforting. A pause, and then the alpha came back. Even over the damaged comms, O'Neill could hear the satisfaction in his voice. *And now we're going to kill you.*

Everything went black.

What the hell? Theta Jackson. Panicking.

Teal'c reported, *I am blind.*

Sensors down, Carter said, like that explained anything.

O'Neill ignored them and groped for the tree next to him, grinding his fingers into the soft, crumbling bark while alerts stuttered across the darkness. After a few seconds, the blackness was pierced by a tiny circle of light that widened and widened until most of his visual field was clear again. But the world he looked at was a watercolor wash, grays on grays. He tried infrared but could access nothing. He focused on his hearing — still operational, but it was like he'd been wrapped up in layers and layers of cotton batting. Everything was muffled. He could no longer hear the heartbeat of the marine closing in on his right. For a moment the forest was eerily silent, the firefight on hiatus, the storm holding its breath, and then some kind of bird started singing, repeating a string of rising notes over and over again like an opera singer practicing scales. But even that stiletto of sound was dull and distant. The storm clouds hung low overhead, heavy and ragged with lightning, but he could no longer feel the static or smell the rain. Under his hand, the tree felt solid, but that was all — no sense of temperature, texture. Nothing. *Carter —*

Movement in his peripheral vision. He ducked, and the tree he'd been leaning on exploded with a hit of staff fire. So, the marine wasn't a marine then. Teal'c got off another shot and then dived for cover before O'Neill could bring his own weapon to bear.

I can't see, theta Jackson said over the comms. At least those were still working, even as the sensory world was eroding.

O'Neill spun around to strafe the bushes behind him, then aimed another short burst in Teal'c's direction. *You can see, Jackson. Stop whining and get the job done.*

Sir, we're compromised. Carter was on the ridge above the alpha now. O'Neill could make out the pale circle of her face between the low-hanging branches.

We're not leaving here without — A shot from behind chewed thick slivers of wood out of the tree trunk right beside O'Neill's head. They couldn't go back now anyway. He still had his speed and he used it, dashing ahead of a series of staff blasts and throwing himself over a fallen tree to roll to his feet in a small clearing.

The alpha was there, Beretta raised. The muzzle was about two inches from O'Neill's forehead. "Hi," the alpha said. Time seemed to slow down as O'Neill watched his finger tighten on the trigger. The alpha smiled. "Bye."

To O'Neill's damaged senses, the shot sounded like nothing more than a distant pop. The alpha jerked as the bullet caught him from behind and spun him around to fall in an awkward slump at O'Neill's feet. Up at the top of the ridge, theta Carter was an indistinct flutter of shadow and light as she lowered her P90 and started to walk-slide down behind a small avalanche of leaves and dirt dislodged by her passing. Above her, a shiny silver bird clapped its way up between the branches and was whipped sideways on the wind, wings angled like boomerangs as it rode the updraft.

Nice shot, O'Neill said.

Theta Carter answered, *You're welcome.*

On her knees in the fallen leaves of the clearing, the human Carter was typing rapidly at a laptop perched on a flat rock. Before her guardians in the bushes could get any ideas about shooting him, O'Neill stepped over the alpha and closer to the human, so that she was in the line of fire. Just as her hand was reaching to tap the Enter key, O'Neill bent down and gripped her wrist.

"Ah ah. I don't think so."

With a thumb planted hard on the back of her hand, he twisted so that she slid off her knees to sit with a thump on the ground, trying to roll into the motion to keep her wrist from snapping. She ended up leaning back against his legs. Her blond hair was washed almost white in the erratic light, just like his own Carter's. And, just like his own Carter would have, the human used her free hand to slip her knife out of its scabbard. O'Neill caught that before she could drive it over her head and into his gut, and he squeezed her wrist until the knife fell, point first, into the loam. Then he raised his head and shouted into the wind, "Come on out!" The branches thrashed and scattered new patterns of shadow across the little clearing. "You know I'll kill her." He was pretty sure the light did a nice job of showing off the edge of the blade he held against her cheek.

Another shifting of branches, and the human Jackson stepped out of the bushes, his Beretta pointing at the clouds in one of his raised hands. Theta Carter took it from him and pushed him down to his knees. O'Neill tried to track the other guardian, but he couldn't get a read. He met theta Carter's eyes and she shook her head. No visual. Distant gunfire told him that Jackson and Teal'c were still occupied north of the gate.

"So," he said to the human Carter at his feet. "Whatcha doin'?"

Keeping her P90 aimed at Daniel's head, theta Carter went down on her haunches to peer at the laptop. She tapped a couple of keys and shook her head. "I don't know for sure, sir, but it's definitely code, and it's set to transmit. First set's already done; second set's waiting to go." She met her counterpart's eyes but got no answer to her implied question. "Something to do with our sensors being down, I'll bet."

On internal comms, theta Jackson reported that he and Teal'c had broken the line and were on their way back to the gate. O'Neill smiled and heaved the human Carter up to her feet. "Trash it and let's get out of here."

The human Daniel's mouth dropped open. He made like he was going to get up but sank back to sit on his heels when Carter pointed her weapon at him with a little more emphasis. "Where can you go?" he said. "What can you hope to accomplish without the control device?"

"We came to acquire a bargaining chip, in case it turned out the alpha was as dumb as we thought and was actually going to kill himself for you people." O'Neill pressed the knife harder to the side of Carter's face. "And we've got that now." He raised his voice to a shout. "Seems like a fair trade, don't you think? One little bit of technology for one life. You bring us the control device, you get her back in one piece." He lowered his head so he could speak right into the human Carter's ear. "That's a good deal, don't you think?"

Instead of answering, she kicked backward, her boot connecting solidly with his kneecap. If he'd been the real O'Neill, that would've sent him howling. But he wasn't, and it didn't.

While theta Carter stomped the laptop to scrap, O'Neill started dragging her human counterpart out of the clearing. Without his broad sensor net to give him a finer picture of the situation, the forest with its strobing light and erratic shadow seemed denser and harder to navigate. And his own counterpart was still out there with the Jaffa. He waited until theta Carter was at his side before turning and hefting the hostage none too gently over the fallen tree and frog-marching her back the way he came.

They didn't get very far. Two blasts from a staff weapon brought them to a stop next to one of the fallen marines, who stared up at them, his face still wearing the expression of surprise he had when O'Neill killed him. Movement everywhere it seemed, and no way to parse it out, so O'Neill shoved theta Carter ahead of him and they took off at a run, slowed considerably by the hostage who dragged her feet and continued to be pretty much a pain in the ass. But there was no way he was letting her go. Not a chance. He stopped long enough to thump her with the butt of his knife and then threw her limp body over his shoulder in a fireman's carry. The gate was close now, just beyond the screen of trees there. It loomed up, a bone circle against the boiling sky, catching a stray lightning bolt so that the chevrons flickered. More staff fire made him change his course, the staccato popping of P90 fire from the other side tearing up dirt and bark as he ran. *Dial it up!* he shouted into comms. In the clearing, Jackson was dodging bullets, zigzagging and finally skidding into the base of the DHD with his hands over his head. As O'Neill and theta Carter broke from the trees, theta Teal'c set down cover fire that drove the marines back into the shadows. The gate started to spin.

Theta Carter ran backward beside him, firing into the forest, and O'Neill risked a glance over his shoulder to see Jack there, ducking for cover and popping out again. There was no shot, though, not with his oh so valuable hostage slung over O'Neill's shoulder. The event horizon bloomed. They were home free.

O'Neill. It was the alpha. He stepped out of the forest and into the clearing. The front of his jacket and vest gleamed with spilled fluid and his hair whipped around his face as the wind bullied through the trees, lifting leaves ahead of it and bringing the first needling drops of rain.

Get moving. O'Neill told his team and they headed up the steps to the platform.

This is for my *team, you son of a bitch.* The alpha smiled. *EXECUTE.*

O'Neill froze. Beside him, the rest of the team was also frozen in awkward poses of flight. Some part of O'Neill's robot brain recognized the message stabbing through comms as code, but for O'Neill it was only pain, lightning inside him that whited out his vision, erased first his body, and then the world. He didn't feel himself fall.

There was nothing. No way to know how much of nothing. And then there was something.

Ow.

Shut up, Jackson. And don't move.

I don't think I can move.

Experimentally, O'Neill wiggled his pinky finger. It brushed against his pant leg, obedient.

What the hell was *that?*

What part of "shut up" don't you understand?

Kill switch, Carter said. *The alpha transmitted the second stage of the code. Pretty clever.*

You don't have to sound so impressed. O'Neill curled his toes inside his boots. He could feel rain falling on his face and hear far-off thunder rolling, hollow like an empty oil drum. Still on the planet then.

What's impressing me, sir, is that we're not dead.

That is indeed impressive. What can account for this?

There was a little crimp in comm space that was Carter shrugging. *Not sure, Teal'c. Maybe the base code is more resilient than they thought.*

A presence above him. O'Neill couldn't tell if his eyes were open or not, but he didn't want to risk the movement, so he stayed still and listened.

"Yes, sir. They're down."

That was Jack. Over the radio, Hammond's voice, fuzzed with static, ordered the return of the bodies to the SGC. That was the other sound then: the low water ripple of the open gate.

"Roger that. We're going to need a medical team and some help with the cargo. What's the status on the mole?"

"We were right about Aaronsen. Picked him up at his apartment as he was packing for a trip."

"Talking?"

"Yes, he is, Colonel. It seems he's more afraid of the NID than of us, so he's willing to make a deal for his future protection."

"Sweet. O'Neill out."

Farther away, almost lost in the steady patter of rain, two

versions of Jackson's voice made halting conversation. The alpha must've been almost out of juice by now. Stupid hunk of junk.

"Carter, you okay?" Jack's voice was closer.

"Yes, sir. OW!"

"That hurt?"

"Yes, sir. That hurts."

"Quite a goose egg ya got there."

"Yes, sir. Please don't touch it."

The blackness O'Neill was staring at was pierced again by a tiny circle of light. As it grew, a number of alerts cascaded across his vision, followed by a scrolling diagnostic. By the time the circle had widened all the way, revealing a boot-level view of Jack and the human Carter, O'Neill had flexed all of his virtual muscles. The sensors seemed to be fried for good, but motor control was, if not optimal, at least acceptable. Energy levels were low. Not quite in the red, but close enough to demand some pretty immediate attention. In his peripheral vision, he could make out theta Teal'c on his back, staring upward, his face streaked with rain. On the other side were theta Carter and Jackson, looking about the same. As he watched, Jackson blinked.

Don't move until I say go.

Obligingly, Jackson set his eyes. *Nobody here but us chickens, said the fox.*

Jack crouched down beside O'Neill, his face scrunched up in a grimace of distaste. "Doesn't really look like me, does it?"

"Not at all, sir," Carter answered at the same time Teal'c said, "You are very much the same."

Jack looked up at them with a crooked smile. "Honesty gets you nowhere, Teal'c. Remember that. Extra cookies for Carter." The smile faded. "What's the count?"

"Six dead," Carter answered. "Three injured, but they'll make it, I think."

Bowing his head, Jack swore at the mud between his boots,

then lifted his eyes a little to glare at O'Neill. "I had my way, I'd slap a brick of C4 to each of them and watch 'em make like confetti," he said.

But this wasn't the day Jack was going to get his way.

At O'Neill's command, all four of the thetas moved at once. It was almost too easy to take out Carter, who was still woozy from the knock O'Neill had given her. The Jaffa was more difficult, but after an exchange of blows that should've dropped a couple of elephants, theta Teal'c brought his counterpart down with a roundhouse to the head. As for Jack, O'Neill scissored his legs around the colonel's neck, twisted — old school wrestling moves never went out of style — and flattened him. Half a second later, he gripped Jack's head and brought it down with a crack against the stone platform under the DHD. The old guy went floppy like a rag doll. Humans. Delicate little things.

O'Neill heard the chevrons engaging even before he got to his feet with Jack slung across his back. Theta Jackson was dialing. Theta Teal'c had the human Carter in a half-nelson and was keeping her between theta Jackson and the remaining marines. When the gate opened, he kicked at her feet to get her moving. Theta Jackson ran ahead of them to meet theta Carter up at the top of the steps. He stopped to wave jauntily at his two doubles, a stolen Beretta in his hand. They stepped through the event horizon and were gone.

O'Neill and Teal'c were halfway up the steps when a streak of motion made O'Neill jump aside. The alpha Jackson narrowly missed tackling him and kept going to barrel into Teal'c. They went down together, the hostage Carter under them both, and rolled back to the bottom of the steps again. By the time O'Neill covered the distance to the blue ripple, theta Teal'c was on his feet. He made it all the way up the stairs again before a staff blast caught him in the thigh and threw him through the event horizon.

O'Neill shifted Jack on his shoulder and paused for just a second to look down at the remainder of SG-1 and their pet robot, soaked by rain, the scene washed a dismal gray by his damaged sensors. "You know what we want, and you know where to find us," he said. "Don't make us wait too long. Your CO's got even less time than we do." Then he fell backward and let the gate take him apart.

Hendek (P2V-861)
October 31, 2002

No one needed to issue the command. Sam, Daniel, and Teal'c flung themselves toward the open wormhole, but they were too late. Only Teal'c was there in time to make a leap for it, but the thing winked out right in front of his face, and Daniel winced as Teal'c fell hard to the ground on the other side.

"Dammit!" Sam said, shoving her P90 to the side. Daniel swiveled around and stared at the DHD. The glyphs were lit for another fraction of a second before they went cold and dark. "Daniel! Did you catch it?"

He squeezed his eyes shut and forced the picture of them back into his mind's eye. With one hand, he fished a pencil and paper out of his vest pocket and flipped open the notebook. "I think so. Most of it." Quickly he scrawled the glyphs down. He had five, but he wasn't sure of the last two. He hadn't had a good enough look at them. But he recognized all five of the glyphs: they were the same as the tattoos on the necks of the acolytes of He-They. He sketched the last two glyphs in and held it up to Sam.

"One way to find out," Sam said grimly.

"There is no strategic advantage to following too closely," Teal'c said, holding out a hand. "You know as well as I that we cannot deliver the device into their hands."

"No," Sam said. "But there's no guarantee they won't find a way to keep going as they are."

"Not much chance of that." They all turned to look at Dan,

who staggered sideways, doubled over, and fell stiffly. By the time Daniel reached him, he'd rolled on his side and was staring at Sam. "The power usage rate is constant. Unless they know something I don't..."

"They did make a stop on Altair," Daniel said, the sickening sense that he was watching some version of his own future too hard to ignore. He dropped down on his knees and rested a hand on Dan's elbow, helped him to roll onto his back. "Maybe they got a boost from that."

"It's possible," Sam said. She crouched beside Daniel and spared him a long look, one that screamed "we don't have time" and a hundred other things Daniel already knew. She glanced at Dan as if she wanted to ask more questions, but Daniel put a hand out, stopping her.

"Dan," he said softly. "Is there anything we can do?"

"Don't...don't tell them," he said, blinking slowly at Daniel.

"Tell...what?" Daniel had no idea how to comfort him. He felt like he was being flayed apart, all the hidden parts of him flung into the open for Sam and Teal'c to see.

"About Sha're," Dan whispered. "Don't...tell them she's dead. Let them go on...hoping."

Them. The other Daniels. Sam's hand was on his shoulder. Daniel swallowed hard. He'd bound Dan to him in mutual misery, and that hadn't been his intention. The truth had seemed so much more important. "I'm sorry," he said, aware suddenly of all their similarities, all the feelings he'd been considering in the abstract, made real.

"Better way to go...than the alternative," Dan said, barely audible. When his eyes closed and he went still, Daniel exhaled a held breath.

Sam patted him awkwardly, a hasty pat, the kind that was meant to hurry him along. He knew she didn't mean it that way, but he had just as much at stake as she did, and he reached for the notebook. "This is the planet the device came from. I think. The glyphs are the same as the tattoos on the acolytes of He-They."

Sam shook her head and looked first at her boots and then
at the gate. "The distortions we saw in the cave on Dunamis
are probably a fraction of what we're looking at on the planet
of the device's origin, if what Asha said was even halfway
true." Sam looked over at Teal'c. "Strategy isn't going to
matter a damn if that's the world they've retreated to."

"Wildfire and howling," Daniel said. He stood, his face
tipped up into the thin rain. Dan's arm lay limp over the toe
of Daniel's boot.

"Well, that certainly looks like the place," Daniel said.

On the monitor over his head, the picture wavered, snowed
out, and cleared again as the MALP's camera swept the scene
in a slow, jerky arc. Clearly the distortions they'd experienced near the cavern on Asha's planet weren't just perceptual, unless the MALP was having some kind of mental breakdown too. That left the ripping universe theory. His stomach
did a slow roll as he tried to make sense of what he was seeing. The landscape was...Daniel groped mentally for the right
word. Indeterminate. Askew. Slippery. He pushed his glasses
up his nose and squinted at the monitor as though he could
force the image into some kind of coherence.

Low rolling hills receded from the gate platform like
swells on an ocean. These hills were marked by flowing, parallel lines of shadow and highlight that could have been made
by silvery grass lying flat before a stiff wind or by grooves
incised in stone. He'd just decided on stone when the lines
seemed to writhe and change their orientation, shadows shifting as though the sun had suddenly slipped to another quad-
rant of the sky. He thought of the turning shadows between
his hands when he'd fallen to the forest floor outside the cavern of He-They, and remembered feeling like time itself was
sluicing away too fast, like he'd been caught in a current, an
undertow. He closed his eyes for a moment, making a point
of feeling his own booted feet firm on the floor of the control

room before casting a glance at the general.

Hammond contemplated the image on the monitor, assessing. With a barely audible huff of frustration, he turned to Sam, who was busy reading the scene in columns of data and cryptic, sinuous graph lines on her own monitor. "Major?"

She tilted her head in a slight shrug and tapped a few keys before answering. "According to the MALP, conditions on the planet are nominal. Atmosphere, temperature, gravity, all within acceptable parameters."

Hammond raised his eyes to the monitor again and said with low-key emphasis, "I'm not sure I'd call this 'nominal,' Major."

On the screen, the land seemed to be changing again, the incised lines on the ground rippling like water—flowing uphill. The clouds above were low and heavy, lit from within by an aimless, diffuse green glow, barely intense enough to cast shadows of any kind, let alone to account for the shifting contours of the land.

"No, sir," Sam said. As Hammond's expression darkened, she added, "But habitable, at least in the short term. Long enough to get the colonel out of there."

Daniel's headache was back, throbbing in his temples. The tightness around Sam's mouth and eyes suggested she was feeling it too. Just looking at the place through the lens of a camera was screwing with his head; he didn't want to think too hard about what it would be like to actually be there. Of course, it was Hammond's job to think about it.

The general was opening his mouth, no doubt to say something about being reluctant to risk more personnel, when Sam got up from her station and came to stand between Teal'c and Daniel. United front. "Sir, we know that the thetas will kill the colonel if they don't get what they want. And if they do get what they want—" She spread her hands.

"Wildfire and howling," Teal'c said, looking askance at the screen.

"Which means what?" Hammond asked.

"We don't know for sure, sir," Sam answered. "But we do know from what Asha told us that the device on that planet is dangerous. The people who made it couldn't get it to work correctly, and I doubt the thetas will do any better." Her gaze flicked to the monitor. The hills were almost gone now, and the new plain stretched off toward an angle of shadow on the horizon. A building, maybe. "The distortion field on Asha's planet is growing. Eventually it will expand beyond the ravine, swallow up the village, the gate. And it's only a residual effect of whatever that is." She lifted her chin at the image on the screen.

Hammond mulled that over for a brief moment, then aimed a piercing gaze at each of them in turn. "We've lost people here today. You reported that the duplicates can't make the device work without our piece, and we know that they're about to run out of power. We could just wait and go in after they've shut down."

Sam shook her head. "Maybe, sir. But if the thetas attempt to jerry-rig the device—and I'm pretty sure they will, because I know I would—the consequences could reach far beyond that planet."

"They will not leave O'Neill alive," Teal'c said.

"We don't know that," Hammond said, but Daniel could tell that he was running this by the numbers, making sure he'd covered all the bases. He knew what they all knew: no one gets left behind. Unless there was no alternative.

Daniel stepped up. "I agree with Teal'c, sir. They're desperate, and from what little I saw of them, and from what Dan told me, they're not just free of conscience. They hate what's been done to them, and they'll take it out on whoever they can. Don't look for mercy or hesitation there." He paused to watch the flowing land on the monitor. In the distance, the angled shadow had resolved into the definite shape of a building, columns and a portico blurred by what could have been heat distortion. Down in the gate-room, the techs were strapping Dan to a gurney so he could be crated up and shipped off. Cargo. "General, I know that you think of the duplicates as nothing but robots, but they made a conscious decision to risk their lives to expose the NID operation. Dan came here knowing we wouldn't—couldn't—save him, but he helped us anyway because he believed in the same things we do. We have to try. We owe it to them to see this through."

"And if they beat the clock and activate that device...Sir, we can't risk the potential consequences." Sam squared her shoulders.

Hammond was about to respond, but Teal'c interrupted him. "Daniel Jackson."

Daniel followed Teal'c's gaze back up to the monitor. "What is it?"

Teal'c didn't answer, but raised his arm to point. After a few seconds he said, "There."

If he'd blinked, Daniel would've missed it, and at first he thought it was a trick of the light. A couple of seconds later it was there again: a boy standing straight and still on the new crest of a hill, barefoot, with white, roughly cropped hair that hung over his wide, colorless eyes. Another blink and he was gone. And then where he stood, Jack, their Jack, slumped to his knees. His face was turned away from the MALP's camera. His neck was smeared with blood. Then the light or the land shifted again, and he was gone.

Without taking his eyes off the image on the screen, Hammond said, "Major, you have a go." As they started to move toward the stairs, he stopped her with a hand on her arm. "You are not authorized to make the trade. This is a rescue, not a negotiation. Take SG-3 for backup."

"Yes, sir."

PART FIVE

inter vivos
between the living

CHAPTER FOURTEEN

Gauss (P49-181), the planet of He-They
November 1, 2002

"You should take better care of your toys." O'Neill leaned back against the smooth, solid wall—the one action that didn't induce a feeling like airsickness and the bends all rolled into one—and watched as Jackson sat back on his haunches next to Jack, who was sprawled across the stone floor where O'Neill had dropped him.

"Very funny," Jackson said. He wiped the blade of his knife on Jack's shirt, smearing it with Jack's blood. "If I break this one I don't get another?"

"Something like that."

"Except for how I'm pretty sure I could get another one any time I like." Jackson eyed him, drilling the point into him, and looked back down at his plaything. "But you're right. There's only one original." Jackson stood up and nudged at Jack with the toe of his boot. "Get up," he said.

It would have been hard for O'Neill to miss the amount of vicious disdain Jackson poured into his wholehearted torture of the human wearing O'Neill's face. O'Neill hadn't seen Jackson show this much enthusiasm in the entire time they'd been conquering worlds together, but then he suspected Jackson was a little bit afraid of him. He was right to be. Maybe it was easier to take out all that anger on something that was too weak to make it a real fight.

Jack stirred, twitching away from Jackson's boot where it dug into his side. Broken ribs, probably. A sliver of memory: the stab of jagged bone spearing into places it shouldn't go, pain the real O'Neill was intimately familiar with. "Bet that hurts," he said, one corner of his mouth curling into a smile.

"I could use some help," Carter said, tossing a handful of corroded, weird-looking components on the ground. "If you can tear yourself away."

O'Neill climbed up onto the raised dais and went to look at the thing Carter was taking apart. The stone surface of the console was waist-high, but Carter was on her knees poking around in the space underneath it. She'd managed to get their own gizmo slotted into its socket quite easily, but the pump was refusing to be primed. Tinkering and jerry-rigging were on the agenda, and while she rummaged around inside the console, time sluiced away, their energy supplies with it.

Beside the console, a stone trapezoid a couple centimeters shorter than O'Neill framed a dull, blank surface. He brushed his fingers across it but got no readings from it at all, not even temperature. Mostly that was because the mirror's surface was about ten kinds of weird. But that wasn't the only reason. Inside his head, queries were pinging and his brain was still looping through the useless diagnostic. The sensors weren't coming back, and his energy levels were so low he felt like he was moving through mud. Around him, the silo rose up, lit by the shifting glow that seeped in through the translucent walls from all directions so that there were no shadows and the place seemed oddly groundless, in spite of the solid squares of polished white stone that made up the floor. Through the gap torn in the domed roof over the partly collapsed entrance corridor, he could see a swath of sky. Without functioning sensors he couldn't even tell what color it was—blue, green, maybe purple, even—but it looked wrong, no matter what color it might be. As he watched, a distortion wave rippled out from the dais and the roof and the hole in it and the sky beyond it seemed to fragment like the surface of a broken mirror, becoming a kaleidoscope of turning slivers that took way too long to coalesce again. Looking at it set off a stutter of confused alerts. It made him feel dizzy, the way touching the inert surface of the quantum mirror made him feel like he

was falling. As the end-point of a heroic quest, this place was
not living up to the dream. He found himself feeling nostal-
gic for the dank blandness of Outpost Hawaii. With an irritated jerk of his head, he looked away from the creepy sky,
stepped back from the mirror and its weirdness, and put his
hands in his pockets. "What is it exactly you think I'm going
to be able to do?"

"Whatever I tell you to," Carter answered, her head all the
way inside a diamond-shaped hole under the console. There
was a snort of laughter from behind him, and O'Neill looked
back to see Jack's face turned toward him, a bruise blooming
over his eye but a smirk on his face.

"Interesting version of Carter," Jack said, pushing up to a
sitting position. If his ribs were broken, he was doing a pro-
ficient job of hiding it. For a moment, as O'Neill looked at
him, Jack split into perfect double vision, like uncorrected
astigmatism, one Jack up and to the right, one below and to
the left. And then he resolved, leaving something in O'Neill's
cyberbrain freaking out at about a hundred decibels.

"Can't you shut that off?" he asked Carter irritably as he
dropped down from the dais to resume his spot against the
wall.

"What?"

"That warning...thing...whatever, that's telling us we're
not right in the head."

"I'm a little busy," she said, every word stiff with ice.
"Pretty sure you can do it yourself."

O'Neill scowled. He just wasn't in the mood for all the
complicated calculations and the power-down and the internal search of his systems and all that crap that reminded him
of being sick. He hated being sick. Even the robot version
of sick.

The section of the wall he was leaning on seemed to fade
suddenly, and he scrambled to catch his balance, only to find
that the wall was still there, solid behind him. "This is getting old," he muttered.

"Be glad you're not human," Jackson said, nodding at Jack, who had his eyes squeezed shut tightly against the wacky and ever-changing landscape. "They can't compensate."

"One more thing to be glad about," O'Neill said cheerfully. He squatted down next to his human counterpart, noting the latticework of glyphs Jackson was carving into his neck. "What's that say?"

"Just a little memento of our time together," Jackson said.

"If they are to bring the control device, it must be soon," Teal'c said to Carter from his spot on the floor beside the platform. He heaved himself up and tested his weight on his damaged leg. Even with the damped sensors, O'Neill could hear the whine of stressed components. After a few experimental steps, though, the mechanism seemed to settle a little. At least Teal'c didn't sound so much like he needed an oil can. The pressure bandage he'd wrapped securely around his thigh was already soaked and gleaming with stiffening fluid. "The instability of this place is increasing."

"I know," Carter replied. "Every component I fix or replace is having an adverse effect."

"The closer we get to making it work, the more this place falls apart," Jackson said.

"Exactly."

"We're not leaving here until it's done." O'Neill stared at the back of Carter's neck and sent her a series of images on comms, likely scenarios of their grisly deaths if she didn't get the damn thing working.

"That's not the problem," she said, shaking her shoulders like she could shrug off the implications. "Assuming SG-1 shows up and we get the control device, I can get this thing running. But then what? The place is coming apart at the seams. There's a space-time—"

O'Neill cut a hand at her. "Spare me the explanation. I already know."

"We could remove the power source, take it with us," Jackson said.

Carter's shrug was repeated about a dozen times as the latest distortion broke her into identical slivers and pieced her back together again, like the planet was emphasizing the doubtfulness of that elegant solution. From outside the silo, the hissing sound like sand driven before a stiff wind added its own derisive commentary. In the light that filtered in through the silo's walls, Jack's face looked pale and he squinted back at O'Neill, clearly feeling not good at all. If he'd been feeling a little more generous, O'Neill might've empathized with his human counterpart. As it was, the further narrowing of his senses as power reserves drained toward critical just made him cranky. He took a mental jab at yet another alert message. Too much more of that squawking in his head and he was going to feel downright happy to go gently into that good night if it meant he could get a little peace and quiet.

"We may escape through the mirror," Teal'c said.

For a moment, O'Neill had the surreal impression that there was a rabbit hole and they were all falling through it, and then he blinked it away. "Into another reality," he said. "With no way of knowing what's over there?"

"Nothing good," Jack said with a little cough. O'Neill looked down at him. Jackson got a handful of his shirt collar and hauled him to his feet. Wincing, Jack swayed, then added, "In every reality we've found, the Earth is devastated, the universe in chaos."

"So?" Jackson gave him an impatient shake. "That's your problem. All we need is a place to set up a home base, and our lifespan is infinite." He let him go and hopped up onto the dais to crouch beside Carter.

Infinite. O'Neill liked the sound of it. The lack of responsibility to an Earth that wasn't theirs was an attractive prospect. An entire universe to make their way through at their own pace. "Can you make it happen?" he asked Carter.

"Maybe. Probably."

Jack was watching him with a bland expression, but O'Neill knew just how many years he'd practiced that look, so it pinged annoyance down deep in that human-remem-brance place. "What?" he said. "Get it off your chest."

With the back of one hand, Jack wiped blood from his lip, then touched his neck. Blood smeared and dribbled toward his collar. "You have a purpose," he said. "And you have a duty to honor."

"Good old Jack. Predictable to the pathetic end," Jackson said. He turned away in disgust and nudged Carter, shoulder-ing in beside her to help with the work.

O'Neill looked at Jack's hair for a long moment. The brown was shot through with gray now, probably as a result of all that purpose and duty. "Easy for you to say. You have choices. Wonderful things, choices. Make life worth living. Not that I'd know much about that, in my present condition." He rubbed at his sleeve. Some of Jack's blood had seeped into the fabric, black on grey. Funny how much he missed color, how flat and depthless the world seemed without it. "I have choices now, though. Who I'll save." He met Jack's eyes. "Who I'll kill."

Jack lifted a hand to rest it against his ribs. "You aren't getting the control device."

O'Neill shrugged. From behind him, Carter chimed in. "Sam will bring it because she knows she needs it. She knows space-time is ripping. There's no question they'll have it with them."

"They will be arrogant enough to assume they can over-come us," Teal'c said, still as a statue on the steps.

"So then we'll take what we want. Or let them give it to us." O'Neill stepped closer to Jack, drove his fist into Jack's injured ribs. Jack crumpled like a wet rag, folding down to lie curled on the ground without a sound. It was disappointing. O'Neill had counted on a good cry of pain to go with that fan-tastically satisfying grimace. Not like it was in the old days, when Jack hung a lantern on the whole honor thing every time he inflicted pain on someone else and told himself it was all about duty. O'Neill wondered how it must be for Jack,

knowing that he didn't have a single private thought in his
head that O'Neill couldn't think before he got around to it.

O'Neill crouched down and patted Jack's shoulder. He
tilted his head and pointed to Jackson. In a conspirato-
rial whisper, he said, "Maybe I'll kill Jackson for you later.
What do you think? A little payback." Jackson didn't break
momentum, though O'Neill knew he was listening. "If he
doesn't kill you first," O'Neill added. "So try to last, would
you? I never get to have any fun."

While the gate cycled, Sam took the control device from
Daniel and zipped it into her vest.

"Would it not be wise to leave the device behind?" Teal'c
asked.

Sam shook her head. "If they really have managed to use
the interface and activate the power source, we might need
this to shut it down."

"But not to negotiate for Jack," Daniel said.

Sam met his eyes with an expression that said about a hundred contradictory things. "We have our orders."

The gate bloomed open and Hammond's voice came over
the intercom, giving them the go. "Bring him home, SG-1,"
he said, just before the gate swallowed them.

For a long moment Daniel thought the gate had put them
back together again upside down. He lay on his back and looked
up at the flat, green clouds while the last sparkling, impossible memory of a very rocky ride ricocheted around inside his
skull and disintegrated into a million shards of pain. "Ow,"
he said. His arms and legs seemed to be missing. No, okay.
There they were, muscles shaking and nerves sparking like
he'd been zatted.

Maybe he *had* been zatted.

That thought made him roll over and clumsily lever himself onto his knees. He got a hand on his sidearm and tried
at the same time to get a grip on his hammering heart. After
two seconds looking out across the slowly undulating plain,

he wished he were on his back again. The sky, although it was sickly and creepy, was at least still. He managed to keep from squeezing his eyes shut, which was a minor accomplishment. Instead he focused on the immediate objective, the gate platform—reassuringly solid stone—and his team. Sam was on one knee beside the MALP, sighting along her P90 at the building in the distance. Blood smeared her lower lip. She must've bitten down on it when they tumbled—careened—through the gate. In the wan light, the blood looked black against her pale skin. Unmarked except for dust on the back of his vest, Teal'c scanned the horizon, his zat powered up and ready. Behind them, three of their four marine escorts were taking up positions flanking the gate. The fourth was on his knees on the other side of the MALP, apparently learning a full stomach was a liability on planets like this.

"I see no sign of the boy," Teal'c said.

"Who could live here?" Daniel was starting to think maybe the boy had been some kind of shared hallucination. But Jack...that had seemed real. Finally managing to get unsteadily to his feet, Daniel drew his Beretta and did a slow 360 himself. The images the MALP had sent back seemed to be pretty accurate. There were no trees, nothing like vegetation. The land around the gate seemed to be slowly drifting and changing. Hills loomed up as he watched and then flattened out again, so that the area seemed by turns claustrophobic and vastly empty. Through the circle of the gate he could see the shadowy angles of a distant mountain range, but a moment later it was gone. All of this happened in complete, unnerving silence. And that morgue freezer smell, arid and antiseptic and dead, that he'd noticed in the cavern of He-They was here too. The whole place gave his brain a slippery feeling, like the land was on the verge of not being there at all, and if he stopped concentrating, he'd come unmoored completely. He cast around for something to focus on and found it on the horizon. The only thing that didn't seem to change was the building with its columns and portico. No matter how the land wavered and shifted, the building was always clearly in sight. "That can't be right, can it?" he asked, mostly to himself.

"What can't?" Sam asked. She was on her feet now and was testing the ground beyond the stone gate platform with the toe of her boot. After a couple of tentative taps, she stomped hard and, apparently satisfied that the ground would hold her weight despite looking like stretching taffy, she stepped out onto the incised stone.

Daniel waved a hand in the direction of the building. "Should we be able to see it if there are hills in the way?" As if on cue, hills rose up between them and the building, but Daniel could still see it. He poked his finger and thumb under his glasses to rub at his eyes. The hills definitely blocked the sightline. He was sure of that. But there it was, the building, clear as day. His head was splitting from trying to reconcile two contradictory realities.

"It is indeed strange." Teal'c scowled toward the building. "The land is very unstable."

"Not land," Sam said. "Space." She looked over her shoulder at them. "It's bent." She licked at the blood on her lip and looked up, as if into the big space inside her brain where everything was laid out in a way that made perfect sense. Daniel could see her trying and discarding explanations. "Space isn't flat—well, it sort of is, in our universe... maybe. The point is, theoretically, other universes have different physical properties. Some of them have positive curvature where parallel lines cross and triangles have angles greater than 180 degrees. Some of them have negative curvature..." Daniel tried to make his expression less blank but had no luck. Sam sighed. "Sometimes you can see around corners," she finished. She turned back to lift her chin at the building. "Whatever that device did or is doing, it's screwed up space here. Light. Time. It's not the land that's changing. It's space."

"O-okay," Daniel said. "So what happens if we—" He

waggled an outstretched finger, this time at the world in general. " — you know, go there?" He had a weird mental image of himself stretched out or squashed like a not-very-fun funhouse mirror reflection. That didn't have much appeal.

"Do we have a choice?"

Teal'c pointed at the building with his staff weapon. "The path is clear. This temple is the only place the duplicates could have taken O'Neill, and it is the only landmark we can be sure of." He stepped off the platform onto the white stone. "We do not appear to be physically debilitated."

The marching band conducting maneuvers in Daniel's head seemed to contradict that theory.

Sam considered for a moment. "You know, the path *is* clear. All of these distortions, and the only constant is that building and the sight line from the gate." She traced the path with the muzzle of the P90.

Stepping out onto the white stone himself, Daniel said, "Not a coincidence, then?"

Sam shrugged. "Something must be maintaining a reasonable level of stability along this path." She tilted her head back and squinted at the clouds. "Maybe the force field has something to do with that."

"Force field?" Daniel put a hand on his boonie to keep it from sliding off and followed her gaze upward. Now he could see it. The uniform cloud cover with its creepy green glow was actually a lot closer than he'd first thought, and it shimmered, faintly iridescent, as if its outer surface were being stroked by rain. "Oh. That force field."

To the marines of SG-3, Sam said, "Stay here and hold the gate. They don't get through under any circumstances. If you get your chance, shoot to kill." She waited for Booker and Kzinsky to get their infrared goggles into place. At least they'd be able to tell a human from a duplicate by their heat signatures.

With the marines situated, Sam headed off toward the temple on the horizon. Daniel followed, with Teal'c taking up his position on their six. It was impossible to tell how far away the temple was. It could be one klick or ten, but Daniel was betting for something on the closer side. Around them, the land—space—kept doing whatever it was doing, but Daniel found that if he kept his gaze on either the temple or Sam's back the ground seemed to remain level under his feet, even if his peripheral vision was telling him he was walking uphill or downhill. It didn't take long before he was feeling decidedly motion-sick. He looked over his shoulder at the gate in an attempt to orient himself, then groped a hand out to catch Sam's vest. "Sam?"

She stopped and turned to him. "What?"

"Where's the gate?"

She stepped to the side to get a better line of sight, but it didn't matter. The gate, if it was still there, was invisible. She keyed her radio. "Booker, what's your twenty?"

"Still on the gate, Major," was the immediate reply.

"Do you have eyes on us?"

This time the pause was longer. "Sometimes, ma'am." Her voice was stretched thin and seemed to warble a little with interference. "We can still see the structure, though, plain as day." Another pause while the radio hissed. "—to rendezvous?"

Sam peered at the structure in the distance and then back toward the gate. "Negative. Hold your position." She started walking again. "No point getting everybody lost. Somebody's got to have a bead on the gate."

Daniel knew without hearing her say it: there was no chance they were heading home without doing their damnedest to find Jack.

They hadn't gone much farther when Sam raised her fist, and they all dropped to a crouch. Over her shoulder, Daniel could see three familiar figures in green fatigues about twenty-five meters away, turned away from them and also crouching. Teal'c shifted up beside him and murmured "Duplicates," as the Teal'c ahead of them moved beside the other Daniel.

"Hmm," Sam said. "Just a second." A bit of one-handed fumbling and she had her infrared goggles in place. "Nope. There's a heat signature. Not robots." Keeping her eye on them, she stuffed her goggles back into her vest, shuffled over behind Daniel and rummaged around in his pack until she came up with the hard case for his glasses. She turned it over in her hands and then straightened up with her arm cocked back, ready to throw. The other Sam, still looking away, did the same.

"What are they looking at?" Daniel asked.

"Nothing," Sam answered, and threw the case as hard as she could.

Daniel ducked reflexively as some kind of projectile zinged over his head from behind. Teal'c swung around and fired his zat, just as Sam shouted "No!" and the world went suddenly white-hot and sparkly. Daniel flopped over onto his face and twitched as the zat charge crackled through his nervous system. After awhile, someone rolled him over and gently slapped his cheek. He opened his eyes to see Sam leaning over him.

"Ow," he said.

"I apologize, Daniel Jackson."

Daniel blinked stars out of his eyes and, once he found his hands — strangely enough, at the end of the numb sticks that were ostensibly his arms — he pointed an accusing finger at Teal'c. "You zatted me." Then he thought about it and the hand dropped to his chest. He wrinkled his brow. "How did you zat me?" He got his glasses settled again and, with Sam's help, struggled up to a sitting position. Sam offered him his glasses case, but he waved it away. "No, thanks. You can keep that."

He followed her line of sight, first in one direction — where another Sam and another Teal'c were kneeling beside a Daniel who was looking away — and then the other — where there was, yes, another Sam and Teal'c and Daniel, only that Daniel was looking away, too. "O-okay," he said. He waved his hand at the doubles behind them. His double waved at someone behind *him*. "Who? How?"

After getting to her feet, Sam took his still absently waving hand and leaned back to leverage him up. "It's us."

"Like, in a mirror?"

Her smile seemed just a little pitying. "You can think of it that way if it helps, but no. It's actually us. Remember what I said before, about space being bent?" She made a cylinder with her hands to illustrate space folding back on itself. "There is here, here is there. It explains why Booker can't see us right now. You see?" When he nodded and then shook his head, she sighed and closed her eyes for a second. "Just don't shoot at them, okay?" she said to Teal'c. "Not those ones, anyway."

Teal'c scowled at the back of his own head, then turned and scowled at the back of his own head in the opposite direction. "It will be difficult to discern an appropriate target if we come under fire. How are we to defend ourselves in this environment?"

"Good question," Sam answered as she moved away, back on the path to the temple.

As they walked forward, instinctively going abreast instead of in a line so that they could all see their doubles clearly, the distance between themselves and the doubles ahead of them shrank. A glance over his shoulder showed Daniel that the same was true behind them, and those doubles—with a Daniel looking over his shoulder—were closer than before. The farther they went, the shorter the gap until, unnervingly, the doubles were pacing just a few steps away. They drew closer and closer, until Daniel found himself tucking in his chin and turning his head away as if anticipating a collision. Then, because Jack was right and Daniel really did have to put his fingers in everything, he reached out in spite of his better judgment and tapped himself on the back of the head.

"Gah!" As he felt his own finger connect with his skull, he jumped forward, colliding—merging, fusing, whatever-ing—with his other self. With a jolt and a snap, there was just one of him again. He stopped walking, closed his eyes and clenched his boonie with both hands for a second. "I don't like it here," he said.

"Me neither," a very young-sounding voice said.

He opened his eyes. In front of him was the boy they'd seen on the monitor. Both Teal'c and Sam had him in their sights. He looked about ten years old. He was wearing what looked like an adult's uniform jacket—epaulettes and what could have been medals of service across the breast—over pants that were long and tattered at the cuffs he'd obviously been treading on for a long time. Everything about him was a sort of antique white, so that he seemed to blend in with the undulating landscape. While he waited for Daniel to get his mouth working again, he looked through his shaggy bangs without much interest at Teal'c's zat.

"Hello," Daniel said.

The kid said nothing.

"I'm Daniel. Who are you?"

At that, the kid laughed, a high, clear sound of amusement. It went on for a long time, even after the boy had stopped and was looking at the zat again. Before Daniel could say anything else, the kid broke into a dozen slivers, just like a mirror cracking and with a similar sound. Each sliver held a boy who was laughing the same laugh; there seemed to be a whole crowd of them. As the laughter went on, it grew deeper and more hoarse and rasping. Finally, the fragments seemed to fuse again and instead of a boy there was a man, bowed and wrinkled and almost translucent with extreme age. His bony hand fumbled toward Sam's vest, and she took a step backward, bringing the P90 up level with the old man's chest, making him laugh again. It sounded like dried leaves driven along the ground by a cold wind.

"You have the *kei*," he said at last.

It wasn't a question, so Sam didn't bother denying it. "We don't want to hurt you. We're looking for others who came here. They look like us. They're dangerous."

Again the hand groped toward her vest. "The *kei* is dangerous." His shrunken mouth turned down in a frown of sadness, and he turned his hand palm upward to indicate the space around them and then the temple itself. "You should not have brought it here. It has done terrible things here."

The voice echoed from behind them, and Daniel started a little when he turned and saw the same man on the next rise making the same gesture. As that hill seemed to collapse and another rose beyond it, there was another man, and another. Grief and impotent anger repeated in both directions to infinity.

"Who are you?" Daniel aimed the question at the man nearest them and stepped away himself when the man slivered as the boy had done, the sound of breaking glass receding away from them as each iteration broke, until the whole landscape was littered with sparkling, upright fragments.

"We are," the voice said, a fugue of repetition.

Daniel put one hand over his ear and tried to focus on the splinter beside him. It was difficult because, like the pillar of blankness in the cave on Dunamis, the surface of the splinter seemed to repel his gaze. He could feel a vast emptiness inside it, behind it, like it was a window onto nothing at all. "He-They," he said. "You sent the *kei* to another world, to protect it."

Again the laughter rose up, multiplied, and coalesced as the slivers resolved into a boy again. "I didn't send it. It was ripped from me. I don't know where. And everything went quiet and strange. There was a woman, and she came and looked at me through the fault, and she sang and we talked sometimes." The pale eyes filled with tears. "I miss her. I miss everybody."

"Yagwen."

The boy nodded and then he was gone, and the man said, "Yes. Yagwen." The tears, though, were the same. "Is she well?"

Daniel exchanged a quick glance with Sam. "The one we saw was fine. She's on Dunamis. That's where the *kei* went. She and her acolytes have been guarding it."

A smile brightened the deeply lined face, and Daniel could almost see a younger man there, a ghost inside the unstable form flickering between childhood and age, someone who might've earned the medals gleaming dully on his uniform. "I'm afraid that the cataclysm damaged Yagwen's people somehow. But it damaged everything, didn't it?" He looked beyond Daniel at the empty world. "Foolishness. We were such fools." His voice hardened. "And now you bring the *kei* here to do it again." This time when he shattered, the word "Fools" trailed off to the sibilant hiss of a hundred snakes.

Sam raised her voice and aimed her question at all the fragments within hearing distance. "We want to stop it, if we can. But we need to know what this device does. We need to know what happened here."

The little boy's laugh sparkled around them. "We thought we could control it all—space and time, space and time, space and time," he sang. "We thought we could reach between the branes and siphon out the light." The old man added, "Fools." Around them, the fragments glittered in the green, undersea light. "Most died, some fled through the gate. I was caught in the flux—slipped out of time, between space—alone. But for Yagwen, who saw me through the fault and spoke to me sometimes." He pointed at the device in Sam's vest again. "The *kei* controls the mirror, focuses the raw energy. They will have to step through the mirror to activate the siphon. They will kill him for it."

As he spoke these last words, the old man coalesced in a bright shard. When the glow died, Jack was there in his place, on his knees. Daniel pushed his glasses up again and stepped closer. Jack's neck bore a fine hatching of lines. Through the blood, Daniel could almost read them. Almost. Jack lifted his head and said to them in the boy's voice, "They'll kill us all. Everyone. Everything. Everywhere."

Unthinking, Daniel reached toward him. Before Teal'c could stop him, Daniel had touched Jack's shoulder, just the barest contact of fingers against glass.

When he touched the fragment of the man, he touched nothing—no hot or cold, nothing solid, no emptiness.

Only howling.

CHAPTER FIFTEEN

Gauss (P49-181)
November 1, 2002

"**D**aniel? *Daniel!*"
    He could hear Sam's voice, but he couldn't see her.
The press of the escaping crowd drove him backward a few steps
before he anchored himself again. He stood his ground as the
people flowed around him and — disturbingly — through him.
There was a momentary chill at their touch, and he wrapped
his arms protectively around himself. They were human or at
least humanoid. Some men and women were in uniforms like
the old man's only deep blue and bright yellow; others were
in civilian clothes, some carrying bags and awkward arm-
loads of possessions he couldn't identify. Their mouths were
open. As they ran, disbelief and terror tore their voices out of
them in screams or prayers. Their eyes were wild. The may-
hem was oddly unified by the headlong drive toward the gate,
and even the cacophony was like a chorus, millions of voices
singing the same litany of loss and fear.
    Daniel swayed in the current and tried to get his bearings.
His fingertips were still numb where they'd made contact
with Jack. But it wasn't Jack, was it? Glass. He knew that was
just an approximation, his brain trying to put a word to something that didn't exist. He could make out the tip of Teal'c's
staff weapon, and over the noise he could hear Sam shouting
his name. In front of him a woman stumbled, and the collection of glass cubes she carried scattered as she pitched forward toward him. He reached out to break her fall, but his
arms passed right through her and she hit the ground hard.
Passersby kicked the cubes away in their rush. She curled

up with her hands around her head, no protection against the running, trampling feet. Daniel tried to help her up, but she was insubstantial, a ghost, and around her the cubes glowed softly, each one containing a floating image, a smiling face, a family. He found himself transfixed by the one nearest to him — children ranged from shortest to tallest — but it was crushed by the stampede.

When he straightened up, Jack was there as before, only a few feet away and watching him steadily as though there was no crowd shoving and crying all around him. "Everything," he said, as the shock wave hit. It came from behind the crowd, from the temple that, Daniel could now see, wasn't a temple at all, but a glass silo. It was blooming — fire so impossibly blue that it burned his eyes to look at it — the wave expanding from it, pushing air ahead of it so that the hot wind ripped the screams from the people's mouths.

"Daniel!" Sam shouted into the sudden silence that followed the wave. But it was only a pause, a brief intake of breath before the real wave hit, blue fire expanding in a sphere, and everywhere it touched there was...nothing. Daniel threw his arms up in front of his face, but he could still see the wave and the people running before it shattering into shrapnel, a glittering haze of remains that were almost, terribly, beautiful.

After the wave passed there was no one, nothing at all. The scoured plain of white stone extended forever in all directions. Only the gate glowed for a moment under the glistening iridescence of its protecting force field and then, with no travelers to swallow, the event horizon winked out. Silence.

"Everywhere," Jack said in the old man's voice. "Everyone."

Daniel's knees gave out. He sat heavily on the lifeless stone and clasped his hands over the back of his neck. "Oh, God," he said. He felt Sam's hand on his shoulder and heard her gasp, and he knew she could see it too. Behind his closed eyelids he watched the fractures crackling — "Subspace," Sam gasped — crazing the universe, time twisting as the eruptions tore space on world after world after world, past, present, future—a vast forest curling and blackened as if its teeming life had been sucked out of it; a moon once green and blue now glowing an arid, deathly white against the stars; a gossamer flock of some vast and semi-sentient beings drifting on the solar winds but now reduced to component particles and dispersed to nowhere. On a green world a familiar shape—the tusked head and shaggy, elephantine bulk of a mammoth—turned, lumbering away from the fissure that opened its ragged maw and coughed darkness across the sky. In a few short breaths that Daniel knew counted eons, the Earth was closed in a fist of ice. On another world millennia later, in a ravine crowned by silver-leaved picket trees, a young woman watched the universe convulse and her eyes burned white at the sight of it.

"Yagwen," the boy said. Daniel opened his eyes to see him standing in the empty world, his hands hidden in the long sleeves of his uniform jacket, his old man's eyes blurred with tears. "We contained it, those of us who survived," he explained in his rasping old man's voice. He poked a finger out of his sleeve to point at the force field overhead. "But it will not withstand another event." His finger slipped past Daniel's forehead as though he was going to touch him, and Daniel flinched away and closed his eyes. In his head, the cataclysm expanded, attenuating as it spread. Seeing to the edges of the universe wasn't helping his headache at all. The boy's laughter danced across the sparking vision in Daniel's mind, multiplied and dwindled and died.

"Are you injured, Daniel Jackson?"

Daniel looked toward the sound of Teal'c's voice. He was standing behind Sam, who was on her knees with her hands raised. He pressed the muzzle of the Beretta to the back of her head. A little ways away, Teal'c—the real Teal'c, Daniel realized as the penny dropped with a painful clatter—was lying on his back, his eyes closed.

"No," Daniel said, raising his hands too. "I'm fine. Thanks

for asking. Theta Teal'c, I presume?"

"Such designations are no longer necessary." Theta Teal'c cast a significant glance at his prostrate double. Then he yanked Sam to her feet and, with one foot, deftly hooked the real Teal'c's staff weapon and hitched it up so he could catch it in his free hand. Without shifting his aim on Sam, he swung the staff and let it go so that it spun end over end through the fractured air, seemed to break into fragments, and disappeared. He motioned to Daniel to get up and precede them. "This way."

Dizziness tipped the world sideways as Daniel stood, and he had to wait for things to even out a bit, relatively speaking, before he could risk walking. "We were heading that way anyway," he said. In his peripheral vision, translucent refugees fled toward the gate, afterimages burned into his mind, and multiple Sams and Daniels and Teal'cs trudged against the current, heading toward the silo. He lifted his hand and all the Daniels he could see lifted theirs. "I really, really don't like this place," he muttered as they left one real Teal'c and all his ghosts behind.

As they got closer to the silo, Daniel realized that what he'd assumed earlier were columns were in fact the girders of the silo's external structure, twisted like licorice sticks and melted at their tops where they bent outward. The portico was the remains of the silo's roof, heat-ravaged and torn open from the inside by the forces that had escaped it. The building's once-transparent glassy surface seemed smoky. Daniel couldn't get much of a sense of what was going on behind it. It was like the walls had been sandblasted. Weirdest, though, was a cloud of debris they encountered about fifty meters from the dark slash of the partly collapsed entrance. Like the girders whose tortured forms traced the contours of the ancient explosion, the debris from the blast persisted as a haze of floating, glittering fragments angled away from the blast zone as though caught in a freeze-frame. Daniel did his best to avoid the larger pieces, ducking and leaning around them as theta Teal'c pushed them forward. Those that he couldn't avoid drifted away from his touch, tumbling into others so that the little procession of captor and captives set out a wave of disturbance like a spreading wake as they passed. To his ears, the displaced fragments chimed softly, but with each point of contact he heard a scream of pain inside his head. The smaller pieces, tiny arrows of light, peppered his clothes and his skin as he moved through them, and these registered to his mind only as a barely-there keening like the singing of a champagne flute rubbed by a wet finger.

"They're people," Sam said behind him, and he stumbled a bit at the realization. "Or what's left of them."

He craned his neck over his shoulder to see her walking backward so she could look at theta Teal'c, her hands clasped behind her neck. "Can you hear them?" she asked. Her voice was equal parts curiosity and accusation. "They're screaming. They've been screaming for thousands of years."

Theta Teal'c looked pointedly away from her along their path and gestured with the Beretta for her to turn around. "I also hear them. I suggest you keep walking."

"If you activate the device, this kind of damage is going to spread," Sam said. "You get that, don't you? The force field won't contain it. It didn't contain it *last* time. The old man showed us. We saw it."

"As did we on our approach to this place."

Maybe the robot was going to elaborate, but a wave of distortion rippled toward them from the silo and, as it passed, the landscape seemed to split into a thousand sharply angled planes of glass, like facets on a jewel or mirrors in a maze. In each was a frozen reflection of themselves seen from a different vantage point. After a second or two, the wave passed, the images released, and the reflections became animate. With this fugue of motion the sharp-edged, polished surfaces faded until there were only ghosts moving off in different directions toward a dozen identical silos. Daniel risked another look back over his shoulder and was met with hazy double-vision versions of Sam and the theta.

"It's like being stuck inside a prism," he muttered, and turned his attention back to the silo directly in front of him. He actually felt like his brain was breaking and the pieces were drifting away. He couldn't help wondering if the robot felt like that too, and if so, what it meant and how they could take advantage of it. Of course, that was going to be tricky given that it was all Daniel could do to keep track of his own two feet and, maybe while he was at it, not go completely insane. A fragment grazed his shoulder and he winced against its howl of anguish. "If we get out of this, I'm never looking in a mirror again."

"If you comply with our demands, you may yet survive this day," the theta said.

Sam asked, "How many more won't?" but got no reply.

Around them, the drifting remnants of a civilization hung glittering in the air.

Jack spread his feet a little wider and pressed his back against the girder behind him, as if somehow a more stable stance might actually make a difference when the space-time continuum finally came apart right under his ass. Which was numb, by the way, from sitting on the cold stone floor. Closing his eyes didn't help with the discomfort, either, because the seesawing and splitting of the distortions that rippled pretty much constantly through the silo felt as bad as they looked. Each new wave that rolled from the machine in the center of the room offered new and exciting variations on freakish and nauseating. He was reminded of one very bad night in college, a bathtub full of something made of grape Kool-Aid and what had to be jet fuel. He'd had two man-sized shots and wound up hanging onto his bed like it was the teacup ride at Disneyland. After that he'd sworn he'd never drink something that toxic again, and so far he'd actually done a good job of sticking to it, that ritual toast on Abydos years ago notwithstanding. After today, he told himself, he was going to make a similar rule about visiting planets that were in the process of falling through the cracks in space and time. He didn't have the stomach for it anymore.

Or the bones. Shifting a little to find a smoother section of the girder to take his weight, he clamped his teeth shut against a groan. Ribs were stupid, he decided. What *Homo sapiens* really needed was an exoskeleton that could withstand repeated kicking. And no amount of probing the cuts on his neck explained what the hell robo-Jackson was carving into his skin with such careful attention. Probably "Jackson was here."

For the moment, though, the Jackson duplicate seemed happy enough to keep one eye and a zat on him while he watched the other two poking around at the Armageddon machine. They didn't say much out loud—that comms thing was a real advantage—but they were definitely talking. At one point the O'Neill robot turned to Jackson with a look that would've stopped the heart of a human being. Interesting.

But heart attacks were never going to be their problem, obviously. Jack could still feel the momentum of the fleeing crowds pulling at him. From his forced march through the shrapnel cloud beyond the silo, the exposed skin of his arms and face was flecked with what had to be tiny points of frostbite or the freaky alien equivalent. That was nothing, though, compared to the wailing that still echoed in his head. It was hard to tell if the robots got that enlightening little show. If they saw it and felt what Jack had, they really were cold-hearted hunks of high-tech junk. Not one of them showed any sign that they were moved to shed a crystalline tear over any of it. Well, that wasn't entirely true. The Carter duplicate seemed pretty morose about coming all this way only to find out that the device was a bust from the get-go, but that didn't stop her from getting elbows-deep inside the damn thing and yanking bits out of it like she was Mr. Wizard. Apparently they'd doubled the ego circuits when they'd pulled out the ethics chip. Another promise to himself: get back to Earth,

find the first NID guy he could lay his hands on, and kick his
ass up and down the street. Twice.

The most pressing issue now, though, was the absence of
the Teal'c robot, who had taken off at a run, Beretta drawn.
Easier to get up close and personal with hostages, Jack figured. He hoped his Carter and Teal'c were paying attention
because, if not, this was going to get ugly pretty quick.

He put that thought aside and focused on the problem at hand,
which meant he divided his attention between the entrance
and the three robots over by the empty mirror with its blackened stone frame. From this angle, he couldn't see much more
than a narrow band of white stone and green sky and the
occasional shadow of rising or sinking hills visible through
the scored surface of the walls. And of course the ghosts: the
robots intermittently multiplying, their reflections extend-
ing into infinity like they were trapped between mirrors and,
always, the fleeing crowds, forever in the process of turning
into the flying shrapnel of broken glass. It was them, he figured, who had pitted the clear surface of the silo, the slivers
of their transformed bodies driven outward by the waves of
destruction, blasting the silo to a smoky translucency. And
the ones not lucky enough to be atomized drifted out there,
screaming. What a miserable way to go.

Jackson was watching him full-on again, and Jack figured
the robot could probably come up with at least a few worse
ways to die. Jack wasn't too keen on learning what they were.
His unblinking stare was getting on Jack's nerves.

"You know," Jack said, "what you need is an evil goatee.
The hippie academic look is all wrong for you." Okay, so
maybe that made Jack feel a little better but on the whole
it was a bad move. Now it looked like Jackson had decided
to abandon the ongoing quest to break the universe into itty-
bitty sparky pieces and return to the more amusing game of
whittling Jack into a personal artistic statement.

Thanks to the latest wave of doom from the machine, Jack
got to watch Jackson slide his knife out of its sheath about

twenty times like some sort of ballet of evil intent. This time, though, Jack was actually conscious, and he planned to demonstrate why it was a bad idea to zip tie someone's hands in front of them instead of behind. Assuming, of course, he didn't pass out in the process. Lightning crackled out from his broken ribs as he tensed, and he practically bit his tongue off. Fighting was going to be heaps of fun. But that's what adrenaline was for. Jackson took another step, adjusting his grip on the knife, and Jack let the pain in his ribs sharpen his attention as he narrowed his focus. He was pretty disappointed when the robot stopped and turned instead toward the door.

Theta Carter snarled something unintelligible when O'Neill dropped whatever delicate and important thing he was holding and stood up with a grin on his face to meet theta Teal'c as he ushered his two prisoners into the silo. At least Jack assumed that was theta Teal'c, since he had a gun pressed to the base of the real Carter's skull.

"Hi, kids!" O'Neill shouted and jumped down from the mirror platform. "Find the place okay? Traffic was good?"

Ignoring him, Carter and Daniel looked around for their own Jack. He leaned out a bit so they could see him better. "Got the jump on ya, huh?" Jack said, smiling bitterly at them. Carter returned his smile with a sheepish, uneasy half-grimace. He lifted his own bound hands and waggled his fingers at them. "Ah, well, it happens to the best of us." He glanced from one to the other. "So, I'm guessing getting captured was all part of the cunning plan?"

Carter lifted her chin in that defiant way she had. "Got 'em right where we want 'em, sir."

O'Neill acknowledged that with a smirk and nodded toward the entrance. "So, Teal'c. Where's your twin?"

"He was incapacitated." The robot Teal'c had Carter's P90 slung over his shoulder and Daniel's Beretta tucked into his holster. No sign of the real Teal'c's staff weapon.

O'Neill's smirk widened to an appreciative smile. "Good."

He sidled over to Carter and stood very close so that he could look down his nose at her. "So." She met his eyes with a glare Jack was sure she'd love to use on her CO some days, but her resolve faltered a little when O'Neill wrapped his hand around her bicep and squeezed hard. Her mouth fell open, but she didn't make a sound. "Samantha. Sam." Another squeeze. "Sammy. You have something of mine." This time, when he tightened his grip, Carter did wince. Jack's hand curled into a fist.

"You don't have to hurt anybody," Daniel said as he stepped forward, but he didn't get to explain why. Theta Teal'c spun him around by the arm and clocked him across the jaw with the Beretta. Daniel went down like a bag of hammers at his feet and stayed there.

"Ooh," Jackson said with an elaborate wince. "That's gonna leave a mark." He checked Jack's lunge forward by raising his knife and aiming its point at Jack's left eye. "I don't think that's a very good idea, do you?" He pushed Jack backward. Jack landed against the wall with a bone-jarring thump, and he warded off the blinding pain with a grunt.

By that time, O'Neill was working his way through the pockets of Carter's vest, taking rather more time fumbling around than Jack figured was strictly necessary. Carter struggled, but Teal'c gripped her hard by the throat and yanked her close to his chest, the muzzle of the Beretta pressed to her temple. Over by the mirror, theta Carter let loose a string of profanity that would've made a marine blush and then disappeared almost up to her shoulders into the opening at the mirror's base. A new wave of distortion expanded, doubling and tripling the population of the silo. Jack kept his eyes on his own Carter and waited it out while his teeth ground each other to nubs.

"Dammit," theta Carter snarled from inside the machine. She poked her head out and directed her frustration at O'Neill. "I need the damn control device. I've got the mirror on line but I can't stabilize the energy from this side of the mirror.

I've got to go through and do it over there."

Another wave rolled through the silo so that a dozen O'Neills smiled a dozen ugly smiles at the real Carter as he finally pulled the device out of her inside pocket and tossed it to the theta. "Since you asked so nicely."

Clawing at theta Teal'c's hand, Carter shouted, "No! Don't do it!" He yanked her back again, but that didn't stop her. "The energy can't be stabilized. It never could. The distortion waves will spread through subspace and hundreds of worlds will end up like this one. Please! I know you've seen it, too."

The robot ignored her and concentrated on slotting the control device into place in the low console beside the mirror. The floor under Jack's knees started to shudder.

"You've been talking to the old man, I see." O'Neill said with a sneer. "You gonna believe him? He's got to be about a million years old."

"Or ten," Jackson said. The tip of the knife was steady at a quarter-inch from Jack's eyeball.

"Or that. Who are you going to trust, some senile ten-year-old or the six million dollar version of yourself?" O'Neill hooked a thumb over his shoulder at theta Carter. "Anything you can do she can do better."

The floor was shaking constantly now, and on the mirror intermittent flashes of light and color chased themselves around and around inside the frame.

"She's wrong," Carter said.

"I'm not wrong," theta Carter replied in the exact same tone and that, Jack thought, was just weird, like listening to Carter hold a debate with her inner demon.

"Well, if she is," Jackson said, "we won't be around to see it. Either we'll be dead or we'll be through there." He angled his head toward the mirror, which was now gleaming like molten silver. "She says there's an infinite number of universes. At least one of them'll have all we need. And with the power pouring through there we'll have all the time we need to find it."

"And what about this universe?"

O'Neill scowled at her. "Who cares? From where we're standing, your universe sucks."

"Maybe, but it's ours," Jack said. "We'd like to keep it."

As the mirror powered up, the ghosts thronging past the silo became more substantial. Jack was sure he could hear them screaming now, and not just in his head. With a blue-white flare, the mirror's surface seemed to solidify, and inside it was not the reflected image of the silo that Jack expected but an open plain of white stone. The sky wasn't green, either, but dark and studded with stars. The star field rippled as waves of distortion chased each other through both universes. In this one, a groaning sound from outside was followed by a crash as one of the silo's twisted girders came down across the entrance like a redwood under the ax.

O'Neill left Carter with her guard and stepped up onto the platform. He didn't look happy. In fact, Jack noted, he was moving pretty slow. "Doesn't look too welcoming," O'Neill said, squinting at the scene in the mirror.

"If I can get this thing stabilized enough to recharge our power supplies and punch through to somewhere better, we won't have to be there long." Theta Carter stood and tweaked the control device. She was leaning heavily on the console.

"Good," O'Neill said and jerked his head toward the mirror. "Get it done." As she was reaching out to touch the surface of the mirror, he added, "And don't get any bright ideas about ditching us."

Her smile wasn't quite enough to instill confidence, but she followed it up with a not entirely sarcastic "No, sir," and stroked the mirror. One bright flash later, she was on the other side. She didn't even pause to wave before hunkering down to start working on the guts of the thing.

Whatever she was doing, the effects were immediate. Around the silo, the crowds surged, and over their muffled screams there was a hissing, pinging sound like sand on glass. History replaying itself in surround-sound-feel-o-vision, Jack figured. Without having to move his head too much and thereby get himself lobotomized by Jackson's knife, he could see a sliver of the sky outside the silo. The green cloud cover that was really a force field was flickering like a fluorescent bulb getting ready to fry.

"If the force field goes down, there'll be nothing to contain the flux," his Carter said in a strangled voice, still struggling against the theta Teal'c's grip on her throat. "We'll never find the gate."

At her feet, Daniel twitched and sat up abruptly, putting his hand over the bruise blooming on his jaw. One glance up at Carter and Teal'c answered his unspoken question. He started to push himself to his knees but fell back on his butt again when Teal'c's foot connected with the middle of his chest. "Okay!" he said, hands up in momentary surrender. "I'm fine here on the floor."

Another squealing groan and Jack could see the shadow of another girder peeling off the outside of the silo. A crack jerked out from under the wall. It crept and then ran across the floor to the base of the mirror platform. Half the floor heaved upward.

Jackson shifted to keep his balance and momentarily lost his bead on Jack's eye. Jack coiled for another lunge, but another wave hit and everyone multiplied, this time not in the endless reflections of facing mirrors but in a bewildering geometry of angled planes. Jack had another chance to get a look at the back of his own head. O'Neill was intent on watching his Carter through the mirror, and Jackson had his eyes on Jack, probably calculating how much force from a knife thrust would cause blindness without actually killing him. Jack's head was splitting, and he entertained the fleeting thought that a lobotomy couldn't be worse than having his brains minced by the universe at large. But, he was able to keep his eyes on his own Carter and Daniel to orient himself.

And while he was doing that he caught a glimpse of the real Teal'c. The distortions shifted and he lost sight of the

Jaffa, only to see him flicker into view in the fun house maze of mirror reflections, moving carefully, eyes intense. Jack did his best not to let his eyes track him, and he willed himself not to react when he confirmed that, yes, one of these Teal'cs was not like the others. In fact, the one he was trying hard not to look at too intently had a wicked welt on the side of his head and a supremely pissed-off expression on his face. Daniel must've seen him too, because, with a shout, he twisted around on the floor, grabbed the duplicate Teal'c's leg, and held on, drawing the robot's attention. By the time the wave passed, the real Teal'c had edged into position. He'd used Daniel's diversion to slip the Beretta out of theta Teal'c's holster and had it tucked in nice and neat at the base of the robot's skull.

He fired.

The gun was angled upward so that the shot took off the back of the robot's head. Gray goo exploded, and the robot made a shrieking sound that was not even a little human. With Carter still in his grip, he toppled stiffly forward on top of her and Daniel.

Beyond that moment, Jack didn't have much of a chance to follow the action since he was busy trying to keep Jackson from making sushi out of him. He managed to catch the downward slice of the knife on the zip ties that bound his hands, but the blade went through them and into his thigh. The floor heaved again, and Jackson stumbled backward, taking the knife with him. The arc of blood that followed the blade out of Jack's leg hung in the air for far too long before it fell. As time jerked into motion again, Jack's body went white-hot with pain. When the static cleared, he caught a glimpse of Daniel—first frozen in midair as a distortion wave caught him and then diving behind the mirror platform just ahead of the small eruptions of bullets tearing into the stone after him. O'Neill was still on his feet guarding the console while theta Carter was on the other side of the mirror, working fast, no doubt, to bring the whole universe crashing down on their heads. O'Neill's aim was off, and a few more bursts sent the real Carter and Teal'c sprinting back toward the entrance but scored no hits. O'Neill was flagging, running on fumes. Jack had half a second to grin when Teal'c got off a shot that caught O'Neill in the shoulder, but the damn robot didn't go down.

Jackson turned to look in the direction of O'Neill's shout. With a roar that was at least as much rage as pain, Jack launched himself toward him. Even slowed by draining energy, the robot was fast and got a foot up to block the tackle, catching Jack on the collarbone and knocking him sideways. Jack managed to hook the leg with his arm as he fell, taking Jackson with him. The robot got hold of Jack's fingers and twisted them back, breaking out of Jack's grip to plant his knee in Jack's gut. Now flat on his back with Jackson above him, Jack dodged another swipe of the knife and a second that rang into the stone right beside his ear. He grabbed for Jackson's wrist, but it was like trying to bend rebar with his bare hands. As they struggled, the floor canted upward and they rolled in a tangle of limbs to crash together into the mirror platform.

Not having a huge gaping wound in his leg, Jackson got his bearings first and ended up behind Jack with his knife against Jack's windpipe. He yanked Jack up onto his feet — only one of which Jack could feel anymore — and started to drag him over the lip of the platform toward the mirror. Close to the mirror, O'Neill was strafing the floor with short bursts of P90 fire. Low on ammo, Jack figured with grim satisfaction. If only the universe wouldn't implode before the ammo ran out and somebody could put a bullet in his duplicate's central processor. Jack's vision whited out each time Jackson gave him another yank, but he could still get glimpses of his Carter and Teal'c hunkered down behind a fallen girder.

"Cover me!" Jackson shouted at O'Neill.

Unfortunately for Jackson, his human shield wasn't cooperating. Even more unfortunately, his robot friend wasn't cooperating either.

The P90 fire stopped. O'Neill said, "Sorry, Danny-boy. You're on your own."

As Jackson twisted around, hauling Jack along with him, Jack caught sight of O'Neill just before the flash took him to the other side of the mirror. Once there, O'Neill raised his hand and waggled his fingers.

"Oh, crap," Jackson said faintly, and started to scramble backward with Jack, trying to keep his hostage between himself and Carter and Teal'c. He made sure his head was as close to Jack's as possible as he shouted, "You think you can make the shot, Sam? I don't." He had them fully on the platform now and dragged Jack backward toward the mirror. They were close; another step and Jack would be down the rabbit hole for real. He didn't even know if there was air over there.

Jack met Carter's eyes. "Oh, I think she can," he said.

She raised the Beretta and took the shot.

The bullet caught the robot in the eye. Jerking with the impact, Jackson then went stiff and began to fall backward, his arm still around Jack's neck and the knife still poised to take his head off. Straining against the pull, Jack worked his hand up between his neck and Jackson's fist wrapped around the hilt. The momentum of Jackson's fall carried Jack backward on top of him, unable to get free, and they bounced off of the console and onto the stone of the dais. The mirror's surface gleamed inches away from Jack's face. Way too close for comfort.

"A little help here, guys!" he growled and kicked at the stone with his good leg, trying to get some leverage against the defunct robot's grip.

It took both Teal'c and Daniel to finally pull the arm far enough away for Jack to wriggle out. He managed to get to his feet but one step proved that he wasn't going to be running any races on that leg anytime soon. It didn't look like he was going to have the luxury of waiting for a better day, though. He let Daniel ease him to the platform and sat staring into another world through the mirror while Daniel pulled a pressure bandage out of his vest and wrapped it tightly around his thigh.

"Nice work, Teal'c," Jack said, breaking off to growl at Daniel who said, "Sorry," but didn't slow down or go any more gently. Daniel was careful to keep his gaze from straying to his duplicate, who sprawled beside them staring upward with one eye. A smoking black circle was all that was left of the right eye socket, and the back of his head was a mess of gray goo and shattered components. Jack followed Daniel's lead and looked away, lifting his chin at Teal'c instead. "What's the situation out there?"

Teal'c looked briefly over his shoulder, where the force field was dancing with arcs of power and the stony plain was crowded with an endless stream of running people. "Very deteriorated," he answered. "Lieutenant Booker holds her ground as ordered but reports a riot on the plain."

"Ghosts," Daniel interjected as he offered Jack three tablets for the pain.

Teal'c nodded. "Yes. The distortions increase in frequency, and she has lost visual on this structure. I believe it will be difficult to find the Stargate if we do not go soon."

"We can't. Not yet," Carter said. She was crouching at the console working at the device. On the other side of the mirror, her reflection was doing the same. It was the big-brain grudge match of the century. "We've got to close the mirror. If we don't—"

The rest of the sentence was lost in a howl of noise, and the entire floor of the silo rose up and fell again with a crash. By reflex, Jack made a grab for Daniel as Daniel was thrown off the edge of the dais. Bad idea. Jack's broken ribs shrieked at him, and he twisted his hand in Teal'c's sleeve.

"M'okay," Daniel called from the floor below the platform. His voice was repeated over and over again as the space inside the silo splintered.

Between the planes and angles, first the boy stood watching them, and then the old man. His mouth was open, but no sound could be heard over the rushing stutter of glass shards peppering the silo and screams from outside on the plain.

Carter's "Oh, no," carried clearly.

Jack twisted back to the mirror to see theta Carter sit up with a triumphant expression on her face. The silo went completely silent. As if he'd been leaning heavily against the wall of constant noise, Jack felt a moment of vertigo when it was suddenly gone.

"I don't believe it," Carter said.

Standing beside theta Carter, O'Neill said something Jack couldn't decipher and, when the duplicate Carter turned and nodded happily at him, O'Neill lifted the P90 with a lightning-fast motion and blew a hole in her head. On the mirror platform, the human Carter jumped back, collided with Jack and started away again like he was red-hot. "Oh, my God."

"What has happened?" Teal'c asked, his voice echoing in the still, empty space.

Carter blinked at him. "He killed her."

"What happened to the machine," Jack clarified, pointing at the console and away from the body slumped on the other side of the mirror.

It took only a second for Carter to recover from seeing herself murdered in cold... well, whatever. She gathered herself and knelt back down at the opening under the console. "She did it. Stabilized the power fluctuation."

In the mirror, O'Neill kicked the defunct Carter out of the way and sat down on his haunches. He was working on something.

Jack watched. "I thought you said it couldn't be stabilized."

"It can't."

"But it is."

"Well, I know that, but..."

Grabbing Teal'c's arm again, Jack heaved himself up onto his good leg. "If we shut this thing down, can he come back through?"

Carter bobbed her head. "I suppose so." She ran her fingers over their control device still slotted into the console. "If he's got a control device on the other side. Which—" She pointed at O'Neill and the familiar beetle of stone the robot was now holding in his hand. He held it up to make sure they could get a good look at it and smiled his smug bastard smile. "—he does."

Jack sighed. "Am I gonna have to go through there and kill him?"

O'Neill stopped smiling. He stepped beyond the frame of the mirror for a moment, and when he stepped back, there were two of him. Then three. Then ten.

"Fools," the old man said, his voice like dry leaves.

From down on the floor where he was watching through the fence of their legs, Daniel said, "Uh oh," just as the wave hit and the world broke into pieces. In the alternate universe, O'Neill was just reaching toward the mirror when the blue-white flare lit up his side. They all threw their arms up to shield their eyes. Then, when the flare died, there was nothing. The plain on the other side of the mirror was empty. Silence like an indrawn breath.

"Guys," Daniel said slowly, his eyes wide and roaming the silo. "I think we should run now."

"Daniel," Jack said, "for once today I agree with you. Carter, let's go."

She looked up at him but went right back to work and in the motion splintered into a dozen pieces, each one moving just slightly slower than the one before. "The control device," she said, and her words seemed to stutter too. "Have to shut it down."

Everything was shaking now, and another girder squealed as it tore away from the silo. Cracks started at the floor and chased each other up the silo's walls.

"We gotta go!" Jack shouted over the rising howl of wind. Awkwardly striding over to her, he grabbed her arm and pulled her out of the way, then turned to Teal'c. "Burn it!"

The staff blast turned the control device and half of the console to slag. The mirror flickered and then flared again, blue-white with a light that Jack could feel like a physical force. A shove from an invisible hand propelled him backward off the platform and into Daniel. He managed to untangle himself and get to his feet as the mirror went dark.

But it was too late. The blue-white light was filling the silo.

He might've shouted at the team to run, but he couldn't hear his voice. It was as if the light itself was noise. Teal'c practically lifted him off his feet as they all turned and ran, scrambling over the fallen girder across the entrance—Teal'c pushing him from one side and Carter and Daniel pulling on the other—and burst headlong into the fleeing crowd. None of the refugees was substantial enough to disturb the debris cloud, but every shard that Teal'c batted away from them as he led the way, half-dragging and half-carrying Jack with one arm, shattered and howled in agony. Jack ducked his head and kept moving. He looked at the ground immediately in front of them and not at the panicked people running with him. There was no way to know how far the gate was from the silo, or even if it would still be where they left it, so they followed the flow of the stampede. Daniel panted behind him with Carter on their six. At one point Teal'c lost his grip, and Jack did a face plant. Daniel and Carter picked him up, Daniel slinging one of Jack's arms over his shoulder and Carter taking the other. Every step sent flares of red across his vision, and every breath ground his ribs together.

Above them, the sky was convulsing and the force field was a maelstrom of livid colors.

"Not much time," Carter said. "The field is collapsing."

Ahead of them, the gate loomed up, at first only a few steps away, and then just a pinprick on a distant horizon.

A burst of static from Teal'c's radio, and Booker shouted, "We see you, Colonel! We're right here at twelve o'clock!"

"Wait for it," Carter breathed, her eyes wide. "Just wait."

They stood swaying with Jack's almost dead weight between them as wave after wave of distortion crashed over them. Finally, the gate was there again. Right there. Booker and the rest of SG-3 were on the steps, almost lost in the crowds swarming up to and through a ghostly event horizon. The ghosts trampled each other, shoved each other away, and climbed over the fallen bodies.

Carter stumbled over to meet Booker at the DHD and stabbed at the glyphs. The event horizon—a real one this time—exploded outward just as the world went dark.

"Force field's down," Carter said in the sudden silence.

There were no stars.

A strong gust of wind buffeted them from behind as Daniel and Teal'c helped Jack up the steps. At the event horizon, they turned to see the sphere of energy expanding from the silo, almost invisible against the black sky except for a gaslight-blue nimbus that marked its leading edge. The last thing Jack saw before Daniel dragged him backward through the gate was the boy in his oversized uniform, alone on the empty plain.

PART SIX

horror vacui
fear of empty places

CHAPTER SIXTEEN

SGC
November 5, 2002

Daniel walked down the wide SGC corridors behind Jack and tried not to hold his hands out like he was ready to catch him. When Jack shot him an irritated look over his shoulder, Daniel stuffed his hands in his pockets and raised his eyebrows. "What?"

"Quit hovering, Daniel. I've been walking on my own since I was a year old." As if to prove it, Jack lengthened his stride and the limp smoothed out. At the same time, the muscles in his neck seemed to wind tighter with the effort of looking relaxed.

Daniel didn't blame him for playing it tough if it meant getting out of the infirmary. Three days flat on his back had made Jack a very unhappy boy, and an unhappy Jack meant an unhappy Fraiser. So maybe she'd protested a little less than she might have when Jack staged a not-so-clandestine escape from captivity.

"Fine!" Fraiser had thrown up her hands in resignation. But as Daniel passed by her in pursuit of his CO, she'd pressed a bottle of blue pills into his hand. "Just make sure he takes them, okay? And bring him back before you leave to get the dressings changed." He'd nodded, but she'd caught his sleeve before he could bolt. "And by leave I mean go home, not off-world."

Daniel had fully intended to drive Jack back to his place and barricade him inside his house, but six hours and four blue pills later, when they were finally on the way to the locker room to change, the klaxon had started its howling.

Harriman had announced an unscheduled off-world activation and so much for good intentions. For a guy who'd been stabbed in the leg a few days ago, Jack was pretty quick on the about-face back toward the elevator. Daniel didn't even bother pointing out that the locker room was thataway or that Fraiser was possibly as scary as Jack and more likely to kick him in the ass for violation of orders. No point. They were already in the elevator. Jack had already thumbed the button for level 28 and was staring at the closed doors, still looking ever so relaxed. Except for the deep notch between his eyebrows that told an entirely different story.

Daniel leaned on the rail on the side of the elevator, folded his arms, and contemplated the bandage across the side and back of Jack's neck. He was going to ask the question, even if it did mean taking his life into his hands. He wanted to see the marks, to know what the theta Jackson had written there. Curiosity was his thing so, if Jack wasn't feeling generous, at least Daniel would go out being true to his nature.

Daniel opened his mouth. Jack's right eye twitched. Daniel closed his mouth.

On the upside, Daniel figured that with the broken ribs and the hinky leg, Jack wouldn't be able to catch him if Daniel hit the corridor at a dead run, so he waited until they passed level 26 and asked, "Did Janet figure out what the marks were, once she got them cleaned up?"

Jack's jaw set. "Latin," he said. He didn't look at Daniel, but took his tablet and scribbled something. He handed the pad back as the doors opened and stepped off the elevator without looking back.

Daniel glanced down at the phrase, mentally supplying the letters the theta hadn't had time to carve. *Cave canem:* beware of the dog. His stomach twisted at the implication, the message straight from his inner id — a repudiation of the friendship and trust Daniel had worked so hard and so long to build with Jack, a slur against Jack's character, most of all. One Daniel didn't believe, not even when he disagreed with

Jack's methods. He hated to think Jack might wonder if he thought it privately,

But he knew they'd never talk about this particular message, or any of the things it might mean. Talking wasn't how Jack dealt with things.

He scratched the words out and caught up to Jack at the stairs to the control room, wanting to offer some indication he understood. What came out was, "Janet said they shouldn't scar."

Jack's thin smile had no humor in it. "Aren't I lucky."

Sam tipped her head back to offer Daniel a quick smile and then sobered as General Hammond came down the stairs from his office, Major Davis on his heels.

"Data burst only, sir, from the Tok'ra," Harriman reported. "No travelers."

Teal'c was standing at ease behind Harriman—who, Daniel noted, hunched his shoulders a little under that shadow—and watched with his usual placid interest as the response teams moved into place and then, at Hammond's command, broke formation and filed out again. Daniel wondered how many holes Teal'c was counting in their defenses. And that made him wonder, as he often did, how Teal'c organized his view of the world, if it was as single-minded as Daniel thought it was. Then he wondered if Teal'c ever daydreamed. And that led him back—as most trains of thought did these days—to the duplicates.

"What?" Jack said, nudging him with an elbow. "You have that look."

"What look?"

"The look that makes me nervous."

"Oh." Daniel licked his lips. "I was thinking about daydreaming."

Jack's soft snort didn't come off half as disdainful as he probably meant it to be, and he was smiling a little as he shook his head. "Only you could think *about* daydreaming, Daniel." They watched Sam unpacking the data from the burst on her monitor. There was a lot of stuff there. Jack waited for another minute. Apparently this was going to take a while. "What about daydreaming?"

"I just wondered if they—the duplicates—if they day-dreamed."

"What would be the purpose?" Teal'c asked.

"I don't know." Daniel thought about it while Hammond ordered Sam and Harriman to contact him when they'd finished unpacking. He and Davis headed back up the stairs to wait for the report. "But," Daniel went on, "there had to be a reason the original designer of the duplicating technology preserved the more messy human functions, like dreaming or emotions, when it would be more efficient to edit them out." He shrugged. "I don't know. Maybe fuzzy thinking is what makes us better than machines."

"I'll try to remember that when you're making your fifth circuit around the mulberry bush in your next briefing," Jack said and started up the stairs to the conference room. "Give us a shout, Carter," he said as he disappeared around the bend, only the slightest hitch in his step and a barely perceptible tightness in his voice.

"Perhaps," Teal'c said after a thoughtful silence, "there is something more than efficiency and function to be considered." He went back to gazing at the now empty gate-room and the closed iris. "This is the difference between a man and a slave."

An hour later, they were still waiting for Sam to crunch the data from the Tok'ra report. Hammond and Davis were still behind closed doors working out the details of the mop-up operation, and Daniel was sitting across from Jack at the conference table. He'd filled two pages of a legal pad with questions he wanted to forward to the brains over at Area 51 regarding the duplicates, should any of the outstanding robots be recovered. He didn't figure any of his questions would get more than a token response from the usual suspects, but there was at least one researcher, Dr. Levine, who could probably be coaxed into entertaining a discussion of the more philosophical side of the duplicate issue.

Jack had his sore leg propped up on a chair and was leaning sideways in his own, concentrating very hard on inventing the best paper airplane ever. He'd already commandeered most of Daniel's notepad and if it came to it, Daniel was considering enlisting Teal'c's help in defending the last few precious sheets. Of course, Jack could pull rank, so Daniel would have to come up with something more compelling than habitual obedience to the chain of command to win Teal'c to his side. For his part, Teal'c was at the observation window, doing what Teal'c did, which was to wait in perfect stillness with no protest whatsoever.

Daniel hunched over his notepad protectively and filled another page with questions he'd probably never get answers for. The gate activated once for a scheduled return—all of SG-12 upright, walking and accounted for, Teal'c reported—and once for some kind of communication, no travelers either way. The fourteenth most perfect airplane ever had just spiraled across the table and bounced off the top of Daniel's head when General Hammond and Major Davis came out of the general's office and met Sam as she came up the stairs. Jack scrambled to gather up the evidence of his aeronautical underperformance as everyone got settled, and Sam dimmed the lights and activated the view screen.

"We're going to have to spend a fair amount of time analyzing the data from the Tok'ra's burst, but we've got a preliminary report," Sam said, pulling up an image of a star field marked with a grid in glowing green. "As they promised, the Tok'ra diverted one of their ships to the vicinity of the planet of He-They. We've designated it P49-181, or Gauss." A small smile surfaced, giving her dimples. "After one of the inventors of non-Euclidian geometry." When nobody seemed to be particularly moved by the wit of geeks, she made a little, very familiar shrug of resignation and got on with the briefing. "That's the planet where the theta team activated the quantum mirror and a device we think was designed to harness energy from the collision between nearby universes. Between branes, as they're called in M-theory."

Jack made a show of trying to get his leg into a more comfortable position. Sam smiled an acknowledgment of the not-so-subtle warning, left behind the finer points of theory, and stepped up to the screen. Her body was marked out in squares by the projected grid as she circled a finger around a conspicuously blank space. "These are the coordinates of the planet."

"I don't see any planet," Jack said.

"Neither do the Tok'ra sensors."

"So, what? It blew up?"

Sam shook her head. "There's no debris of any kind. In fact there's nothing there. And I mean nothing. Nothing at all."

"That's space for ya."

"I don't think you understand, sir. Even the emptiest space you can find in our universe has *something* in it. Radiation, at least. This—" She poked the blankness in the centre of the grid with the end of her remote. "—this is absolutely, completely empty. There are no readings at all."

Davis glanced around the table and opened his hands with a brief, confused grin. "So... it's just been erased?"

"I don't know," Sam said. She hit a button on her remote and the star field shifted its orientation, bringing another nearby star system into focus. "The Tok'ra released a probe and almost immediately lost all telemetry. However, a few hours later they picked up the subspace signal and followed it here, to a planet in a system just slightly less than fifteen light years away." The magnification jumped and jumped again, and a bright moon came into view around the curve of a green-and-blue planet. Sam clicked through a few more similar views until she came to a ground-level shot. A phosphorescent sea stretched all the way to the horizon, where the moon hung, round and heavy, in a gap between silvery clouds. "A minor Goa'uld did a general survey of this area of space a few years ago looking for planets suitable for settlement of human and Jaffa populations. This one was flagged but eventually rejected because the surface conditions weren't optimal. The Tok'ra have access to that Goa'uld's database. They sent this image."

"Pretty," Jack said flatly, like he knew what was coming.

"This is the planet where the Tok'ra found the probe. It *was* a planet with an oxygen atmosphere and surface water, bacterial life forms, some algae, which accounts for the green." She clicked her remote again, and the image shifted back into space where the same moon and planet glowed against the black, only this time both bodies reflected the distant sunlight away from their barren, stony surfaces. "This is the planet now. The Tok'ra located the probe *inside a mountain*. There is no life there now at all. Nothing."

She left the image on the screen and sat down at the table next to Teal'c.

"You think the events on 181 did this?" Hammond asked.

"We can't say for sure, sir, but it can't be coincidence that the probe sent into the phenomenon ended up there."

"So, it's like a wormhole?" Daniel asked, groping mentally for all the things he'd absorbed about wormhole theory listening to Sam over the years. "It transported the probe."

"Initially, we considered the notion it might be a something like that, maybe an intermittently stable connection left when the planet collapsed. But that doesn't seem to be the case. Although we say that nothing escapes the event horizon of a black hole, that's not entirely true. Even though the singularity itself is invisible because its enormous gravity traps everything, even light, we can tell it's there because of the way its gravity deforms the space around it. Plus, the uncertainty principle means that quantum particles will leak out past the event horizon, not to mention the radiation shed by matter being pulled into the singularity. If there was a singularity there, we should be able to detect at least the ambient effects on the space around it. But there's nothing. Whatever this is, it's not space, at least not any kind we're familiar with."

Daniel picked up his pen again and clicked the point in and out as he thought it through. "If what the old man—or whatever he was—showed us on the planet is true, the first cataclysm had pretty far-flung effects."

Sam nodded. "And the effects may not be synchronic. If space is distorted, time likely is too. We saw that on the planet, the way that the past events were folded into the present. We may never know the scope of the damage. We may be looking at the effects right now and not be able to trace them back to the origin there, either to the first or the second event a few days ago. If in fact there were two, and we didn't just fall into the first one."

"Gah," Jack said and pressed the heels of his hands to his eyes. "I hate time travel paradoxes." He dropped his hands heavily to the table and scowled at Sam like tying knots in time was a personal hobby of hers. "No more time travel paradoxes. That's it. Nada. Got it?"

"Yes, sir." She waited for him to get more comfortable before bringing up another image, this one familiar: a scored plain of white stone. "However, we do know of one planet that had a direct link to 181."

"Dunamis," Teal'c said. "Yagwen's and Asha's planet."

The pen dropped out of Daniel's hand onto his note pad. "*That's* Yagwen's planet?"

"Yes. After we got the burst from the Tok'ra, we opened the gate to try to download some telemetry from the MALP we left to monitor the fault in the cave there. The MALP was mostly fried, but we managed to get the camera up and running again, and it sent this footage." The MALP's camera panned across the empty plain. At the far right they could still make out the gate and the forest beyond it, looking like autumn had come early but otherwise still standing. "The cave, the ravine, and the surrounding trees are all gone, but as you can see, the damage isn't nearly as extensive."

"Extensive enough," Major Davis said, looking appalled.

Sam nodded her agreement. "The upside is that this suggests that the effects might be attenuated, that every point of contact won't face the same degree of disturbance. But look here." She fast-forwarded to a reverse shot of the plain. There in the middle of the frame was a woman in white robes, slumped on her knees and almost invisible against the stone. The beads still screened her eyes. Beyond her, the rest of the acolytes were huddled together, vulnerable-looking. The MALP's microphone was damaged, but Daniel didn't need it to imagine the sound of their keening voices.

"It's Asha," he said.

Hammond took a deep breath, considering. "Take a med team," he ordered.

The villagers on Asha's planet weren't taking any chances this time. The few who had been near the gate when it opened scattered before the event horizon even disengaged. Daniel closed his mouth and swallowed his greeting and declarations of peace and interplanetary love.

Jack watched the people rabbiting into the sparse cover of the trees and muttered, "This is getting so old." He turned to the medical team and their marine escort. "Just stay by the gate until we get a read on the situation." Before he turned away to lead his team off the platform, he added for Fraiser's benefit, "And don't worry, doc, if there's any running or jumping to be done, I'll get Teal'c to do it for me."

The scene was pretty much as the MALP had shown them. To the west, the forest of aspenlike picket trees was as it was before, only the silvery leaves seemed to have tarnished to a brittle gray. Daniel could hear the rustle and rattle of the dry foliage shifting in the wind. Above the trees, the sky was still bright with the setting sun, but overhead it was deepening to evening. Their shadows rippled across the grass, pointing in the direction of the village and what had been the ravine. Now there was nothing in that direction but white stone, as if the land had been scraped clean, a knife on bone. The village itself was gone. He hoped that the people had seen it coming, that they'd been warned, that they'd fled. He also hoped there were many more of them hiding in the trees than he'd seen when they arrived.

In his mind, the blue corona of the shock wave expanded against the black sky. For a second, ghosts pressed against him. He blinked hard and turned to Teal'c. "Did you—?" But Teal'c only tilted his head, curious. "Never mind," Daniel said. "Just my imagination." Still, he felt the pull of exodus dragging against him like an undertow.

By unspoken agreement, they stopped where the grass gave way abruptly to stone. At the seam, the grass was burned black. About a hundred yards head of them, burnished a little by the angled late-day light, the MALP squatted on the stone. It was listing drunkenly to one side.

Sam said, "Seems pretty stable," and pulled out her binoculars to sweep the horizon. "And the forest starts up again on the perimeter. I'd say we're looking at a disturbance zone about twenty-five klicks square. A pass with a UAV can give us a more accurate picture."

"A local apocalypse then," Jack said. "How nice for them." He stepped off the grass and paused, waiting. When nothing weird happened, he set off again.

It was getting dark—the sun behind them was balanced on the pointed tops of the trees—but there was more to it than that. Daniel thought of the starless sky on 181 and tipped his head to look upward. It was just a sky like a hundred others he'd seen. He lifted his hand and turned it in the slanting rays of sunset. Plain as day. So maybe it was his imagination too, the sense that he was groping his way through a lightless place.

Jack's voice prodded him into a jog. "Get the lead out, Daniel. It's getting dark."

Or maybe not just *his* imagination.

Maybe it was because of the encroaching darkness—real

or illusory—that they almost tripped over Asha before they saw her. On the empty plain, she and her acolytes should have been conspicuous, but Daniel had to peer closely, following Teal'c's pointing arm to make them out. As the team got closer, the women, about a dozen of them, seemed to coalesce out of the stone itself, their heads turning toward the sound of SG-1's arrival like the figures of a frieze coming to life. They were bleached, all of them, a dead, antique white—clothing, hair, even the bead veils that hung before their eyes.

"Who's there?" Asha called, rising to face them obliquely.

"It's okay. It's just us," Daniel answered.

Her head jerked in the direction of his voice. "Who?"

"Um." Daniel turned to Sam and her frown was a reflection of his own. He stepped closer to Asha but at the sound of his boots scraping the stone she lifted her hands warily to ward him off. "It's okay. It's me, Daniel Jackson. You remember?"

Her hands fell from their defensive posture and she straightened to her full height. "Yes. I remember." She began to twist the sleeve of her robe tightly around her fingers. "The others. They are here, too?"

Daniel nodded and then, realizing his mistake, said aloud, "Yes, we're all here." He waved the rest of his team forward and whispered to them, "Say something so she knows where you are."

After they'd each said an awkward hello and Asha had turned her head toward them, as if pinning them in the landscape by their voices, she nodded. "You all survived, then, the danger you spoke of."

"Yes, we're mostly in one piece. Asha, what happened h—"

"Yagwen is dead." When Daniel didn't answer she turned in his general direction and said it again. This time, the words seemed to draw all the energy from her, and she slumped to her knees before Daniel could catch her. He knelt beside her on the stone. "She broke into a thousand pieces." With that, she held up her arms and the sleeves of her robe fell back to her elbows. Her skin was flecked with the same marks, points of frostbite, that Daniel and the rest of them had brought back from 181. "I felt her shatter." She let her hands fall to her lap and sat staring blindly. "He-They called her, and she went to him. And…" Behind her, the other acolytes cried together softly as her silence grew, and Daniel's memory filled it with an expanding sphere of nothing, limned in blue. "We see nothing now. There is nothing," Asha finished, her voice a fine, colorless thread stretched taut, almost inaudible in the stillness.

Jack stepped away and keyed his radio. "SG-one-niner to evac unit."

Over the murmur of his exchange with Fraiser, Teal'c asked Asha, "Why remain in this desolate place? If you have been blinded, why do you not seek assistance?"

She lifted her face to him and the veil of beads parted to reveal the opaque whiteness of her eyes. "They fear us. Our people. They will not let us leave this place." She bowed her head again and, after a long moment, whispered, "We are very thirsty."

"There's help on the way," Sam told her as she dropped her pack and detached her canteen.

Fraiser and her team were visible, silhouettes against the livid sky.

When Daniel tried to guide Asha's hands to the canteen, she pulled away. "We do not want your help."

"I know," Daniel said, his own hands falling to his knees. "But you need it."

CHAPTER SEVENTEEN

NID Beta Site (P4H-268)
November 8, 2002

"Mendez," Siebert said, drawing Carlos's attention without so much as a hint of deference. "We're in orbit."

Carlos sat up on the floor, where he was wedged between two stacks of cartons, trying and failing to sleep. Maybe Siebert's usual drummed-in military deference was a casualty of the evacuation, or maybe it was just because they were all irritable and annoyed after their little jaunt across the cosmos in a ship barely big enough to contain them and all their junk. Didn't matter much. He stretched, popped his neck, and rose easily to his feet. At the back of the hold, the two gamma robots were watching him, tracking his movements with their eyes like some kind of creepy living sculptures.

He moved closer to the cockpit, glanced out at the planet the NID had chosen to house its secondary site. Shimmering clouds drifted across the broad continents. "Set us down between the gate and the facility."

Siebert nodded and placed her hands around the controls. Within a minute, they had broken through the atmosphere. Clouds streaked by and gave way to sky, and the half-constructed backup facility with its generator sheds, skeletons of buildings, and Quonset huts peeked up from the lone cleared area among thickets of trees and winding streams. They hadn't planned on needing it so soon. Carlos had hoped never to need it at all, but here they were.

"Sir." Kutrell stirred from his perch on the only crate big enough to hold his large frame comfortably. "Will replacement personnel be arriving once we've cleared the perimeter here?"

Carlos glanced back at the gamma Carter and Jackson, his free labor for the next little while, until the facility was ready to house personnel. "Looking for a vacation, Kutrell?" he asked, one corner of his mouth curling up in a smile.

Kutrell flashed an easy grin. "No, sir. This job suits me fine."

"I'll bet it does." Carlos dug a finger in under his loosened collar and rubbed an itch. "Good thing, because you're it, for now."

"Yes, sir." Satisfied, Kutrell adjusted his weapon across his lap and pulled a leg up beneath him, looking for all the world like he was ready to eat someone for breakfast. Carlos was just about that hungry himself. But there were supplies at the site, enough to tide them over until they could reestablish communications and arrange for a delivery.

He'd be able to feed some power to the gamma duplicates, too. Their preservation had become important to the survival of the few personnel he had left, so that had to be a priority.

The minute Siebert set the ship down, Carlos sent his ex-marines into the open to clear the gate and their temporary shelters. Peterson lingered near Carlos, pacing nervously around the ship as if he expected to be scared back onto it at any moment. "Shouldn't you start unpacking?" Carlos asked him finally, eyebrows raised. Peterson shot him a grateful look and clambered back on the ship.

"All clear, sir," Siebert said, coming up to his left, the others trailing behind her. "Looks like there's nothing here but us and some birds."

"Good." Carlos nodded to Kutrell, who was coming around the corner, bringing up the rear. "Gate in good order?"

"Appears to be. DHD looks fine."

"Siebert, set up communications and gate-dialing protocols. Make it your priority." She nodded and climbed into the ship. "McDonald, Pitchner, Kutrell, use the duplicates to help you set up their power source. Get the generator online and get us some power."

"Will do." Kutrell crooked a hand at the others. They followed him on board, then streamed back out again a moment later with boxes in their arms. A few seconds later, the duplicates emerged, carrying heavy pieces of machinery twice as big as their torsos as if they were made of fluff. They gave him an appraising look as they passed by, but neither of them spoke.

Carlos climbed back into the ship, where Peterson was wielding his familiar clipboard, having apparently pulled it out from where he'd stashed it. "It'll only take me a few minutes to get power up," he said, and it took Carlos a second to realize he was speaking of the duplicates, not the facility.

"You should get on that then." He gestured to the pilot's chair. "I'm going to grab some quick shut-eye. You can find me here if you need me."

Peterson nodded, absorbed with whatever scribbles he was making on the clipboard.

Carlos eased into the chair and blinked slowly. His eyes were gritty, as if ten pounds of sand had settled in his eyelids. From the front viewport he could see the stream defining the far edge of the new compound. Probably cold, but he was betting it'd be the best bath he'd ever had. He'd get to that. Right after his nap.

It seemed he'd barely closed his eyes when a familiar sound wrenched him fully awake: chevrons engaging, a Stargate spinning to life. He shoved up from his chair, stumbling to the back of the ship to shout, "Siebert! Kutrell!"

No one answered.

His Beretta was secured underneath his suit jacket, which was in a rumpled heap in the far corner of the hold. He retrieved it and made his way in a low, loping run to the corner of the main building, a perfect vantage point to see the gate—a gate without an iris, since this was not yet a fully functional base. Which, clearly, was turning out to be a liability. The Carter duplicate was standing in front of the DHD,

Jackson behind her, watching as the wormhole opened.

Mendez raised the 9mm and stepped out into the open. "Get away from the gate," he said, low. He kept his distance. They were much faster than he was, and he figured there was a better than average chance they'd either disabled or killed the rest of his people.

Carter turned to him, an amused expression on her face. She made no move toward him, and Jackson didn't even bother to turn. His back remained to Carlos as he gazed into the shimmering wormhole. It winked out suddenly, and Carlos breathed a soft sigh of relief. The last thing he needed was another debacle like the thetas.

"You should put that down," Carter said, pointing at the 9mm.

"You should explain why you were activating the gate," he answered, edging slightly closer. He raised his voice, pulling the sound from deep in his belly. "Siebert! Kutrell!"

"They're not going to answer," Jackson said, ever so casual. His back was still to Carlos.

A shiver went down Carlos's spine. "What have you done?"

Carter looked as if she planned to answer, but just then, the Stargate began to activate, spinning as chevrons snapped into place. She waited until the sixth chevron locked, then said, "We haven't done anything you wouldn't do."

The wormhole burst to life, and O'Neill and Teal'c stepped through—his missing gammas. They moved leisurely down the steps, stopping only when they'd reached Carter and Jackson. "You have it?" O'Neill asked Carter.

"Yes, sir. All the necessary equipment was moved whole during the evacuation."

"We have found a suitable location," Teal'c said.

"Let's get a move on then." O'Neill turned, and as if just noticing Carlos, he frowned. "Carter? Why is he still alive?"

"We haven't gotten around to him yet, sir." Carter gave Carlos a dismissive glance. "We assessed him as a less immediate threat."

"Hmm." O'Neill reached for his own sidearm, which pushed Carlos into action. He sprinted low across the short distance to the building, darted around the corner and burst through the unsecured doors of the main facility, looking for a more suitable weapon. The duplicates could certainly be stopped, though it would take a significant and concentrated burst of ammo to do so. To the left of the door, most of the power source equipment the duplicates would need was stacked neatly, as if someone was packing for a trip. And the duplicating equipment was smashed, all those fine, mysterious components crushed and twisted. The incubation unit was torn open and all the internal connections looked like they'd been fried with a blowtorch. Goddamned duplicates. He swore under his breath and sprinted across the room and down the corridors, scanning for his people.

Kutrell was sprawled in the hallway, half in and half out of what was to have been the new duplication room, his face on the wrong side of his body. So that was why no gunfire had awakened him; the duplicates had been snapping necks. Carlos sucked in a slow breath and glanced into the duplicating room. Peterson was crouched behind one of his consoles, looking pretty much like he'd wet his pants. Complete terror distorted his features.

"Hide," Carlos said, in a stage whisper. "Now."

Peterson stood on shaky legs and made a run for it, shoving past Carlos and beating feet down the corridor toward some unknown hiding place. Good for him. Carlos wasn't going to get off that easy. He tucked his Beretta into the back of his pants and snatched up Kutrell's P90. Behind him, quick footsteps—the duplicates. He stepped over Kutrell's body and retreated into the lab.

When Teal'c pushed open the doors, Carlos hit him with a constant stream of gunfire, strafing him even as Teal'c approached with heavy steps, determined. The duplicate was only a foot away when it jerked, twisted sideways, and fell in a heap on the floor, oozing that gray goo that lubricated their insides.

Carlos backed toward the unfinished console and away from the duplicate, just in case. He had less than half a clip left. For a moment, he considered trying to negotiate for his life and Peterson's, but he didn't have a thing left to bargain with. Carter had already taken all the technology—duplicating and power equipment. That had been their strategy, he guessed: play nice and maneuver into a position to take what they needed from the inside.

Smart. But then again, they were walking computers, so it wasn't such a stretch for them to plan ahead.

O'Neill stuck his face into the open doorway, apparently unafraid of having it blown off. He stepped into the open, and Carlos raised his weapon, fired the few token bullets he had left. One caught O'Neill in the shoulder, another four in the belly and chest. The duplicate froze in mid-step, then continued slowly on into the room, halting beside Teal'c's body. "What a waste," he said, looking down at the destroyed duplicate.

"You're next," Carlos said.

"No," O'Neill said. "You are."

The last thing Carlos saw was a blur of fire from the dark barrel of O'Neill's Beretta.

NID Beta Site (P4H-268)
November 10, 2002

"I'm just saying," Daniel started, and then the wormhole took him. On the other side, he continued his sentence. "—there's no reason they have to be destroyed."

"Out of our hands," Jack said, stepping to the left to allow Carter and Teal'c to come through, as well as the three teams of marines behind them—the cleanup crew. They'd managed to persuade their mole to give up most of his vital information, which led them to this secondary base, though Jack had no real expectation of finding anything with the program so compromised.

They'd pop up again somewhere else. The NID were government cockroaches. They could survive anything.

He glanced over at Daniel. "What, no arguments about sentience?"

Daniel's gaze lingered pointedly on the healing wounds covering Jack's neck. "Not today."

They followed the marines across the open field toward what looked like the main building. A few smaller buildings were scattered across the compound, and Daniel could make out a couple more in the trees where there was an intermittent glimmer of water — a stream or a small lake. The place had a half-finished look to it and off to the right of the main building, a supply shack gaped open, no door, and empty inside. He double-timed it to catch up with his team and with them followed the marines into the building, down a long hallway and through what looked like it was going to be a lab. The consoles — the ones that had been unpacked — were dark. Carter stopped and gave them a cursory once-over, then said to Daniel, "Any duplicates we find will be taken to Area 51, like every other piece of technology."

"Interesting way to put that," Daniel said, but there was no heat behind it.

"It remains to be seen if any of the additional duplicates will respond to the summons," Teal'c said. "We must assume they have exhausted their power. If they have not, it is unlikely they will return to face certain destruction."

"Maybe they have faith in us," Daniel said.

"They know what we'll do," Jack said. "Would you come back?"

"Point taken." Daniel cleared his throat.

"Sir." Colonel Souter rounded the corner into the lab, one prisoner in tow. The guy had a round face and pale eyes that blinked at Daniel through the cracked lenses of his glasses.

He looked like he couldn't decide if he was afraid to be captured or relieved to be rescued. "We found him hiding in the head."

Jack jerked a thumb back toward the gate. "Save him a spot on the trip home."

"Yes, sir." Souter dragged him by.

"Lab coat," Carter said. "Scientist."

"Yes, that makes it all better," Jack said drily. He lifted his P90 and pointed toward the door and the rest of the building beyond it. "Might as well take a look around. See if we want to buy."

They proceeded steadily down the wide hallway, Carter flanking Jack, Daniel and Teal'c at the rear. Jack sighed once or twice, and finally said, "I'm going to be glad when there are no more of me trying to take over the galaxy."

"Won't we all, sir?" Carter said brightly. Daniel made a sound between a snicker and a cough.

"SG-one-niner." Vara this time. His voice was thin through static. "Sir, there's something here you should see. Right away, sir."

"Your twenty?" Jack turned, followed Teal'c at point back down the corridor.

"Off the rear entryway, sir. Another lab. To the left, and then the right."

"On our way."

It was a short jaunt, and aside from themselves and their lone prisoner, the place was empty. Vara was standing near the lab, over the body of a burly operative with a broken neck. He nodded toward the room, then pushed open the doors and let them swing back.

In the middle of the room, one of the Teal'c duplicates was sprawled in a puddle of gray goo. Not far away, an NID operative—or what had been one, before he'd been shot—was crumpled beneath a long, low console of smashed and disassembled equipment. Jack looked to Carter, who gave a tight nod of confirmation. This had likely been the duplicating technology. Jack stepped closer. The empty eyes of the agent seemed focused on some faraway place where all this had made sense, and his neatly striped, blood-dotted blue tie was curled under.

"Sir," Vara called, from his left. "Over here."

Jack turned.

"Huh," Daniel said, in that uniquely understated way he had.

Across the room, Jack, version 2 point whatever, sat motionless in a desk chair, legs crossed, 9mm still clasped in his hand. A piece of paper was across his chest, one corner of it folded down into his pocket, a hasty method of pinning it in place. Scrawled across it in Daniel's overly neat handwriting:

You're welcome.

Jack lifted the paper and handed it to Daniel. Beneath the paper above the pocket of the duplicate's shirt was the only identifying label, the stitched designation: GAMMA.

"Guess that solves that problem," Jack said, glancing back over his shoulder at the NID agent. Whoever he was, one less roach to propagate the agenda next time around. "Thanks to…me."

"Yes," Daniel said. He stared at the handwriting, then looked at the duplicate's lifeless face. The duplicate had been damaged, but he didn't look like he'd fallen from those injuries, taken down in the heat of battle. He looked at peace. Like he'd sat down and waited quietly for his death. When Daniel raised his eyes to Jack, a frown creased his brow. "But where are the rest of the gammas?"

EPILOGUE

emeritus

NID Primary "Hydra" Project Site, Perseus (P66-421)
November 21, 2002

The base had never been busy at the best of times, but now that Piper was the only person left—the only name on the list of "essential personnel"—the place was completely dead. The unofficial decommission of the post had come fast and with explicit instructions from Mendez as he beat feet to get to the *tel'tak*: get your crap together and get on the transport. Everyone but Piper, of course; someone had to stay behind to manage any last-minute issues. The two tech guys who glued together Piper's equipment when it went down had practically broken their arms to cram all their little gadgets into their foam crates and get the hell out of there. Ditto the ex-military bruisers whose job it was to make sure nothing went on unless the brass approved of it.

Mendez hadn't seemed to have any problem leaving him there alone. Mr. NID had told him what to monitor, and for how long, and what frequency to make the extraction call to the beta site on. Piper had dutifully taken notes. Good thing, because they'd only left him with two weeks' supply of food. He supposed he was lucky to have that much.

He swiveled around in the ancient metal desk chair. The green seat was covered in duct tape, and the central spring protested every time he sat forward. *Creak*, creak. *Creak*, creak. It echoed off the walls. He ran a hand across the communications array, dozens of dedicated channels, each dutifully broadcasting an automatic return call. All his teams, his responsibilities, were dead—destroyed, Mendez would remind him—or off the grid. No one was going to answer.

Creak, creak.

The coffeepot with its liquid gold was in the break room, which had been the broom closet, just down the hall. Piper got up with a sigh and loped across the room toward the double doors. Quonset hut decor abounded: metal walls, concrete, and wide square windows, with the occasional poster to break the monotony. A pretty girl looking over her shoulder, black hair draped just so over a sexy tattoo; the French Riviera at sunset; a US Air Force recruitment poster, improved with graffiti.

He took them down as he went and rolled them into a cylinder, then deposited them in the trashcan that no one was around to empty.

The coffee was burned into the bottom of the glass pot, but that didn't stop him from pouring a cup, sugaring it up, and taking a long sip. "Ugh," he said, scrunching his face at the bitterness. He scratched his head, looked around the room at the tables without chairs, the randomness of abandoned equipment.

It was more cheerful in his little comms center.

On the way back up the hall, he thought maybe he should have waited to take down the posters. Gray metal didn't exactly make for a fabulously cheery view.

As he neared the comms center, a faint beeping pulled him into a jog—old habit. He rounded the corner and stopped dead, staring. There was a signal. His chair squawked in protest as he landed in the seat with a thud and focused on the signal, ignoring the coffee he'd sloshed all over himself. It only took him a second to zero in, to narrow down, and then...

"Come in, Piper, are you out there?"

Piper shoved the headset down over his ears, tuned to

the gamma comms channel. "I read you," he said quickly.

"Piper! Stand by, I, uh, I have quite a story to tell you."

Piper grinned and slung spilled coffee from his damp hand. "I'll bet you do, Daniel. I'll just bet you do."

ACKNOWLEDGMENTS

We owe a tremendous debt of gratitude to our first readers, whose notes and excellent suggestions helped us sort out and revise our rough drafts: Ellen Ross, Terry McGarry, and Jeanie Oriold. Sue Factor's fantastic, thorough copyedit on the revised draft was a thing of beauty. With her hard work, she saved us from ourselves on nearly every page, and polished away the confusing parts.

Thanks also to Sally Malcolm, for her edits and for the opportunity, and to Tom Reeve as well. And a thousand thanks to those who have encouraged each of us in one way or another — especially our friends, family and co-workers who bought the first book (even if they'd never heard of *Stargate SG-1*) and wished us well with the second.

STARGÅTE
SG·1

STARGATE
ATLÅNTIS™

Original novels based on the hit TV shows, STARGATE SG-1 and STARGATE ATLANTIS

AVAILABLE NOW

For more information, visit www.stargatenovels.com

STARGATE SG-1 © 1997-2008 MGM Television Entertainment Inc. and MGM Global Holdings, Inc. STARGATE SG-1 is a trademark of Metro-Goldwyn-Mayer Studios Inc. All Rights Reserved.
STARGATE: ATLANTIS © 2004-2008 MGM Global Holdings, Inc.
STARGATE: ATLANTIS is a trademark of Metro-Goldwyn-Mayer Studios Inc. All Rights Reserved.
METRO-GOLDWYN-MAYER ™ & © 2008 Metro-Goldwyn-Mayer Studios Inc. All Rights Reserved.

Series number: SG1-11

STARGATE SG-1: THE BARQUE OF HEAVEN

by Suzanne Wood
Price: $7.95 US | $9.95 Canada | £6.99 UK
ISBN-10: 1-905586-05-1
ISBN-13: 978-1-905586-05-9

Millennia ago, at the height of his power, the System Lord Ra decreed that any Goa'uld wishing to serve him must endure a great trial. Victory meant power and prestige, defeat brought banishment and death. On a routine expedition to an abandoned Goa'uld world, SG-1 inadvertently initiate Ra's ancient trial – and once begun, the trial cannot be halted. Relying on Dr. Daniel Jackson's vast wealth of knowledge, Colonel O'Neill must lead his team from planet to planet, completing each task in the allotted time. There is no rest, no respite. To stop means being trapped forever in the farthest reaches of the galaxy, and to fail means death. Victory is their only option in this terrible test of endurance – an ordeal that will try their will, their ingenuity, and above all their bonds of friendship…

STARGATE SG-1: DO NO HARM

Series number: SG1-12

by Karen Miller
Price: $7.95 US | $9.95 Canada | £6.99 UK
ISBN-13: 978-1-905586-09-7

Stargate Command is in crisis – too many teams wounded, too many dead. Tensions are running high and, with the pressure to deliver tangible results never greater, General Hammond is forced to call in the Pentagon strike team to plug the holes. But help has its price. When the team's leader, Colonel Dave Dixon, arrives at Stargate Command he brings with him loyalties that tangle dangerously with a past Colonel Jack O'Neill would prefer to forget. Assigned as an observer on SG-1, hostility between the two men escalate as the team's vital mission to secure lucrative mining rights descends into a nightmare of pestilence and death. Only Janet Fraiser can hope to save the lives of SG-1 – that is, if Dave Dixon and Jack O'Neill don't kill each other first…

Series number: SG1-9:

STARGATE SG-1: ROSWELL

by Sonny Whitelaw & Jennifer Fallon
Price: $7.95 US | $9.95 Canada | £6.99 UK
ISBN-10: 1-905586-04-3
ISBN-13: 978-1-905586-04-2

When a Stargate malfunction throws Colonel Cameron Mitchell, Dr. Daniel Jackson, and Colonel Sam Carter back in time, they only have minutes to live. But their rescue, by an unlikely duo — General Jack O'Neill and Vala Mal Doran — is only the beginning of their problems. Ordered to rescue an Asgard also marooned in 1947, SG-1 find themselves at the mercy of history. While Jack, Daniel, Sam and Teal'c become embroiled in the Roswell aliens conspiracy, Cam and Vala are stranded in another timeline, desperately searching for a way home. As the effects of their interference ripple through time, the consequences for the future are catastrophic. Trapped in the past, SG-1 can only watch as their world is overrun by a terrible invader…

STARGATE SG-1: RELATIVITY

Series number: SG1-10

by James Swallow
Price: $7.95 US | $9.95 Canada | £6.99 UK
ISBN-10: 1-905586-07-8
ISBN-13: 978-1-905586-07-3

When SG-1 encounter the Pack—a nomadic space-faring people who have fled Goa'uld domination for generations—it seems as though a trade of technologies will benefit both sides. But someone is determined to derail the deal. With the SGC under attack, and Vice President Kinsey breathing down their necks, it's up to Colonel Jack O'Neill and his team to uncover the saboteur and save the fledgling alliance. But unbeknownst to SG-1 there are far greater forces at work—a calculating revenge that spans decades, and a desperate gambit to prevent a cataclysm of epic proportions. When the identity of the saboteur is revealed, O'Neill is faced with a horrifying truth and is forced into an unlikely alliance in order to fight for Earth's future.

Series number: SG1-4

STARGATE SG-1: CITY OF THE GODS

by Sonny Whitelaw
Price: $7.95 US | $9.95 Canada | £6.99 UK
ISBN-10: 0-9547343-3-5
ISBN-13: 978-0-9547343-3-6

When a Crystal Skull is discovered beneath the Pyramid of the Sun in Mexico, it ignites a cataclysmic chain of events that maroons SG-1 on a dying world. Xalótcan is a brutal society, steeped in death and sacrifice, where the bloody gods of the Aztecs demand tribute from a fearful and superstitious population. But that's the least of Colonel Jack O'Neill's problems. With Xalótcan on the brink of catastrophe, Dr. Daniel Jackson insists that O'Neill must fulfil an ancient prophesy and lead its people to salvation. But with the world tearing itself apart, can anyone survive? As fear and despair plunge Xalótcan into chaos, SG-1 find themselves with ringside seats at the end of the world...

• *Special section: Excerpts from Dr. Daniel Jackson's mission journal.*

STARGATE SG-1: ALLIANCES

by Karen Miller
Price: $7.95 US | $9.95 Canada | £6.99 UK
ISBN-10: 1-905586-00-0
ISBN-13: 978-1-905586-00-4

Series number: SG1-8

All SG-1 wanted was technology to save Earth from the Goa'uld ... but the mission to Euronda was a terrible failure. Now the dogs of Washington are baying for Jack O'Neill's blood—and Senator Robert Kinsey is leading the pack. When Jacob Carter asks General Hammond for SG-1's participation in mission for the Tok'ra, it seems like the answer to O'Neill's dilemma. The secretive Tok'ra are running out of hosts. Jacob believes he's found the answer—but it means O'Neill and his team must risk their lives infiltrating a Goa'uld slave breeding farm to recruit humans willing to join the Tok'ra. It's a risky proposition ... especially since the fallout from Euronda has strained the team's bond almost to breaking. If they can't find a way to put their differences behind them, they might not make it home alive...

STARGATE SG-1: A MATTER OF HONOR

Part one of two parts
by Sally Malcolm

Price: $7.95 US | $9.95 Canada |£6.99 UK
ISBN-10: 0-9547343-2-7
ISBN-13: 978-0-9547343-2-9

Five years after Major Henry Boyd and his team, SG-10, were trapped on the edge of a black hole, Colonel Jack O'Neill discovers a device that could bring them home. But it's owned by the Kinahhi, an advanced and paranoid people, besieged by a ruthless foe. Unwilling to share the technology, the Kinahhi are pursuing their own agenda in the negotiations with Earth's diplomatic delegation. Maneuvering through a maze of tyranny, terrorism and deceit, Dr. Daniel Jackson, Major Samantha Carter and Teal'c unravel a startling truth—a revelation that throws the team into chaos and forces O'Neill to face a nightmare he is determined to forget. Resolved to rescue Boyd, O'Neill marches back into the hell he swore never to revisit. Only this time, he's taking SG-1 with him…

STARGATE SG-1: THE COST OF HONOR

Part two of two parts
by Sally Malcolm

Price: $7.95 US | $9.95 Canada | £6.99 UK
ISBN-10: 0-9547343-4-3
ISBN-13: 978-0-9547343-4-3

Returning to Stargate Command, Colonel Jack O'Neill and his team find more has changed in their absence than they had expected. Nonetheless, O'Neill is determined to face the consequences of their unauthorized activities, only to discover the penalty is far worse than anything he could have imagined.

With the fate of Colonel O'Neill and Major Samantha Carter unknown, and the very survival of the SGC threatened, Dr. Daniel Jackson and Teal'c mount a rescue mission to free their team-mates and reclaim the SGC. Yet returning to the Kinahhi homeworld, they learn a startling truth about its ancient foe. And uncover a horrifying secret…

STARGATE SG-1: TRIAL BY FIRE

By Sabine C. Bauer
Price: $7.95 US | $9.95 Canada | £6.99 UK
ISBN-10: 0-9547343-0-0
ISBN-13: 978-0-9547343-0-5

Trial by Fire follows the team as they embark on a mission to Tyros, an ancient society teetering on the brink of war. A pious people, the Tyreans are devoted to the Canaanite deity, Meleq. When their spiritual leader is savagely murdered during a mission of peace, they beg SG-1 for help against their sworn enemies, the Phrygians. Initially reluctant to get involved, the team has no choice when Colonel Jack O'Neill is abducted. O'Neill soon discovers his only hope of escape is to join the ruthless Phrygians—if he can survive their barbaric initiation rite. As Major Samantha Carter, Dr. Daniel Jackson and Teal'c race to his rescue, they find themselves embroiled in a war of shifting allegiances, where truth has many shades and nothing is as it seems. And, unbeknownst to them all, an old enemy is hiding in the shadows…

STARGATE SG-1: SACRIFICE MOON

By Julie Fortune
Price: $7.95 US | $9.95 Canada | £6.99 UK
ISBN-10: 0-9547343-1-9
ISBN-13: 978-0-9547343-1-2

Sacrifice Moon follows the newly commissioned SG-1 on their first mission through the Stargate.

Their destination is Chalcis, a peaceful society at the heart of the Helos Confederacy of planets. But Chalcis harbors a dark secret, one that pitches SG-1 into a world of bloody chaos, betrayal and madness. Battling to escape the living nightmare, Dr. Daniel Jackson and Captain Samantha Carter soon begin to realize that more than their lives are at stake. They are fighting for their very souls.

But while Col Jack O'Neill and Teal'c struggle to keep the team together, Daniel is hatching a desperate plan that will test SG-1's fledgling bonds of trust and friendship to the limit…

STARGATE ATLANTIS: MIRROR MIRROR

by Sabine C. Bauer
Price: £6.99 UK | $7.95 US | $9.95 Canada
ISBN-10: 1-905586-12-4
ISBN-13: 978-1-905586-12-7

When an Ancient prodigy gives the Atlantis expedition Charybdis — a device capable of eliminating the Wraith — it's an offer they can't refuse. But the experiment fails disastrously, threatening to unravel the fabric of the Pegasus Galaxy — and the entire universe beyond. Doctor Weir's team find themselves trapped and alone in very different versions of Atlantis, each fighting for their lives and their sanity in a galaxy falling apart at the seams. And as the terrible truth begins to sink in, they realize that they must undo the damage Charybdis has wrought while they still can. Embarking on a desperate attempt to escape the maddening tangle of realities, each tries to return to their own Atlantis before it's too late. But the one thing standing in their way is themselves…

STARGATE ATLANTIS: RELIQUARY

by Martha Wells
Price: £6.99 UK | $7.95 US | $9.95 Canada
ISBN-10: 0-9547343-7-8
ISBN-13: 978-0-9547343-7-4

While exploring the unused sections of the Ancient city of Atlantis, Major John Sheppard and Dr. Rodney McKay stumble on a recording device that reveals a mysterious new Stargate address. Believing that the address may lead them to a vast repository of Ancient knowledge, the team embarks on a mission to this uncharted world. There they discover a ruined city, full of whispered secrets and dark shadows. As tempers fray and trust breaks down, the team uncovers the truth at the heart of the city. A truth that spells their destruction. With half their people compromised, it falls to Major John Sheppard and Dr. Rodney McKay to risk everything in a deadly game of bluff with the enemy. To fail would mean the fall of Atlantis itself — and, for Sheppard, the annihilation of his very humanity…

STARGATE ATLANTIS: CASUALTIES OF WAR

by Elizabeth Christensen
Price: £6.99 UK | $7.95 US | $9.95 Canada
ISBN-10: 1-905586-06-X
ISBN-13: 978-1-905586-06-6

It is a dark time for Atlantis. In the wake of the Asuran takeover, Colonel Sheppard is buckling under the strain of command. When his team discover Ancient technology which can defeat the Asuran menace, he is determined that Atlantis must possess it—at all costs. But the involvement of Atlantis heightens local suspicions and brings two peoples to the point of war. Elizabeth Weir believes only her negotiating skills can hope to prevent the carnage, but when her diplomatic mission is attacked—and two of Sheppard's team are lost—both Weir and Sheppard must question their decisions. And their abilities to command. As the first shots are fired, the Atlantis team must find a way to end the conflict—or live with the blood of innocents on their hands...

STARGATE ATLANTIS: BLOOD TIES

by Sonny Whitelaw & Elizabeth Christensen
Price: £6.99 UK | $7.95 US | $9.95 Canada
ISBN-10: 1-905586-08-6
ISBN-13: 978-1-905586-08-0

When a series of gruesome murders are uncovered around the world, the trail leads back to the SGC—and far beyond. Recalled to Stargate Command, Dr. Elizabeth Weir, Colonel John Sheppard, and Dr. Rodney McKay are shown shocking video footage—a Wraith attack, taking place on Earth. While McKay, Teyla, and Ronon investigate the disturbing possibility that humans may harbor Wraith DNA, Colonel Sheppard is teamed with SG-1's Dr. Daniel Jackson. Together, they follow the murderers' trail from Colorado Springs to the war-torn streets of Iraq, and there, uncover a terrifying truth... As an ancient cult prepares to unleash its deadly plot against humankind, Sheppard's survival depends on his questioning of everything believed about the Wraith...

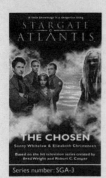

STARGATE ATLANTIS: THE CHOSEN

by Sonny Whitelaw & Elizabeth Christensen
Price: £6.99 UK | $7.95 US | $9.95 Canada
ISBN-10: 0-9547343-8-6
ISBN-13: 978-0-9547343-8-1

With Ancient technology scattered across the Pegasus galaxy, the Atlantis team is not surprised to find it in use on a world once defended by Dalera, an Ancient who was cast out of her society for falling in love with a human. But in the millennia since Dalera's departure much has changed. Her strict rules have been broken, leaving her people open to Wraith attack. Only a few of the Chosen remain to operate Ancient technology vital to their defense and tensions are running high. Revolution simmers close to the surface. When Major Sheppard and Rodney McKay are revealed as members of the Chosen, Daleran society convulses into chaos. Wanting to help resolve the crisis and yet refusing to prop up an autocratic regime, Sheppard is forced to act when Teyla and Lieutenant Ford are taken hostage by the rebels...

STARGATE ATLANTIS: ENTANGLEMENT

by Martha Wells
Price: £6.99 UK | $7.95 US | $9.95 Canada
ISBN-10: 1-905586-03-5
ISBN-13: 978-1-905586-03-5

When Dr. Rodney McKay unlocks an Ancient mystery on a distant moon, he discovers a terrifying threat to the Pegasus galaxy. Determined to disable the device before it's discovered by the Wraith, Colonel John Sheppard and his team navigate the treacherous ruins of an Ancient outpost. But attempts to destroy the technology are complicated by the arrival of a stranger — a stranger who can't be trusted, a stranger who needs the Ancient device to return home. Cut off from backup, under attack from the Wraith, and with the future of the universe hanging in the balance, Sheppard's team must put aside their doubts and step into the unknown. However, when your mortal enemy is your only ally, betrayal is just a heartbeat away...

THE OFFICIAL MAGAZINE

STARGATE
SG·1 ◆ ATLANTIS

- Interviews with cast & crew
- Latest *Stargate SG-1* & *Stargate: Atlantis* news!
- Behind-the-scenes secrets revealed

Subscribe now and save 10%

UK call 0870 428 8217 or visit www.titanmagazines.co.uk
US call 1877 363 130 or visit www.titanmagazines.com

STARGATE SG-1 © 1997-2006 MGM Television Entertainment Inc. and MGM Global Holdings Inc. STARGATE SG-1 device, all names, characters and likeness thereof are trademarks of Metro-Goldwyn-Mayer Studios Inc. STARGATE: ATLANTIS is a trademark of Metro-Goldwyn-Mayer Studios Inc. STARGATE: ATLANTIS © 2004-2006 MGM Global Holdings Inc. All Rights Reserved.